LOCH NESS

A monster stirs at the bottom of Loch Ness.
For centuries it has lived in peace,
rising to the surface,
from time to time,
to become a legend in the hills of Scotland.

Now something has arrived to disturb its tranquility—
the violent, greedy thrust of men in search of oil.

Now the monster must strike back to survive,
in an explosion of unimaginable fury
that will rock the world.

A TALE OF THE BEAST

Also by Jeffrey Konvitz
Published by Ballantine Books

THE SENTINEL

MONSTER

A Tale of Loch Ness

JEFFREY KONVITZ

BALLANTINE BOOKS • NEW YORK

Library of Congress Catalog Card Number 82-90501

ISBN 0-345-29447-5

Manufactured in the United States of America

First Edition: October 1982

To Robert Littman, without whom this book would not have been written. And for my father, who hung in there to see it happen.

CONTENTS

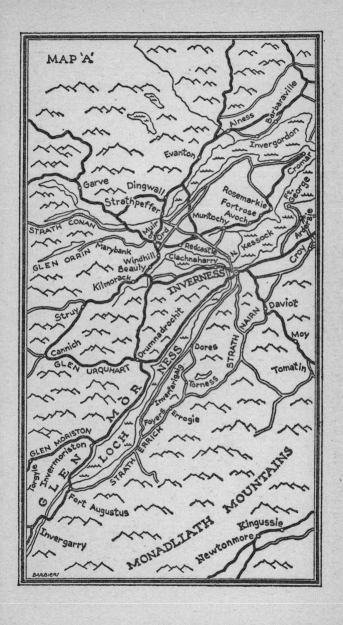

MAP 'A'

Part I

$\approx$

THE
COLUMBUS

Preface

Rolf Kreibel, chief design engineer of the Highland Fabricators Company, maneuvered the Rover sedan past affluent mansions to the top of the hill on Old Edinburgh Road and looked down at the city below.

"Inverness," he announced, spreading the word with a heavy Bavarian drawl.

Jerry Foster, director of public relations, Geminii Petroleum International, a portly man with an effusive personality, placed the stem of a pipe in his mouth, then squinted toward the west where late-morning sunlight splashed brilliantly against the Highland Mountains. "Not a bad-looking little place," he said, fingering his thick crop of handlebar moustache, barbered to perfection.

"And it's a hell of a lot more colorful than Deenie," added Bob Reddington, the third member of the group.

Inverness, which lay around the horn of Scotland and inside a shield of bays, the huge Moray and the smaller Inverness and Beauly firths, did not remotely resemble Aberdeen, the center of the North Sea oil industry on Scotland's east coast. First, there were no oil companies and few modern buildings. And second, the city possessed an architectural style far more pleasant than Aberdeen's ponderous stoniness, quarried to withstand the fierce winds and the pounding rains of the North Sea.

Kreibel, who had picked up Foster and Reddington just minutes before at Inverness Airport, eased the Rover down the hill on to High Bridge Street, a long avenue of colorful storefronts, curiously embellished.

Pastry stores had little cookie and cake monsters displayed in their windows. The kilt-maker shops were cluttered with toy Nessies and inflatable souvenirs. And one bookstore had an extensive exhibit of monster posters on its portico as well as an eye-catching welcome sign across its façade: GREETINGS FROM INVERNESS—HOME OF THE LOCH NESS MONSTER.

It was May. Tourists would be arriving in June. Inverness was ready.

"Do you think the locals take the thing seriously?" Foster asked.

Kreibel shook his head. "Would you if every summer you had to answer the same ignorant questions? I doubt it."

Kreibel steered the car across the River Ness Bridge toward the Caledonian Canal, an artificial offshoot of the River Ness. The canal, like the river, was fed by Loch Ness and emptied into the Inverness Firth.

"We're taking a detour," he said, turning the car to the west. "The big shake knocked out part of the Dores Road on the south bank. We'll have to pick it up outside the city."

"Funny," Foster said. "We didn't feel the quake in Aberdeen."

Kreibel's eyes widened. "Well, it was a corker here. We took a lot of superficial damage. We were lucky, though. At six-eight on the Richter, it could have been a lot worse."

"What about aftershocks?" Reddington asked.

"Two days' worth," Kreibel replied.

"That's reassuring news before a dive," Foster said facetiously.

Kreibel waved away the thought. "I spoke to a quake expert with the Forestry Commission this morning, and he said the activity had played itself out."

Reddington shook his head. "From what I hear about those guys, we shouldn't lay the odds."

Reddington, a big man with a boisterous sense of humor, laughed alone. Currently the drilling supervisor for Geminii Petroleum's wildcat venture in the Dundee North Sea sector aboard the semisubmersible rig *Valkyrie*, he'd come over to the North Sea four years before when Geminii, the operating partner in the multilayered international consortium, had received its first license to explore in the British Offshore Sector. Since then, he'd overseen three exploratory Dundee wells, the third of which had encountered a large pay zone of hydrocarbons and several delineation wells, which had established the boundaries of the Dundee field, now forecast to produce at over 30,000 barrels of oil a day. While waiting for completion of a permanent steel Dundee production platform being built by Highland Fabricators just north of Inverness, he was preparing to move with the *Valkyrie* to a separate license area and begin another round of wildcat exploration.

Shortly before noon, they intercepted the Dores Road at Loch Ness about eight miles from the city, then headed toward the village of Foyers on the south loch shore.

A year before, a friend of Kreibel's named Harry Bailey had discovered an underwater fissure while diving off Foyers. Lacking sophisticated diving equipment, Bailey had chosen not to explore. Having been told the story, however, Kreibel, a monster buff, had decided to make the dive and had convinced Reddington and Foster, both scuba enthusiasts, to join.

"What do you know about the loch?" Kreibel asked as they rumbled along.

"Not much," Foster replied.

Kreibel smiled. He was a pleasant fellow, soft-spoken, likable, athletic. Consumed by a burning curiosity about unexplained enigmas, he was also a thorough man who prided himself on research and preparation. "Ness and two other separate lochs lie in a giant geological fault which cuts Scotland in half," he began. "Loch Ness, though, which sits fifty feet above sea level, is the largest, about twenty-four miles long and a mile and a half wide at its widest point as well as nine hundred eighty feet deep, making it one of the deepest fresh-water lakes in the world."

"It looks as cold as hell," Reddington declared.

"Colder," Kreibel said, chewing into a stick of gum. "Though it never freezes. And it's murky dark because of the runoff of peat. That's why I ordered special headgear with torches designed specifically to accommodate loch conditions."

"Do you have the dive coordinates?" Foster asked as the car moved along the narrow road whose sloping borders were gradually merging into the steeper walls of the rising mountain sides.

"Yes," Kreibel replied. "If we're lucky, we'll find the fissure."

"Then what?" Reddington asked.

"You and Foster will perch outside. I'll go in with a camera."

"What if you find the monster?" Foster asked, laughing, his thoughts on cookies and cakes.

"I'll take its picture," Kreibel answered. "Close up." He pulled three envelopes off the dash, opened one, and withdrew a stack of photos. "This is some of the photographic evidence accumulated so far."

Jerry Foster relit his pipe, while Bob Reddington examined the photographic plates.

"The first reference to a monster was made by St. Columba, the Irish monk who brought Christianity to Scotland around 550 A.D., though we can pinpoint the rise of the modern legend to 1933, when engineers blasted the northside road from Inverness to Fort Augustus. Now I've studied hundreds of eyewitness reports. Most are frauds. But a good number appear to be legitimate." He noticed Foster's skeptical expression, then pointed to the pictures. "These are the best above-water photographs of the monster ever taken. The first was shot in 1933 by Hugh Gray. The second by a surgeon in 1934. The last by Tim Dinsdale in 1960."

Foster craned his neck. "They all look like floating logs to me."

"That's arguable," Kreibel said, glancing at Reddington. "What do you think, Red?"

"Don't know," Reddington observed, shrugging.

Reddington placed the plates back in their envelope for Kreibel and opened the second as instructed, pulling out another set of exhibits.

"These are sonar records," Kreibel said. "The first trace was recorded by the *Rival III* trawler in 1954. Some have claimed the trace was made by an undulating eel. But it's unlikely." He pointed to another exhibit. "That was recorded in Urquhart Bay by a team from the University of Birmingham. The object was calculated to be moving at four hundred fifty feet per minute. Now no Ness current moves that fast, eliminating the possibility of water-carried flotsam." He quickly noted several other tracings. "Convinced?" he asked.

"Not yet," Reddington said as he pulled up the sleeves of his military surplus shirt. He never bothered much about clothes. He was an outdoorsman. Very unpretentious.

"Open the last envelope!" Kreibel suggested.

Reddington tore the folder and placed the final exhibits on his lap as the jeep moved past Urquhart Bay.

"That's Urquhart Bay," Kreibel said, pointing. "The loch's widest point. The ruin is Urquhart Castle."

"How deep is the loch there?" Foster asked.

"We're at the deepest point," Kreibel replied. "The locus where most of the researchers have worked, including the group responsible for the final photos and sonar tracings. The group's called the Academy of Applied Sciences, and they hit pay dirt in August '72, after they'd lowered their sonar equipment and an aligned strobe camera into the bay. On the night of August 7, the sonar scope printed out a large trace." He indicated the record. "Excited, the team theorized the camera must have photographed the object, too. They developed the film, and this is what they got." He held up a series of photos, apparently worthless, a mélange of lines and shadows. "It doesn't look like much, I know. It didn't look like much to the academy team, either. That is, until the photos were enhanced by a computer. The computer picture looked like this." He pulled another photo. "Now tell me if that's not a goddamn animal's body and a giant flipper!"

Astounded, Reddington and Foster examined the plate.

"What was the reaction?" Reddington asked.

"A team from the Smithsonian concluded the object was probably animate. Now I won't lie to you. Others dismissed the evidence as inconclusive. But you form your own conclusions."

Jerry Foster pointed, curiously subdued. "And those?"

"Those are the pictures," Kreibel said, "taken during the academy's 1975 expedition. Two sequences of photos were obtained. A whole body photo and a head picture. Once more, the Smithsonian supported the findings, and once more, there were a whole slew of official and semiofficial detractors."

The jeep moved through the village of Inverfarigaig, nearing the outskirts of Foyers.

"What's happened since '75?" Reddington asked.

"Not much," Kreibel said. "The academy has returned several times. So have other groups. There've been interesting sonar tracings but no pictures of consequence."

Foster glanced at the German. "Do you think it exists?"

"Sure. Why not? And the fissure might well be its home."

They arrived in Foyers ten minutes later. Foyers was a small village divided into two districts, upper and lower. Upper Foyers lay on the side of a mountain. Lower Foyers stood along the loch.

Kreibel drove down to a dock.

"The diving point is fifty feet eastward by thirty-seven offshore," Kreibel said.

"Thirty-seven?" Foster asked, eyebrows raised.

"I guarantee you'll find it deep enough. The shore of Ness

is virtually nonexistent. In many parts of the loch, its under-water walls drop straight down to a near maximum depth within only a few feet of land." He laughed. "You'll find it a little unsettling at first."

Kreibel stopped the Rover and jumped down. Reddington handed out the diving gear, which Foster and Kreibel carried on to the quay. When the equipment was in place, they checked their valves and oxygen tanks, then watched as Kreibel illustrated the use of a tether rope.

"I'll lead," he said, spitting out the wad of gum. "Bob, you'll trail. Bailey estimated the strike depth as seventy-five feet. Once we find the fissure, I'll go in alone."

They put on the scuba gear. Reddington and Foster tied a life line between themselves, then Foster attached one end of the tether to his belt. Reddington followed Kreibel and Foster into the water. They bobbed on the surface momentarily, eye contact assured, then went under.

The water was cold, black, inky. They could feel the density of peat. Several feet below the surface, they began to lose light. Kreibel moved away from shore. Suddenly, the base-ment fell away. Kreibel started down. Foster and Reddington followed. They switched on the helmet torches. Streams of light pierced the murky blackness.

The wall of the descent steepened. They were moving down alongside an underwater cliff, nearly vertical. When they had reached target depth, Kreibel moved horizontally, searching. Moments later, he waved. He'd found it. Reddington and Foster approached. No doubt. There was a huge opening in the rocks.

Kreibel attached the tether line firmly to his diving belt, then moved inside the fissure. Several seconds later, he was gone, no trace of his beam in sight.

Reddington and Foster watched the tether rope move through their hands. The line, marked every five feet by in-soluble chalk streaks, ran to fifty feet, stopped, then continued out to one hundred and ten. Suddenly, the water began to cloud. Puzzled, they looked around, then heard it—a low rumble. Foster glared at Reddington, terrified. They waited. The water disturbance got worse. So did the muffled roar.

Quake! The goddamn quake!

They were jolted. Reddington grabbed tighter to the tether. The shaking and vibrations increased. The tether line brushed hard against the edge of the fissure. They pulled. The rock wall shook, then shifted, tearing the tether in half.

Stunned, Reddington and Foster watched the free tether end disappear. Reddington moved to follow just as a huge tremor surged through the water, disorienting them. Panicked, Foster headed to the surface. Reddington followed. By the time they had broken water, the quake had subsided.

They climbed on to the dock. The end of the tether line lay by Reddington's side, one end sliced clean. A small aftershock hit, then quiet. It was over.

"What the hell do we do now?" Foster asked.

"I'm going down!" Reddington said.

"Are you crazy?!"

"We've got to do something."

Reddington returned to the water. Foster waited on shore, trembling. Reddington was not gone long.

"I can't see a goddamn thing down there," he said, surfacing.

"The torch?" Foster asked.

"Useless!"

Reddington climbed from the loch and fell to the ground, exhausted. Foster moved next to him. Immobile, they watched the water, the now-quiet surface. Above them, residents of Lower Foyers had emerged from their homes, looking for damage. Eventually, Reddington glanced at his watch and stood.

"His tanks must be empty by now."

Foster stood, too, wobbling toward the Rover. "We'd better call the police!"

Frantic, Rolf Kreibel moved quickly along the wall of the cavern. He could feel his lungs pulling desperately, his entire body wracked with pain. Shortly before, he had opened the emergency reserve valve, but now even those tanks were almost empty. And God, he was exhausted, having moved in endless circles, fighting to get out of the maze and back into the open waters of the loch.

Blood was pouring from a deep gash on his forehead. Part of his wet suit was torn. His fingers, too, were raw, eaten to the bone, the flesh shorn by desperate lunges along the rock wall.

The torch was still working, barely illuminating the black, glistening walls. He continued to search, spearing at threads of hope. However, he'd begun to feel the final ebb of the reserves. He clutched his throat, holding off suffocation, then darted quickly ahead and slammed into a wall. Directly above, the cavern was spreading; he might be near the entrance. Gasping, he surged through the quake debris. Yes, he was certain; he was near the mouth. He moved even quicker. Suddenly, however, the view grew dark again, as if the exit had been sealed. Puzzled, his body bursting inside, he committed himself to a final assault, exploding forward.

He was jolted aside. As his vision clouded, he whirled about and felt a surge of terror accompanying the onslaught of unconsciousness.

Something was there.

Directly in front of him.

There!

Two days after Rolf Kreibel's disappearance, Jerry Foster and Bob Reddington were summoned to Foyers by Detective Constable James MacKintosh, Fort Augustus Division, Northern Constabulary, Criminal Investigations Division. Since the accident, they had been staying at the Clachnaharry Inn near the Beauly Firth. The first day had been consumed by interrogation, the second by an interminable wait for the procurator fiscal's ruling concerning the nature of Rolf Kreibel's disappearance. The crown's chief prosecutory official in Inverness, the procurator was charged with determining cause of death and, in criminal cases, bringing indictment under the jurisdiction of the lord advocate. As such, he held their immediate futures in his hands.

Reddington and Foster arrived in Foyers in the late morning. Two police vans were already at the site. MacKintosh was there with several uniformed constables.

"Gentlemen," MacKintosh said perfunctorily as Reddington and Foster climbed from the Rover, "the procurator has ruled the disappearance an accident."

Foster and Reddington strained to pick up the words. MacKintosh, an expatriate from the Glasgow Lowlands, had a very heavy brogue and mountainous illiterate style.

Reddington looked up at the sky, which was heavy with clouds and moisture. "Then I suppose we can go?"

"Sure as the Word is good," MacKintosh said. "But we'd like you to look at something first. For identification purposes. A villager was fishing this morning and found a diving helmet along the shore. He called us. We assumed the helmet belonged to Kreibel. We'd like you to take a look."

MacKintosh motioned to one of the uniformed officers, who brought over a helmet covered with dirt and a grayish-blue film.

"That's Kreibel's," Foster said. He reached into the Rover and took out one of the other helmets, handing it to MacKintosh. "We each had an identical one."

"Do you agree, Mr. Reddington?" MacKintosh asked.

Reddington did not reply.

"Mr. Reddington?"

Reddington's eyes shifted. "Yes," he said, running his fingers across the helmet's torch.

"Good," MacKintosh declared. "Gentlemen, I'm sorry this had to happen. But I'm right pleased we were able to expedite things quickly. You have my number if you need speak to me, and we have yours in case there are further questions or in the event the body is recovered."

Reddington and Foster thanked MacKintosh, who offered a few quick words about the dangers of Loch Ness and a peculiar philosophical statement about life and death in the Highlands.

"Let's head back to Aberdeen," Foster suggested sheepishly after the police officers had disappeared.

Reddington walked to the shoreline and kneeled. Sniffing the edges of his fingers, he remained trancelike until Foster had moved to his side.

"What the hell's the matter with you?" Foster asked.

Reddington held out his hand, extending his fingers. "Smell that!"

Foster sniffed the substance. "Christ!" he said, astonished.

"Yeah," Reddington declared. "The quake must have opened a fissure."

Foster changed thoughts to words. "There's oil down there? Under Loch Ness?"

And Bob Reddington, senior drilling supervisor, Geminii Petroleum International, just stared.

Chapter 1

The music and words had been filtering through his thoughts ever since he had stepped off British Airways Flight 7425 in Aberdeen. *You take the high road and I'll take the low road and I'll be in Scotland afore ye. . . .* A strange sense of Scottish earthiness or some bizarre notion of history, he guessed, rather than his heritage or an overromantic persona had created a bridge to barely familiar melodies. Oh, sure, Peter Robert Bruce, he'd been told, was a Scottish name, but his father had died when he was three, and if he professed any roots, it would have been to his mother's Irish ancestry. No, there was something about this country that culled emotions, something unaffected by two days of orientation at Geminii Petroleum's Aberdeen complex and by the long hours spent analyzing drilling and geophysical reports. Nor did this something relinquish its hold during the quick flight to Inverness or along the route into the city in a stretch Mercedes limousine to the rented home on a domineering hill. No, it was there, and goddamn, he couldn't quite put his finger on it.

"I hope you like Travis House," Jerry Foster said as the limousine stopped in front of an old stone mansion overlooking the city. "I took particular care choosing it. In fact, I must have looked at half the vacant mansions in Inverness and even some that were occupied."

"I don't think the effort was necessary," "Scotty" Bruce replied. "I would have been very comfortable in a sleeping bag."

"It wasn't an effort. It was a pleasure, Mr. Bruce."

"Mr. Bruce? Hey, if I'm going to call you Jerry, you're going to call me Scotty."

Foster smiled broadly while patting down the lapels of an

ostentatious plaid suit, unflatteringly styled. "All right, Scotty. But I've got to tell you the formality is part of idol worship. I lived in Los Angeles when you were at USC, and I was a real fan of yours."

Scotty smirked; the memories were almost petrified. "That was a long time ago."

Foster puffed his chest as they entered the grounds, proud of his good memory. "You were the best tight end I ever saw. There might be faster ballplayers today but no one who could block like you could."

Scotty pulled off his Amarillo Stetson. "I hope you're the only football fan in Inverness 'cause I don't want anyone to remind me how old I am."

Foster laughed, his moustache rising up his cheeks, his pudgy body and rotund face expanding. "Well, there are a lot of football fans, but football is soccer here. They're bonkers about it."

They entered the mansion. Foster led a tour: living room, dining room, kitchen—a housekeeper would be forthcoming— the upstairs bedroom area, and then the den, where they sat and attacked some beers pulled from the refrigerator.

"I was also in Washington with the State Department when you were traded to the Redskins," Foster began again. "I didn't miss a game. In fact, if you ask me, Scotty, those years with Washington were your best."

"My coldest, too."

Foster lit his pipe, impressed with Scotty's appearance. Scotty did not look like the athlete long retired. He was muscular and slim, and his handsome, angular features, aggressive eyes, and inviting smile still carried a message of enthusiasm. "You may wish you were still there once you get a load of the Scottish winter. They say it's warmer than one would expect because of the Gulf Stream, but when those gales come raging in off the North Sea, no one takes much comfort with a few extra degrees of temp. The rain isn't God's gift, either. Oh, yeah, it snows, but the rain's the curse. Drops as big as golf balls and blown horizontally by the wind so they whiz around like artillery shells. It gets so bad you can hardly stand. Everyone winds up slushing around in the mud. It's worse than playing football on a rainy field, and you'd know about that 'cause of the torn knee!"

Scotty slugged some beer, subconsciously flexing his scarred kneecap. He didn't like memories of the NFL, and he rarely indulged himself, but it was hard to prevent others from doing so. Notoriety always carried a ponderous curse even many years after the fact.

Foster pulled some papers from his pocket, continuing to speak. "I've got a message for you from Jim Barrett."

Scotty massaged his burnished cheeks. "I tried to get in to see Barrett in London, but he'd just been flown back to the States."

Foster shook his head. "The man's fortunate to be alive. I tell you, Scotty, it was one scary night. We were lucky we had a doctor on the plane. Barrett was sitting right next to me when he started to complain about shortness of breath. I told him he'd eaten too much. But when he started to sweat, I knew he was in trouble. It wasn't ten seconds later, he turned blue, his eyes rolled into his head, and he went out like a light. I called for help. A doctor ran over, tore off Barrett's shirt, and went to work, pumping his chest. He said Barrett'd had a coronary and his heart was fibrillating. And he was trying to get it back in rhythm. Yeah, let me tell you, Scotty, Barrett's a lucky man to be alive."

"How's his condition now?"

"Not good."

"You said he had a message."

Foster didn't flinch. "Yeah. He said; 'Good luck. You'll need it.' "

"Is that so?"

"Some say yes. Some say no."

"What do you say?"

"Not much. Remember, I'm the press officer. The official PR man. I keep locals at bay, newspaper reporters subdued, and company egos massaged. I try to stay away from controversy. Out of everyone's way. I talk and write and make up little press releases like the one in my hand announcing your arrival, education and work experience listed, plus your membership in the Pro Football Hall of Fame."

Scotty grimaced. "Do we need the last?"

"Absolutely. Stateside management demanded it. They like the PR potential."

Scotty stood and walked around the den, examining bookshelves, then sat down again. "Have you got some time?" he asked.

"Sure," Foster replied. "And it's at your disposal." He looked at his watch, a relic on a gold chain. "Call it nine-thirty.

Mr. Whittenfeld suggested I bring you by just after one. You'll be asked to call him Bill. Just about everyone does. He may be the boss, a high-powered executive and a man not unaware of position and station, but he's human, too. A member of the team. A first-name sort of guy."

"I see."

Foster laughed. "You'll like him . . . like him a lot."

Scotty closed his eyes, thinking. Foster watched, bemused. There was silence. Several minutes passed.

"Well, if you're at my disposal," Scotty suddenly said, "talk to me."

"About what?"

Scotty once more subconsciously flexed his knee. "I've just joined the company. I'm in Scotland for the first time. I don't know anything about anything."

"You do know I was with Reddington and Kreibel the day Kreibel died?"

"Call that the beginning," Scotty said. "Start from there."

Foster poked at the end of his moustache. "I wasn't privy to all the technical stuff. You'd know more about that than I would. Oil wasn't supposed to be here. The oil slick suggested it was. The company obtained a preliminary exploratory license from the Department of Energy in London and quietly went about its business. Divers dove. Seismic crews doodle bugged the area. When Geminii was sure everyone had been wrong about the region, it approached Energy, obtaining a license to drill for and produce oil. Then it petitioned the local authorities through the Highland Regional Council for land access and development approval, and that's when the fireworks began." Foster repacked his pipe. "The Department of Energy only licenses the company. The local elected councils must license the land and approve a development plan." He paused thoughtfully. "The company applied for local cert. It presented a comprehensive development statement. The on-land application was quickly approved. But the Loch Ness request hit a shit storm. A councilor named MacKenzie from Foyers put up a hell of a fight, forming an opposition group, the Caucus, which recruited environmentalists, the Free Church, and the Scottish Nationalist Party. After the Caucus lost in committee, they tried to stop the initiative in the full council as well. They lost again. But this didn't end the matter. No way. Throughout the entire process of public hearings, the secretary of state for Scotland, who is a member of the British

Cabinet, head of the Scottish office, and sort of Scotland's prime minister, could have taken jurisdiction himself. But the loch application was a nasty political issue, and the secretary left it in the Highland Council's lap and would have kept it there had MacKenzie and company let the matter die. They didn't. They put so much pressure on the secretary, he buckled and held a new round of public hearings. Once again, the application was approved, and once more MacKenzie rebelled, bringing suit, claiming the secretary had ignored pertinent testimony. The case was thrown out of court. And that's where we are now. Moving ahead. Slowly. Under the watchful eye of the crazies who opposed the Loch Ness application and who hope something goes wrong so their cause will be vindicated."

"Is MacKenzie a crazy, too?"

"No. MacKenzie gathered the army, but MacKenzie led from conviction. All the Caucus members legitimately felt strongly. Most of them live near Loch Ness, and the loch is an emotional issue. It has a national identity, and strong reactions were provoked when the drilling proposal openly discussed oil spills and other catastrophes."

"There'll be no spills or catastrophes. Barrett's procedures were very strict. Mine are even stricter."

Foster threw out his arms. "Hey, Scotty. I'm not suggesting anything. I just said the area is sensitive, certainly more sensitive than the North Sea fields. The North Sea rigs are so far out no one can see a goddamn thing. But Loch Ness isn't very wide, and the *Columbus* sits right at the mouth of Urquhart Bay. You can't miss her, and no one does. She attracts a big audience, and anyone with binoculars can see just about everything happening on board."

"What about the Loch Ness monster? Anyone seen it?"

"No. And no one will. Because there's no such thing. Along with the planning application, the company commissioned an environmental impact report. To compile it, the contractees did a thorough sweep of the loch with side-scan sonar, underwater submersibles, and subsurface television. They even explored the closed cavern where Kreibel died. There's nothing down there except fish, flotsam, the wreck of a World War Two RAF bomber, and a couple of sunken barges. And there have been no sightings, though one newspaper reporter, sympathetic to the Caucus, headlined after seeing the *Columbus*, 'Nessie has arrived, crew and all.' "

Scotty was staring, half smiling. "You got any family here?" he asked, suddenly changing the subject.

Foster pulled his wallet, opened it, pointed. "Sure. The girl is Jennie, the boys Michael and Adam. That's the wife. Name's Amy. Unfortunately, we're all buried in those grotesque company apartments. You're a lucky man, Scotty. You live in a palace. The man who designed the company complex was a sadist."

"There wasn't enough housing?"

"There was some. But Whittenfeld wanted to bring in a shitload of English workers, so the company felt it advantageous to build. To keep the pressure low. The Scots ain't too fond of the English."

The grandfather clock in the hall chimed twice. Scotty adjusted his watch.

"I haven't eaten breakfast yet," he said. "What say we find a place for a snack?"

"Formal or otherwise?"

"Otherwise."

Foster looked relieved. "Good. Because that's all there is!"

Foster returned Scotty to Travis House at eleven and vowed to reappear at twelve-thirty to ferry Scotty to Geminii's office complex.

A Brunhilde-sized woman of fifty, carrying a satchel, was perched on the front doorstep.

"My name's Mrs. Munro," the woman said sternly as the limousine disappeared into the distance. "I'm your new housekeeper, cook, and guard."

Scotty smiled, approaching. "I didn't expect anyone so soon!" he said, attempting to help the woman with her bag.

"Never you mind," Mrs. Munro scolded, defending her belongings. "The company didn't hire you a tulip in the spring. I can carry my own things."

Scotty gaped. "Anything you say, Mrs. Munro. By the way, my name's Scotty Bruce."

Mrs. Munro looked at the paper in her hand. "Bruce. You're the one. Says so right here. Bruce! District superintendent! Let me say, Mr. Bruce, you've got the right woman at the right time. I specialize in oil. Have had me a dozen or so petroleum executives to look after over the last six years ever since I come down from the north."

They entered the mansion and walked about the first floor.

"I've worked for Geminii people all along," Mrs. Munro said, continuing, "and I've built a good reputation. You know, it takes more than hole diggers to make an oil company run. It takes people like me to keep people like you in one piece."

They moved into the kitchen.

"Now this is one smart-looking house, Mr. Bruce," Mrs. Munro declared, diddling with the appliances. "You should only get a chance to see the shack I was born in. It would make you appreciate luxury such as this."

Scotty showed Mrs. Munro to the housekeeper's quarters. "I hope this will do," he said.

Mrs. Munro waved her finger in his face. "If it doesn't, you'll hear from me. But it will. 'Cause I don't intend to spend much time in here. I like to keep busy. So just stay clear 'cause I move around right quickly."

"You have my promise."

Mrs. Munro dug into her satchel and pulled out a simple little bag with a tasseled flap. "This is a sporran," she said, handing it to Scotty. "It's a gift. Made it myself."

He examined the piece. "It's very pretty. But what do I do with it?"

"Use your brain, Mr. Bruce," she scolded. "You wear the sporran around your waist in front of you, hung from a strap over your kilt. You know what a kilt is, don't you?"

"Sure as hell."

"Then hell be damned. You know something."

"Unfortunately," Scotty said, "I don't own a kilt."

Mrs. Munro seemed aghast. "Then you're going to have to get yourself one. Along with a proper kilt jacket and bonnet. So you can wear the sporran."

He was flabbergasted.

"Let me see the bedrooms," Mrs. Munro demanded.

They walked upstairs, inspecting the master.

"Mr. Bruce," Mrs. Munro said, "you might know how to stab a length of drill pipe, but I'll bet you don't know a damn about putting your own clothes away. So you leave it to me. You go be important and save the world from its woes. I'll save you."

Mrs. Munro led Scotty back downstairs and set him on the lounge in the den.

"This is a good place for you while I get this house under control," she said, handing him the sporran. "Now will you be in need of dinner?"

"No. I'll be spending the night on a company installation."

"Good. Then I'll have plenty of time to devote to the premises. And God be praised, 'cause I can see there's lots of things to do. Now, you hear me, Mr. Bruce. You are not to worry about Travis House. She's well taken care of now. Munro of Ross and Cromarty has arrived."

Head raised, Mrs. Munro stalked from the room. Scotty watched her ample body move down the hall, then laid his head back on the arm of the lounge and smiled.

"Christ," he mumbled to himself, yawning. "What a piece of work!"

Chapter 2

The huge sign on the fence surrounding the Geminii company complex at Dores read:

LOCH NESS CONSORTIUM ENTERPRISES
OPERATING PARTNER:
GEMINII PETROLEUM INTERNATIONAL, LTD.

Next to the sign stood the main gate, overseen by an admitting station. Beyond was a multistoried glass and steel building, fronted by a jammed parking lot. The loch shore-line itself contained a separate enclosure, harboring two large pontoon loading docks. Both were crammed with equipment. A tug was moored. A seismic craft was in transit, several miles away. And there were numerous armed guards. Obviously, someone was very paranoid and unconcerned with local public relations.

Scotty looked across the road. Fields overrun by sheep extended toward the foothills of the Grampian Mountains. Up the way, he could see the Dores Inn and several small homes.

He sat back in the limousine. Fortunately, he would never have to ride in the damn thing again. A jeep had been ordered and would be available in the morning.

"So what do you think?" Jerry Foster asked.

"Interesting," Scotty replied. "But who the hell are they expecting, the Russians?"

Foster laughed; the question had unexpectedly amused him. "I don't know," he replied. "Perhaps you should ask Lefebre."

"Lefebre?"

"The security chief. As you can see, he believes in George Patton tactics. But I shouldn't prejudice you."

Foster signaled the chauffeur to proceed. The limousine lurched past the guard post and stopped in front of the executive building's main entrance. Climbing out of the car, they entered the lobby, checked through security, rode an elevator to the third floor, and located William Whittenfeld's suite.

Whittenfeld's secretary, a young Englishwoman, ushered them into Whittenfeld's private office and told them Whittenfeld had stepped out for a moment but would soon return.

The office was luxurious, bordered by a huge picture window and furnished with opulent couches, lamps, rugs, a conference table, and a magnificent antique desk.

It was neat, clean, almost too perfect.

"Impressed?" Foster asked.

Scotty surveyed the room. "I think Mr. Whittenfeld has a keen sense of what he likes."

Several minutes later, Whittenfeld returned and excitedly closed the office door. "Peter Bruce!" he cried, his deceptively slim body held posture perfect. "Welcome to Scotland." He took off his blazer and draped it carefully over a chair. "And Christ, I'm embarrassed. You get here and I'm nowhere to be found. Problems always seem to pop up when you want them the least. Forgive me. The interruption was unavoidable." He glanced at Foster. "Fortunately, you had Jerry Foster with you, so I know you weren't left flopping about. Foster can make time hustle like the wind."

"It's my job," Foster said.

"Can I call you Scotty?" Whittenfeld asked, shaking Scotty's hand.

"Of course," Scotty replied.

"And you call me Bill, or 'hey' if the occasion demands." He laughed, very self-assured. "Foster get you settled?"

"He couldn't have been more conscientious. The house is perfect."

"Did he also give you the grand VIP tour of the base?"

"We didn't have a chance," Foster advised. "We came right up."

Whittenfeld smiled. "Precision timing."

Foster nodded graciously. "I'll be in my office, Scotty. If you need anything, you just let me know." He inched toward the door. "It was a pleasure."

Foster disappeared. Whittenfeld offered Scotty a cigar, which Scotty accepted.

"Scotty!" Whittenfeld declared, his manner of speech, narrow Nordic features and graying temples accentuating a visible air of authority. "It's a goddamn thrill to have you here. Really a thrill. Though, of course, we all miss Jim Barrett." He paused, thinking. "Barrett was one hell of an engineer, a gentleman, too."

"So I've heard."

"And he was an integral component in the inception of the project."

"From day one?"

"Day two. I supervised the initial exploratory work alone. I brought in Barrett after the ball had started to roll, and I couldn't have chosen a better man. Hell, he deserved to be here. Deserved to receive the proper credit, to see results. Damn heart attack! He is as responsible as anyone for our progress. Not only did he design the drilling program, but without him we wouldn't have been able to get the *Columbus* into the loch."

"You barged the ship through the Caledonian Canal, didn't you?"

"Yes, but that was no easy exercise. The old locks were falling apart, and the chamber's beams were too narrow. We would have had to chop the *Columbus* into a million pieces. I asked Barrett to get us off the hook, so his team lengthened the lock chambers and widened the beams. In order to keep commercial navigation alive, they built the new system right over the old and then tore out the inner structure." He smiled thoughtfully, winding his Piaget watch, everything about him reeking elegance. "The entire region came out to watch the *Columbus,* split in thirds, in transit. It was a social and media event, the biggest noise heard around here since St. Columba announced the presence of a monster."

"I've seen the canal sections in miniature. They have the mockup in London."

Whittenfeld nodded. "A monument to Barrett's inventiveness and our perseverance." He had just passed fifty, the lines on his face appropriate for the age. "When Barrett went down, there was panic in New York and London. Fortunately, Bob Reddington recommended you. And after I had researched your background, I bought the recommendation too. I flew to the States and told them to stop jerking off. Get me a good man. Get me Scotty Bruce. Of course, I wasn't too sure they'd be able to lure you, but when the home office told me you'd expressed interest in abandoning private consultancy, I nearly jumped up to the top of Carn a Bhodaich across the loch."

"I appreciate the sentiment," Scotty said, puffing his cigar.

Whittenfeld walked to the window, staring at the finger of water stretching into the distance. "There it is! Loch Ness. The big prize. Sitting and waiting. Waiting to get angry. I know it looks like a docile child, but that's just a perverted little game it plays. Beneath the child is a vile little bitch with a nasty temper. Like a sorcerer, it can invoke the wrath of hell, and when it does, it is none too pleasant. The wind funnels between the mountains. The water surface waves to enormous proportions. The sky hangs heavy, black, brooding. I've seen it from here, and I've witnessed it aboard the *Columbus*. And I've seen the fear it instills."

Scotty listened, watched, fascinated.

"But what intrigues me most," Whittenfeld continued, "is what lies beneath. A colossal anomaly. A freak of nature. A renegade oil field." He held up several maps. "Look at these seismics and isopachs. Every day the project starts to look better. And every day the company's opponents look more and more like babbling fools." He laughed. "Mr. Bruce, the world is very illogical, its population almost devoured by its own stupidity and ignorance. Fortunately, there are enlightened men determined to see the battle through against onerous odds!"

Scotty just stared. "If I'm to get started tomorrow," he suddenly said, "I'd like to get a feel of the place, walk around, meet the staff."

Whittenfeld laughed. "The profile is accurate. Scotty Bruce: a man of action, few words. That's good. Your impatience with profundity will dewind me!" He walked to a free wall and pulled down a chart. "This is base personnel. I'm at the top. You're underneath. You have a chief district engineer, his staff, a district geologist, and the normal administrative personnel." He pointed at another graphic. "Here's the operational profile for the *Columbus*. Below is security. That's about it. You're familiar with general organizational procedures. Now you just need to meet the faces."

Scotty stood. "It's a big staff for an exploratory base."

Whittenfeld shook his head. "The company is very optimistic. We're sure there's plenty of oil here." He put on his jacket. "Shall we?" he asked, indicating the door.

They walked out into the secretarial area. Pierre Lefebre was waiting for them.

"I was told Mr. Bruce had arrived," Lefebre said in an appealing but heavy French accent. "So I came up to meet him."

"I'm glad you did," Whittenfeld declared, introducing the two men.

"It's a pleasure," Lefebre announced with a flourish. "I've heard a lot about you, Monsieur Bruce."

"I hope not all bad," Scotty said.

"All good!"

Impossible, Scotty thought, allowing a touch of realism to invade opening-day pleasantries. "Thanks" he said.

Lefebre was slim, scarred, blandly complected. At first glance, he looked the type of man who would rarely smile. But he was smiling effusively, almost overdoing it.

"So good," Lefebre continued as he buttoned the bottom button of his tightly tailored, epauletted Eisenhower jacket. "I'm anxious to discover if the man lives up to the legend."

"Don't believe all the propaganda," Scotty declared. Was the Frenchman referring to his football and engineering careers or his infamous reputation for corporate radicalism, his addiction to anticorruption crusades and causes?

"Propaganda or not, I look forward to working with you."

"Thanks. The feeling is mutual."

They entered the hall.

Whittenfeld turned to Lefebre. "What are you up to?"

"A security check."

"Can it wait?"

"Sure."

Whittenfeld pointed to the elevators. "Good. Come along and help me introduce Scotty to the base."

Shortly after two o'clock, Scotty, Whittenfeld, and Lefebre returned to Whittenfeld's suite.

They were joined moments later by Tony Spinelli, the senior district engineer, whom Scotty had already met downstairs.

"I made the arrangements," Spinelli said, spanking out a precise English accent. He was Italian by race, British by birth. "They're preparing the Black Isle hole. We'll give them a sendoff next week. We'll also copter over to Beauly Highpoint, which is near depth. Then we'll check Highland B, which is about a third of the way along."

"Sounds good," Scotty declared. "Though I want to make sure I spend as much time as I need on the *Columbus* first."

"No problem."

Whittenfeld interceded. "A dignitary named Farquharson arrives tomorrow. He's a Scottish Office undersecretary. He has considerable clout in energy matters, though he's never been near a rig in his life. I want the *Columbus* team to give him a thorough indoctrination. Since you'll be going out today, prep Reddington and the crew."

Scotty bit off the end of a new cigar. "It's as good as done."

"I also want you to be on board in the morning."

"I'd intended to stay out overnight, anyway."

"Good. And I want you to act as Farquharson's tutor. Teach him something. It will be a good way to orient yourself, make yourself at home."

"I'll do my best."

Whittenfeld gestured to Lefebre. "I want you there as well."

"Of course," Lefebre said.

Whittenfeld turned to Scotty again. "Why don't you join me for lunch?"

"I'd rather have a raincheck," Scotty declared. "I'd like to get out to the ship."

"Right to work," Whittenfeld said with a smile. "That's what I love to see. Raincheck given."

The helicopter hovered momentarily over the Geminii complex, then pitched southeastward.

"Look at those thunderheads," Scotty said, pointing toward the northeast.

The chopper pilot shook his head. "Just window dressing. I spoke to flight service this morning. The prevailing winds will take them due south through the North Sea sector."

Scotty looked at the surrounding countryside. Damn beautiful, he thought. High mountains. Acres of green pasture land. Bare granite pinnacles. Fingers of firths and inlets along the rugged west coast.

The pilot gestured. "There! The peak. It's Ben Nevis, the highest in Scotland. The city just beyond is Fort William, right at the west end of the Great Glen."

Scotty glanced out the side window. Below them was one of the company's seismic vessels, trailing its long hydrophone cable, picking up echoes for geophysical interpretation.

"We're home!" the pilot announced a short time later.

Scotty looked ahead. The *Columbus* was less than a half mile away, perched just beyond the mouth of Urquhart Bay. She looked magnificent, her huge derrick and drilling assemblage sticking high into the air above the moon pool, the midship access hole down through the hull to the water.

The pilot maneuvered the chopper over the forward helipad and set the bird down. Scotty opened the side door and stepped out. Bob Reddington rushed up and embraced him.

"You old grizzled son of a bitch!" Reddington said, laughing.

"Me? Old?" Scotty pulled away. "Why, you big jerk. I ought to heave you into the moon pool!"

Reddington suddenly lay down on the side of the helipad, bracing his elbow and raising a massive forearm. "Ready?" he asked.

Scotty dropped down, too, grabbing Reddington's extended palm. "You bet your ass. This one's for a case of beer!"

"Why not two?"

"Two? You'd think I'd never beaten you before."

"You haven't!"

Scotty gritted his teeth. "Well, I've been practicing."

Several crew members gathered. The chopper pilot lifted off but hovered nearby to watch the outcome. The arm wrestling match was over in seconds.

"All right," Scotty said, rising. "I owe you two cases."

Reddington could not stop laughing. "You've been practicing?"

They climbed down from the helipad and walked toward

ship center, passing several roustabouts who were unloading one of the *Columbus*'s supply tugs.

"That's one hell of a way to greet your best friend," Scotty said. "And your boss!"

"What do you want from me?" Reddington asked coyly. "You named the price and took the challenge. It's not my fault you're a schmuck!"

Scotty put his arm on Reddington's shoulder. "I took this job because of you. But now I'm having second thoughts."

"Here comes the bullshit," Reddington said, still laughing.

Climbing on to the drilling platform, Reddington introduced Scotty to the members of the current shift who were pulling the drill pipe out of the well.

"Why the trip?" Scotty asked, referring to the maneuver. "We lose a bit?"

"No," Reddington explained. "We hit some hard chert-silica strata, and we need a real chomper down there or we'll be here forever."

Scotty watched the movement, listening. He loved the noises, the smells, the chatter.

"I saw the kids before I left," he said.

"You did?" Reddington asked, beaming. "How'd they look?"

"Great. I've got the two handsomest godchildren in the world."

"Did they tell you I'm bringing them over in July?"

"Sure did. They also asked me to ask you if you'd bring over mama, too."

Reddington frowned. "That's some thought. I've got the divorce papers back in the apartment and a slew of letters from Margaret's lawyers as well as a couple of nasty ones from Margaret herself." He shook his head, leaned against a deck crane, which was offloading a supply tug, then looked out toward Drumnadrochit, a small village nestled in the crook of Urquhart Bay. "You should have married her yourself. She was your friend." He shook his head again, as if to clear it. "All right, what's done is done. So let's forget the bullshit. You're here, you bastard. Right here. I told you one day we'd work together. I told you I'd make it happen." He punched Scotty in the arm, a habit retained from the days he was fourth-string defensive end at USC, a pincushion for weekly simulation drills. "So let's go. Into the valley of death. I've got a load of executives waiting on pins and needles for your appearance. They think some godlike football hero is going to walk into the room."

They climbed down from the drilling platform, entered the executive quarters beneath the forward helipad, and walked through the dining, rec, and radio rooms. Reddington introduced Scotty to the staffs, then accompanied Scotty into the superintendent's office, where Bill Nunn and Mike Grabowski were waiting.

"These are the slaves," Reddington announced as he slid his way into a chair. "Bill Nunn, our well-site geologist. Mike Grabowski, our engineer." He pointed to Scotty. "The hero. Scotty Bruce." He laughed as the three men shook hands, exchanging quips. "Careful, Scotty. Don't make the standard operating error. Don't mistake Grabowski for a rabbi. I know he looks it, especially with the beard, but he's not. Though his parents never got over the fact that he didn't become one like the rest of his brothers. Grabowski will tell you. His parents nearly croaked when he burned his yarmulke and announced he was going to spend his life drilling holes."

"Is that so?" Scotty asked, stern faced, positioning himself at a work table, which was covered with the drill ship's mud and bit records, the morning and daily drilling reports, and the team's most recent blowout-prevention calculations.

"Red has a way of exaggerating," Grabowski said.

"The hell!" Reddington declared, looking at Scotty for support. "Grabowski's parents made life so miserable for him in the States, he had to pack his bags and transfer here to Inverness. In fact, he arrived just in time to watch Bill Nunn confront the Free Church."

Nunn cringed. "Oh, Christ, must you," he said. "I'd almost forgotten the damn incident."

"Bull," Reddington snapped. "Scotty, Nunn may be a geologist, but once he reaches shore, he Dr. Jekylls into a regular A. J. Foyt, equipped with a suped-up motorcycle and black crash suit. He plays the trumpet, too, though we had to prohibit the thing from the *Columbus* because the men started to complain." Nunn shook his head in mock disbelief. "Anyway," Reddington continued, "Nunn got drunk one Sunday and rode his cycle into town, taking the trumpet, too. Now that might be okay in some places, but this is Inverness. The Church of Scotland is bad, but the Free Church is comatose, and they control Inverness with an iron fist. They hate tourists. They hate noise. They're even against heavy breathing." He laughed.

"Well, Nunn slurped a couple of beers, roared the motorcycle up to the gathering hole of the Free Churchers, and blasted the 'Star Spangled Banner' on the horn. The parishioners stormed out like rabid dogs. Undeterred, Nunn drove the motorcycle through the church. Well, there was some uproar. Whittenfeld's as religious as Karl Marx, but after the Free Church threatened to boot every oil worker out of the region, Whittenfeld gathered the entire company and gave a fire-and-brimstone speech. You should have seen his face! I nearly laughed my balls off. But Nunn didn't. Whittenfeld almost guillotined him."

"I see you survived," Scotty said, patting Nunn on the back.

"Barely," Nunn observed.

"Where's the trumpet now?" Scotty asked.

"Locked in my closet. I may be dumb, but I'm not stupid."

"And you, Grabowski? You none the worse for wear?"

"I'm breathing."

Scotty smiled. He'd expected Reddington to bombard him with a story or two; Reddington had always had a penchant for whacko tales.

He picked up the drilling reports, mentioned Farquharson's impending visit, his own lack of familiarity with the drill ship's progress, Whittenfeld's concern for precision and preparation, and then pointed toward the work table.

Reddington glanced at Nunn and Grabowski. "Recess is over, gentlemen," he said.

The sun had just dipped below the horizon. The dark, majestic mountains surrounding the loch looked stern against the colored sky. The temperature had dropped suddenly. Scotty raised his collar and buttoned his jacket. He was dressed in his habitual jeans and boots. Hell, even back in the days when he'd roamed the clubs with the other football players, he'd been most comfortable in Western garb.

He smiled, examining the last trace of his reflection on the polished bulkhead wall. There were few streaks of gray in his hair and only several lines under his eyes. Not bad. Even nearing forty, he still looked young.

He turned, staring first toward the east, then the west. Loch Ness was one of the most magnificent places he'd ever seen. It was a sanctuary, and the sound of drilling, the movement of men, made him very aware they were intruders.

Yet there was something about this place that reminded him of home, the small town in the foothills of the Rocky Mountains outside Denver where he'd grown up as an all-American jock. There was a serenity that seemed to have already taken an enormous weight off his back. Never again would he allow himself to be the professional hero, the rallying flag for all kinds of causes, the conscience of his peers. He'd never been cut out for it. Had never aspired for it. It had just happened. Christ, that one crack-back block in Philadelphia, that one broken neck, that one poor bastard confined to a wheelchair, had changed his life. Led to martyrdom. The pursuit of his conscience. And what had he accomplished? Not much. He'd made a lot of noise. He'd punched out some crooked asshole executives who'd deserved a good thrashing. He'd uncovered some legitimate wrongs and cabals, pursued some worthy causes along with the bogus, those figments of his imagination. And he'd ultimately screwed up his life but good, been fired from a handful of companies, been branded a pariah.

Now he wanted peace, quiet. He did not want to confront management, any management, anymore.

He just wanted to do his job.

Geminii might very well be his last if he fucked up again. He wasn't kidding himself. He'd disrupted too many corporations already. He'd caused too much financial and personal damage. And private consultancy had been a sham. He hadn't been able to get an assignment in two years. So what if the populace and the press considered him a crusader, a hero? He was broke!

Thank God Reddington and Whittenfeld had come to his rescue. And even though he wasn't sure why Geminii had gone out on the limb to hire him—hell, there were better, certainly less controversial petroleum engineers around—he damn well was going to keep his nose to the grindstone, avoid questions and controversy, become a normal wage-earning executive once again.

He walked along the main deck, hugging the railing, then glanced up at the drill floor, smiled, and disappeared into the interior of the ship.

Chapter 3

Jerry Foster, Pierre Lefebre, and William Whittenfeld disembarked the huge Bell helicopter—followed by an older, white-haired gentleman supported by a cane, a young man, and a woman.

Scotty Bruce and the *Columbus*'s executive staff were assembled on the main deck. It was four o'clock.

"Getting a bit rough up there," Whittenfeld said, adjusting the handkerchief in his blazer pocket.

The crew members on the drill floor were in position, watching. The rotary table was still. The drill bit had already been changed, and the drill pipe had been run back into the bore. And everyone was holding steady, waiting for the entourage to pass and enter the forward cabins.

"Well," Reddington said. "The Bell looked beautiful coming in. Like a big prehistoric bird."

Everyone smiled except the woman. She was about thirty, attractive, brown haired, full faced, and blue eyed. Unlike most Highland women, she had a ballerina's figure and walked with an effortless, feminine grace. Her facial expression, however, was rigid, her features frozen into a leer of defiance.

Whittenfeld introduced her as Mary Ann MacKenzie.

Scotty turned to Foster. "*The* MacKenzie?" he asked, whispering.

"Yeah," Foster whispered back.

"Why the hell didn't you tell me MacKenzie was a woman?"

"You didn't ask."

"What's she doing here?"

"She's part of the package. Yes, Farquharson's here for an orientation visit, but that's only part of it. This is a political gambit. A sop to the opponents of the loch project. The theory is we bring them out, show them how it works, convince them

30

it's safe, and then hope they buy the caviar treatment and go into hibernation." He smiled as Whittenfeld began to detail the history of the *Columbus.* "The young bureaucrat is Peter Droon, a member of the Development Department in the Scottish Office. He was a rising star until he took the side of the Caucus. Since then, he's been given nowhere assignments, but he wouldn't be here unless they were considering resuscitating his career. Of course, the old gentleman's Andrew Farquharson, the undersecretary of state for Scotland and a member of the House of Commons. Apart from his new oil and gas duties, he's the secretary of state's trouble-shooter."

Fascinated, Scotty stepped away from Foster, then turned his attention to Whittenfeld.

"The *Columbus,* Mr. Farquharson," Whittenfeld was saying, "is a true ship as opposed to North Sea submersibles. Subs are basically pontoon-supported decks specifically designed for extreme conditions. We were able to use a drill ship here because the waters are nowhere near as rough as those in the offshore sector." He smiled. "The *Columbus* is operated completely by Geminii, which is one of the only integrated oil companies to own an offshore drilling subsidiary."

Farquharson hobbled around on his cane. "Ay, she's a big ship!" he said matter-of-factly. "Haven't been aboard one like her in some time. Since the war, in fact. That's where I injured the leg. I was a gunner on a destroyer running convoys. We got trapped by a phalanx of U-boats and Messerschmitts. Lost a lot of tonnage. Men, too. I took a big-caliber round. Wound up spending the rest of the war in the hospital." He laughed, far more raucously than his reserved appearance would have indicated. "But I didn't leave warfare behind me, Mr. Whittenfeld. I just exchanged Messerschmitt attacks for forays by the Labor opposition in Parliament."

Whittenfeld smiled politely, then introduced the members of the *Columbus* executive staff, taking particular care to pinpoint Scotty Bruce.

"So this is your first time in Scotland, is it, Mr. Bruce?" Farquharson asked.

"First time," Scotty declared, watching MacKenzie, who seemed extremely aloof. "Though I hope and expect to be here for a while."

"Scotty's your real name?"

"No, it's Peter Bruce. Peter Robert Bruce."

Farquharson coughed—slightly consumptively—then dabbed

his mouth with a handkerchief. "That's very parochial of Geminii."

Scotty shielded his eyes from the receding orb of the sun. "Sir?"

Farquharson limped to the ship's railing and looked down at a small tender tug. "Bruce was a noble family. Robert Bruce himself became Robert the First, King of Scotland."

"I feel humble," Scotty said.

"A Bruce humble?" Mary Ann MacKenzie asked, finally speaking in a near brogueless voice. "Come now, Mr. Bruce, you don't look the humble sort. Robert the First crowned himself king. Today, oil makes kings. And you look like the type of man who would be king. That reality might prove irresistible."

Scotty smiled awkwardly. "I'm sorry. I have no aspirations toward kingship. Do you?"

MacKenzie said nothing. Instead, she glanced at Droon, who offered no response as well.

Farquharson rapped his cane against the deck and laughed. "You give a Highlander a chance to fight and swords will flash within minutes. Right, Mr. Droon?"

"I wouldn't know," Droon said. "I'm not a Highlander."

Farquharson bristled. "That's nit-picking, Mr. Droon. You've got a Highland head filled with all kinds of rebelliousness. You and Miss MacKenzie are a fine pair. A wrong word and it's war."

"I don't war over words, Mr. Farquharson," MacKenzie said. "Only the ideas they represent and the problems they cause."

Farquharson turned to Whittenfeld. "MacKenzie is a proper Highland lass, Mr. Whittenfeld. Filled with courageous sayings. Morals. Proverbs. And valiant clichés. And she has the will of a lion. She's been a worthy opponent as well as fitting heir to the spirit of Robert the First."

Whittenfeld arched his brow. "I'm sure Robert the First was a brilliant warrior and king. But he didn't know a damn about the oil business." He bowed slightly in the direction of Mary MacKenzie. "Scotty Bruce does."

Whittenfeld climbed the steps to the drill floor. Farquharson followed, bemused. He understood people, politics, personal conflicts. He was enjoying the show.

"I've asked Mr. Bruce and Mr. Reddington to explain the operation of the vessel," Whittenfeld said, moving in front of the drill crew, all protected by hard hats, their clothes covered with grease. "As soon as you've all donned protective headgear, we'll begin."

One of the roustabouts doled out helmets.

Scotty moved to the fore. "Most of the procedures and equipment are identical to those used on land. There are four systems: power, hoisting, rotating, and circulating. Simply, the power system consists of diesel and electric engines, located below deck." He paused, looking upward. "Above is the derrick." He pointed across from where they were standing. "The big drum is the draw works, the main hoist, which lifts and lowers the rotating drilling assembly. The drilling assembly consists of the swivel, the square Kelly pipe, the rotary table, the drill pipe, drill collar, and drill bit. As the rotary table rotates, it turns the Kelly, which turns the drill pipe and, thus, the collar and bit downhole."

Farquharson pointed to the swivel. "And the purpose of the hose entering the swivel?" he asked.

"To introduce mud to the system," Scotty replied. "Mud pumps, located below deck, pump mud through the hose and down through the drill pipe to the bottom of the hole. From there the mud turns right around and comes back up the hole between the drill pipe and the bore wall. The mud cools the rotating bit, carries cuttings up from the bottom, fortifies the bore wall, and most important of all, exerts tremendous downward pressure, balancing any upward pressures from gas, oil, or other fluids. It keeps the well from flowing inadvertently or kicking, as we say." He paused, glancing at Lefebre, who poked his thumb into the air. Lefebre approved of his performance; he hoped, however, the others did, too. "The mud system is closed. Mud coming up is cleaned, then recirculated back down into the hole. Now we can vary the content of the mud. If we need more downward pressure, we add weight by adding solids. If we need a greater cleaning capacity, we add other substances." He pointed at the drill-floor crew. "The men you see," he said, continuing, "work in twelve-hour shifts. The tool pusher is the boss on the drill floor. The driller operates and monitors all the drilling and blowout-prevention equipment. The derrick men and rotary helpers attach and disconnect equipment, add additional lengths of drill pipe as the well gets deeper, change drill bits, run wall-support casing into the bore hole and cement casing in place, using cement pumped from tanks below deck."

Whittenfeld led the entourage off the drill floor and on to the main deck.

"Mr. Whittenfeld," MacKenzie suddenly called out. "Mr. Bruce said the mud exerts a downward pressure to prevent an inadvertent upward flow from the well. What if there is a flow?"

"It can't happen," Whittenfeld explained. "The downward pressure is always kept higher than the upward."

"Excuse me, but I've come to understand this is often not the case. That pockets of very high pressure can be inadvertently penetrated, causing a kick."

"Downhole conditions are closely monitored by the mud logger and mud engineer."

"But it can happen!"

Whittenfeld stared at MacKenzie before answering. "Yes," he said deliberately. "It's rare but possible. And if it does happen, we take care of it very quickly."

"Or else there can be a catastrophic blowout? Isn't that correct?"

Reddington quickly interceded. "No chance. A blowout preventer sits on top of the wellhead. We communicate with the preventer through two control hoses which run down to the well from the ship. If we detect excessive upward pressures, we stop drilling, and we hydraulically close the blowout preventer's rams. Then we increase the weight of the mud to counteract the upward pressure, pump the heavier mud into the hole, and open the preventer once the pressures have been balanced."

"But sometimes a kick goes unnoticed!" MacKenzie charged.

"Not on the *Columbus*," Whittenfeld said.

"Who says so? God?"

"Every precaution has been taken."

Droon joined. "What if the blowout preventer malfunctions?"

"It can't," Reddington said.

"They have in the past," MacKenzie challenged, playing to Farquharson. Having taken part in the public hearings, she knew the questions and answers already, and she knew Whittenfeld was well aware of it. "The *Ekofisk* platform blew out on the North Sea several years ago. Everyone knows the *Ekofisk* engineers installed their blowout preventer upside down. Maybe you've installed yours upside down, too!"

Whittenfeld laughed, very calm, very amused. "Mr. Farquharson, this tour was undertaken for your edification. It was not planned as a review of arguments made during licensing procedures. Those are all part of the public record, which I would be happy to supply."

Farquharson smiled obliquely. "I have a copy already. And I shall be reading it soon."

"Good," Whittenfeld said. "I encourage it." He waved toward the forward cabins. "Dinner is ready. I suggest we let Mr. Bruce explain the riser system. Then we can go into the dining room."

"You are our host," Farquharson said. "We are merely guests. We bow to your wishes."

There was silence. Nobody moved. Least of all Whittenfeld.

Scotty climbed up to the storage racks. Foster had revealed the existence of emotional opposition. Observing it first hand, however, was far more interesting. "Those large pipes are components of a system peculiar to offshore drilling. They are marine riser sections, which we join together. Essentially, the assembled marine riser connects the ship to the blowout preventer and the wellhead. In fact, if we were to go below deck into the moon pool area, we could see the riser descending down into the water under the ship. Now the drill pipe runs to the wellhead through the riser, and mud is circulated inside. And we have a tensioning system on board which helps keep the riser firm and mitigates against overstressing." He led them back toward the drill floor and pointed out several sets of pneumatic tensioning cylinders feeding wire lines down into the moon pool. "Those larger wires are attached to the top of the riser. The cylinder winds the wires in and out as the ship moves up and down. The smaller cylinders to the side perform the same function for the ship's guide wires, which descend to the wellhead and facilitate the movement of television cameras and other equipment. Both systems alleviate the problem of vertical motion, keeping the riser and guide wires taut."

"What if the wires were to break?" Farquharson asked.

"It's unlikely," Scotty replied. "However, if they did, we would close down the tensioners to prevent damage and replace the broken wires as quickly as possible."

He looked to Whittenfeld. What now? He'd just about covered everything. Whittenfeld asked if there were any questions, expecting some from MacKenzie and Droon. There were none.

Satisfied, Whittenfeld led everyone toward the bow.

The executive dining room was located on the lower-bridge deck. It was large, elegantly furnished. There were five tables. The *Columbus* staff and Whittenfeld's guests were clustered about the center three.

Undersecretary Farquharson was speaking. "What intrigues me is how you begin to drill in the first place. From up here to down there. From nothing to something. It's all very fascinating."

"Believe it or not," Scotty said, sipping from a wine glass, "we don't use divers, though we keep them available in case some of our underwater connections don't grip properly or the television cameras fail. Basically, it's pretty much a mechanical operation. Once the ship is positioned over the well site, we lower a temporary guide base on the guide wires to the ocean floor, along with television cameras. Then we guide down the drill pipe, cut an initial hole, insert casing, lower a permanent wellhead, the blowout preventer and marine riser, and begin to drill. Fact is, Mr. Farquharson, in a short time, you've become an expert in offshore drilling."

Farquharson laughed facetiously. "If I could make you an expert on British politics as quickly, Mr. Bruce, I would be hailed a genius."

Smiling, Scotty listened to the sound of the pumps and rotary table. The crew was drilling ahead with the new bit.

"For example, the Labour Party," Farquharson said, "ran the country for years, burying Britain under mountains of costly social programs. And the electorate correctly threw them out. But . . ."

Farquharson's words were suddenly muffled by a roar, followed by a violent jolt that sent dishes and food all over the floor.

"What the hell was that?" Whittenfeld screamed, jumping to his feet.

The boat lurched again. The rotary table stopped.

"Topside!" Scotty yelled.

"Monsieur Farquharson," Lefebre commanded. "You and your people stay here with Monsieur Foster!"

Scotty, Reddington, Whittenfeld, Lefebre, Nunn, and Grabowski ran up to the drilling platform.

The tool pusher rushed over. "We lost one of our anchors. Damn thing just pulled right out."

"That's impossible," Reddington countered. "They're cemented in place."

"Impossible, my ass!" the tool pusher screamed.

"Are we stable?" Whittenfeld asked.

"Yes," Reddington replied. "As long as we don't lose any others. We shift our position too much, we'll bust the drill pipe and maybe even rip the riser right off the wellhead."

They waited, everyone perspiring heavily. A popping sound turned them all around. Two of the ship's four guide wires had snapped somewhere below the water line and had spiraled upward; their pneumatic tensioners were beating furiously, fighting to restore tension, building up internal pressure to critical levels.

"Close the tensioners down!" the tool pusher yelled.

The driller shut down the system, then called everyone to his control panel and pointed to the riser position indicator screen, which illustrated the riser's vertical position relative to the wellhead. "The riser's way out of line."

"Current?" Whittenfeld asked.

"No way," Scotty shouted. "The current's minimal tonight. The wind's nowhere near critical, and there are still five anchors holding. There! Feel it? The ship is moving." He looked at the screen. "The riser is pushing the ship, and something is pushing the riser!"

"Close the preventer!" Reddington ordered, shoving the driller to his control panel.

Hands shaking, the driller manipulated the dials on the blowout preventer control panel. Lights flashed, indicating the signals sent down the control hoses had been received.

The blowout preventer had sealed off the well.

"Goddamn riser is all over the place!" Scotty said.

The drill pipe began to bang off the inside of the riser.

"The drill pipe's bending," the driller cried. "This keeps up, we're going to be in big trouble."

Below they could hear the top of the riser sloshing in the water in the moon pool, pushing the resisting ship farther out of line. The clanging of the drill pipe increased. The Kelly bushing, which held the drilling assemblage in the rotary table, shot out, nearly decapitating a rotary helper. The ship's movement eased momentarily. Then another jolt hit. Tools and pipes bounced off the derrick lattice. A tong smacked the tool pusher across the face, sending him sprawling to the floor, covered with blood. Several men moved to help, ducking beneath a swinging pipe, which pinned a roustabout against the rear stairwell. Mud shot up through the deck planks to the rear of the derrick, covering everyone with wet clay.

Reddington closed down ship electrical.

"A mud tank ruptured!" a derrick man called.

"Get someone downstairs," Scotty cried.

A crewman ran forward through the melee. "There's tremendous pressure on the other anchors. They're going to rip out, too!"

The derrick started to vibrate. Tools secured to the upper derrick walkways showered down. Men cried out, running away from the downpour.

"What the hell can we do?" Whittenfeld asked frantically.

"Nothing!" Scotty advised. "We just wait."

They watched the driller's controls. Listened to the clank of the drill pipe inside the riser. Felt the ship sway beneath them. Heard the creak of the anchor lines.

Then, suddenly, the ship stopped moving; it was over.

No one said a word. Everyone wiped the sweat and mud from their clothes and faces. The injured roustabout and tool pusher, both still bleeding heavily, stumbled off to medical, assisted by several crew members.

Whittenfeld walked across the drill floor, eyes wild, hands clenched into fists, finally turning toward the bridge deck to return to Farquharson and the others.

However, the bridge deck was empty.

Undersecretary Farquharson, Mr. Droon, Mary MacKenzie, and Jerry Foster were all on the drilling-platform staircase, covered with mud, spackled with blood, staring.

Chapter 4

William Whittenfeld examined the equations on the lead page of the differential workout, then stopped pacing and returned to the conference table.

It had been a week since the *Columbus* disruption. As expected, there'd been flak. Fortunately, though, there'd been no press leaks, and he'd been able to keep the interested parties on hold, pending the outcome of Geminii's internal investigation.

"Continue," he said.

Scotty glanced at Reddington, Foster, Lefebre. "Before we dispatched the contract diving team from Aberdeen," he said, examining several sets of documents, "we recalculated the mooring equations for the ship's six anchor lines. Those are the ones you just read. And you've seen the results. The anchor pattern was appropriate, and it was certainly capable of withstanding much higher current and wind forces than were being exerted at the time of the breakdown."

Whittenfeld glanced at the equations again. "Agreed."

Scotty looked at another document. "The divers carefully inspected the anchor hole and its cement plug. There was no sign of disintegration or decomposition. The plug itself was intact, and the anchor hole did not fail. We're certain something grabbed the anchor line and pulled the plug from the wall!"

Whittenfeld was shocked. "Are you sure the *Columbus*'s own movements couldn't have done it?"

"Absolutely. The driller noticed the position display panel just before the disruption and the drill ship was right over the wellhead."

"Were there any marks on the line?"

"No. We ran microinspections. The line's clean."

Whittenfeld turned to Reddington. "Do you agree, Red?"

"Yes," Reddington said. "We're also convinced the jolts we felt on board were caused by the anchor wire being yanked against the weight of the ship."

"Could there be another explanation?"

"Not really," Reddington replied. "The direction of the ship's movements after the initial pullout jerk back were toward the anchor pile, and one member of the crew said he saw the shipboard end of the broken anchor line pull taut several times after it had certainly been ripped from its foundation."

"What about the broken guide wires?" Whittenfeld asked.

Scotty pulled a cloth off the center of the table. Beneath were four pieces of wire line, set in two parallel rows. "The points where the ends meet is where each wire was cut."

"Cut? Not broken or ripped?"

"No. Something cut the guide wires at approximately two hundred and ten feet. Fortunately, whatever it was came in from the side because if it was cutting indiscriminately, it might have axed the two blowout prevention control hoses."

"What cut the wires?" Whittenfeld asked after placing two of the cut wire ends together.

"A scissorlike tool," Scotty said.

Whittenfeld thoughtfully tugged the cuff ends of his sleeves into alignment. He was relatively calm; he had not shown real anger since the day of the incident. "What about the riser?"

Scotty placed the cloth back over the guide wires. "I said at the height of the confusion that I thought something was pushing the riser. Well, we're convinced of it now!"

"Is there any firm evidence?"

"No. Certainly nothing at the point of attack. We had the divers inspect the riser sections. There were no dents of any kind on the riser's steel shell, no remnants—paint, oil, grease—nothing."

"Then how did you reach your conclusion?"

"By carefully reviewing the facts. By questioning the crew, analyzing movement, the ship's momentum, direction, eliminating possibilities."

"Did the riser come close to failing?"

"No, but it was severely stressed. I had the divers inspect most of the joints. The joints were given a good jostling. The divers also did a magnetic-particle inspection for cracks. None were found. The drill pipe is okay, too. All in all, I think we got away lucky." He looked around the table. "Whatever pulled out the plug and moved the marine riser had tremendous power. Whatever cut the guide wires had a very sharp tool face. We have to make the assumption that all three events were initiated by the same culprit."

"There were no unknown vessels on the loch surface at the time of the attack," Reddington added, joining. "No one on the ship saw anything other than our seismic boats, two of our tugs, and a transglen navigational barge. Since the guide wires were cut at over two hundred feet beneath the surface, we have to eliminate anyone breathing air because you just can't effectively use air diving systems at that depth. Scuba is out. Diver lockouts are out. So are wet vehicles."

"No," Scotty said. "We've analyzed the information ad nauseam. The only culprit that makes sense is a manned submersible."

"Are you serious?" Whittenfeld asked.

Scotty shrugged. "We know it sounds incredible. And believe me, we're not comfortable with it. But yes, we're serious. It's the only conclusion that rings true. What we can't imagine is who would have been sophisticated enough to have gotten an operating submersible into the loch undetected."

"A lot of people, Monsieur Bruce!" Lefebre suddenly said. "If you pay the price, you can buy anything you need. Submersibles. Experienced crews. Certainly secrecy!"

Whittenfeld stiffened. "The *Columbus* was attacked by a submersible?" he asked incredulously, his anger beginning to resurface.

"Yes," Scotty said.

"Under whose control?"

"I don't know."

"Lefebre?"

Lefebre stood. "The three guests come on ship," he said. "As soon as they get here, all hell breaks loose. Even an idiot would realize it was timed to happen." He jabbed the table. "Make a list of every radical nationalist group in the region. Make another which includes everyone who opposed the loch application. Someone on those two lists instigated the attack. And I wouldn't dismiss the two who were aboard the drill ship. This MacKenzie and Droon. I've dealt with fanatics all my life. They live for their causes. MacKenzie and Droon would have sacrificed themselves. I heard it in their voices. Saw it on their faces."

"I want the *Columbus* protected," Whittenfeld snapped.

"Shouldn't we notify the police?" Scotty asked.

Whittenfeld vehemently shook his head. "No. The police will only interfere. We'll do what must be done ourselves. Lefebre! I want you to place armed guards on the *Columbus* and around the loch shore!"

Reddington sat forward, distracted. "Armed guards on the ship can't protect it from a submersible," he said. "They'll just invite dissension."

"From whom?"

"The crew. The rig team. The union."

Whittenfeld's expression hardened. "Geminii Petroleum. The *Columbus*. The completion of the Loch Ness exploratory well. Those have to be our priorities. Not the feelings of the rig crew nor the position of the union. There will be armed guards aboard the drill ship!" He pointed to Scotty. "I want a guard tug permanently on line as well. I know we don't have any to spare, so call Aberdeen or speak to the London office. Make arrangements. Get it here. And have it loaded with sonar equipment and stationed near the *Columbus*. If anything attempts to approach the riser or any of the anchors again, I want us to know about it before it reaches its target." He ambled toward the conference table. "The Energy Department license gives us four years to operate. If we comply with license conditions, we get an additional thirty. I don't want to see us closed down. I don't want to see us lose out when the Moray Firth offshore bids come up, either. And Lefebre is right. There are legions of opponents who would like to see us booted. They don't understand the real world. They're fanatics. And damn, I'm not going to let a bunch of fanatics delay or run us out!" He caught his breath. "There will be guards and sonar, and our installations will be protected!"

"Do we try to track down the saboteurs ourselves as well?" Scotty asked, realizing Whittenfeld's protective decisions were realistic in view of the findings.

"Yes," Whittenfeld replied, turning to Lefebre.

"The environmentalists," Lefebre said. "The Scottish Nationalist Party. The radical nationals. The unions. It was one of them or all of them."

Whittenfeld leaned toward his security chief. "You're to see that the ship and our other installations are guarded. Then you're to try and uncover the parties behind the attack. Do what must be done. But do it carefully. I don't want any confrontations. I don't want any violence. I don't want to alert the constabulary. And I certainly don't want to provoke the local governing authorities. No, I want done just what must be done to protect this project and this company. Only that!"

Shortly after Whittenfeld had adjourned the meeting—he had ended the discussions by commissioning Foster to compile a report on the *Columbus* incident for Farquharson as quickly as possible—Scotty accompanied Reddington to the roof, where a helicopter was waiting, then re-entered the building, taking an elevator down to the first floor.

Locating Lefebre's suite, he entered. Lefebre's secretary was not at her desk, but Lefebre's door was open. The Frenchman was on the phone. Scotty began to retreat, but Lefebre waved him in.

The office surprised him. He expected something sparse and uninviting. But this place was fascinating. There were potted plants about. Shelves filled with books. Hanging lithographs. An open volume of Shakespearean plays on a reading stand. A half-dozen mounted ivory carvings. And one carving in progress on a work bench in the corner.

Lefebre ended the phone conversation—he'd been talking to a perimeter security officer—and put down the receiver. "Monsieur Bruce?" he said, smiling.

"I was down the hall," Scotty explained. "I thought I'd drop in and sit for a minute. See your office."

"Make yourself at home," Lefebre said, shifting in his seat. Behind him was a duty roster clogged with names. "Would you like something to drink? Some coffee, tea, water?"

"No, thank you," Scotty said, looking about, admiring the carvings.

Lefebre smiled. "I see you have a roving eye. See anything interesting?"

"Yes. The ivory work."

"My menagerie."

"The elephant in particular. It's spectacular."

"I appreciate the compliment."

Scotty pointed to the work bench. "You carved these yourself?" he asked, very impressed.

"With considerable difficulty."

"Where'd you learn?"

Lefebre paused, thinking, then answered. "In the army. In Marseilles. There was a soldier in my regiment who'd been raised in the Cameroons. He learned the skill from a native. I learned from him."

"Are you from Marseilles?"

"No, Calais. I was stationed in Marseilles. And I remained there after my discharge. Working."

"For the Marseilles police?"

Lefebre laughed. "You seem to be compiling a dossier. So please, allow me to complete it. Parents dead, childhood status: orphan. No wife. One child . . . a bastard . . . location unknown. Six years as security director for various industrial concerns. A tenure in the French army. A long career with the Marseilles police. A degree from the Sorbonne in classical literature."

"Classical literature?"

"Does that surprise you?"

Scotty glanced at the shelves, the books. "Not really. I see the evidence." Lefebre's manner of speech included; it was perfect. "No, I guess I just find it incongruous that someone with a degree in literature would become a security man."

"Life's convolutions can never be accurately foreseen. There are roadblocks, circumstances, twists of fate, which often lead men down uncharted roads. Yes, I enjoyed literature. I still do. But long ago I found other pursuits far more rewarding."

"Like what?"

"My job. This job."

"I hope I'm not prying?"

Lefebre shook his head, laughing. "I'm flattered by the attention." He extended a pack of Gitanes. Scotty declined. Lefebre pulled one out. "So," he said, lighting the cigarette and blowing a ring of smoke across the desk, "what else can I tell you?"

Scotty looked about. The blotter was filled with papers. There were several books piled on a corner of the desk and, strangely, two boxes of chewing tobacco, something he would not have expected to find in the possession of a Frenchman.

"Tell me about the submersible," he said.

"What do you mean?" Lefebre asked as he flipped some pages of the Shakespeare compendium.

"My conclusion."

"I accept it."

"Do you think it was right?"

"If you're asking whether or not I think there could actually have been a submersible in the loch, the answer is 'yes.' If you're asking whether there are people who would attempt such an attack, I refer you to my speech upstairs, and again the answer is 'yes.' And if you're asking whether I will uncover the identity of the malicious parties involved, the answer is . . ."

" 'Yes'?"

"Definitely yes."

The telephone rang. The secretary had not returned yet, so Lefebre picked up the phone himself. The caller was Whittenfeld. They spoke briefly; then Lefebre walked Scotty out into the hall.

"Duty calls, my friend," Lefebre said. "But we should have lunch soon. Talk some more. Compare dossiers."

"Absolutely," Scotty declared.

The elevator arrived. Lefebre disappeared. Scotty sorted out impressions. Though Lefebre had tried to make a sincere and friendly impression, he'd failed. Scotty wasn't quite sure what he sensed, but he suspected a completely different kind of man lurking inside the smiling shell of the security chief.

He left the building.

It was raining the following morning when Scotty walked down the second-floor corridor past frenetic secretaries and popped into Jerry Foster's office.

"You look bright eyed and bushy tailed," Foster observed as he collated some papers on his desk.

"Hardly," Scotty said, picking up the bottom of the drawn window blinds. "You going to show movies in here?"

Foster laughed. "No. The rain depresses me. I also work best under artificial light."

Scotty sat, noticing a ludicrous picture of Foster in scuba gear hanging on the wall.

"That the *Columbus* report?" he asked, pointing at the papers.

"You bet."

"You have a full draft already?"

"Already? Hey, Scotty, that's a funny one. I haven't left this place since yesterday afternoon." He glanced down at the report. "God knows if the damn thing makes any sense. I'm so bleary-eyed I doubt I'll be able to tell. And hell, a lot of the stuff is Greek to me."

"You need my expertise?"

"No. Whittenfeld will be down in a while to dot the i's. He's been hovering around me like a bat since I started this thing. But who can blame him. The ship gambit backfired. There's been pressure from New York and London. And while you and Reddington were working on the loch, Whittenfeld was fielding some stinging phone calls from the Scottish Office and the Highland Council. No, he has every reason to make sure this report hits the mark, some special incentive, too. Loch Ness, this place, this operation, all of it is very personal to him. He lives for it. Christ, I'm surprised he's been as restrained as he's been this week, though, I tell you, when you laid the submersible thing on him, I thought he was going to explode like a bomb."

"Maybe I have a calming effect on him."

"Could be."

Thoughtful, Scotty picked up the draft, glanced over it, then laid it down and stood. "You call me if you need me."

Foster stood, too. "You got it," he said, smiling.

Chapter 5

Several days later, Whittenfeld summoned the executive staff to his office and distributed the *Columbus* report. The report recapped the events aboard the drill ship, the results of the investigation, and the conclusions reached by management. It declined to point an incriminating finger but acknowledged the company was undertaking steps to ensure the safety of its installations.

He asked for comments. There were none. He said he'd expected none, so he had taken the liberty of previously forwarding the report to Farquharson.

He dismissed everyone except Scotty and told Scotty about a meeting he'd arranged with the planning committee of the

Highland Regional Council. Having already forwarded copies
of the report to committee members as well, he asked Scotty
to take the meeting and answer any questions that might be
forthcoming.

The planning committee convened the following morning.
Scotty fielded questions, again avoiding incriminating accusa-
tions. Specifically, the committee asked why the company had
not requested the assistance of the Northern Constabulary.
There was no permanent damage, he replied. No fatalities.
And the company had stiffened its security to ensure there
would be no repetition. In fact, he said, the entire affair had
been put to bed, and the meeting with the committee had
been called solely as a courtesy.

Most of the committee members were satisfied. However,
he wasn't sure how Mary MacKenzie had reacted. She'd said
absolutely nothing.

The meeting adjourned.

He left the council building and waited in the parking lot.
MacKenzie appeared several minutes later and walked briskly
to her car. He approached.

"I'd like to speak to you," he said.

"I'm late for an appointment."

"Mrs. MacKenzie," he said, "this is important."

"It's miss," she snapped.

"All right. Miss. But what I have to say is still important."

She looked at her watch.

"I won't keep you long," he said.

She slid into her car, opened the shotgun door, and waved
him inside.

"Did you read the report?" he asked, moving next to her.

"Of course I read the report," she said. "I read it twice."

"I should have known. You had all those comments. Observations."

She glanced at him, fire in her eyes. "I said nothing,
Mr. Bruce, because there was nothing to say. I read the
report. I heard your arguments. I listened to the conclusions."

"And?"

"They're absurd! Is that clear?"

He held up his hands, nonplussed. "Don't get angry at me.
I'm only doing my job."

"And I'm doing mine. Which means I have to represent the
people of this region. And protect their lives, their homes. I

have to sift through lies and see the forest for the trees. And what I see I don't like."

"Neither do I," he shot back. "I see a closed-minded woman with predetermined opinions, little or no courtesy, and no patience."

She cranked her head toward him. "I've been listening to Geminii for years. Till it's almost choked me. I'm no novice at this."

"I didn't say you were."

"I was on the ship. I was there! Something disastrous happened. Something occurred that endangered us all!"

"I don't deny that. No one does. But you've been given all the facts. The results of the investigation."

"And am I supposed to accept them as the gospel?"

"Yes."

"Then you take me for a fool, Mr. Bruce."

He breathed deeply, frustrated. "I conducted the investigation, Miss MacKenzie."

"I see," she said, glaring wickedly. "Does that entitle you to some kind of award?"

"No!" he challenged. "But it entitles me to defend the truth. And the report reflects the truth."

She laughed. "We were all told Geminii had just hired a saint. You, Mr. Bruce! The conscience of the world. The essence of integrity. But don't delude yourself. Don't think I attribute more to your panderings than I would to the word of any other employee of Geminii. You are an employee of Geminii, aren't you? District supervisor, if I'm correct. A senior executive?"

He sat back. Thoughtful. Did everyone know about his background? "Yes. I work for Geminii. Yes, I'm district supervisor."

She looked him square in the eyes. "Mr. Bruce, let me ask you an honest question. Do you really believe someone operating a submersible vehicle attacked the *Columbus?*"

"The evidence suggests so."

"I haven't seen any evidence. I've just heard what representatives of Geminii said they found."

"That's what we found!"

"All right. That's what you found. But even looking at this so-called evidence, these findings made by divers. A manned submersible? Attacking a giant ship? You must be senile."

"It's possible."

"Who, Mr. Bruce? Who?"

"What do you mean, 'who'?"

"Who was in the submersible? Who organized this attack? Tell me who."

"That's the exact question Whittenfeld asked me. I couldn't give him an answer, and I can't give you one. I just joined the company. I wasn't here during license application. I wasn't here at the start of active exploration. I don't know the players, so I couldn't possibly make a guess at who might have tried to sabotage the *Columbus*."

"Sabotage is a very serious charge, Mr. Bruce."

"Yes. Especially when lives might have been lost."

She smiled archly, paused. "Now, Mr. Bruce, you can't tell me no one at the company named names. Identified parties who might have engineered such an attack!"

"There were suggestions."

"Well, then. You didn't tell the council this."

"It's not the type of speculation one indulges in publicly."

She looked around. "We're not in public."

He glanced at her severely. She was almost too attractive to be so goddamned stubborn and contentious, too feminine and sensual to be a clarion for local public outrage. "It's common knowledge there were opponents to the company's application."

"Like?"

"Environmentalists."

"I'm an environmentalist, Mr. Bruce."

"The Scottish Nationalist Party."

"I'm one of them, too."

"The unions fought aspects of the plan that called for the importation of English and American workers."

"I'm a union sympathizer. You know, Mr. Bruce. It seems you're pointing a finger in my direction. Or in the direction of my close associates."

"I'm doing nothing of the kind."

"Then what are you doing?"

He didn't respond.

She stiffened, angrily twisting her features. "No submersible attacked the *Columbus*. And that leaves one of two alternatives. Something *did* go wrong beyond the control of the crew. Something that endangered everyone. Or the event was planned. Planned and executed by Geminii executives."

"Are you crazy?" he asked, dumbfounded.

"No," she said calmly. "Not in the least. It makes a hell of a lot of sense. Whittenfeld invites us all on board. The breakdown is engineered. Everyone is taken off the ship. A report is issued. Saboteurs are blamed. But there are no saboteurs. Nevertheless, these imaginary saboteurs serve a very useful purpose. The specter of sabotage allows the company to close down access. Increase security. Keep everyone away. Keep oversight at a minimum. That's the way oil companies like to work, isn't it?"

"No."

"Spare me, Mr. Bruce. Because there's more. There's something else this supposed conspiracy serves to do. It serves to protect Geminii Petroleum."

"How's that?"

"In case something does go wrong internally. Something beyond the control of the company. A breakdown. A disaster. Anything. The company can blame it on sabotage. Plain and simple. Blame it on sabotage and no one will question whether the company should be allowed to continue operations. Have everyone out chasing ghosts and the company itself is free from scrutiny!"

"You're crazy."

"You've said that already."

"Look. I can see you and I have to have a long talk."

She leaned across and snapped down the handle of the door. "We've *had* a long talk, Mr. Bruce. Good day."

"Please . . ."

"Good day," she repeated, interrupting.

Scotty climbed out of the seat. MacKenzie turned on the engine, revved it momentarily, maneuvered the car out of the parking lot, then sped away.

Scotty closed the front door to Travis House, walked down the hall, and entered the den. Mrs. Munro was puttering about with a feather duster.

"Home early, aren't you, Mr. Bruce?" she asked.

"Yes," he replied.

"You wouldn't be wanting me to fix up some food for you, would you now?"

"No."

"That's good. Very good. I only have two hands, and the dust is creeping over this place like the moor fog at night."

He bobbed into the kitchen, built an impressive turkey sandwich, then returned to the den, sitting down on the lounge.

"If you sit there, Mr. Bruce," Mrs. Munro said, waving feathers, "you're going to have a side order of dust."

"I'll cover up when you roam by."

He sipped his beer as Mrs. Munro whizzed past him, her plain drape of a dress catching nearly every article in the room.

"Do you know anything about the Scottish Nationalist Party?" he asked moments later.

Mrs. Munro stopped dusting and turned, a gaping expression on her face. "Now that's some question, Mr. Bruce. I'm Scottish. Was born and raised here. My poor dead husband, too. I'd be a boob if I didn't know about the Scottish Nationalists."

"That's fine, Mrs. Munro. Then perhaps you can give me some insight."

"The Scottish Nationalist Party is a political party," she said a trifle condescendingly, as if she had found his ignorance pathetic. "Just like Labour, the Tory Conservatives, and the Liberals."

"Are you a member?"

"No, but I'm a Nationalist. Everyone in Scotland is a Nationalist."

"What does the party stand for?"

"What do you think it stands for, Mr. Bruce? An independent Scotland! Scotland for the Scots!"

"Makes sense."

"Darn right it makes sense."

Having finished his sandwich, he laid his plate on the coffee table. "How do these Nationalists feel about the oil companies?"

"They don't like them much."

"Why is that?"

" 'Cause the oil companies bespoil the land. 'Cause they bring in foreign workers when it's the Scottish worker who should be in employ, and they take out Scottish oil and give it to the British government, which is controlled by the English. We get no benefit. Or almost none. The government in London bleeds Scotland dry, and when there's no oil left, it will let Scotland rot in the sun!"

"You don't really believe that, do you?"

Mrs. Munro was indignant. "Get a history book, Mr.

Bruce. Read it! Then tell me whether I should believe it or not."

"Would you think the Nationalists disliked the oil companies enough to try to sabotage their installations?"

"I wouldn't know anything about that kind of thing, Mr. Bruce. I wouldn't even try to make a guess."

"I have one more question."

Mrs. Munro breathed deeply. "What is that, sir?"

"Do you think the Loch Ness monster is a member of the Scottish Nationalist Party?"

Mrs. Munro stopped in her tracks and shook her head incredulously. "Geminii hired me out to a crazy man. A loon. Mr. Bruce! Monsters don't join political parties. They don't vote. Even if they exist, they don't do such things."

"Does it exist?" What a ridiculous question, he thought. Thank God Red hadn't heard it!

"I don't know."

"You must have an opinion."

"I believe in goblins. There are goblins in the mountains."

"That's very interesting. But I'm not asking about goblins. Just monsters. Does it exist?"

She stared. Then nodded.

"Thank you, Mrs. Munro," he said, walking out of the room.

Chapter 6

The limousine glided quietly along the two-lane highway, heading east out of Inverness.

William Whittenfeld sat in the back seat reviewing the contents of a folder—a pair of lists—that Pierre Lefebre had given him that afternoon. A security man was perched next to the driver. A tape cassette played softly.

Whittenfeld examined one list, then the other. The first contained the names of company opponents, the second the names of radical Scottish nationalist groups. In addition, there were detailed notes and recommendations as well as a special document, denoted *important*, describing the modus operandi of a group known to the authorities as the New Jacobite Coalition, a virulent nationalist organization that had broken away from the Scottish Nationalist Party several years before.

Geminii had received three threatening letters from New Jacobite operatives within the last week, and although the Jacobites had historically confined their activities to the southern cantons of Scotland, the letters clearly indicated that the coalition had arrived in Inverness in force. An inquiry by Lefebre had uncovered evidence indicating that Jacobite operatives worked almost exclusively under the protective umbrellas of existing organizations—trade unions, merchant associations, business groups, and the like—but so far Lefebre had been unable to pinpoint the identity of any operatives, let alone the man who had written the letters. And a question certainly remained whether or not this group was involved in the *Columbus* conspiracy at all since Lefebre had uncovered no information as of yet creating an inference one way or the other.

The group deserved watching.

The limousine turned off the main road. Nearby, he could see the lights of the Inverness Airport. Beyond was the Inverness Firth. Ahead, the Culloden Moor.

Whittenfeld placed the folder in an attaché case as the limousine swept between gate posts. Beyond the posts stood the Culloden House. It had two stories, about fifty rooms, and was brightly lit by floodlights.

The limousine stopped in front of the main entrance, behind Scotty's jeep. Whittenfeld stepped out. Above him loomed the mansion's stone walls. There were numerous windows, turrets and parapets, too, as well as oblique turns of the architecture that hid clandestine stairways and nooks.

He climbed the main staircase and looked through the front door's glass partition. He could see the bar. Scotty Bruce was there, waiting. He looked at his watch. He was twenty minutes late. He did not like tardiness. Especially his own!

Quickly, he opened the door and entered.

* * *

"I've listened," Whittenfeld was saying as they attacked their main courses and sipped from partially filled glasses of Mouton Cadet. "I've heard it all. I've heard the scuttlebutt. That I'm consumed by Loch Ness . . . the prospect of finding oil . . . a bonanza. That the whole thing has become a fixation."

Scotty looked around the dining room. It was elegant. All the tables were filled, conversations subdued.

"Has it?" he asked.

Whittenfeld eased a grin. "Perhaps. But I don't find an intense commitment unwarranted. Loch Ness is important. To the world. To Geminii." He looked out the dining-room window. "And to me."

"That's understandable," Scotty said, staring at his host, who was dressed in an elegantly tailored black suit, white shirt, and black tie. "You did say you were here from day one."

"From day one and before," Whittenfeld declared. "I was comanaging director of the Dundee field when the Loch Ness oil slick was discovered. Sure, the Dundee field was special. You see, the North Sea represented my first opportunity to work outside the United States. But this loch thing; this was something else. It was . . . well . . . exciting. An incredible opportunity. Something a man waits for all his life. Though the company was skeptical, I grabbed for it, urged them to pursue. I led the first seismic crews and geology contingents. Hell, Scotty, I got my hands dirty. I was there with the doodle buggers, laying seismic cables. I rode the seismic launches. I spent nights awake, reading charts, knocking possibilities around." A look of pride crossed his face. "Damn, *I* was the one who cracked the puzzle. *I* pinpointed the anomalies. *I explained* the unexplainable!" He pounded the table. "My guts are riding with success. No, I will never allow the Loch Ness enterprise to fail. I won't allow it."

Scotty looked at Whittenfeld's eyes. He'd seen the look many times before. Obsession. But there was more. Contention. Whittenfeld was something other than just a company manager. He was a challenger who might very well have come to hate his opponent.

"I don't think you will fail here," he said.

"Is that a compliment?" Whittenfeld asked.

"Absolutely."

"I want you to feel like I do. I want you to be committed. To this place. To the loch. To the battle. The loch has thrown down a gauntlet. It has dared us to beat it. It is a vile little bitch!" He laughed smugly. "You know, I remember the licensing hearings. There was such a hue and cry from the hearing committee once its members had learned you can start a well in one place and directionally bend it to drill into a producing horizon many miles away. Why put a ship on the loch? they cried. Why drill down through the water? Why endanger Ness?" He shook his head. "I explained the facts of life. That you can only bend a well a few degrees at a time and that if a producing reservoir is too near the surface, you cannot directionally drill into it because you cannot drill deep enough to bring enough bend into play. And that the Loch Ness field fit the negative criteria precisely since it lay only four thousand feet below the surface. And I remember then thinking about just how clever this renegade was. To have insulated itself so well!"

Scotty sat back. "To state the obvious, the loch is definitely an emotional thing to you," he said.

"Yes. I'll confess. It is."

"I have to confess, too. I don't think I'll ever be able to generate the same kind of involvement."

Whittenfeld lifted his glass, bowed his head, sipped, then stared. "You will," he said. "If I have anything to say about it, you will!"

They finished dinner by nine o'clock, entered the lounge, and ordered two glasses of anisette.

"I respect devotion," Whittenfeld was saying. "I covet enthusiasm. I expect everyone on the Geminii payroll to work as hard as I do. But I don't mind eccentricity. In fact, Scotty, a little eccentricity is good. It makes men more creative. It makes them more valuable." He laughed. "But look who I'm talking to about eccentricity. Scotty Bruce. Famous football player. My God, you must have seen your share of talented eccentrics. From what I've read—and I'm not one for athletics, mind you—professional sports are filled with them."

"They're about," Scotty admitted as he popped some pretzels into his mouth. He glanced at his watch; it was almost ten o'clock. He looked through the parlor door into the hall. The place was very old, and there was a musty smell in the air, a peculiar sensation of history. If he'd never seen a candidate for haunting before, he'd seen one now. "But you have to be a little off the wall to pound your brains into the dust day in and day out, to beat your body black and blue, to literally risk your life."

"You did it. Did you consider yourself off the wall?"

Scotty stared; he knew Whittenfeld knew the answer already. "No," he said. "Not in the beginning. Not until my Götterdämmerung."

Whittenfeld smiled. "You're a smart man, Scotty. An asset. I made the right move bringing you here, and I want to clear the air right now. Set the record straight once and for all. I hired you because of what you are and what you've done and not in spite of it. Yes, I heard the worst. I heard you're one of the best engineers around, but also one of the most unreliable and dangerous. I heard you're too honest, too much a magnet for cause mongers, too quick to fight a battle of conscience. I know about all your crusades. I know where you succeeded and where you screwed up. I wasn't frightened. And I'm not now. Because I know everyone makes mistakes, and good men learn from them. Scotty, you're exactly the type of man we wanted, an honest man with principles. Because Geminii is an honest company with principles. A company that's not afraid to be questioned. Yes, you and Geminii were made for each other."

Scotty uncomfortably sipped his drink. Did Whittenfeld mean this? Or was it a speech born of necessity? "I told you when you hired me that those days were over. That I was tired of causes and bureaucratic battles. That I just wanted to mind my own business and do a good job. I said it then. I say it now. And I mean it."

"I know you do," Whittenfeld declared. "You're the gun fighter who's killed his last man, right? Put the guns away forever? Well, don't bury the guns completely because I want you to be able to take them out any time your conscience demands it. And I want you to keep them ready if we have to tackle any violent radical groups."

"What's the chance of that?"

"Well, based on your experience with the *Columbus*, I'd have to say odds are good. Though I must also admit, in fairness, that the majority of the Scots have lost their ancient warrior personas." There was some disdain in his voice. "But you'll see. You will get to know the Scots very well."

"I hope so."

"Now I've got a confession to make."

"To me?"

"Yes."

"Are you joking?"

"No. I failed you."

"I don't understand."

"I wanted to welcome you with pride, not horror."

"Hell. The *Columbus* thing wasn't your fault."

Whittenfeld was adamant. "On the contrary. I am in charge. The Loch Ness project is my child. I gave birth to it. A father must not only love a child, he must protect it. I failed."

"I don't think an apology is needed."

Whittenfeld shook his head. "I'm being honest. Open. I'm declaring my trust. You're my new right hand, and I will always try to deal with you in a straightforward manner. Therefore, the apology." He lifted his glass, toasting. "To openness, honesty, trust!"

Scotty stared, thinking, sensing. Then he raised his glass, too. "Yes," he said, "absolutely."

The limousine pulled down a residential street about a mile from Travis House and stopped in front of Whittenfeld's home, a three-storied mansion similar in style to the Culloden House. Moments later, Scotty's jeep screeched up as well. Whittenfeld stepped out of the limo, Scotty from the four-wheeler.

Scotty looked around. The neighborhood was affluent. The streets were dimly lit. There were no moving cars. However, he could see a car parked near the corner with two men inside. He could also see a man in the shadows nearby. He pointed them out to Whittenfeld, who said they were security, cogs in Lefebre's normal arrangements. He dropped the subject.

"There was no way I was going to let you get away without showing you the collection," Whittenfeld declared as they entered the house.

"Believe me," Scotty said, "it's my privilege."

Whittenfeld turned up the parlor lights and pointed to the large interior wall. "My pride and joy."

Scotty moved close. There were six huge framed maps of

Scotland and about a dozen smaller cartographs of the Inverness region.

Whittenfeld indicated the legend boxes on the map corners. "These are the cartouches. They give you title, scale, the map maker's name, and other pieces of background, and as you can also see, they give a good indication of the craftsman's sense of art." He pointed to a particular map. "For example, this projection of Scotland was drawn by French maritime cartographers from the Dépôt de Marine. It was printed in 1757." He moved to the side of another. "This was drawn by Gerhard Mercator in 1575. It's one of the earliest maps of the Inverness region as well as one of the best. It's nearly priceless. You might have heard of Mercator."

"The Mercator projection?"

"Right."

Scotty admired the exhibits as Whittenfeld pontificated. He was impressed; Whittenfeld knew his subject. He was also enthralled. If the man's obsession with Loch Ness and Inverness had not been clear before, it certainly was now.

Whittenfeld pointed to one last cartograph, a tracing of Great Britain.

"Great Britain!" he declared admiringly. "A torch of enlightenment in a barren world. Scotty, Great Britain is England. It is England that has given Britain greatness. It is England that has engendered the whole with nobility and might. You know Scotland and England merged in 1707. And I tell you, England's gift of partnership was the greatest gift one nation ever bestowed on another. England gave Scotland its history, its knowledge, its power, its grace. Every Scot alive should thank God the English saw fit to join hands and bring Scotland up to glory."

Scotty sat on the couch. Next to the couch was a table. On the table, a picture.

"Your son?" Scotty asked.

"Yes," Whittenfeld replied. "He was fifteen when the photo was taken. He died at seventeen in an auto accident."

"I'm sorry."

"Don't be. It happened a long time ago."

Scotty could tell Whittenfeld did not want to discuss it. "Any other children?"

"No."

"A wife?"

Whittenfeld's expression froze. "No."

Scotty could not only tell this subject was taboo as well but could see it had invoked the same reaction of hatred and distaste he'd seen during Whittenfeld's "vile bitch" speech several days before.

After a drink, Whittenfeld walked Scotty to the door.

"You're welcome here anytime," Whittenfeld said as he shook Scotty's hand. "Call. Come over. We'll talk about football, maps, whatever. You make yourself seen. You're one of the family now."

"I appreciate the invitation," Scotty said.

"See you in the morning," Whittenfeld declared.

"Right."

Whittenfeld closed the door. Scotty returned to the jeep, looking for the security man who'd been standing on the street. The man was gone. However, the occupied car still remained. Scotty started the jeep, pulled slowly past the car, and looked inside. Two men looked back, their faces obscured by the darkness.

Strange.

The following day, a staff meeting was called for ten. Scotty arrived five minutes early. However, by ten-fifteen, Whittenfeld, Lefebre, Foster, Spinelli, the company's labor relations officer, a starched Englishman named Fullerheim, and the local representative of the Transport and General Workers Union, Malcolm Abercrombie, had joined him in the first-floor conference room.

Abercrombie was a dignified-looking Scotsman, overweight and red cheeked, who appeared out of place as a union rep.

He began the meeting by vehemently denouncing the company's plan to place visibly armed guards aboard the drill ship.

Whittenfeld listened attentively, then explained the company's position and launched into an impassioned monologue about Loch Ness, oil, union responsibilities, and union interests.

Scotty felt the emotion, the intensity, noting that Whittenfeld had a flair for alliteration and prose.

He also gazed through the window, observing the compound's perimeter fences. There were guards everywhere, but base security had not really been increased since the

Columbus incident. It had been excessive from the beginning —the same number of men, the same preparedness.

There were also men outside the perimeter fences—unemployed workers—men who he'd seen gathering near the base intermittently since the day he'd arrived. Foster had said local displeasure among the unskilled work force was a price they had to continually pay for importing the best men available from abroad.

Whittenfeld finished his speech. A minute of silence followed. Abercrombie once again stated the union's position, but less adamantly. Whittenfeld cajoled, complimented, and massaged.

Abercrombie caved.

Abercrombie did not have a stiff enough backbone to compete with a William Whittenfeld.

In fact, Scotty doubted there were many men who could. Ever.

While drinking coffee in the executive lounge after the Abercrombie meeting, Lefebre treated Scotty to additional erudition, in particular, a discourse on selected subjects in anthropology. Besides literature, Lefebre, it seemed, had a deep interest in primate history, and based on his discussion of *Australopithecine* man, *Pithecanthropus,* and *Homo Neanderthalensis,* an extensive knowledge as well.

They also spoke about Lefebre's approach to uncovering the identify of the suspected saboteurs—private interviews, meetings with known contacts, discussions with paid informants.

Scotty did not ask about the excessive security.

Lefebre asked if Scotty had any particular interests; petroleum was Scotty's reply.

Coffee finished, Lefebre invited Scotty to his office.

"Here," Lefebre said, handing Scotty the ivory elephant.

Scotty examined the sculpture. "What do I do with it?"

"You take it. It's yours."

"I don't understand."

"It's a gift. You like it. I appreciated your compliment. I have other figures. And can carve more."

"I don't . . ."

Lefebre interrupted. "I appreciate your appreciation. And art is to be shared."

Scotty gestured appreciatively. "Thank you," he said.
"Don't mention it," Lefebre declared.

Scotty returned to his office and inspected the room. The desk? The window sill? The shelves?

Yes, the shelf opposite the desk wall.

A perfect place for the elephant.

He placed it between two volumes of technical literature.

Chapter 7

The view across the pub room of the Clachnaharry Inn was mired in a haze of smoke. It was nearly ten o'clock in the evening. Scotty and Bob Reddington had been there since eight, Scotty drinking lager, Reddington downing heavier Scottish beer.

"Scotty," Reddington said, slurring his words, "it's hard to believe it was so long ago. 'Cause I can see it as if it were yesterday. Joe Dumbrowski. Straight from the coal fields of Pennsylvania. I'll never forget the first day he came in. Will you?"

"I wasn't there," Scotty said.

"Why not?"

Scotty's thoughts seemed far away. "I don't know, Red. An exam or something."

"You missed practice 'cause of an exam?"

"Guess so."

"Too bad," Reddington said, slapping Scotty across the back. " 'Cause when Dumbrowski walked into the training room, we nearly shit. Who in the hell expected a four-hundred-pound load of a defensive tackle, especially with all the emphasis coach had placed on speed. Speed? Dumbrowski couldn't have outraced a boulder. And he had on those overalls of his that looked like a tent for the caliph of Baghdad. Remember those?"

"Sure as hell," Scotty said.

"Fosberg, the equipment man, tried to fit Dumbrowski into some gear," Reddington said a bit wistfully. "And that was something to see. Did I ever tell you this story before?"

"Nope."

"Did anyone?"

Scotty ordered another round of beer and lager, then belatedly said "no" again.

Reddington wiped his mouth on the sleeve of his flight jacket. "They got him into a helmet but couldn't get the helmet off because his nose was stuck between the rungs of the face guard." He laughed, burped, and laughed again. "Then Fosberg put him into pants. Dumbrowski sat; the pants ripped right off. Coach ordered the field tarpaulin cut to size. You sure no one ever told you this?"

Scotty looked at the faces in the room. Narrow. Weatherbeaten. Tinged with alcoholic redness, filled with toothless smiles. "I told you, Red," he said. "I never heard this before."

"Right," Reddington said, straightening up. "Well, to get Dumbrowski into a pair of cleats, they cut out the toes. Pads didn't fit, so they tore up one of the trainer's mats and tied the rubber around Dumbrowski's shoulders and neck. Poor Dumbrowski. Every time he hit the tackling dummy, he nearly bounced out of the stadium. The funniest thing, though, was when coach tried to show Dumbrowski the proper technique to ward off a cross-block."

"What happened?"

"Dumbrowski fell on him, that's what. Coach turned blue. If they hadn't gotten Dumbrowski off, coach would've asphyxiated."

Scotty laughed, though he still seemed very distant. "Dumbrowski might have been doing us a favor."

"You didn't like coach?"

Scotty shrugged and drank some beer. "I didn't hate him. But I didn't love him, either. He was a little too much of a sadist. Too much of a taunt. Hell, I didn't mind when he got on me, but I didn't particularly enjoy seeing him rip into the fifth stringers to satisfy his lusts."

"Well, he's on the rag, anyway."

"What do you mean?"

"I heard he's on the bread line. Unemployed."

"Busted?"

Reddington nodded, then took a letter from his pocket and placed it on the table. "Got a note here from the kids. They want to know how I am and when they're coming. But, more important, they want to know about Uncle Scotty."

Scotty read the letter. "I'll drop them a card tonight."

Reddington took out a second. "Now this poetic specimen is from the Dragon Lady. I weakened. Wrote her. Asked her to come back. Don't hold the letter too long. It's dripping with poison."

Scotty skimmed the note. "Guess she's not coming back."

Reddington laughed, slugging beer. "Guess not. I'm surprised she didn't include a pipe bomb. That would have been a fitting good-by."

Scotty tore the letter in half.

Reddington fingered the pieces. "Ripped up," he said, smirking. "Just like my marriage. Scotty. Let me tell you. You were smart never getting hooked."

Scotty laughed, dripped some lager on his jeans, then wiped the brew away. "Listen, jerk off. The only thing I've gained from bachelorhood has been the absence of alimony. I've had affairs break up just like your marriage, and the pain has been just as bad. Why don't you just step away from yourself for a moment and stop personalizing everything. It won't work right away. You just can't say, 'All right, I'm cured,' but you've got to try!"

Reddington embraced him. "You're a buddy." He pointed to the bartender. "Give this ace a lager. And I'll take another beer, too."

Two muscular men wearing T-shirts entered the pub, snaring Reddington's attention.

Reddington nodded to them; they barely acknowledged.

"Who are they?" Scotty asked.

"Special security guards. Information hounds."

"Lefebre's?"

"Yeah."

The drinks arrived; the noise continued.

Scotty shook his head thoughtfully. "Red, I don't understand what's going on here. This is Inverness. Not Los Alamos. And we're not manufacturing atomic warheads. What the hell are all these ex-Gestapo officers doing around?"

"Guarding!"

"I'm aware of it, wise guy. I know we have to watch our

flanks. But I've never seen anything like this. And I saw it before the *Columbus* was attacked! Hell, if you act like you expect big trouble, you usually get it."

"You may have a point. We certainly got it."

"You haven't answered my question."

"Has Whittenfeld?"

"I just arrived in Scotland. I swore I'd keep my mouth shut for once in my life. You know it and encouraged it. I didn't ask Whittenfeld a thing. I'm asking you."

"Has Whittenfeld given you the *child-emotion-vile-bitch* speech?"

"Yes."

"Well, then. There's your answer. Only you didn't think he meant it. He does. He loves this project. He eats and sleeps Loch Ness. He's as paranoid as hell about it. And, in a way, you can't blame him. There was plenty of opposition. There were threats. He brought in Lefebre and company to protect the nest. He felt tight security was necessary. London and New York respected his opinion because they respected him, and based on the *Columbus* incident, I'd have to say he might have been right."

"Maybe."

"Someone did try to sabotage the drill ship, remember?"

"Maybe."

"Sabotage was your conclusion, too!"

"I've been wrong before. And even if I were right, we might be suspecting the wrong parties."

Reddington was confused. Scotty repeated Mary MacKenzie's challenge. Reddington nearly fell off his chair.

"Are you out of your mind?" he mumbled. "Yeah. You've been drinking too much. That's it. Tell me, Scotty. Tell me how that lunacy crept into your head!"

"It just did."

"Well, forget it. I'm in command of the *Columbus*. Nothing goes on board her I don't know about. No one from Geminii could have rigged her without my knowing, and you know goddamn well I never would have been a party to such a thing!"

"You're forgetting the submersible."

"The company doesn't have a submersible in Inverness!"

"It could have brought one here."

"You're nuts if you believe that!"

Scotty smiled. "I don't. I just wanted to see if you did."

Reddington slugged some beer. "You old son of a bitch."

A bald, emaciated man entered the pub from the inn proper, stopped at the bar for a Scotch, looked around, noticed the security men, then quickly walked out, leaving his drink untouched.

The security officers followed.

"What's that about?" Scotty asked.

"Beats me," Reddington replied.

Scotty listened. A car drove slowly away. Another followed, marking time. Interesting, he thought. All of it. Interesting.

It was darker than hell as Scotty and Reddington emerged from the pub door and climbed into the jeep. A strong wind blew off the firths, carrying a night howl along. The lights of several boats were visible. Clachnaharry Road was dead.

Scotty primed the jeep to life and edged it on to the road.

"You know," Reddington said as Scotty steered the jeep toward Inverness, "this was where we stayed after Rolf Kreibel died. It's hard to believe it was so long ago."

"Ain't that the truth."

"I wonder if Kreibel's watching from somewhere, if he knows what his death brought about."

Scotty smiled as he turned the jeep around a bend; the lights of the city had still not appeared. "We'll never know."

"You don't think a séance would be worthwhile?"

" 'Fraid not."

Reddington slapped his knees. "Well, I bet we haven't seen the last of Kreibel. He was a money-hungry bastard. If we hit oil under the loch, he'll come back and lay claim."

They both began to laugh. Suddenly, a Renault shot out of a side street ahead of them.

"Slow down, you asshole," Reddington screamed, waving his fist.

Another car, a Volkswagen, careened out of the tributary. Scotty turned the jeep's wheel quickly. The Volkswagen rammed into their side, tearing off the jeep's front fender. Scotty's head crashed against the steering wheel. The jeep skidded into a ditch. The Volkswagen roared off.

"Lefebre's sons a bitches!" Reddington screamed.

"Fuckers tore off the damn fender," Scotty fumed, dabbing at his bleeding lip.

Reddington jumped out of the jeep and started to push. Scotty pounded the accelerator.

They were back on the road in less than a minute.

"I want to find them!" Scotty said. "And I don't want to wait until tomorrow. Damn fuckers ruined my car!"

They drove along, seeing nothing. However, as they neared the edge of Inverness, Reddington jerked Scotty's arm.

"There!" he cried, pointing.

On top of a bare bluff were two cars, the Renault and Volkswagen.

Scotty gunned the jeep up the hillock into a clearing. The car's headlights framed three men. The bald man from the Clachnaharry was on the ground, his face covered with blood. The two security officers were standing over him, beating him with crow bars.

"Get off him," Scotty yelled as he and Reddington jumped from the jeep.

The security men bolted toward the Volkswagen. Scotty tackled one. The other made it inside the car. As Scotty wrestled with the first, Reddington rushed to the injured man, who was nearly unconscious. Suddenly, the first security officer kicked Scotty in the head, broke from him, and jumped inside the Volkswagen, too. The driver gunned the engine. Scotty grabbed the Volkswagen's rear-view mirror; it ripped off in his hands. The Volkswagen spat dirt and pebbles into the air, then tore down the hill.

Gasping, Scotty ran to Reddington's side.

"How is he?"

"Not good."

"Damn!"

They carried the man to the jeep.

"We'd better get him over to the hospital," Reddington advised.

Scotty nodded. "Whittenfeld and I are going to have a talk about this!"

They stared down the hill. A billow of dust was rising into the night sky. The car was gone.

Whittenfeld looked down the conference table, shaking his head.

"Was the man able to talk?" he asked.

"Not last night," Scotty replied. "But he was able to speak this morning."

"What did he say?"

"He said he'd been attacked by two men he didn't know

but who'd been following him off and on for twenty-four hours. They forced his car off the road. Then they accused him of sabotage and beat him, warning him they would continue to beat him until he talked."

"Have the police been called in?"

"No. I also don't think they will be. The man said he didn't want more trouble. He didn't want to be killed. He just wanted to be left alone."

"What's the man's name?"

"Reynolds."

"And his occupation?"

"Laborer. And a part-time volunteer organizer for the Scottish Nationalist Party."

"Fanatics," Whittenfeld said. "How can you be sure the attackers were Lefebre's people if the man couldn't identify them?"

"Red identified them. He recognized them at the Clachnaharry Inn. He pointed them out to me."

The office door opened. Lefebre entered and sat next to Scotty. He was chewing a wad of tobacco.

"Monsieur Bruce," he said sympathetically, "I'm sorry about your car and your lip."

"Both can be fixed," Scotty declared.

"Yes," Lefebre said, smiling. "Of course."

"Well?" Whittenfeld asked.

"They were my men," Lefebre admitted. "I checked with Special." He turned to Scotty. "Monsieur Bruce, my friend. I'm sorry about the entire incident. Very sorry."

"So am I."

Lefebre looked back to Whittenfeld. "It was Girard and Lennox. Two good men. Company men. Men with character and self-control."

"Self-control?" Scotty declared, shocked. "Character?" He laughed wryly. "They're punks and cowards."

"My men are not punks and cowards, Monsieur Bruce," Lefebre said calmly. "And they had every right to do what they did."

"Is that so?" Scotty asked.

"Lefebre!" Whittenfeld said. "I told you no violence."

"Monsieur Whittenfeld, the man Girard and Lennox were beating tried to run them down with his car outside the Clachnaharry Inn after they had asked him some questions about the *Columbus*. Obviously, the man had something to hide. Girard and Lennox followed the man and stopped him to ask additional questions. They still had no intention of hurting the man until the man pulled a knife."

"I heard the cars leave the inn," Scotty protested. "They drove off slowly. There was no commotion. And I didn't see any knife on the bluff."

"That's because you didn't look, my friend. My men said the man had a knife. And my men don't lie. Certainly not to me."

"Then why'd they run from us?"

"They couldn't tell who you were in the darkness."

Scotty gestured to Whittenfeld. "This is the biggest crock of shit I've ever heard!"

Lefebre's entire expression changed. His face turned red. His eyes flared open. "Are you calling me a liar, Monsieur Bruce?"

Scotty stood and looked to Whittenfeld again. "They were beating the man for information. Trying to uncover a lead. Acting under Lefebre's orders. Christ, if I hadn't followed the security men because of the accident, God only knows what would have happened. God only knows the problems we'd have right now. Bill, we can't operate this way. No company can!"

"I see the six-guns have already been brought out of mothballs," Whittenfeld said sympathetically. "And the gun fighter is back. Scotty, I know you're upset. Understandably so. I'm upset, too, and would be furious beyond control except that Lefebre said the men were only protecting themselves."

"I checked security," Scotty said. "Lefebre's orders did not exclude the use of force."

"Monsieur Whittenfeld," Lefebre said, standing. "I swear to you . . ."

Scotty grabbed Lefebre's arm and whirled him around; he could feel Lefebre's body react angrily, almost unnaturally to the touch; he could also see the most sudden and intense look of insanity he'd ever seen on a man's face. "You're lying," he snapped.

The Frenchman spat a wad of tobacco into his face.

"Lefebre!" Whittenfeld cried.

Scotty grabbed Lefebre by the collar, a reflex. "Your animals could have killed that man. They could have murdered an innocent human being!"

"Stop it!" Whittenfeld ordered.

Lefebre's eyes blazed; a strange smirk crossed his lips. He punched Scotty in the throat. Scotty fell back on the conference table, choking. Lefebre pinned Scotty down, then pulled Scotty's head back into a neck-snapping position. Scotty fought to breathe. Lefebre's hands shook, his face twitched, his eyes rolled with lunacy. And tobacco-stained spittle drooled out of his mouth on to the table.

Whittenfeld rushed over and tried to pull Lefebre off.

"I should break your neck," Lefebre growled through gritted, rotted teeth. "And I will if you ever so much as touch me again. Nobody touches me. At any time. For any reason. Ever! Understand?"

"Goddamnit," Whittenfeld roared, trying unsuccessfully to subdue the Frenchman.

Fighting to breathe, Scotty couldn't reply.

Lefebre dug his nails into Scotty's face. "Understand?" he screamed.

Scotty mumbled, nodded, spat up blood.

Lefebre's whole body rocked; he pressed his hold. Whittenfeld pulled harder, his strength nearly exhausted.

Then, suddenly, Lefebre stood and backed away from the table.

Whittenfeld wiped the sweat from his face. Nearly paralyzed, Scotty coughed in spasms. Lefebre dispassionately looked into space.

Whittenfeld wanted to speak but couldn't. He was shaking too hard.

Nobody moved. Nobody talked.

Lefebre calmly walked out of the room as if nothing had happened.

Whittenfeld, still shaken, appeared in Scotty's office several hours later.

"How are you?" Whittenfeld asked.

"I'm all right," Scotty replied.

"I want to apologize to you for Lefebre's actions," Whittenfeld declared. "They were vile, disgusting. And since Lefebre's not the type of man to make apologies, I've come myself. Lefebre's ears are still ringing. He will keep his revolting temper under control. No ifs, ands, or buts. I swear to you, if I didn't know him better, if he had not had such a good record with Schlumberger in Paris, if he had been less of a faithful employee here, I would have fired him on the spot. Scotty, what can I say? Lefebre's explosive, unpredictable, headstrong, eccentric. He has a horrible temper, though I never saw it explode like it did today. But I need him. He's a trustworthy man. Effective. And he lives for Geminii."

"I understand," Scotty said stone faced. He understood the nature of the ridiculous self-serving rationalization. He'd heard them before. What's a fight when placed against the overall good of the company. Christ, he was boiling! He did not like being beaten and nearly strangled! He damn well knew that if Lefebre tried again, it would be the Frenchman whose neck would wind up in a sling. But he also knew the realities; he would have to try to avoid another confrontation with Lefebre no matter how strong the impulse to lay one back on the bastard. Although he was determined to pull Lefebre's company dossier and examine the lunatic's background, he was going to have to try to leave it at that. Hell, he'd just gotten here and had just assumed his post. There was the *Columbus* incident. His own previous history. Another confrontation with the Frenchman was the last thing he needed right now. He would try to keep his fists to himself no matter how hard it would be to do!

"Scotty. I appreciate your restraint," Whittenfeld continued. "And again, you have my promise. There will be no other incidents. Between Lefebre and you. Or Lefebre and anyone else for that matter."

"Good," Scotty declared. He prayed Whittenfeld was right.

"For your information, we did a further check on Mr. Reynolds. He has two arrests for assault on the police blotter. And an unsavory background, to boot. He might very well have attacked Girard and Lennox. As for Lefebre's people in general, I've issued a very restrictive authorization. They will continue to investigate the *Columbus* incident, searching for the guilty parties. But there will be no violence of any kind." He patted Scotty on the shoulder. "I detest violent incidents. I promise you there will be no more."

"I appreciate the consideration," Scotty said. He held up a telegram. "This just arrived. The sonar tug will be here on Monday and will be deployed Thursday."

"I'll want to inspect the vessel before it goes on line."

"Of course."

"I'll also want the *Columbus* and loch security forces to begin duties simultaneously. Please advise Lefebre."

Scotty massaged his throat—it was covered with bruises—then nodded. "No problem," he said.

Whittenfeld smiled and stepped out the door.

"I'll see you later" were his final words.

Scotty sat at the den desk, shrouded in darkness. It was midnight. He was tired. He'd returned from dinner two hours before. Since then, he'd been frozen in place, sifting through an avalanche of thoughts.

There were several documents on the desk. Lefebre's company resume and security clearance. A telex from Schlumberger Corp., Paris. A telex from the Marseilles police.

Early that afternoon, he'd pulled Lefebre's records. He'd been determined not to look for trouble. But trouble had already found him.

The resume and security clearances did not match the information contained in the telexes. Lefebre had worked for Schlumberger Corporation, but he'd not been a model employee. Twice he'd been implicated in brutal security excesses. Another time he'd nearly beaten a company superior to death during an argument. Several times he'd been suspended from duty but rehired. He'd also been with the Marseilles police, but the resume had listed a tenure of ten years, while the telex had only reported two terms of one year each, six years apart. Eight years of Lefebre's life were missing, and Scotty had never known a security clearance to be so inaccurate.

Lefebre was hiding something, and based on Whittenfeld's attitude, he suspected Whittenfeld might well be aware of it. Although he kept telling himself to hold to his promise and mind his own business, he damn well was going to make a quiet exception in this case.

Pierre Lefebre. The son of a bitch.

Yes, he'd challenged the Frenchman but certainly his action didn't warrant the response. Lefebre's attack had been the knee jerk of a madman, the reflex of a man out of control, a man on whose shoulders rested the safety of the project and every individual involved.

Was he the only one in Inverness who understood the danger this man presented?

Chapter 8

Scotty leaned over the ship's rail, watching whitecaps surge across the water toward Urquhart Bay. The surface conditions were a shade toward the perilous for most loch vessels, and so there were few in sight. However, the sonar tug had arrived and was lingering nearby, waiting for Whittenfeld's appearance.

Scotty had risen early, feeling even angrier than he'd felt before going to bed, an anger fed by the prior evening's smoldering solitude and a telex received at Travis House that morning from the London office that had announced it knew of no information concerning Pierre Lefebre apart from the material contained in Lefebre's resume and clearances. Completing breakfast, Scotty had retired to the den to place the same transatlantic call he'd unsuccessfully tried to place the night before to Michael Wessinghage, State Department, Washington Intelligence Bureau, an old friend. This time, however, Wessinghage had been in his office.

Their conversation had been short. He hadn't asked for much. Only a rundown on a man known to him as Pierre Lefebre, a Frenchman. Certainly, if anyone could pinpoint Lefebre, it was Wessinghage. However, even Wessinghage could only make a commitment to diligent effort, promising to call as soon as he'd located anything of interest.

Leaving the house, he'd picked up Tony Spinelli and had toured the three exploratory on-land well sites. The Black Isle hole, located on the Black Isle, a peninsula north of Inverness, had just been spudded. Highland B, situated across the firth, was a third of the way along, and Beauly Highpoint was almost at depth and, unlike the other two locations, a beehive of excitement because preliminary core tests had indicated

72

they might very well be on the verge of a significant hydrocarbon find.

Subsequent to a conference with British Midland field executives at Beauly—Midland had won the drilling concession for all three wells—he'd returned with Spinelli to the base and had helicoptered out to the *Columbus*.

Bob Reddington, who'd been standing quietly alongside, moved closer. "What are you going to do?" he asked.

"Nothing," Scotty replied, deciding not to mention his continuing inquiries even to Reddington. "I don't want more trouble here. If the situation had been different, if Whittenfeld hadn't been there . . . God knows what might have happened."

"Damn thing is incredible."

"What do you know about Lefebre?"

"Not much. Whittenfeld brought him in last year with little fanfare. He's apparently done a good job. And he's never attacked anyone that I'm aware of. Oh, sure, there've been some problems. Barrett didn't like the excess security. He unsuccessfully lobbied Whittenfeld to curtail it. And consequently argued heatedly with Lefebre, who did not appreciate Barrett's interference. But this kind of thing? Never."

They descended into the drill ship to the second deck and inspected the condition of equipment at the heart: the mud pumps, the liquid mud containers, and cement pods. Satisfied, they checked the electric and engineering workshops, moved forward into the moon pool, then returned to the main deck and entered the superintendent's offices.

A summons from Grabowski drew them topside moments later.

Several members of the crew and staff were gathered on the forward helipad, babbling excitedly, pressing in on one of the helipad workers, identified by Grabowski as a crewman named Simpkins.

"What's this all about?" Reddington asked, trying to still the commotion.

Simpkins jostled excitedly in place. "I saw it, sir. Damn, and may God strike me if I didn't see the monster."

Scotty glanced at Reddington, smiled, then placed his arm around Mr. Simpkins's shoulder. "The Loch Ness monster?"

"Yes, sir. One and the same."

"You sure you ain't been drinking?" Reddington asked, once again hushing the group.

"On the ship! No way. I haven't been hallucinating, either. No. I was standing right here washing some petrol off the deck. I looked out at the south shore, and there it was."

"What exactly did you see?" Scotty asked.

"A hump."

"What kind of hump?"

"A hump hump, Mr. Bruce. What other kind of hump is there?"

Scotty stifled a laugh. "It was just floating in the water?"

Simpkins pointed, moving his arm toward the west. "No, first it was moving. Kind of zigzag. Then it disappeared below the surface, popped up once more for just a second, and was gone for good before I could puff a breath again."

"Did anyone else see this thing?" Reddington asked.

"No," Grabowski advised. "I've already checked every member of the crew."

"How long was it on the surface?" Reddington questioned, scanning the horizon.

"Maybe ten seconds," Simpkins replied.

"And you didn't call for anyone?"

"You have a good sense of humor, Mr. Red. No. I was shaking like hell. Couldn't talk. Besides, I was trying to get my camera working."

"You took its picture?" Scotty asked.

"Sure enough."

Simpkins handed Scotty a Polaroid glossy. Scotty and Reddington looked close. Oh, the hump was there all right, but it looked more like a floating log than a big monster.

"This doesn't help us much at all, Mr. Simpkins," Scotty said, commenting on the poor resolution.

"I didn't say it would, sir. I only said I took the monster's picture."

Scotty looked out toward the south shore. There was no sign of any floating riffraff. "Beats me." He turned to Reddington. "What about you?"

"Beats me, too."

"Well, it was there," Simpkins said, defending himself.

Reddington nodded. "How long have you been on shift?"

"Six hours."

"Then you're relieved. Go down and relax for an hour or two."

The crew members began to congratulate Simpkins. Then,

as Simpkins started off the helipad, he turned. "Can I have my picture, sir?"

"Of course," Reddington said, handing Simpkins the undistinguished glossy.

Simpkins put the snapshot in his pocket. The clutch broke up. Scotty and Reddington remained on the helipad, searching the horizon.

Whittenfeld's chopper appeared. Turning to each other, they laughed, then moved off the pad to clear the chopper's approach.

A chill wind had begun to gust mercilessly across the main deck as Whittenfeld, Lefebre, Foster, Reddington, and Scotty Bruce emerged from the bridge deck after an exhaustive meeting.

"I want one guard stationed in the moon pool area at all times," Whittenfeld was saying as they stopped alongside one of the deck cranes. "And the other two on the stern and the bow."

"Two shifts?" Reddington asked.

"Yes," Whittenfeld replied. "Twelve hours each to run concurrently with the drill-crew tour."

Reddington looked up at the drilling platform. One of the guards was already in position, holding an automatic rifle; the others were below deck in the cabins assigned to security.

Whittenfeld turned to Reddington. "The guards have been instructed to inform you of anything suspicious. If that occurs, you are to call home base and speak to Lefebre." He looked down the catwalk. "Is the launch ready, Scotty?"

"Ready and waiting," Scotty said.

Whittenfeld smiled. He hadn't smiled much during the meeting. He'd been very businesslike, very preoccupied. "Then let's go for a ride," he said.

They walked to the gangway, then carefully descended on to a motor launch, moored to the ship's side.

"Take us out," Scotty ordered.

The launch pilot steered the launch away from the drill ship and then, several minutes later, pulled up to the sonar tug.

They climbed aboard. The tug was rolling heavily on the swells. The tug captain, a stalklike Norwegian named Sven

Olafsen, ushered them into the bridge room and introduced them to the sonar engineer.

"You all set?" Whittenfeld asked, examining instruments and scope displays.

"Absolutely," the engineer said, flipping a switch. "We've got passive sound, side scan, and heat detect." He pointed to a panel of instruments. "That's the passive. Standard Royal Navy issue, antisubmarine. It's a basic sonic receiver. Particularly sensitive to engine noises. If anything with a drive shaft and propeller comes waltzing along, we're going to pick her up." He pointed to another scope. "Again, Royal Navy, standard issue, antisubmarine ordnance. It's a heat seeker. It will spot any mechanical vehicle, even if the vehicle's running silent."

"Will it pick up the *Columbus?*" Reddington asked.

"Sure," the engineer replied. "But we have a clear picture of the *Columbus*'s pattern, so we can factor out its influence. However, the drill vibrations will give us distortion on the side scan." He moved to another console. "We've got a high-resolution, computerized Marine Tech, Model 800 Side Scan sonar on board, equipped with a very advanced sonar fish, which we're trailing a couple of hundred feet behind the tug."

"How reliable is the unit?" Foster asked.

"As reliable as they come. We used its forerunner to survey the Loch bottom when we were trying to fix a position for the *Columbus.*"

Whittenfeld impatiently walked out of the cabin, followed by Olafsen and the rest of the group.

"I want the system on 'go' at all times," he said after everyone had returned to the launch.

"Of course," Olafsen replied from the tug.

The launch returned to the *Columbus.*

"Are you coming back with us?" Whittenfeld asked as he, Lefebre, and Foster marched to the helipad's steps.

"No," Scotty said. "I'm going to hang around for a while."

Whittenfeld stepped on to the pad along with Foster and climbed aboard the helicopter. Lefebre remained on the steps, staring down at Scotty, motionless. Lefebre had not said a word since arriving on board. In fact, this was the first time Lefebre had even looked at Scotty. The look was not pleasant.

Scotty restrained himself; God how he wanted to unload on the bastard!

The helicopter loudspeaker belched Lefebre's name; Lefebre hopped on to the helipad and disappeared as well.

Moments later, the helicopter was gone.

At eight o'clock, Scotty called Geminii base and spoke to the director of helicopter operations. Since Whittenfeld's departure, a heavy fog and drizzle had socked in the loch. Both agreed visibility was unfavorable for shipboard landing. Scotty decided to remain on board until the morning and joined Bill Nunn in the lounge.

Reddington appeared moments later.

"One of the sonar scouts just called," Reddington cried. "They've got something already."

"What?" Scotty asked, standing.

"They're not sure. But they want us out. Right now."

Leaving Nunn, they hurried topside, climbed on to the launch, and raced toward the tug, whose night lights were shining a half mile away. Once aboard, Captain Olafsen led them onto the bridge.

"We don't know what the hell we've picked up," Olafsen stammered, "but it's very strange."

"How many tracings?" Reddington asked as they poked through the doorway.

"Several, so far."

Three crew members were huddled together behind the sonar engineer, who was carefully monitoring scopes.

"What's up?" Scotty asked, pushing to the fore.

The engineer glanced over his shoulder. "Take a look at these printouts."

Scotty and Reddington leaned over the side-scan display.

"It looks like a Rorschach of a big eel," Reddington said.

"What is it?" Scotty asked.

"I don't know," the engineer replied. "But whatever it is, I think we've just picked up part of it. You can see the trace broadening out as it leaves the paper."

Reddington breathed deeply. "Could it be a submersible?"

The engineer emphatically shook his head. "No submersible traces like that. First of all, if the thing was inanimate, its trace would be composed of straighter rebound lines. No, I'd bet it's alive, whatever it is."

"Is it moving?" Reddington asked.

"Yes," the engineer replied. "Straight down! And no submersible dives straight down. Especially at five hundred and fifty feet per minute!"

Scotty pointed to the displays. "Could the thing be a fish or a school of fish?"

The engineer tried to increase resolution. "I doubt it. The rate of descent makes it unlikely."

Reddington moved closer. "Are you sure, absolutely sure, the traces aren't being made by a submersible?"

The engineer annoyedly pointed to the other displays. "The sound detect hasn't registered a damn thing other than the drill ship's drilling track. There are no motors running. No propellers turning. There's negative on heat. There's nothing mechanical down there, period!"

Seconds later, another trace plotted out. The engineer analyzed it.

"My guess is the object's in excess of one hundred feet. And it's moving at close to seventeen knots."

Reddington flinched. "Seventeen knots? Over a hundred feet long?"

Stunned, they huddled around the instruments.

"It must be gone," the engineer finally said shortly before ten o'clock, a half hour after the last trace had been taken. "Whatever it was has headed for the hills."

Scotty tore off the trace sheets, folded them, and placed them in his pocket.

"You've been doing this for a long time?" he asked.

"That's correct," the engineer replied.

"Then tell me. Have you ever seen traces like these before?"

"No. Absolutely not."

Scotty turned to Olafsen. "We'll be on the drill ship. If the object returns, call us immediately."

"Of course," Olafsen declared.

Scotty and Reddington returned to the launch.

Reboarding the *Columbus*, they entered the supervisor's office. A tremendous jolt hit the ship moments later, throwing them off their chairs and against the cabin wall, upending every standing piece of furniture in sight.

"What the hell!" Reddington said as he struggled to his feet.

Another jolt hit, shoving the drill ship sideways, once more adding to the disarray.

They ran out the door. Bill Nunn intercepted them on the main-deck catwalk.

"Man overboard!" he cried. "The jolt knocked him off the forward helipad."

"Who?"

"We don't know yet."

Reddington pushed close. "Have the floods picked him up?"

"No. The fog's too thick for visual contact. We don't have much time. There. Listen. You can hear his screams."

"The life rafts?" Scotty asked.

"They're being lowered."

"Any damage to the ship?"

"Don't know yet, either."

"Something hit us?"

"No one's sure."

Scotty and Reddington raced to the gangway. A sizable portion of the crew had already crowded around. The life raft was in the water. Scotty and Reddington jumped aboard with two other men. They listened. They heard cries. Scotty pointed. They began to row, accompanied by the hazy lights of the ship's floods and their own torches.

"We're coming," Reddington cried.

No response.

"Can you hear us?"

Splashing sounds echoed, then screams.

"Hang on!"

Water spat up into the raft, water cold, damn cold, as was the air, thick as shit, as Nunn had said, visibility nil.

"To the right," Reddington ordered.

"We're coming," Scotty repeated, responding to a cry.

Goddamn if they would ever reach the man. The current was strong, swells heavy. They were confused, too.

An echo reverberated, a cry.

"Hang on."

Suddenly, the raft set into a peculiar position as if it had been sucked downward. Water spilled over the sides. The raft lurched rightward, spun hard, then moved quickly against the current. Terrified, they held on tight, sensing something might have moved with great force beneath them, causing an underwater wake, which had grabbed the raft.

A terrible yelp of pain, a death cry, refocused their attention on the lost crewman.

"Can you hear us?" Scotty called.

Another call of pain and then nothing.

They continued to search. They found a torn-off shirt sleeve covered with blood. Nothing more. Concluding they'd done all they could, they returned to the ship.

Grabowski walked down the gangway to meet them.

"We've got an ident," he said.

"Who?" Scotty asked.

Grabowski paused, then said, "Simpkins."

"The man who thought he saw the monster?"

"Yes."

Simpkins!

The flat light of the Scottish morning highlighted William Whittenfeld's features as he sat behind his desk, examining the sonar traces.

"This is it?" he asked.

"Yes," Scotty replied.

Whittenfeld's thoughts were flying. "Positive traces. No mechanical echo. Negative heat report."

"We all agreed. The object was alive, very big and very fast."

Whittenfeld laughed. "The Loch Ness monster?"

Scotty shrugged. "I don't know."

Whittenfeld dropped the traces on the blotter, then stood. "Scotty, I put the tug out there to watch for submersibles, not monsters."

"I know. But those traces were recorded. They exist. They are reality."

"Scotty. They are nonsense. A school of fish. An electrical error. Flotsam. But not a monster."

"The sonar engineer considered every possible alternative."

Whittenfeld shook his head. "I want this matter deep sixed. I want you to inform the sonar tug team to deep six it, too. There are no monsters in Loch Ness. No one at Geminii can ever infer such a thing. One word of this and every Nessie freak in creation will descend on the loch. The environmentalists and the university community will go berserk, and we could have our asses reamed right out of here."

"But how do you explain the traces?"

"I told you. A school of fish. Mechanical error. Or perhaps the work of saboteurs."

"Saboteurs?"

"Think, Scotty. They try to wreck the *Columbus*. They fail. Then they decide to introduce something to the loch which will record unnaturally. Suggest a monster. Everyone knows we've put the tug on line. It's the next logical move. Create a monster, a rallying flag. Cause the government to review our environmental impact report in light of developments. And then stick it up Geminii's ass!"

Was Whittenfeld serious? "You're assuming vast technical knowhow."

"I'm assuming the obvious."

"Suppose we pick up similar traces again?"

Whittenfeld smiled. "I expect you will." He tore up the trace pages and threw them in the wastepaper basket. "Then we'll file them away just like I filed these." He laughed again. "Don't worry. We haven't destroyed the world's only record of the Loch Ness monster. There are books and books written by monster freaks filled with similar stuff. Buy some. Read them. They're great fiction."

"I may just do that."

"Now, more important. What about this man who drowned?"

"His name was Simpkins. We did not find the body."

Whittenfeld solemnly shook his head. "This is a risky business."

"Very risky."

"Does he have family?"

"Yes."

"Are we helping out?"

"Yes."

"Good. Poor man! Damn accident!"

"It wasn't an accident. Something hit the ship."

"Yes, I know. But what? The sonar tug picked up nothing near the *Columbus*."

"That isn't conclusive. The tug might have been scanning the wrong sector at the time."

"Did anyone see anything?"

"No."

"Was a calling card left?"

"No."

"Then let's label the incident *unexplained* and file it away. Or, at worst, attribute it to the work of our saboteurs."

"The dead man's shirt was covered with blood."

"He probably injured himself in the fall."

"I think the ship is in danger."

"We've recognized that as a matter of operating policy."

"I think we should cease operations temporarily."

Whittenfeld flushed. "I'll pretend I didn't hear that, Scotty. I'll pretend it was never suggested. Nothing stops operations. Ever." He paused, then approached, put his arm around Scotty's shoulder, and said, "Scotty. This is natural. Everyone gets this goddamn monster bug sooner or later. There've been sightings, sonar contacts, pictures. Rubbish. As soon as something happens to defy explanation, the monster is blamed. It's an out. An excuse. And a poor one. You, an experienced engineer, should know better. Clear your head and address reality. The last thing any one of us can do is to engage in fantasy, and I must be very firm about this because I cannot allow it to happen. The world is full of the jealous, the weak. It is not full of monsters." He paused. "Now please, forget about this monster." He led Scotty to the door. "You're an important man. Think about important things."

Scotty walked out but stopped halfway down the hall, looking back.

Important things? Yes, Whittenfeld was right. He had to think about important things. Only he suspected Whittenfeld had not focused the emphasis in the right place.

The death of the man was important. The cause of the death even more so. And possibly the man's claimed sighting the most important element of them all.

For some strange reason, he was convinced of it!

Chapter 9

Scotty drove the jeep along the Dores Road and the loch shore. The view was breathtaking, almost mystical, the road seemingly churning into eternity. And Christ, he was actually starting to feel at ease behind the wheel as well.

Stopping once or twice to look back at the *Columbus*, still visible at its moor site, he whisked through Inverfarigaig, then bypassed Lower Foyers, guiding the jeep up the mountainside to the Carn Dearg Inn, a provincial little cottage with a woven thatch roof. Leaving the car in the empty parking lot, he entered the inn's pub. It was only ten A.M. The place was empty, quaint, very parochial. There were tables for dining and others for dominoes, though the only domino pieces in sight had been molded into a sculpture of a Highland clansman. Music was playing in the background, too, and a hypnotizing shaft of light was dancing colors in the middle of the room.

"Is anybody home?" he called, settling on to a bar stool. He lit a cigar and let his mind wander. The place reeked of history. Of Highland clans. Battles. Shifting tartan colors. "Hello?" he called out again; he'd heard movement inside the inn proper. "You've got customers."

The bar door opened. Mary MacKenzie entered. Seeing Scotty, she froze.

"What are you doing here?" she asked.

"I'm thirsty!" he answered. He felt his pulse race unexpectedly. He'd carefully rehearsed what he would say, but would he say it right?

"There's fresh water in the loch. Go drink!"

"I'm more interested in lager."

She took off her apron. "We're closed."

"The sign on the door said 'open.' "

"Open means closed as far as you are concerned!"

83

He leaned over the bar and drafted a lager.

"What the hell are you doing?" she cried, moving threateningly toward him.

"Serving myself," he replied, grinning.

"You're out of here right now or I call a constable."

He drank deeply from the mug. "Look, Miss MacKenzie. I came to talk to you. We don't need constables for that."

She gestured defiantly. "How did you find this place?"

"I called the Highland Council offices and asked where I might write you a letter. They were very helpful."

"You drove all the way here when you could just as well have put your questions on paper?"

He laughed. "The half hour drive from Dores was very pleasant. Besides, it's not a long trip when one considers the fantastic reception I've received."

She grabbed a towel and wiped the bar. "I think I heard everything you had to say in the car."

"Most of it, but not all."

"Mr. Bruce. What do you want?"

He puffed heavily on the cigar. "It's imperative I get to know someone who lives in Inverness. Someone who has a vested political interest. As I said in the car, I'm the new boy in town. You can help me, and I may be very well able to help you."

"Of course you can help me. You can get Geminii the hell out of Loch Ness."

"I can't do that. But I have considerable clout. It would not be a mistake on your part to at least have my sympathetic ear."

She stared, thinking. "Keep talking," she finally said.

"Only if you promise to listen."

She cracked a half smile. "You've invaded my home, and unless I call a constable, I'm afraid you hold me hostage."

"Nonsense. If you ask me to leave right now, I'll be out of here like a shot."

She paused, considering the alternatives, then called through the door. Her niece appeared moments later. She asked the girl to tend bar, then turned back to Scotty.

"If we stay here, we won't be able to talk. Soon there'll be a good deal of commotion. There's a quiet veranda behind the inn, a good place to sit."

Scotty stood and smiled. "Sounds fine," he said.

*   *   *

The air was clear, filled with the scent of pine needles. There wasn't a cloud in the sky, it was autumn brisk, and the view from the veranda was spectacular.

"I wasn't really sure what I wanted to do with my life other than play professional football," he was saying, "until one day I read the story of Spindletop, America's first oil gusher. And I tell you, by the time I had finished, I was hooked."

"Where was this thing?" she asked.

"Texas," he replied. "And it blew out on June 10, 1901. The site was operated by a one-armed hell raiser turned Sunday school teacher named Bud Higgins and a geologist named Lucas. However, on the day of the strike, only their employees were about. The men first heard a rumble. Then the earth began to shake. A geyser of mud shot from the well, destroying their rig. When the flow had stopped, the men turned off the boilers. Then the rumble began again. More mud funneled; the men fled for their lives. Then came a spout of gas and an explosion of green crude rising two hundred feet into the air. It blew out for nine days, spewing eight hundred thousand barrels of oil before being capped. And before you could say Spindletop, the countryside was covered with drilling rigs, and the modern oil industry was born."

"That really inspired you?"

"Damn if it didn't. The next day, I began to study petroleum engineering. Then, after graduation, I earned a master's degree between football seasons and worked for Exxon part time. When I retired from the NFL in 1965, I began to specialize in drill-ship operations, and the rest is history. A lot of years passed around grease monkeys, oil rigs, and drill ships. A lot of dry wells. And now Loch Ness."

"And you retired from football to try to conquer the oil business."

"No, not really. I had some good years left in me."

"This knee of yours?"

He hesitated. "No, the knee had healed." He stared. *Why not?* he thought. "I retired because I was determined to change things. You see, I broke a man's back. I crack-back blocked an opposing linebacker and damaged his spine. The accident had a tremendous impact on me. I'd never thought of football as violent before. It was just fun, a game. I'd grown up with it. I didn't think about hitting people. I just did it. When I saw the opponent, I cut him down. But then I crippled a man, and for the first time in my life I began to think about what I was doing. I was told the pangs of conscience were normal—a psychiatrist said so—but I began to realize there were things happening on the field that were dangerous and unnecessary. I started to make public statements. I found there were other ballplayers who felt like I did. So, for the first time in my life, I took up a cause. We tried to work out changes with the ownership. But, hell, the ownership didn't want to change a thing. The sport was doing great. Why mess with it? Go out and play ball like the All-Pro you are and don't let guilt cloud your vision, they all said! But I refused to fold. I fought. I got nowhere. I didn't like getting nowhere, losing. So I became a martyr. As an All-Pro, I had a lot of influence. I decided to make a real impact, sacrifice myself for the cause. I quit the game!"

"Did martyrdom accomplish anything?"

"Yes and no. Over the years, there've been changes. Many of the things I fought to clean up have been eliminated. But I'd attribute the changes more to the efforts of others. I didn't stay around to continue the war."

"You're being modest." She smiled; he didn't respond. "What about the paralyzed ballplayer?"

"He's still paralyzed. I used to keep in touch with him. But over the years the contact ended. He's bitter. And I can't blame him. I just sort of drifted away."

"Because of guilt?"

"Maybe."

She examined his features, the intensity. Good-looking man, she thought. "I take it the owners and management weren't too fond of you."

"That's an understatement," he said, smiling. "I was Judas. An unappreciative man who had no right to open his mouth."

"But you did have a right! You were a participant!"

"It could be argued either way."

She seemed puzzled. "If they disliked you so much, why did they elect you to their Hall of Fame?"

He laughed. "The owners don't vote. Only sportswriters. To them, I was a bit of a—I hate the word—hero."

She stared, looking especially attractive in the vibrant sunlight. "A hero son of a Scotsman."

"The son of a Scotsman part is correct. Though I never knew my father. And he didn't know the hero. He died when I was a kid."

"Did he name you Scotty?"

"No. He named me Peter, and it was Peter until college. You see, one night after a football game, our fraternity threw a bash. I got drunk. A frat brother owned a bagpipe. I found it, marched into the party, and played the thing until all the guests were screaming for mercy. My friends took the bagpipe away and tied my hands so I couldn't cause any more damage. Someone called me Scotty during the melee, and Scotty I became." He paused, drinking his beer. "Now, Christ, I've been talking about myself too damn much. I'm not that interesting. So it's your turn." He couldn't bring himself to tell her about the raw years that still scarred his life, the corporate battles, the failures.

She blushed slightly. "I'm not that interesting, either."

"Why don't you let me be the judge of that?"

She looked out at the lake, saying nothing.

"How did you get into the inn business?" he asked, prompting her.

"I was born into it," she answered almost by rote. "The inn's been here a hundred years. My father purchased it in 1930 after the family had moved down from Dornoch."

"Is your father still alive?"

"No. Nor my mother. But they were wonderful people. You would especially have liked my father, Mr. Bruce. He was a big man. With very square features and a rock-hard constitution. Though he could be as stern as the Lord, he could also be as soft as a lamb. That's very important, Mr. Bruce. Strength and gentleness. Few people possess both. My father did."

"He ran the inn?"

"Yes. And dabbled in politics. He was one of the founding members of the Scottish National Party."

"You're also a member?"

"Yes. I said so in the car."

"I'm told the SNP is a radical organization, a gang of irresponsible fanatics."

"Nonsense. The fact you've even mentioned such a thing shows you are completely ignorant of Scottish history."

"Not completely. I'm aware Scotland chose to unite with England in 1707, surrendering her independence."

"A strategic surrender, Mr. Bruce. An act of survival. And, therefore, as nationalistic and pragmatic an act as any ever contemplated by the Scots. But don't get the wrong idea. The union of states wasn't popular. Nor did it kill our sense of nationalism. In fact, though Scotland ceased to be a state, its parliament dissolved, its institutions dismembered, it has remained a nation."

Scotty sat once again. "If the union wasn't popular, why was it done?"

"Union was Scotland's only choice! England was a major trading power, a colossus. Scotland was impotent, near economic ruin. A vassal for her southern neighbor. Scotland tried to found her own colonies in the new world to finance her independence, but the colonies failed. England was also at war with France, a historical Scottish ally, and England wanted to secure her northern borders. So the pressure was increased, the economic screws tightened. No, Mr. Bruce, union was only the means for Scotland to survive. Without it, this land would have become just frozen sod filled with starving people."

Scotty finished his mug of beer. Mary MacKenzie fetched him another, then sat down once more.

"After the Act of Union, there were numerous uprisings, and when they were crushed, all vestiges of Scottish independence were destroyed. But by the end of the eighteen hundreds, an organized nationalist movement began to gain widespread support, and Parliament allowed for some home rule by establishing the Scottish Office and the Cabinet position of secretary of state for Scotland. Many thought this wasn't enough. After the First World War, a group of Nationalists formed their own party. My father was there, twenty-one years old, a fighter, a visionary. He and his cohorts were idealists and firebrands, and at first they didn't have much of a party because they spent more time intellectualizing than organizing. And there were a lot of divisions. My father wanted the party to fight for elected office, to separate completely from Great Britain, to keep ties only as a commonwealth member. Others wanted only more home rule, while some wanted to work through the established parties and not contest elections separately. In truth, it wasn't until the 1960s, after several compromise oriented groups had split away, that the party began to achieve success, principally by emphasizing the economic issues instead of the historical and emotional perspective, which had already been widely accepted." She paused, then began speaking again. "Mr. Bruce, at the time of the Act of Union, England was a world power, a great trading nation. It made sense for Scotland to join her.

Today, things are different. England is a shadow of her past, eclipsed by much of the world. The longer Scotland remains part of Great Britain, she, too, remains eclipsed. Scotland has oil. If Scotland were an independent state, she would be a world power." She smiled wryly. "England fears dissolution would leave her in tatters. And that may be so. But we owe England nothing because England has sucked our lifeblood for centuries."

Scotty was fascinated. "I suppose you hate the English."

"No. I understand them, their society, their history. Besides, I spent a great deal of time in England when my father was a member of Parliament."

"Then I assume you have English friends?"

"Yes. And I sympathize with their point of view." She grabbed Scotty's hand and touched it momentarily to her own. "You see, I am flesh and blood. I am not a bogey woman. A fanatic. Yet I am still for Scotland."

Scotty nodded, impressed with her brightness, her strength, her vibrancy. "There must be some fanatics within the SNP. There always are."

"A few. And there are some spinoff groups espousing violence. But the SNP has always been nonviolent. A free Scotland will only be achieved by rational compromise and the development of mutual respect between the English and the Scots. It is not going to happen all at once. It will come in stages. And even when it comes, I hope there will be close contact between England and our homeland. That is as it should be."

"What about the recent history?"

"There was a vote on the establishment of a domestic Scottish parliament. It was defeated. Most thought the proposals did not go far enough. Some thought they went too far. Nobody liked them much."

"Did you?"

"My feelings were mixed."

"Did you vote for it?"

"Let's just say I believe in momentum."

Scotty stood and began to pace the veranda, looking at Mary MacKenzie out of the corner of his eye. She was watching him, too, almost surgically dissecting his hidden thoughts.

"Is something bothering you, Mr. Bruce?" she asked.

"Yes, but not you or the SNP. No, it's something else."

"Perhaps I can help you."

"Perhaps you can. If you're willing to discuss the *Columbus* incident again."

"I will if you accept one stipulation. There were no submersibles in the loch. And no Scottish group sabotaged the ship."

He nodded, tacitly accepting her position. "What do you know about the Loch Ness monster?"

"Are you serious?"

"Damn serious."

"Are you suggesting a living thing attacked the *Columbus?*"

"I'm not suggesting anything. I'm just asking a question."

"I know what the populace knows."

"I've spent the last two days reading everything I've been able to find on the subject." He paused, smiled. "Have you ever seen it?"

"No."

"You've lived here all your life and you've never caught sight of it?"

"Unfortunately not."

"Then you don't believe in it?"

"I didn't say *that!* There are too many people I respect who claim to have seen it."

He massaged his jaw, thinking. Could he tell her about the tracings? No. She might say something, repeat the information to members of the Highland Council.

"Why have you so suddenly become a naturalist, Mr. Bruce?"

"I've always been a naturalist."

"I see."

"You said you know people who claim to have seen the monster."

"There are many. Some more reliable than others. Some more interesting."

"I'd like to speak to one who is both."

"It could be arranged."

"Give me a name."

She didn't hesitate. "Father James MacPherson of Drumnadrochit."

"Can you take me to talk to this man?"

"Yes."

"When?"

"Now is as good a time as any."

They discussed an itinerary, then returned to the pub.

"One thing," he said just before they popped out to the jeep. "Since we're no longer at war . . ."

"It's not a peace, either," she declared, interrupting. "Only a truce."

"All right. Only a truce. But since we are at truce, I'd like you to call me Scotty, not Mr. Bruce."

She thought for a second, then nodded. "And I'm Mary," she said.

The trip from Foyers around the loch was pleasant. Passing through the tiny village of Drumnadrochit at Urquhart Bay, Mary MacKenzie directed Scotty northward into the mountains toward Loch Meiklie, about nine miles away. The final leg of the drive took fifteen minutes. Parking the jeep in the church's crowded parking lot, they entered the small chapel and located two seats in the rear just as MacPherson was positioning himself in front of the congregation to deliver his sermon, the opening prayers of the service having been concluded.

MacPherson was a striking-looking man, gaunt through the face and body. Very tall and bony, his anemic appearance and wrinkles helped accentuate an impression of age, although Scotty doubted the man could have been less than seventy-five.

"I saw a wild beast come out of the sea," MacPherson began, his voice rising in pitch and power, possessed of a fearful resonance, eyes blazing. "The beast was like a leopard, but it had paws like a bear and the mouth of a lion. I noticed one of the beast's heads seemed to have been mortally wounded, but this mortal wound was healed. In wonderment, the whole world followed the beast. And they said, 'Who can compare to the beast or come forward to fight against it?' " He began to beat his hands against the air, his white mane violently tossing about. "The beast hurled blasphemies against God. The beast waged war against God's people and conquered them. The beast was worshiped by all who did not have their names written in the book of the living."

The priest stopped and looked searingly down at the audience. The room was silent, everyone expectant. Scotty leaned close to Mary MacKenzie to whisper. She stopped him.

"Then I saw another wild beast come up out of the earth," MacPherson began again. "It made the world's inhabitants worship the first beast. It led astray these inhabitants. It forced all men to accept a stamped image on their right hand or their forehead, the name or number of the beast, and that name is Satan and that number is 666. And the second beast is the son of Satan, the false prophet. And woe be to us for he is upon us!" He was suddenly screaming, his face red, his eyes almost sprouting from their sockets. "Woe to us, Yes, he is upon us!"

Father MacPherson began to move around the stage, wailing, alternately stabbing his fist into the air and punching at his chest. The parishioners, predominantly septuagenarians, also punched at their chests, forcefully inflicting pain. Scotty was mesmerized.

"Woe be to him who is clutched by the beast. Woe be to him who embraces the beast. But sink not into despair, for I have seen a vision. The heavens open, and a white horse appears. Its Rider is called the Faithful and True. Justice is his standard. He wears a cloak dipped in blood, and his name is the Word of God. The armies of heaven are behind him, riding white horses and dressed in fine white linen. Out of his mouth comes a sharp sword, striking down the nations as he blazes the wrath of God, the Almighty. A name is written on part of the cloak: King of Kings and Lord of Lords." He began to wrench in spasms, sweat pouring, face defiantly contorted against an inner pain. "Next I see the beast and its armies do battle with the One riding the horse and his army. The beast is captured along with the false prophet. Both are hurled down into the fiery pool of burning sulphur. And the rest are slain by the Word."

Suddenly, there was silence, though MacPherson's cries still echoed between the building's ramparts. Scotty turned, confused. Mary MacKenzie showed no emotion, no reaction, her attention riveted on the figure who had been haranguing the audience.

Father MacPherson walked forward, then raised his hands. "Who is the beast?" he cried out.

"Satan," the congregation replied in unison.

"The second beast?" he screamed.

"The false prophet," the congregation replied. "The son of Satan."

"And the Word," MacPherson declared, "carried by the Rider on the white horse is God's Word. And the Rider is the Son of God, Christ our Lord. And we are his army!"

An enormous clamor erupted through the church as everyone began banging their pews. "We are his army!" they cried.

"Will we die if we must at the side of our Lord?"

"Yes, we will die if we must!"

Father MacPherson walked back to the pulpit. He waited, watching the exhausted expressions. Then he returned to the Latin of the Mass, reciting a series of prayers and bringing the services to a close with the consecration of the host and wine, the Holy Communion of the faithful and final prayers.

The formal service completed, he waited for his altar boys and then followed them out of the room.

Father MacPherson rose from his chair and shook Scotty's hand. "Bruce. King of Scotland. Yes, Bruce! You look like King Robert, and I know, for I saw his visage in a dream as he entered the battle of Bannockburn to fight against the English." He sipped at the steaming cup of tea, then turned to Mary MacKenzie. "And King Robert has a fine lass for an escort. A lass with Christ in her heart." His expression deepened as his eyebrows twisted. "And we must keep Christ in our hearts, for Satan and the false prophet are upon us."

MacKenzie smiled. "How are you feeling, father?"

The priest held up his hand. "Steady as a rock. My gout and arthritis have been assuaged by the Lord's kindness. He is preparing me for the great battle, curing my wounds. And I shall not fail him. I shall carry his banner. For I am a soldier of Christ on earth."

Scotty smiled, amused by the image of a toothless, barking dog. "I take it you've lived here a long time."

"Ay, you take it right, my son," MacPherson said. "Was born and raised here. I've served the Lord at this very spot for more years than I care to count. I've seen heathens come and heathens go, and I've seen the Word of the Lord cut its swath across the land. Yes, these are hallowed grounds, Mr. Bruce."

"Father, I noticed there were no young people in the church."

MacPherson seemed to rise with indignation. "The young have been perverted. They have taken to the beast, to the false prophet. But they shall return. They shall find their way back to the house of the Lord."

Mary MacKenzie pointed to bound volumes on the book shelves. "Father MacPherson is a scholar. An expert on the history of the region. These shelves are a treasure of folklore and personal chronicles."

The priest giggled. "All covered with cobwebs and dust, as I am, Mr. Bruce. You must admit, I'm a bit hoary."

Scotty shook his head. "I heard you speak from the pulpit. You may be hoary, but I don't think they're going to put you out to pasture yet."

"At least not until I have helped fulfill the prophecy!"

"What prophecy?"

"You heard the sermon, young man, the ultimate cataclysm. God's war against Satan. When Christ rides forth against the black host, I shall be there, too!"

Mary MacKenzie cleared her throat. "Father. Mr. Bruce would like to speak to you about the Loch Ness monster."

"The beast!" MacPherson cried, face ablaze with confrontation. "It is not a monster. It is the beast itself. Hell's master."

Scotty moved to the edge of his chair. "So you believe it exists?"

"Believe? I have seen it! I have felt its breath upon my skin!"

"You actually saw it?"

"And touched it! Confronted it! Overcame its overtures! Sent it back into the depths!"

Scotty was enthralled. "When did this happen?"

The priest's thoughts seemed to dart rapidly away. "In 1935," he suddenly said.

"Tell me, father. Tell me what happened."

MacPherson's voice grew deeper. "Fortunately, senility has not overcome my memory, and the image of what happened stands as vivid as ever, as if my confrontation had occurred just moments ago." He waved his hand, painting a picture. "I remember the feeling. Something came into my heart, carrying the Word of the Lord. The Lord told me to proceed on to the loch's waters. I did not question the Word, though I was filled with trepidation and fear. The midnight hour had already struck. I had feared for a long time that the forces of evil had taken ascendance and might achieve the ultimate destruction of God's kingdom. I had prayed to the Lord, asking him to tell me this was not so. And his call had suddenly come. I knew he was about to show me the truth of his ascendancy."

Mary MacKenzie settled into a seat next to Scotty. Both

were riveted on the priest's animated face, though MacPherson's eyes were ablaze with distance, probing through mists of time.

"I left the chapel and drove to the loch. There was no one about, and a veil of hell was upon the waters, a fog so thick you could not see the end of your hand. There was a death-like silence, too. I was afeared. My heart was pounding. But the Word of the Lord in me said go on. So I did. I located a rowboat, and out on to the waters I went, alone, cold, and defenseless. I cannot remember how long I floated aimlessly, but deep into the hours of darkness I asked the Lord for a sign. The Lord said I would soon witness his power and I would know my fears for his ultimate survival were ill founded. So I waited. Then it happened. The loch waters rose, drenching me to the quick. Ay, I was filled with terror as from out of the depths a wild beast appeared with ten horns and seven heads. And on its heads were blasphemous names. I noticed one of the beast's heads seemed to have been mortally wounded, but this mortal wound was healed." He stopped, stared at MacKenzie and Bruce, marveled at their astonished expressions, then continued. "Yes, I was staring at the face of the beast. I did not know what to do, but I stood my ground as its hot breath seared my skin. It moved to me, churning water, then took me up in its mouth and cried into my soul: do you follow the beast and the son of the beast, the false prophet? Or do you curry to the Word of the Lord, God, and his hated son, the Christ? I was afraid to answer. But I felt God give me strength. I defied the beast. He asked me to follow him. I told him I follow the Lord. A red bolt of lightning struck the lake, the sword of the Almighty. The beast shook and fought, trying to destroy me. When he could not, he disgorged me and receded beneath the water. I was nearly sucked down, too, by the undertow, but I managed to swim back to the boat and get the boat back to shore, where I fell upon the land and lay unconscious until the darkness and fog had lifted away and the kiss of the sun hit my face."

"Did you ever see the monster again?"

"It is a beast, Mr. Bruce. *The* beast."

"Right—*the* beast. But did you ever . . ."

"Never," the priest said, interrupting. "I never saw it again. But I will. I am a member of Christ's legion. And the Lord has promised I shall do battle with the beast and the false prophet before I die."

"Is the false prophet here, too?" Scotty asked.

"The false prophet's word is everywhere, but his manifestation is also in the loch."

"I don't understand."

"The ship!" the priest screamed, awash with anger. "The drill ship! It is the manifestation of the son of the beast, and I have been called to do battle with it."

Scotty stared. Had Mary MacKenzie told MacPherson he was part of Geminii? He didn't know.

"How will you battle with the ship, father?"

The priest raised his fist. "I do not know. But the Lord will show me. I shall battle the ship. The men of the oil company, who are followers of the false prophet. And then the beast itself."

Scotty glanced at Mary MacKenzie. "What if I told you, father, that I work for the oil company?"

The priest stood. "I would look at you to see if that were true. If I felt you were of the beast, I would try to bring you back to the Lord. If that were not possible, I would smite you dead. But I have watched you carefully. Because I cannot be deceived, I am satisfied. You carry the Word of the Lord, Mr. Bruce."

"Thank God," Scotty said, relieved.

Father MacPherson walked around his desk and placed his hand on Scotty's shoulder. Turning to Mary MacKenzie, he said, "This is a good man. He is welcome here at any time. If I did not have to perform another Mass, I would most enjoy talking some more. You bring him back, you hear, lassie."

Mary MacKenzie smiled. "Absolutely, father."

They spoke several minutes more; then Father MacPherson led them to the door.

"May God be with you" were his last words.

Scotty stood next to the jeep, staring back at the church. Mary MacKenzie moved to his side.

"What do you think?" she said.

"I think he's crazy," he replied.

She nodded noncommittally, then climbed into the jeep. He climbed in, too, and started the engine, heading back toward the Carn Dearg Inn.

Chapter 10

The next week was a busy one. A drill-stem test, run on Beauly Highpoint, recorded a significant flow of oil. Excited, the senior staff charted follow-ups, authorizing Beauly delineation wells, additional wildcats, and new cost and revenue projections. A letter was also received from Farquharson. Having read the *Columbus* report, the undersecretary expressed satisfaction with Geminii's investigation and, although not completely accepting the company's conclusions, at least considered the possibility of sabotage as real, asking to be apprised of further developments.

Scotty spent most of the week locked in meetings. He did not see Mary MacKenzie again, though they spoke twice on the phone, and he ran into Lefebre only once, passing him without so much as a nod. On Thursday, Whittenfeld asked Scotty to fly to Edinburgh to pay a courtesy call on Farquharson and then to proceed to London to present the new projections to company management. The assignment could not have come at a better time. Michael Wessinghage had called Wednesday night, having located a lead to Lefebre's past in London. Scotty's contact was to be a man named John Leslie Houghton, and a warning accompanied Houghton's phone number. No substantive questions were to be asked over the line, nor was he to ever publicly use Mr. Houghton's name or ask Mr. Houghton anything about himself, his business, or his acquaintances. The entire bent of their forthcoming conversation and possible liaison was to be confined to Lefebre.

The next day, early afternoon, he called Houghton's number from the privacy of Travis House, spoke to Houghton's secretary, and arranged a meeting for Saturday night at Houghton's office. Informing Mrs. Munro to pack his suitcase, he drove to Geminii base for the final matter on the weekly agenda, an orientation session with the new district organizer of the Transport and General Workers Union. According to the information they'd received, Malcolm Abercrombie, though still a district union official, had been stripped of his senior position, and a man named Hugh Sutherland had been transferred there to fill the void.

"Mr. Abercrombie was unable to make the meeting," Sutherland began irresolutely moments after Scotty had arrived. "He had some district branch matters to attend to, so he could not do the honors of introduction. That I will have to do myself. But perhaps we're fortunate." He smiled at Whittenfeld. "You've all spent more than enough time with Abercrombie already. Perhaps too much."

"Abercrombie has been a credit to the union," Whittenfeld said. "It's been a pleasure to do business with him. And we, of course, look forward to his continued friendship as well as a new and fruitful relationship with you."

"Yes," Sutherland said in an offbeat manner, his callused hands laid on the table, his gaunt face and orbited eyes inactive. "I certainly look forward to a new relationship."

Whittenfeld smiled; the smile was stilted. "I'm sorry Mr. Fullerheim couldn't be here, either. He's not feeling well. However, I'm sure you'll find him to be one of the more attentive labor relations executives in the business."

"So I've heard," Sutherland said, examining faces.

"Is this the first time you've worked in the area?" Foster asked.

"No," Sutherland replied. "But I haven't been here in a bit. I've concentrated on national duties the last couple of years, though I've committed myself to field work whenever the situation has become nasty enough to warrant special action."

"There are no nasty problems here," Whittenfeld said. "Isn't that so, Scotty?"

Scotty massaged his jaw. "No. Our relationship with the union is top notch."

Sutherland smiled sardonically. "Unfortunately, I'm not of that opinion."

"Oh?" Whittenfeld remarked.

"I have a list of grievances," Sutherland said. "And I would like to see if we could work out an accommodation."

"We're always willing to talk," Whittenfeld said. "Though, as you know, our actions are already governed by the parent agreement as well as by the local contract worked out with Abercrombie, which, I might add, was enthusiastically accepted by the rank and file."

"Don't hold Abercrombie up to me!" Sutherland said. "Abercrombie is a mouse. A man without strength. A man easily swayed by those he views with awe, which includes the management of Geminii Petroleum and most everyone else with power. Because he is a weak man, he has surrendered the interests of his union membership. We cannot allow that to continue. No, gentlemen, Mr. Abercrombie has been a disappointment. Perhaps a Quisling as well."

"You're making an inference about our integrity," Whittenfeld said. "And I don't think it's warranted."

"We'll see," Sutherland remarked, bowing.

"Did the membership vote out Abercrombie?" Foster asked.

"No," Sutherland replied. "The National Executive Committee stripped him of his authority."

"I don't understand," Foster countered. "If Abercrombie had been doing such an inadequate job, then why didn't the district membership act first?"

"They probably didn't realize they were being shortchanged," Sutherland declared.

"Can we hear your list?" Whittenfeld asked.

Sutherland smiled. "The first demand is based on a new development. You've put heavily armed men on the *Columbus*. Vigilantes. We want them off."

"I'm sorry," Whittenfeld declared. "They have to remain on board."

"Why? To intimidate the men?"

"No. To protect them."

"We had an unfortunate occurrence," Scotty said. "The ship was attacked by a submersible, as you no doubt know. We need the guards to protect her as well as your men."

"Come now! You don't expect armed guards to shoot and kill a submersible as if it were a herring, do you? So please don't play me for an idiot!"

Reddington's words exactly, Scotty thought.

Whittenfeld stood. "The men are aboard to prevent attempts at internal sabotage."

"Attempts? By whom? Geminii executives and staff?"

"No."

"By union members?"

"Let's say neither."

Sutherland lit a cigarette, self-rolled. "I will restate our position. The men are to come off the ship. I would also like the safety officer to come off as well. We want to replace him with our own man, someone who will look after the interests of our membership with a more devoted sense of diligence. Since one of our men has already drowned and several have been injured as well, I don't think the request is unreasonable."

"Not excessively," Whittenfeld said. "But unreasonable enough. We've discussed this matter with the union many times. We reached a consensus long ago."

"A consensus is not embodied in the general agreement."

"Correct. But it's been verbally accepted by both sides. And, anyway, there's no compelling reason to open the issue again."

"On the contrary," Sutherland charged. "There is a strong compulsion. Namely, as I said, casualties."

Whittenfeld scribbled a note. "Believe me, I sympathize. But if I have a union safety rep on board, complaints will be nonstop, and, well, progress will slow. I cannot allow that to happen."

"Do you prefer dead men to dead dollars?"

"Of course not," Whittenfeld said. "And I don't understand why you think I don't have the men's interests at heart. Hell, I respect the union and encourage its activities even though my first obligation is to Geminii."

"Don't make me retch, Whittenfeld. I'm not here to be coddled, conned, or entertained. I'm here to do a job, and may be the first rep around here in a while who's had such a desire."

"Mr. Sutherland," Whittenfeld said. "There's no reason to roar in here flinging antagonisms all over the place."

"I'm just stating our positions as clearly as possible."

"I said we'll talk."

"Talk alone is worthless."

"Talk leads to other things."

"Like more talk. And if that happens, we'll just have to . . ."

"Sit down?"

Sutherland stared noncommittally, then smiled. "We also want a union representative to attend your management meetings."

Whittenfeld tried to stifle a laugh. "You're not serious, are you?"

"Yes," Sutherland declared. "And practical. These are very special circumstances. As you said in your own explanation to the union, Geminii suspects the *Columbus* was attacked. As such, we wish to be privy to security and operational decisions."

"Out of the question."

"Let us blaze new territory."

"The consortium is not a government enterprise."

"Let's treat it like one."

"Unfortunately, I can't. Now is there anything else?"

"The issue of local union workers."

"I didn't know there was an issue."

Sutherland grimaced. "You've imported planeloads of English, German, and American personnel. Utilized the services of very few locals."

"We've hired the best men available. Unfortunately, we could not find qualified people here."

"Nonsense."

"This is a nonunion matter. We hire who we want. If they desire to join the local and live by union rules, then that's their business. We respect their decision."

Sutherland stood and began to pace. "There are experienced men in Scotland. Union men who have learned their trade in the North Sea and elsewhere. Union men who live in this region. Union men who have been overlooked."

"We have figures," Foster said. "A breakdown on nationality and . . ."

Sutherland exploded. "I don't care about figures. I care about jobs. Men's lives. Their families' well-being."

"Let's not get acrimonious, Mr. Sutherland," Whittenfeld cautioned.

"I'm trying not to."

"You must understand. I cannot fire good men just to employ locals. Even your union won't stand for that."

"I agree. But we want you to make a commitment to local employment."

"I assume this is an unofficial position."

"Semi."

"Then I will treat it as such."

Sutherland leaned close. "What are you going to do about the first three demands?"

"I'm going to take them under consideration."

"And then?"

"I'll repeat myself again. We're going to talk. We're going to find a way to compromise and work together. Hell, Sutherland, this is not *us* against *you*. It's a partnership. We're all working toward one thing. The discovery of oil. That one thing will benefit everyone, benefit Scotland. It's our duty to compromise. It's our duty to work together. You let me think about the demands. Then you come over for dinner where you and I can exchange ideas and get to know each other."

"Forget it."

"We must allow trust to grow."

"I will grow to trust you when you agree to the demands."

Whittenfeld stared, saying nothing. Seconds slowly passed. Then Sutherland stood and ambled decisively to the door.

"I've taken up enough of your time, Mr. Whittenfeld," he said. "You've heard what I have to say. I've heard your reply. Think about the demands. Then let me know. You know where to find me."

"Of course," Whittenfeld said.

Sutherland excused himself and walked out of the room.

"Sutherland sounds more like an SNP politician than a union rep," Whittenfeld said.

"He may be both," Foster reminded. "Everyone around here talks that way, anyway. Abercrombie did, for one. The Scottish Office does, for two. So do the regional domos."

Whittenfeld shook his head. "One-third of them believe what they say. The next third say what they say because they think that's what we expect to hear. And the last third talk like nationalists just to impress the other two-thirds with their piety. No, it's not what Sutherland said but how he said it. Something strikes me off key!" He turned to Scotty.

"I want you to talk to him. See if you can start up a relationship. Maybe reason some sense into his head."

Scotty walked down the first-floor hall toward the reception desk. Hugh Sutherland was standing by the front door Scotty had called down from the conference room, asking reception to hold the union rep.

"You wanted to speak to me, Mr. Bruce?" Sutherland asked as Scotty moved to his side.

"Just for a moment," Scotty answered. "I know you have things to do, and I have to prepare for a trip to Edinburgh."

"All right," Sutherland said. "I'm listening, though you had every opportunity to talk in the conference room."

"I wanted to observe. Hear what you had to say."

"Admirable."

"You certainly did not pull any punches."

"Mr. Bruce, I'm a union rep. My business is to represent the Transport and General workers. Whether I'm liked by Geminii management or not is irrelevant. I say what has to be said. I don't mince words. I do my job."

"I understand. And since I'm the number-two man here, I would like to understand more."

"Admirable."

"I know you rejected contact apart from business, but I'd like to talk to you—at length. I'll be involved in union relations from now on, and it will help if I have a good grip on the issues."

"I have little time or patience for bullshit."

"I promise—no bullshit."

Sutherland stared suspiciously. "All right, Mr. Bruce. You stop by the union offices sometime. Yes, that will be all right."

Scotty smiled. Sutherland's offer was efficiently stated. He understood. He would also take the man up on it.

"Good day," Sutherland said, exiting.

"Yes," Scotty replied. "Good day."

It was eight o'clock. He would have to leave for the airport by eight-thirty to catch the nine-twenty flight to Edinburgh. In between, he would merely have to contend with Mrs. Munro.

"Now you take my advice, Mr. Bruce," Mrs. Munro was saying as she carried two of Scotty's bags to the front door. "You watch yourself. Edinburgh is a big city, but London is bigger and more dangerous, too. And I should know since I nearly met my maker there several times."

Scotty popped out of the den holding an attaché case. "Is that so?"

"There are no rules, Mr. Bruce. None whatsoever for lorries or cars or anything. There's no place to cross the streets, and I tell you, the English try right hard to hit you on purpose. As God's my judge, it's the truth. And that just doesn't apply to the Scots. It goes for nice plump Americans, too."

Scotty laughed. "There must be crosswalks, Mrs. Munro."

"No. They have underground walkways to pass under the streets. But when you're in a hurry, Mr. Bruce, you've got to do it straight. And since I've been with you, I've come to know you like to hurry."

Scotty whisked into the kitchen, then returned to the den where Mrs. Munro had planted herself.

"I assure you, I will return in one piece."

She giggled. "Well, I think I'm not the only one who'd be right glad to see that?"

"Oh?"

"The MacKenzie woman called just before you arrived."

"Why didn't you tell me?"

"I can't remember to tell you everything, Mr. Bruce. Besides, it doesn't matter since she said she couldn't be reached."

"What else did she say?"

"She wished you a good trip."

"Is that all?"

"Yes. That's all. Mr. Bruce, do I detect a little bit of the old romance beginning here?"

Scotty stuffed some additional papers into the case. "I'm afraid not, Mrs. Munro. Miss MacKenzie tolerates me at best."

Mrs. Munro sat on the arm of the sofa. "Now I'm not so sure, Mr. Bruce. I'm no novice, you know. Though I look like a battleship, I was an attractive lass at one time, with my share of suitors. So I know something about love. I know a woman gets this little sound in her voice when she fancies a man."

"What sound?"

"Just a sound. I can't describe it. But I know it when I hear it, and I heard it in MacKenzie's voice."

Scotty couldn't disguise a smile. "I think you ought to get your ears checked, Mrs. Munro."

Mrs. Munro was indignant. "I'll have you know I got hearing like radar. And that's 'cause I always treat my ears good and dig out all the wax. Now I heard this sound in the lady's voice, and if you don't believe me or don't care, then that's your problem. And let me tell you something else. Another problem you have. You don't listen to me enough. You buzz around like a bull in a china shop, and you don't take note of all the intelligent things I try to teach you. And you're still a mess. No matter how hard I try, nothing works. I went into your closet this morning and looked at how everything was hung, and I nearly got sick. You had the sporran dangling upside down! Now you got to be crazy to treat a good sporran like that!"

"Now Mrs. Munro—"

"Don't *now* me, Mr. Bruce!"

Scotty's expression deepened; he was suddenly very serious. "You know, Mrs. Munro, when I was growing up back in Colorado, we had a family dog named Fuzzy. In fact, my mother still has Fuzzy's grandson. But Fuzzy was my dog. He'd follow me everywhere. He'd go to school and wait outside until the school day was over. He'd go to football and baseball practice. He'd follow me around the house. Wherever he went, he'd have his big mouth open, barking advice to my teachers through the school windows, to the coaches from the stands, and to my mother from the floor. The damn dog never stayed quiet for a minute. And, believe it or not, the nonstop yakking led to a terrible tragedy."

"Pray tell me what, Mr. Bruce," Mrs. Munro said, skeptical already. "I can hardly wait to hear."

Scotty fudged a scowl. "His tongue fell out. God help me, it's the truth. He yakked so much the muscles holding his tongue disintegrated, and the damn thing fell out."

"Pshew, Mr. Bruce! Pshew!"

Scotty quickly looked at his watch, barely able to control his laughter, then grabbed a jacket and hustled toward the door.

"I'm going to teach you a thing or two when you get back," Mrs. Munro continued. "That's if you get back." She followed him to the hall and watched him grab his luggage. "There you go, running off again and not listening. The plane will wait. There's plenty of time. You just don't like to know someone knows more than you do and—"

Mrs. Munro stopped. Scotty was gone, the door slammed shut. She moved to the window and watched him get into the jeep. Then, as she turned away, she heard the jeep roar off into the distance.

"Fool man!" she mumbled.

Chapter 11

Scotty arrived in Edinburgh at ten-thirty and spent the night at the George Hotel, a touristy relic to days past, only a short walk to New Andrews House, the modern building housing the Scottish Office.

He checked out early in the morning, walked around the streets beneath Edinburgh Castle, which was situated high on a domineering hill, then arrived at his destination shortly before ten.

Several minutes later, he was in Andrew Farquharson's office, an unimpressive cubicle with an impressive city view.

Farquharson was there, smiling, waving his cane, full of questions and observations. Mr. Droon was with him as well, more subdued than at their earlier meeting. Droon was Mac-Kenzie's alter ego; he could not possibly have accepted the *Columbus* report at face value. Scotty could only guess that Farquharson had warned Droon to keep his opinions within the confines of their offices.

They spoke briefly about the *Columbus* incident. Scotty explained that no additional information had surfaced, though he was careful to avoid any mention of the tracings. The rest of the meeting consisted of small talk. Congratulations were offered for the Beauly find. Then Farquharson mentioned he had read the Geminii file and had agreed with the secretary of state's decision. Finally, Scotty offered to convey Farquharson's pleasure to Whittenfeld, punctuating the offer with a gift, a box of Havana cigars, which Farquharson gladly accepted.

The meeting was adjourned.

Scotty flew to London and checked into Grosvenor House, Hyde Park, Mayfair District.

As soon as he was sequestered in his suite, he called

Houghton and spoke to Houghton's secretary once more, confirming the scheduled meeting, eight o'clock precisely, the address provided, 113 Elizabeth Street, Belgravia.

It was five o'clock. He had several hours to kill. He would take a shower, a shave, and then a short nap, expecting the switchboard operator to call at seven.

The street was dark, the building's windows boarded. Scotty rang the bell. The door speaker crackled, its mounted television eye focusing. Upon request, he announced his name. The door opened. No one was there.

He walked down a long, dark hall. Nearing the end, an attractive young woman appeared, identified herself—Mr. Houghton's secretary—then frisked him thoroughly. Dumbfounded, Scotty said nothing.

They entered a suite.

The suite's outer office was small. A file cabinet stood in the corner. The walls were white.

The only visible interior door opened, and a man appeared dressed in a vested suit.

"Mr. Bruce," he called, rushing to shake Scotty's hand.

"Mr. Houghton?" Scotty asked, still a bit put off by the reception.

"Of course, Mr. Houghton," Houghton said, leading Scotty into his office, another spartan room, white as well, with a solitary desk, one couch, and an eye-startling bank of telephones. "Please take a seat and relax." He nodded approvingly as Scotty sat. "Would you like some coffee?"

"No, thank you," Scotty said.

Houghton walked behind the desk. "Well, you just tell me if the need arises." He smiled effusively. "Now I hope your trip from Inverness was without incident."

Scotty examined the man. Houghton was far more pleasant than he had expected. Far more gregarious, too. In fact, Houghton was a rather agreeable, elegant chap, equipped with a proper upper-class English accent, a soothing demeanor, and an engaging personality.

"The trip was fine," Scotty said, relaxing.

"Good. I'm happy to hear that. I hope you've taken a liking to the country up there."

"Yes. Very much so."

Houghton sat. "I love Scotland myself. In fact, I have a small farm in Nairn, not far from Inverness. I use it as a vacation cottage, though, I'm sorry to say, I don't get up there often. Business consumes far too much of my time."

Scotty was tempted, but he didn't ask. "I appreciate your meeting with me, Mr. Houghton."

"Don't mention it. Wessinghage is an old friend. Although I haven't seen him going on about ten years, we still transact business over the phone. A request from Wessinghage is an honored request. Besides, this one was easy."

"You were able to obtain information on Lefebre?"

Houghton looked puzzled. "Of course. I had information long before Michael Wessinghage called. Mr. Lefebre is not an unknown quantity."

Scotty's curiosity began to peak. "Might I smoke?"

"Of course."

Scotty lit a cigar while looking about the room.

"I notice you've noticed," Houghton said. "The place is sparse. Quiet and colorless. But I find it comfortable." He removed his glasses. "Wessinghage told me you were a famous football player."

"An exaggeration."

"You're being modest. And evasive with the wrong person. I know everything there is to know about you, Mr. Bruce."

"How did that come about, Mr. Houghton?"

"I do not impart information to unknown quantities. Though Wessinghage's word is uniquely trustworthy, my associates still compiled a normal profile. I hope you don't mind, but we try to keep our procedures standardized."

"We?"

"Yes. We. I am only the tip of the iceberg. These telephones put me in contact with a great many ears and mouths. I am not as insular as I might appear." He smirked. "I can see you are brimming with curiosity. What does Mr. Houghton do, you are asking yourself. Is he a spy? A secret agent? A master criminal?" He laughed broadly. "None of those, Mr. Bruce."

Scotty remembered Wessinghage's careful admonition. "I am only concerned about Pierre Lefebre's background."

Houghton smiled. "I approve your sense of discretion." He rifled through the pages of a dossier. "The life of Mr. Pierre Lefebre."

Scotty craned his neck; Houghton kept the file out of reach.

"Why do you wish to know about Lefebre?"

"I work with him. There's no love lost."

"I see. But that is rarely the reason for such intense curiosity."

"I think he's dangerous. I don't understand what he's doing with Geminii. I'm concerned about the future consequences."

Houghton's expression deepened. "Mr. Lefebre is a very evil man."

"I'm not surprised."

"And yes, very dangerous, too. More dangerous than you think. You might be better served without the information contained in this dossier."

"Why is that?"

"Sometimes ignorance is bliss. Be aware of the real man and you will treat him differently. If Mr. Lefebre were to ever know you possess intimate knowledge of his past, he might become very ill tempered."

"I appreciate the warning."

Houghton broke the barest of smiles, glanced at his watch, and rose from his desk chair.

"It is time for dinner, Mr. Bruce. I have made reservations at the Ritz."

"At your pleasure," Scotty said, glancing at the lights on the telephone panel that had been silently flashing, nonstop, since he had entered the room.

Houghton walked to the door. He followed. They entered the outer office. The secretary called a car. They entered the hall, took an elevator to the basement, climbed into a limousine behind a driver and bodyguard, and left the building.

The limousine slowly moved along London's side streets.

The Ritz had been superb, dignified, cordial. The food had been equally inviting, but as Scotty had listened to Houghton recite a chronology of Pierre Lefebre's achievements, he had quickly lost his appetite. In fact, by the time the message which prompted their departure had arrived, he'd become positively nauseous.

The Black Angel of Algeria. The general's master of castration and decapitation. The death man of Katanga. Maimer and crippler of blacks on both sides of the Congolese insurrection. The Frenchman. The Chief of Torture in Idi Amin's State Research Bureau. Bearer of death and pain for thousands of Ugandans. All these evils. All one man. Pierre Lefebre.

He'd heard it in detail. The events of Lefebre's orphaned childhood. His undistinguished career in the French army. And, of course, the particulars of his long, satanic romance with Africa.

Some of the facts matched the information Lefebre had provided himself; however, Lefebre had left out most of the interesting particulars.

What the hell was Lefebre doing at Geminii?

Unfortunately, Houghton did not have the answers, but he'd promised to uncover them. And Scotty was certain Houghton could turn the trick.

The limousine crossed the River Thames, scooted through side streets, turned past a fish market, then angled into a dead-end alley and stopped. Houghton ushered Scotty from the car.

"I thought some first-hand knowledge would be proper punctuation," he explained.

"An eyewitness?"

"Unfortunately so."

Houghton pulled back a dangling door and stepped into a small room lit with a solitary lantern. Scotty followed. Inside the room was a cot. On the cot, a black man, both his legs mangled.

"How are you, Kabugo?" Houghton asked, slipping the man a roll of sterling.

"Very good," Kabugo said, gutturally forming words by forcing air from his throat.

Houghton turned to Scotty. "You will have to be patient with Mr. Kabugo. He does not have the services of a tongue. It was summarily removed with a machete. But he has learned to overcome his disability through practice and the rejection of pain."

Kabugo smiled, then laughed. He had a patch over his eye. No right ear. No teeth. A massive scar crossing his face.

"Sit," Kabugo said, pointing to a pair of crates.

Houghton and Scotty sat down, their feet immersed in dust. Scotty lit a cigar, Houghton a cigarette, poised at the end of a holder.

"Mr. Bruce would like to know something about Pierre Lefebre," Houghton said.

Kabugo's smile turned to a scowl. "May he die. Die in pain."

Houghton glanced at Scotty. "There are many who have

wished the same end for Lefebre." He gestured to Kabugo. "Mr. Bruce would like to know specifics."

"Mr. Bruce wish to hear of the devil?"

"Yes, he wishes."

Kabugo's eyes blazed. "I only meet Lefebre once, but the name Lefebre known in Kampala like the name devil. Most evil man. But no one ever see. Head of torture at State Research Bureau."

"Go on," Scotty said, after Kabugo had paused, searching through memories.

Kabugo coughed consumptively. "Uganda bad place once Amin throw out Obote. Many die. Many tortured. But wife and I poor persons, no politic, so we never think there be a problem. But Amin a Moslem. And for Catholics like we, Amin no good." He lit a hand-rolled cigarette that soon emitted a distinctive odor—hash. "One day we at Makerere Church of Christ singing, and Amin's soldiers under orders from General Adrisis enter, searching for Pastor Musotebi. But Musotebi no there, being somewhere near Namasaga at time. Soldiers have arrest order charging Musotebi with treason. They ask us where pastor be, but we no say. So soldiers take us to basement of Research Bureau, the place of the dead." His speech became stuporous. "Nubians come and beat us with sticks. When no one tell where the pastor be, we be forced to lie face down on ground until we hear voice of Frenchman Lefebre. Frenchman say he want to release married couples and all those who be that should raise hands. I try to stop wife, but she raise hand, and then Lefebre pick us out and have us taken to a little room where we be tied to the wall. For whole day we hang, then Lefebre, the Satan, come in, smiling. He say I am to tell him whereabouts of pastor, but I no do. So Frenchman Lefebre, he beat me all over legs with lead bar while he laugh. He break legs, but I still no tell him nothing. Lefebre he come and go, and each time he come, he beat me more and cut my face with knife. Finally, he say, if I no tell him, he kill wife. I tell him pastor in Namasaga. Lefebre leave, then come back next day to tell me I lie." He stopped, choking, tears beginning to come down his cheeks. "Then he kill wife."

"Tell him how, Kabugo," Houghton prompted gently.

Kabugo wiped the tears from his face. "He dig out her heart and leave it at my feet."

Scotty nearly threw up. Unable to believe. Unable to fathom how such a thing could take place in this day and age.

"Tell him the rest, Kabugo," Houghton ordered.

Kabugo cleared his throat, trying to force more strength into the muscles. "Lefebre make me hang there another day with dead wife on floor; then he come back and tell me I am to be let go. But I am to be punished for lying." He began to cry again. Houghton soothed him, urging him on. "Lefebre, he cut out my eye, cut off my ear, then cut out my tongue. Lefebre leave. Nubians come and take me to Kampala hospital. And I no ever see Lefebre again."

"I can't—" Scotty tried to say, looking at Kabugo, trying to impart some sympathy.

Houghton stood. "Kabugo doesn't need sympathy. Sympathy does not buy food."

Squeamishly, Scotty handed the cripple a ten-pound note.

"You be a kind man," Kabugo said, rocking back against the wall.

The conversation ended abruptly; Houghton and Scotty returned to the limousine. Houghton ordered the driver to proceed to Grosvenor House. Scotty remained quiet, reflective, confused. As the car neared Park Lane, though, he turned to Houghton.

"Can I believe all this?" he asked.

"Of course," Houghton replied.

"Will you get me the remainder of the information?"

"It may take time, but I will get it."

Scotty glanced out the window as the driver pulled the limousine up to the hotel. "One more question, if I may."

"Of course."

"Why is Lefebre loose?"

"There is a price on his head in Algeria and Uganda."

"No. I mean why isn't he in jail here?"

"He'd done nothing wrong."

"He's killed, tortured, maimed."

"In Africa."

"Africa exists. Africa has laws."

"Lefebre is in Great Britain. He has done nothing wrong here. Broken no laws. And as far as this society is concerned, he is thoroughly welcome."

Scotty stared. Houghton smiled. Houghton was a thorough professional.

He and Houghton shook hands.

"Thanks," Scotty declared, easing out of the car.

"You will hear from me," Houghton said in reply.

Scotty stepped back from the curb. Houghton bowed. The limousine disappeared.

The Monday-morning session was the last on his schedule. He arrived early at company headquarters, the home base for Geminii's European and African business ventures, and left shortly before two, early afternoon. In the interim, he met with senior executives, discussing the exciting discoveries in Inverness. He truly admired the London contingent. They were professional, considerate, likable. And that was doubly true for John Fallworth, the managing director of Geminii International Limited, a man widely respected not only in the oil business but in the general community as well. Unfortunately, Scotty was ill at ease most of the time, painfully trying to refrain from asking any pointed questions about Lefebre. Of course, questions would have been ill advised. He was new to the company, and his relationship with Fallworth was still embryonic. As Houghton had said so pointedly, Pierre Lefebre had done nothing wrong in Great Britain, and for all he knew, Lefebre's background was known to top-level management, albeit the gruesome details submerged by time and distance.

He lunched with Fallworth and several other executives, spent most of the time dodging questions about the National Football League—most of the men were American—then returned to the hotel midafternoon, rested until five, and caught the company limousine to Heathrow.

He disembarked his British Airways' flight to Inverness shortly after nine o'clock. It was dark and cold at the airport, and his jeep, which he'd left in the terminal parking lot, was nearly frosted over. As he climbed inside, his thoughts rambling, he was unable to forget Kabugo.

Shivering, he headed toward home.

Chapter 12

Eyes closed, Bob Reddington listened to the soft music emanating from the cassette deck. It was dark. Quiet, too. He'd been lying on his back in the cabin the last two hours half asleep. It had been a long day.

The door to the stateroom suddenly flashed open. A shaft of antiseptic light invaded the room. A derrick man followed.

"We've got problems," the derrick man said.

Reddington opened his eyes. "Like what?"

"Possible kick!"

Reddington jumped to his feet. "The indicators?"

"A drilling break and stroke increase."

"Has there been a change in the drill-pipe weight?"

"Yes."

Reddington put on his clothes; something less buoyant than the drilling mud had entered the well bore, providing less support for the drill pipe and thereby increasing its observable weight.

"Did Grabowski and Nunn return to the ship?" he asked, bursting into the hallway ahead of the derrick man.

"No. They stayed on shore in the lab. The chopper returned, though, bringing out a new security guard."

"That's just what we need right now. Goddamn bastards!"

They emerged from the cabin. Rain was pounding against the catwalks. The sky was darker than hell, the wind as fierce as legend.

Reddington climbed on to the drilling floor. Even through the fog and rain, he could see tense faces, trauma.

"Any primary indicators yet?" he asked.

"Not yet," the driller replied, nervously scanning his instruments.

Reddington looked downship. A helicopter was tied to the

forward helipad. The crew seemed to be moving in slow
motion. Off the ship, whitecaps were churning.

"Let's do a flow check," he ordered, moving between the
tool pusher and the driller.

A roughneck appeared on deck, settling the issue. "We've
got a volume increase in the mud pits," he screamed, trying
to be heard over the howl of the wind. "And gas in the
cuttings."

"It's a gas kick," the driller cried.

Reddington rushed to his side. "Shut the goddamn well and
prepare to kill it!"

The shut in and kill procedure was dangerously complex.
They had to close the blowout preventers, record bore pressures, calculate new mud weight, circulate heavier mud into
the bore to kill the kick, then open the preventers again and
proceed with normal operation.

The driller manipulated his controls, sealing the blowout
preventer's rams.

"Close down the electrical," Reddington ordered, turning
to a rotary helper. "You! Tell the radio operator to inform
base we've taken a gas kick and we're now employing shut in
and kill procedures."

The rotary helper raced to the radio room as Reddington
ordered the drill-floor guard to leave the area.

"I'm under orders to remain at this post," the guard declared, confused.

"I'm in charge of this vessel," Reddington cried. "And I
want you off!"

"Mr. Whittenfeld and Mr. Lefebre ordered—"

"I don't care what they ordered. We have an emergency. I
don't want us blown away because of some fool mistake made
by someone who had no reason to be here. Now get off."

The guard didn't move.

"I said off," Reddington screamed, grabbing the guard by
the collar and hurling him down the steps. "And off means
off!"

The guard reached for his gun. A tremendous wave swell
hit the ship, upending him. Looking up at Reddington, he
rose to his feet, then wobbled toward the cabins and disappeared.

Reddington returned to the drill floor. The driller had completed his procedures. Reddington recorded bore pressures,
calculated the additional weight of mud required to kill the

kick, entered the mud room, ordered the derrick men to add a required volume of solids, then set new pump rates and returned to the teeth of the storm.

Captain Olafsen leaned close to the cabin's window, staring at the beads of rain.

"Can't see a damn thing," he said, coughing. "What a night to be without a radio."

"I'm trying my best," the radio man said, his head obscured within an open console.

Olafsen lit a cigarette, coughed again—smoker's cough—then turned to the first officer. "You'd think we were out in the North Sea. The loch don't know how to treat visitors with respect."

The first officer laughed. The captain poured a cup of coffee, then roamed into the surveillance area where the sonar engineer was perched over the sensing equipment and side-scan displays.

"I'd like to be back on shore with a good woman in a warm bed," the engineer said.

"Yah," Olafsen remarked as he sat down. "But then again, things could be worse. You could be on board the *Columbus*, fiddling with ice-cold pipe. Yah, think about that for a while and you'll be thankful you're at least in a dry cabin."

Laughing, Olafsen opened a magazine, scanned the pages, glanced up at the deck clock—eleven P.M.—then yawned.

"I can't fix her," the radio man announced a short time later.

"Keep trying," Olafsen called back, his worn, scarred features shifting slowly, experience called to thought. "We have plenty of time!"

The patter of rain grew heavier, almost hypnotic.

"We've got something!" the engineer yelled a short time later.

"Like what?" Olafsen asked.

"My God!"

Olafsen examined the side-scan printouts, then ordered a realignment of the mechanical fish. "It looks like the same object we had last time."

"It *is* the same object!"

They examined the succeeding traces. The radio man joined them. Huge rebound images continued to plot out.

"It's starboard," the engineer said, examining the blips. "And it's turning toward us."

"A submersible?" the radio man asked.

Olafsen pointed at the other instruments. "No heat. No noise." He searched the side scan. "It's the same thing we had before! No mistaking it. The damn thing is alive!" He pushed the radio man back toward the cabin. "Get that radio fixed. I don't care what you have to do and what instruments you have to cannibalize but get it fixed."

The radio man disappeared. Olafsen leaned over the instruments. "It's diving," the engineer said, puzzled. "And twisting crazily."

Olafsen looked away, then shook his head. "Damn!"

Totally drenched, Scotty Bruce sloshed up the path to Travis House and knocked on the door, shielding himself under the eave of the building.

Mrs. Munro appeared moments later. "Mr. Bruce," she cried.

He slipped past her, dropping his bags in the foyer.

"I need to talk to you," she said.

"Not now," he said, removing his jacket. The last thing he wanted was a lecture from Mrs. Munro. "Let me clean up first."

"This is right urgent."

"What's the matter?"

She pulled a note from her pocket. "The people at Geminii just missed you at the airport. They called here and left a message. It says: 'Gas kick on *Columbus*. Shutting in and attempting to kill.' "

Startled, he suddenly put on his jacket once more. "When did it come in?"

"Five minutes ago."

He pointed to the phone. "Call the night operator at Geminii. Ask for helicopter operations. Tell them I'm on my way. Have them prepare a chopper. Immediately!"

Mrs. Munro hurried to the phone. However, by the time she had picked up the receiver, Scotty was gone.

Informed the mud weight had been increased as ordered, Reddington instructed the driller to begin kill procedure by pumping the mud down narrow tubes attached to the marine

riser, tubes intersecting the bore below the blowout preventers.

Within minutes, the kick had been killed, and the gas in
the marine riser had been evacuated. The well was dead.

Reddington rechecked pressures and inspected equipment.
There was no damage. According to his readings, the downward weight of the new mud was now more than sufficient to
overburden the upward flow of gas. Although they were still
drilling through a section of very high pressures, the pressures
were under control.

He ordered normal operations to resume.

The sonar engineer wiped away an accumulation of sweat.

"I've never seen anything like it," he said, mesmerized. "It's
incredible."

"I know," Olafsen observed.

Reams of printouts lay on the floor, displaying unaccount-
able motion. First, the target object had dived, then ascended.
Then it had seemed confused, even angered, moving in ever-
narrowing circles.

"The radio?" Olafsen called, trying to be heard over the
howl of the storm.

"Still out!" the radio engineer called back.

"Any progress?"

"No."

"Son of a bitch."

"It's gone under us," the sonar engineer cried.

"Where's it headed?"

"To the *Columbus!*"

Olafsen raced forward to the wheel. "Full speed," he ordered, ignoring the weather danger.

The first officer pushed the throttle forward; the tug's
engine roared.

"Take us in," Olafsen added.

"To base?" the first officer asked.

"No," the captain replied. "To the drill ship!"

Scotty emerged on to the roof of the Geminii office building. He'd just left the radio room. The radio operator had not
been able to raise the *Columbus.*

The director of helicopter operations walked briskly out of
his bunker.

"We set?" Scotty asked.

The director waved his arms. "You can't fly out in this."

"Don't tell me I can't!"

"The pilots have refused."

"Screw them!"

"Without them, you can't get out!"

"Give me the keys."

"What?"

"I'll fly her myself."

"Mr. Bruce—"

"I can handle a bird as well as any of your pilots!"

"It's suicide."

"My suicide."

"But my responsibility!"

Scotty entered the control bunker and grabbed a key off the call board.

"You can't do this!" the director cried, following him.

"You bet your ass I can. I'll take the responsibility. They're taking a kick out there. I'm going. Understand?"

The director stared, then nodded.

Scotty climbed into the chopper.

As the tug raced toward the *Columbus,* the sonar engineer called for the captain again.

"What is it?" Olafsen asked, approaching.

"Look!" the engineer cried, white as a ghost.

Olafsen examined the side-scan tracings. The drill ship's riser was clearly visible, descending from the ship to the well head. But there was something else, the target object, moving several hundred feet below the surface, heading directly for the ship at incredible velocity.

"Thank goddamn God!" Reddington cried, ignoring the stinging rain. He was thrilled. The kick had been killed.

The crew was elated, too; he could hear it in their voices!

He poured himself some coffee from a thermos. Hot coffee tasted good on a bitter night.

He returned to the bridge deck.

Chewing a dead cigar, switching its position from side to side in his mouth, Scotty quickly scanned the instruments, highlighted by a red console light, then looked out the windows, searching the horizon through the glare of the chopper's floods. The rain was dropping diagonally, a sheer wall of

water. The air was misty black. The loading docks were
barely visible, the Dores shore a melange of merging lines,
shifting relentlessly as the helicopter rocked askew from the
violent blasts of wind.

He held tighter to the stick as the chopper's wipers surged
across the windshield. Rising to five hundred feet, he tilted
the chopper northward and steered away from the Geminii
complex. Maintaining visual contact with the loch surface, he
crossed the Lochend finger, aligned the chopper with the loch's
north shore, then descended to three hundred feet, pushed his
controls forward once more, and began to negotiate the intervening distance to Urquhart Bay.

It was the most incredible sight Captain Olafsen had ever
seen, and though he doubted his senses, it lay right in front
of him, captured on paper. As before, the marine riser was
prominent on the sonar record. But so was the target object,
though its position had changed. The target object had the
marine riser in tow at three hundred feet, and it was pulling
the riser out of whack, trying to tear it in half.

"Full speed ahead," Olafsen cried, realizing the *Columbus*
was probably unaware of the peril.

A roustabout was the first man aboard to notice impending
disaster. Standing near a control hose reel, which held the
upper end of one of the blowout control hoses, he saw the
hose go slack. Checking the equipment, he realized the hose
must have broken below the water line. Alarmed, he informed
the driller, who affirmed the conclusion and then checked the
riser azimuth indicator. The riser was visibly way out of line
again.

"Get Red!" the driller screamed.

The roustabout summoned Reddington.

"What the hell?" Reddington cried after returning and
glancing at the screen.

The roustabout told him one of the control hoses had
broken.

"Close the preventers," Reddington ordered as the sound of
the bending drill pipe exploded against their ears.

The driller manipulated the blowout preventer controls. No
closure lights. Frantic, Reddington pushed the driller aside
and repeated the procedure. Again nothing.

The drill pipe clanked more fiercely; the Kelly bushing flew out of the rotary table.

Reddington ran to the other control-hose spool. Its hose was limp, too, broken below the surface. There was no way to close the blowout preventer.

Captain Olafsen ripped off a segment of the sonar tracing and studied the hideous trace of what had been one long, straight integral marine riser, now bowed terribly.

"The thing has bent the riser," he cried, suddenly panicking.

The sonar engineer took the tracing. "What can we do?"

Olafsen fell against the console, the tug shifting heavily against the swells. "I don't know."

"We've got to do something!" the sonar engineer screamed, looking through the cabin windows in the direction of the *Columbus*'s night lights.

Olafsen raced past the partition into the cabin proper.

The first officer turned, having heard Olafsen's frightened voice.

"Faster!" Olafsen said softly, fearing the worst.

Bob Reddington spat out a series of orders, then ran toward the bridge deck, trying to reach the radio room. A tremendous vibration overran the ship, knocking him back on his rear. He looked up, terrified. A ball of gas-fed flame erupted through the ship's center, shooting the drill pipe out, destroying the derrick, and taking the drill floor and all the men along.

Sparks and flaming debris fell around him as he stood, only to be knocked back again, jolted off his feet by an enormous explosion that shattered equipment and smashed bodies into pools of flesh and blood.

Reddington stumbled ahead, bleeding heavily.

The deck was strewn with metal. The center of the ship was afire. Several crewmen, too. The off shift had appeared on deck, as had members of the ship's crew, tending to the injured, brandishing fire extinguishers.

A death wail rang through the air. Far off port, the lights of the sonar tug seemed to be moving toward them.

Frantic, singed by flames, Reddington picked his way through the desolation, shuddering. They were drilling through a gas zone. God help them if the gas evacuated the riser beneath the ship!

The helicopter pitched furiously about in the wind as Scotty hugged the shoreline, nearing Urquhart Bay. Several times, he'd nearly lost control. Certainly he was mad, having attempted the flight. But he'd had a premonition for days, and it had never been stronger than it was at this moment, the vision of a bright burning light on the water curdling his blood.

Tortured by the cries of the mangled, Reddington mounted the bow and stared at the water. He saw it immediately. Bubbles. Gas. The pressure zone was blowing out below them, aerating the water, surrounding the ship with less bouyant fluids, gas that would not support the vessel's weight.

He'd heard about it. Now he was a participant. He would take the experience to his grave.

Screams turned him around. Several uninjured men, having noticed the bubbles, had climbed on to the helipad where the pilot had primed the helicopter. The men were swarming all over the chopper's runners. The chopper lifted off, over-weighted, bludgeoned by the wind. It careened down into the pad and exploded, killing everyone.

Flames and burning debris seared Reddington's flesh. He stumbled forward. The wait wasn't long. He felt it within seconds, the loss of support and control. Slowly, the vessel began to wobble sideways, then, began to sink.

The *Columbus* was going down.

Scotty felt terror rise up his spine as he watched the fire reach into the air, spiraling like fireworks against the black sky.

He pushed the throttle forward.

The *Columbus* had blown out!

The tug's crew members were confused. The *Columbus*, which was burning only several hundred feet away, seemed to be listing, bow into the water. That was understandable; it had been attacked. But they'd been unmolested. Yet they had lost control, too, and the tug was turning like a top, listing terribly in the direction of the drill ship.

"Reverse full!" Olafsen cried.

The first officer juggled controls, but the tug didn't respond.

Suddenly, a crewman ran into the cabin. "There's a gas blowout," he screamed, terrified. "The water's aerating. And we're in it!"

No one said a word.

Fire. Blood. Twisted steel. Mangled bodies. All before his eyes. All horrible. Almost as horrible as the hideous panic gripping the men who remained alive, diving hopelessly into the water, screaming.

Gripping a post, Reddington held on as water started to overflow the deck. Rain whipped his face. Blood clouded his vision. He thought of his children. Then he looked off starboard. The sonar tug was bearing in on them, carried by the collapsing suction of the water. It rose over the drill ship, then crashed in like a spear, its bow ripping through the rear of the drill ship, severing it, igniting additional explosions, decimating the stern. He listened. The ship screamed a death knell, then jerked downward. Walls of water surrounded it and the remains of the tug. He felt a kiss of death hit his face.

Then he felt nothing.

Scotty was sick. There was nothing he could do but watch. The *Columbus* was almost gone.

Only her bow was visible within the collapsing well of water.

And then, suddenly, the ship vanished, though the marine riser remained still visible, spewing gas and fire.

Disoriented, confused, he searched for survivors and then, realizing it was hopeless, turned the helicopter into the teeth of the gale and directed it toward the base.

Part II

INTERREGNUM

Chapter 13

Jerry Foster exploded from the ballroom of the Claidheamh Mor Hotel pursued by a frantic group of reporters. Behind him, he left scores of international correspondents who had been pouring into Inverness for the last two days along with busloads of tourists, the flow starting the moment word had gone out that the *Columbus* and a support tug had gone down.

Because the Geminii complex was off limits, the press center had been set up in the city. This had been Foster's sixth scheduled press conference. The company line was simple. The *Columbus* and tug had gone down in the death claws of a gas blowout. That was it. As of yet, divers had not been dispatched, and the causes of the disaster were unknown. Sonar had located the wreck, the largest piece of which had settled over the wellhead, but more specific information had not been accumulated, and everyone had been advised they would just have to wait.

"That's all for today," Foster was screaming as he pawed his way through the lobby, joined by two press aides and Tony Spinelli, who had emerged just moments before from a technical press orientation. "The next Q and A will be at five tomorrow."

The reporters responded angrily.

"Gentlemen, please," Foster pleaded, nervously poking the air with his pipe. "You'll just have to have patience."

"This way," Spinelli advised, tugging at Foster's jacket.

Foster instructed the press aides to remain at the hotel. The aides blocked the doorway. Foster and Spinelli squeezed out, barely avoiding a screeching lorry.

"They're nuts," Foster said as he and Spinelli closed themselves into a limousine.

"The Geminii complex," Spinelli ordered, shaking his head.

Foster glanced out the window as the limo began to move; the streets were clogged with traffic. "Look at this place," he said, so disconcerted he nearly placed the wrong end of the pipe in his mouth.

"Goddamn incredible," Spinelli observed.

"I sent the wife and kids to London," Foster added. "They're going to be better off away from here."

The limousine crawled through the town center, then turned on to the Dores Road. Foster continued to stare out the window, arranging his priorities. Suddenly, the discovery of oil at Beauly seemed to have lost its significance.

He grimaced. Thoughts of the *Columbus* provoked questions. But there was no reason to ask them.

The only men who had the answers were dead.

"Those poor goddamn men," he kept whispering to himself instead. "Those poor goddamn men."

The Volvo stopped in front of the mansion. Bill Nunn and Michael Grabowski eased out, walked through the front gate and knocked on the mansion door.

Mrs. Munro appeared. "Can I help you?"

Bill Nunn smiled. "Is Mr. Bruce in?"

"Yes, but he's asked to remain alone. No visitors."

"Tell him it's Nunn and Grabowski," Grabowski said.

Mrs. Munro retreated, then returned moments later and invited the men inside, leading them into the den where Scotty was perched at the desk scribbling a letter.

"We thought we'd drop by," Nunn said.

Scotty berthed his pencil. "I'm glad you did."

Nunn eased on to the lounge. Grabowski took the couch. Scotty smiled and quickly reread the beginning of the letter, shaking his head.

"A status report?" Grabowski asked.

"No. A letter to Red's kids." He paused. "I called the mother, and she responded like a human being for the first time in her life. But there has to be a note from Uncle Scott and it has to be straight. No bullshit. Hell, when I heard bullshit as a kid, I shot off a finger and a fuck you, closed my eyes, and lit off." He laughed. "Reddington. What an asshole. I always knew he'd go down like a flaming Viking. Get some free press. Make his old lady feel guilty. Th miserable son of a . . ." He put the letter back on the desk. "Thing reads like shit."

Grabowski stood and walked around the room. The place was spotless. Mrs. Munro had stormed through with a vengeance the night before.

"What's next?" Grabowski asked.

"We go back to work," Scotty replied. He placed an unlit cigar in his mouth. "I'll know more this afternoon. I have a meeting with Fallworth and Whittenfeld. I'm sure one of them has some ideas."

"You don't?" Nunn asked.

Scotty looked momentarily bewildered. "Apart from salvage, not a one." He paused, thinking. "You see the last transmission?"

"No."

"Gas blowout. Crew dead. Ship going down. The radio man sent three others as well, though the last was cut off midstream. The second two were identical to the first. No hint of what caused the blowout, though he did say they had completed the kill procedure."

"Could they have screwed it up? Miscalculated?"

Scotty shook his head after examining the possibilities. "I doubt it."

"What about equipment failure?"

"We inspected the ship's systems a hundred times, and we never found a speck of trouble. The riser was checked by the diving crew after the first mishap and the guidelines were replaced. No. Equipment failure just doesn't jibe."

Grabowski was puzzled. "Then what? The crew?"

"Maybe. But they were crack. You worked with them, and I read every key man's profile. They'd all been through a shitload of kill situations."

"One mistake," Grabowski said. "It was late. It was raining. The crew must have been tired. All it took was one mistake."

"Or no mistakes," Nunn said, interrupting. "And no failure."

Scotty looked up. "You've got some ideas?"

"Don't you think it's peculiar that the tug went down with the ship?"

"What do you mean?"

"The tug wasn't supposed to be anywhere near the *Columbus*."

"Granted."

"Well. Then what the hell was it doing out of position?"

"I don't know, and I don't think you do, either."

"You're right. But let's go back to square one—the first attack."

"I've been doing that since I saw the *Columbus* go under. I've been banging every alternative around. I've got to see the remains."

"Something attacked the ship." Nunn pointed to his stomach. "And the tug was involved. I know it. I feel it here. In my gut!!!"

Scotty buried himself in silent speculation. Nunn and Grabowski remained quiet, too. The phone rang. Scotty answered it, then informed Nunn and Grabowski that Whittenfeld's secretary had summoned him to the first of what promised to be a strenuous succession of meetings. He would have to leave. However, he invited them back for dinner. Mrs. Munro would cook. They agreed and left, with Scotty following moments later.

Scotty entered William Whittenfeld's office alone. Four men were already inside. Whittenfeld, John Fallworth, and two other officious-looking gentlemen in tweed coats, Detective Chief Inspector James MacKintosh, and a massive, athletically built man, Detective Superintendent Angus MacGregor.

Fallworth shook Scotty's hand. "I did not think we'd meet again under circumstances such as this," he said. "When you left London, Scotty, I felt very positive about the future. I felt disturbances aboard the drill ship were history, and I certainly felt extraordinarily sanguine about local management. You made a strong impression in London once again. Yes, an even stronger impression than you made on your first trip through, and the consensus was that you and Whittenfeld would make the best of teams with the best of ships. Unfortunately, one element in the equation has been removed." Fallworth seemed genuinely upset; the *Columbus* had not just been a piece of equipment and its men mere payroll numbers. "Yes," he said. "This is a nasty reason to meet again."

"The worst," Scotty observed.

"Please take a seat," Fallworth suggested.

Scotty sat; Whittenfeld tossed him two separate worksheets.

"The first is a crew list," Whittenfeld said. "The second

s a compendium of salvage firms and equipment-leasing
companies. Hold on to it." He pointed down the table. "Mr.
MacGregor is chief of detectives, Criminal Investigation
Bureau, Northern Constabulary. Mr. MacKintosh is his
deputy. They've been informed of our prior experiences, the
possibility of sabotage, and as you can see, they've been
given copies of the *Columbus* report. The police are now
officially involved, both the CID and the Special Branch,
which work with Scotland Yard and are responsible for the
surveillance of subversive organizations. We have also been
contacted by the Ministry of Defence, various units in the
armed services, and by MI5, but for the time being Mr. Mac-
Gregor will look after Ministry of Defence and British Secret
Service interests and will coordinate his investigation with the
Special Branch."

"I see," Scotty said ambivalently, trying to sort out the
proliferation of interests.

"You look pained, Mr. Bruce," MacGregor said, bellowing
a thunderous brogue. He had impressive features, which
evoked a myriad of impressions. "Do you object?"

"To what?"

"To my representational capacity."

"Of course not. I wouldn't have the right. I'm just surprised there are so many people involved."

"It's not by whim," MacGregor suggested. "Defence, MI5,
Scotland Yard, and the Northern Constabulary coordinate
many operations and share many responsibilities, including
home and internal defence, natural-disaster contingency
planning, the infiltration of the regional narcotics trade—"

"Narcotics? In Inverness?"

"Does that surprise you?"

"Inverness just doesn't seem like the type of place. And
the people certainly don't look like drug users."

"For the most part, they're not. Because there's little or no
retailing. Inverness is a distribution depot for cocaine and
heroin. Ships sailing from Latin America and the Near East
use the North Sea as a dump-off. There's quite a bit of
play on the Inverness waterfront. As well as aboard various
North Sea oil installations."

Scotty was surprised.

MacGregor continued. "Narcotics are transferred from
ships to the installations and then transported to shore by
helicopter. There are several oil service companies whose

income derives predominantly from the drug trade. Oil
service is small potatoes to them."

Scotty digested the information. "There's no narcotics problem here. No natural disaster occurred. No defense matters
are involved. So why MI5 and the Ministry of Defence?"

Fallworth interceded. "Although the protection of installations is the responsibility of the company, there has been
a long-standing official and unofficial working relationship
with Defence and MI5 operatives in the offshore sector, and
even though the *Columbus* was technicallly onshore, their
services were utilized by us in the initial stages of *Columbus*
sector planning."

"There's also a potential nationalist terrorist element in
Scotland," MacGregor said, completing the picture, "whose
actions would fall under diverse jurisdictional scrutiny. The
Northern Constabulary, the Special Branch, and Scotland
Yard would most certainly be involved, as well as MI5, if
British national interests were affected." MacGregor tapped
his hand against the table for emphasis. "Scotland does have
its fringe groups. Though their barks are often bigger than
their bites, we've uncovered links to the Provisional IRA, and
that raises an inference of real trouble—if not now, then later.
There have also been some isolated instances of violence
already. The Tartan Army bombed our oil pipelines several
years ago. So did the Army of the Provisional Government.
And a violent fringe group called the New Jacobite Coalition
has been implicated in a handful of political murders. In
fact, even the Scottish Nationalist Party, although officially
opposed to violence, has its activities monitored by the
Special Branch because it stands almost by definition for the
breakup of the British state and therefore its activities are
technically considered to be subversive. No, Mr. Bruce, each
governmental group has a right to have its interests represented because until we know more, I'd be hesitant to ex
clude any possibilities."

Whittenfeld's secretary entered carrying a tray of cups
a pot of coffee. She doled out servings, then retreated.

Whittenfeld stood. His face was a mirror of emotion; hi
cheeks were burnished. He was in control of his temper fo
the first time since the disaster, having finally accommodate
the shocks. "Scotty," he said, "you are to coordinate th
salvage operation."

Scotty just nodded.

Fallworth glanced through Scotty's dossier. "I was surprised you had asked for the assignment."

Scotty stiffened. "The *Columbus* was my responsibility. I will bring her up!"

"I had no idea," Fallworth continued, digesting Scotty's remark, "that you had amassed so much salvage experience."

"The opportunities were there."

"And so much diving expertise."

"Yes, sir."

"In addition, Scotty," Whittenfeld declared, "you will coordinate our investigation with the Department of Energy."

"When will you begin the salvage work?" MacGregor asked as he sipped his coffee.

"Right away," Fallworth said. "Under international law, we have no choice. We have to bring the derelict off the loch floor as quickly as is practicable."

Whittenfeld turned to the detective. "Do you have any questions for Bruce?"

MacGregor tipped back his chair, placing his enormous hands on the table edge. "Not now. Though I think Mr. Bruce and I should meet as soon as salvage planning actually begins and as often as possible thereafter. Of course, I expect to be informed of all developments. All findings."

"Absolutely," Scotty said.

"One more thing, Mr. Bruce," MacGregor advised. "There's quite a bit of tension about because of this thing. Tread lightly. The Scots have received a shock and they do not react warmly to shocks applied by foreigners. I'm sure you can appreciate that."

"There'll be no problems," Scotty said.

The police officers smiled. Whittenfeld noted MacKintosh's relation to the Loch Ness enterprise—he had investigated the death of Rolf Kreibel as a junior officer—then escorted MacGregor and MacKintosh through the door, returning moments later, taking a seat.

"New York management will be here in the morning," Fallworth said. "I'll try to absorb the brunt. If I need either of you, I'll call."

"I'll be home until noon," Whittenfeld said. "Scotty?"

"I'll be in my office."

Fallworth stood. "The *Columbus* incident monopolized debate in Parliament all day Wednesday. Apart from an outburst by an SNP minister, the debate followed party lines.

Energy was put on the spot. So was the Scottish Office. The government agreed to an interbranch inquiry before a select tribunal. There will be representatives from the Scottish Office, Energy, Home, Trade, and the Highland region. It is essential we protect our position within the confines of the law. I want a thorough investigation. If the *Columbus* was sabotaged, let's know it. If mistakes were made by us, then so be it." He paused, waiting for comment; there was none. "Anything else?"

Whittenfeld and Scotty shook their heads. And that being the case, the meeting was adjourned.

Whittenfeld looked through the office window at the loch. The vile bitch!

He could feel anger still surging through his body. Yet he could also feel strength and resolve. He'd had a temporary setback, but he'd never allow Geminii to be stopped.

No, they would bring the *Columbus* up. They would start operations again, and he would make sure the infamy would never reoccur.

Lefebre entered the office carrying a folder. A Gitanes was dangling from his lips. He handed Whittenfeld the folder. Whittenfeld examined the two lists inside.

"Is that all?" he asked.

"Yes," Lefebre replied. "You've seen the names we pinpointed after the first attack on the ship and the names we added as we looked closer." He pointed to the bottom of the second list. "These are new."

"Did you meet MacGregor?" Whittenfeld asked, studying the names.

"Yes."

"What did you think?"

"I think he's incompetent and dirty."

"You think most human beings are incompetent and dirty."

"They are. This MacGregor is also stupid. He tried to intimidate me by stomping around the room like King Lear. I find him to be pathetic. One doesn't achieve authority with words, nor does one achieve it by attempting to intimidate the nonintimidatible, by underestimating the intelligence of higher intellect. One conquers authority, claims it for his own." He laughed derisively. "MacGregor is a fool."

Whittenfeld ignored the lecture. "I don't think the police

will get anywhere. We'll take it upon ourselves again. Open up everyone on these lists. Tail the most suspicious. Tap phones if you can. Rifle private files. You have some good moles on staff. They're overpaid, too. Put them to work. But concentrate on this Jacobite group."

"All right."

"Anything else?"

"Yes. As you suggested, we did a run on Sutherland, and we've come up with something interesting."

Whittenfeld's attention perked. "What?"

"It seems Mr. Sutherland has turned up as the Transport Union representative in the precise locations of and just prior to the last four Jacobite terrorist attacks. We checked with the union national, and we learned in each instance Sutherland requested the assignment because of a real or imagined problem with local union representation. And, in each instance, he did not remain in the area long after the mutinous events."

"Interesting," Whittenfeld remarked.

"We also checked with the SNP. Sutherland was an active member in Strathclyde. However, he espoused a more violent line than the SNP membership was willing to accept. They wanted him to tone down the rhetoric. He balked and disappeared, only to reappear in Northern Ireland, organizing secret militant Catholic cells for the IRA. Then he unexplainably returned here three years ago to work with the Transport Union."

"How'd you get the information?"

"Stools. Payoffs."

"Nothing firm? No usable proof?"

"Not yet."

"Get it for me. But quietly. I do not want a repetition of the Bruce incident!"

Lefebre began to laugh.

Scotty left his office late, descending to the first floor. He doubted anyone remained in the building apart from the night staff. He was wrong. Pierre Lefebre emerged from the security office just as he appeared.

He had nearly forgotten the horror of London but Lefebre's presence made it re-emerge. A taste of bile surged up his throat.

"Men live," Lefebre said cryptically with a mysterious

smile, "men die. The cycle continues. When men die, they are forgotten. All men. Including you, Mr. Bruce."

Scotty stopped and stared. Brilliant, he thought derisively. A philosophical statement and an intimidation all in one breath. What a diseased mind! Christ, he still wanted to bash the bastard's brains all over the place, although he'd promised himself he wouldn't. Hell, he'd gone back on that promise before. After paralyzing the ballplayer, he'd sworn he'd never hit anyone again—intentionally or unintentionally—but, over the years, he had belted a couple deserving bastards. He wasn't a total angel. On the other hand, he was going to try to stick to his pledge of docility right now. The fight with Lefebre had happened some time ago; things had been quiet between them since. More importantly, Reddington and the crew of the *Columbus* had just been lost. He was not in the frame of mind for a personal confrontation, nor did he think it proper. Then again, he had to admit the truth. The information he'd received from Houghton had been intimidating. Christ, he wasn't a coward, but he was now aware he was dealing with a mass murderer who had killed hundreds without remorse. No matter how brave he thought himself to be, he wasn't a gunman nor did he think he could ever kill anyone. Lefebre could and had! Only a complete imbecile would fail to tread softly.

"The *Columbus* tragedy is more important than our feelings. We have to put the project first." He had difficulty getting the words out.

"Monsieur Bruce. In American baseball, they give the batter three strikes. In my world, I give only one. You have had your strike! I would prefer to have broken your neck, and I would still prefer to do so, but for the time being, I am constrained. I am forced to tolerate your existence. Believe me, monsieur, it is a painful task—made possible only by my ability to deny your existence. I have no reason to talk to you. Nor do I desire to. You are nothing to me. Do I make myself clear?"

"Yes. Very clear."

"Good."

"But let me make something clear to you. I don't like to be threatened or attacked!" So much for treading softly.

Lefebre stared condescendingly. "Nobody touches me," he finally said. "Ever!"

Chapter 14

Stateside management arrived, remained in Inverness several days, then returned to London with John Fallworth for meetings with the secretary of state for energy. A number of salvage experts flew into Inverness. Under Geminii supervision, they analyzed several recovery methods and adopted one after a team from the Department of Energy's Petroleum Engineering Division had joined the deliberations. In addition, they prepared a requisition analysis and drafted a salvage proposal for presentation to the Highland Regional Council and Scottish Office.

Two days after the disaster, Scotty had called the Carn Dearg Inn. Unable to locate Mary MacKenzie, he had phoned several more times in the interim, speaking to MacKenzie's niece. Twice he was told she was out of town, the third time that she had no desire to speak to him. Angered, he'd decided to wait for the Highland Council-Scottish Office meeting to confront her.

The meeting took place at the council offices in Inverness behind closed doors. Mary MacKenzie was there, though she did not look directly at him even once. However, the session over, he was able to corner her alone in the council lounge.

"Why the hell have you been ignoring me?" he asked.

"Now look, Mr. Bruce—"

"I thought the name was Scotty."

"Only during the truce."

"We're not at truce anymore?"

She breathed deeply, annoyed at his naïveté. "Are we on the same planet, Mr. Bruce? Do we hear, see, and comprehend the same things? Did I not just listen to you present yourself as a senior Geminii executive, the man responsible for Geminii salvage operations? I fought Geminii. I predicted

137

disaster. I was forced to adopt a truce. Forced by politics. Practical considerations. The facts of life. But a disaster has happened. The well has blown out. The loch has been polluted with gas, drilling mud, chemicals. There is the specter of more trouble ahead." She smirked. "So all bets are off, Mr. Bruce. The truce is ended. War declared once more."

"Does the state of war go to me personally, also?"

"As I said, you are senior Geminii management."

He faced her squarely. "I think you think I'm putting on an act. That I'm not upset. That all I care about is Geminii. Proving Geminii blameless. Getting Geminii back into operation. Getting a new ship at the wellhead."

"Perhaps I do."

"My best friend was on the *Columbus!*"

"I'm aware of that!"

"There were also a lot of other men. Friends. Acquaintances. All dead. How goddamn callous do you think I am?"

"I'm afraid you have to answer that question. I can't. But I never knew what callous meant until the word *oil* became more personal to me than a definition scrawled in a dictionary. Yes, I understand how crucial the search for oil has become in this insane world. And yes, I realize the despair the absence of oil creates. I am aware of all the arguments. I am a compendium of rehearsed monologues and convoluted legal presentations."

"Then you should understand the difference between the corporation and the individual."

She ran her tongue against her lips. "I've developed a terrible fear for the individual, Mr. Bruce. A premonition he has been swallowed by something far more powerful."

"The beast?"

She grinned diabolically. "Perhaps. But perhaps you should admit there are times when corporate policy or your own corporate survival prevents you from saying the things you would like to say. Prevents you from defending the truth until you've become so programmed, you cannot even identify it."

He bristled. "You've got the wrong guy, lady. And the wrong malady. Hell, I made a career out of fighting corporations. I made a career out of defending the 'so-called' truth. I didn't just turn on the football owners. No way. It accelerated from there. I liked the feel of martyrdom. And I have a whole list of conquests. I rebelled against the oil industry when I felt it was about to endanger restricted areas in the Santa Barbara Channel off the California coast. I sniffed out executives—senior execs—who were taking kickbacks. And to this day I defend those actions. They were worthwhile. With worthwhile rewards. And yes, the accolades poured in from the public. I ate up the tribute. And suddenly, Christ, I found causes everywhere. Good ones. Bad ones. I became a clearing house for crusades. I got to the point where every word spoken and every move made had a sinister motive behind it. There were conspirators and conspiracies everywhere. I smelled rats in all the woodwork. I became a walking bloodhound, even if it meant identifying evils that didn't exist. I was just like a sixties, anti-Vietnam war-flower child, protesting everything that was protestable. And lady, you remind me of me!"

"But you're no longer you. You've changed! Abandoned your crusades."

"Right."

"You let the corporations win."

"Wrong. I chose to regain my soul. I chose not to remain a cause-spouting zombie. I re-established contact with reality."

"Reality?" she asked angrily. "Try this reality on for size. A drill ship and a tug lie at the bottom of the loch. Soon, armadas of surface support vessels, loaded with chemicals and dangerous equipment, are going to swarm over the graveyard, desecrating the dead. And I'm not saying that should not be so. The wreckage must come up. The water must be cleansed. The precise cause of the disaster must be discovered. But look what has happened. A beautiful loch, a national treasure, has been turned into a grotesque junkyard and battleground, and an important part of our heritage has been stomped on like so many blades of grass."

"Don't you realize I understand? Why is this so hard for you to accept?"

"Because I've heard the rhetoric too many times."

"Well, then. Perhaps you're the one who can't recognize the truth. Perhaps you've so buried yourself in utopian dogma, you've lost the ability to see the forest from the trees. . . . I did!"

She tried to walk away; he grabbed her by the arm.

"Running?" he asked. "Hiding?"

"No!" she replied. "Trying to leave this room so I can go about my work."

"You want Geminii out. I want Geminii in." He paused. "I know there's a middle ground."

"You were convinced Geminii was occupying a middle ground before."

"I might have been wrong. There's a possibility our investigation will prove so, and I'll be the first to admit it. But you should also be aware the investigation may uncover some very incriminating facts. Facts which may point a finger at the Scots. Facts suggesting sabotage and murder."

"Nonsense."

He tried to organize his thoughts. "Look, you. Why the hell can't you be a woman for just one goddamn minute?"

She was indignant. "I am a woman, and because I'm a woman, I have to work that much harder to defend what is right."

"Yes. I know all about it. I know all about the feminine burden. But no burden should allow a woman to turn herself into a Sherman tank. Christ, let some human warmth get out! Then maybe you'll be able to tell when a man is trying to be a man, not a machine, a corporate number. I'm crying inside because of what's happened! If you'd just look for one minute, you'd see it."

She stood tall, staring back at him, lowering her voice. "This is a hard country, Mr. Bruce. We've all grown up with a little bit of stone in us. Poverty, war, the climate, the rape of the nation, the usurpation of our identity—all of it has served to petrify a portion of our innards. There is very little left."

"Christ. I know all this! I'm not asking you to abandon your crusade. I'm the last person who could do that. I'm just asking you to become a little more human, understanding, open."

"I do not have the right."

"Says who?"

"Says the dead men in the loch. Says all that was once Scotland but is no more. We have sworn away the privileges of the unburdened."

She started to walk again; he followed.

"So you're going to get in your car once more and speed away," he said, moving close, trying to stick his face in front of hers.

"You're in my way."

"There's more to be said!"

"No, there isn't. There are no words to be passed between you and me. Out of personal choice and out of duty. I have been nominated to sit on the investigation commission panel. As such, I can have nothing to do with anyone at Geminii until the commission has issued its findings."

"Bullshit."

She turned, her anger building even further, and then burst through the council building door out into the parking lot.

He watched her disappear. "Damn woman," he said.

The sight made him sick. Urquhart Bay, Drumnadrochit, the entire north shore of Loch Ness, overrun with tourists.

Why the hell couldn't they appreciate the horror—the *Columbus* down, his best friend dead, the crew buried beneath hundreds of feet of water! Why the hell couldn't they all have stayed away!

Resigned, he drove along the north shore, past Urquhart Bay and the still visible top of the marine riser, and arrived in Fort Augustus at the west end of the loch about a half hour later. Pausing to watch a boat enter a chamber on the St. Augustus track of the Caledonian Canal, he meandered from one lock to another, then returned to the jeep, drove by the St. Augustus Abbey, and rumbled out of Fort Augustus along the south highway. Passing an endless extent of sheep meadow, he headed toward Foyers on a narrow road, barely capable of handling one car, then returned to Inverness, arriving at his home exhausted, his frustrations purged.

Detective Superintendent MacGregor was waiting, seated on the mansion's front porch.

"I thought you'd never return," MacGregor said.

"If I'd known I had a reception committee," Scotty said, "I would have hurried back sooner."

"No matter," MacGregor advised, displaying a very melodic brogue. "I enjoyed the rest. You know, resting and waiting are part of the job. If you can't get used to both, you might as well leave the constabulary." He smiled, pointing northward. "Besides, I've had a good view of the Black Isle, and it's one right soothing view for the eyes after a long day."

Scotty looked down from the hill, past the city and the Beauly Firth—a heavy fog lay over the water—and toward a green expanse of farmland rising in the distance.

"I assume," MacGregor said, "you've been there."

"Yes. We have an exploratory well at Munlochy."

"Of course. I've passed it many times on my way to Cromarty."

"Cromarty?" Scotty asked, puzzled why the superintendent would be spending much time in the little village.

"I have a good amount of family there," MacGregor said as he pulled some nuts from his jacket pocket and popped them into his mouth. "Some of whom work over at Nigg."

"Are you from Cromarty, too?"

MacGregor shook his head. "Kessock," he announced, pointing toward the near shore of the Black Isle. "There's Kessock, right across from Clachnaharry. It used to be the Black Isle docking point for the ferry from Inverness." His expression turned slightly wistful. "Before they built the big bridge, there was a ferry route, and it was right well needed because to get to the isle without the boat necessitated a thirty-mile drive around the Beauly Firth through Beauly. Ay, and the ferry was one fun thing, especially for us kids. I used to ride it all the time when I wasn't out stealing fruit and vegetables from the big-corporation farms."

Scotty laughed. "You? Stealing?"

Superintendent MacGregor laughed, too. "I'm not such a saint that I've never erred. Rob Roy, who was the most famous Highland outlaw of all time, was a MacGregor. When my cousins and I were children, we all wanted to be just like him. I even had my father take me down to Balquhidder near Loch Tay when I was twelve years old so I could see Rob Roy's grave dug right in the soil of Clan MacGregor country." He tossed some more nuts into his mouth, then stood. "Ay, up until my midteens, I wanted to be an outlaw like Rob Roy."

"But you became a detective instead," Scotty said facetiously.

"What better man to deal with crime than a criminal at heart."

Scotty invited the superintendent inside. MacGregor demurred, preferring to stay on the porch. The day was pleasant; he did not want to waste it, especially since the weather service had predicted that the offshore fog would move in rapidly once the wind had changed.

"So?" Scotty asked. "What can I do for you?"

MacGregor adjusted his tweed jacket. "You can answer a few questions," he said.

"Fire."

"Besides the current tragedy and the previous attack on the *Columbus,* I've learned another suspicious accident occurred aboard the drill ship. A drowning. I'm told you're familiar with the particulars."

Scotty sat on the porch railing. "I was there."

"Tell me about it."

Scotty recapped the events.

"Why wasn't the drowning reported to the police?" Mac-Gregor asked.

"There was nothing to report," Scotty replied. "It was an accident."

"A matter for the procurator fiscal to determine."

"We thought we could handle the whole thing internally. Cause less of a stir."

"In retrospect, do you think that was wise?"

"I can't answer that."

"I see."

"Why the sudden interest?"

MacGregor smiled; he had sparkling white teeth, an aggressive face. "I'm trying to fill in background."

"A paycheck well earned?"

MacGregor waffled about in place, thinking. "Did anyone try to ascertain what caused the jolt which threw the crewman off the helipad?"

"Of course. We checked the ship. There was no damage and no clues left behind. I wish there had been." He decided not to mention the sonar tracings; why create the inference he was a bit off his rocker? "I doubt the drowning incident had any relation to the blowout."

MacGregor waxed ambivalent. "Maybe. Maybe not." He took another nut from his pocket, tossed it into the air, and caught it dramatically in his mouth. "Well done," he said, complimenting himself.

"Is there anything else?" Scotty asked impatiently.

"Yes," MacGregor replied. "I'd like to backtrack to the 'so-called' attack on the ship several weeks ago."

"All right."

"You were there?"

"You know I was because I'm sure you've read the *Columbus* report."

MacGregor smirked, caught. "It was very interesting. So were your conclusions."

"They were educated guesses."

"Do you think they were accurate?"

"What I think is irrelevant. What I know for a fact carries weight."

"And?"

"I honestly can't answer your question."

"Do you think your educated guesses might be applicable to the current tragedy?"

"I don't know. I may never know."

MacGregor paused, thinking. "When all is said and done, the police may have no involvement here. These strange and tragic events may be explained away naturally. No crimes may have been committed, nor may there have been any criminal malfeasance. I may very well be wasting my time, sniffing for the unsniffable."

"Could be," Scotty said with a smile.

MacGregor walked to the porch staircase. "Yes, could be," he said. "But I doubt it. Something tells me the police will be heavily involved." He smiled. "Thank you for the information, Mr. Bruce. You've saved me considerable time and effort."

"My pleasure," Scotty declared.

The detective departed.

Scotty drove into town alone that night through the heavy fog that had raced in over the Great Glen like an express train just before sundown. He also ate dinner alone, had a lager or two, then returned to Travis House shortly after nine.

"He just insisted he had to talk to you and wouldn't leave," Mrs. Munro was saying as she indignantly followed Scotty through the foyer. "I told him I don't approve of such things. Uninvited visits are not proper, and I know proper from improper 'cause I got a good mind for manners. But he wouldn't take 'no' for an answer. I tell you, Mr. Bruce, he's a bit of a hard head 'cause he stood up to me and pushed into the house even though I had a fire stoker in my hand."

"There's no need for any violence, Mrs. Munro," Scotty said, moving to the den. "You know Mr. Foster!"

"Don't matter a bit if I know him or not. Right is right."

"Thank you, Mrs. Munro!"

Mrs. Munro retreated with a huff. Scotty entered the den. Foster was seated in the armchair; his expression was serious.

"What's up?" Scotty asked as Foster stood.

"More bad news," Foster said. "I thought I would bring it to you personally." He shook his head. "I know you didn't know the man, but I do know you've been interested in his progress."

"What are you talking about?"

"Jim Barrett died last night."

Scotty sat behind the desk puffing heavily on a Havana cigar. It was late. The room was deadly quiet. The window glass was covered with a gray mist; the fog still hung heavy. He heard Mrs. Munro lumber across her room, then began sifting through a stack of photos—underwater pictures taken by the diving crews of the remains of the *Columbus* and the sonar tug. The prints were precise and grotesque, making his skin crawl. He put the stack to the side and began to examine three large charts. One was a schematic-composite diagram of the derelicts, drawn from the referenced pictures. There were several large red marks near the drill floor and deck lines representing the crucial material the divers had not been able to locate—the blowout preventer control hoses and the guide wires. Preliminary inspection suggested the missing parts had been burned off their surface connections by the blaze. Damn, he was convinced the parts would be needed if they were ever going to know the true cause of the disaster. Hopefully, though, the parts had been pinned beneath the drill ship rather than having spun free into oblivion. He examined the other two diagrams. The first was a plan chart of the salvage operation that set the position of the salvage vessels and diving barges. The second was an operational plan depicting the stages of the underwater recovery. They were not futures; they were immediate. All the salvage vessels were on their way and would soon arrive. Recovery would start in a week. Though the operation was not going to be easy, he was anxious as hell to get on with it.

He dropped the charts, walked away from the desk, and poured himself a glass of wine from an open bottle sitting on the coffee table. He sat looking out the window. The news of Barrett's death continued to disturb him. He hadn't known the man, but there was an affinity. They both had been trained in the same discipline. They both had held the same job, and according to Bob Reddington, they both had disliked Pierre Lefebre.

He finished the glass, poured himself another, then stood, turned off the desk lamp, walked to the window, and looked out. The fog was eerie. So, too, had been the news of Barrett's death.

He did not know why.

Chapter 15

The Sunday-morning sun caromed sharply off the bright-blue water of the Moray Firth, splashing against the jeep's windshield as Scotty maneuvered the vehicle down a narrow macadam road.

Ahead he could see a solitary farmhouse perched on a bluff. Arriving at the farmhouse, he jumped from the jeep, walked to the front door, and rang the bell. As expected, a mounted television camera responded first; then Houghton's secretary appeared, frisked him, and invited him inside.

The farmhouse was rustic, simply furnished, its den equipped with another impressive telephone bank. Apart from Houghton's secretary and an energetic West Highland terrier, however, the place seemed deserted.

"Mr. Houghton is waiting for you on the rear patio," the secretary said, leading Scotty through the living room.

"Have you been in Scotland long?" Scotty asked as he followed.

"No," the secretary replied. "We arrived just two days ago."

They emerged on to a tiled patio; the rim of the sea was just beyond. Houghton was seated, fiddling with a crossword puzzle in *The London Times*. Seeing Scotty, Houghton dropped the newspaper on the patio table and stood.

"Mr. Bruce, my friend," he said, bubbling with energy. "It's so good to have you here."

"It's good to be here," Scotty countered, "though I've got to admit, your call took me by surprise."

"I suspected it would," Houghton said, indicating one of the chairs, which Scotty dutifully occupied. "But since I was to be in the area and since I had uncovered information I thought you might find interesting, I decided I should not let the opportunity go wanting." He sat as well. "And it always pleases me to show off the farm, especially to distinguished visitors such as yourself."

"The house is super and the view—"

"Magnificent?"

"The very word."

Houghton looked out at the huge expanse of water. "The North Sea, Moray Firth. It awes me, Mr. Bruce. It's power. Longevity. History." He gazed away wistfully. "I sometimes can sense the ghosts of Nazi U-boats gliding silently beneath the waves, and I can certainly feel the presence of the Soviets. One need not invoke spirits to be aware of the hammer and sickle. No, Mr. Bruce, these waters are brimming with Russian nuclear submarines." He laughed. "There's a spectacular game of cat and mouse invisibly underway right before us. A game with the most dire of consequences."

Scotty scanned the horizon. "You don't seem overly concerned."

Houghton smirked, then lit a cigarette. "What I seem does not reflect what I am: I *am* overly concerned. But because I understand the game, I have been able to come to grips with it."

Scotty glanced around the enclave; the borders were sealed by a barbed-wire fence. Curiously, however, there were no guards in sight.

"So," Houghton said, "how are your salvage preparations faring?"

"They've been completed. We've begun the actual work."

"I'm pleased for you."

"You're obviously familiar with the *Columbus* tragedy."

"Yes. The trials and tribulations of Geminii Petroleum have been vigorously heralded by the London press, and, of course, I have my private sources."

"Of course."

"Your method of recovery?"

"Standard stuff. We have bell diving crews on the loch. Hoisting barges. Flotation equipment. We've carefully examined the remains. Parts have proven almost airtight. Others have not. Those that haven't have been sealed, welded shut. As soon as practicable, we're going to pump small buoyant flotation bags into the hulks, attach hoists to their outer shells, jack the remains to the surface, then drydock and study them carefully."

"Do you suspect sabotage?"

"I don't suspect anything yet. Do you?"

Houghton smiled, blowing a thin mat of smoke between his lips. "How could I?"

Scotty refused to snap at the bait.

"You'll be pleased to know I've made some added progress with Mr. Lefebre," Houghton said. "I acquainted you with Lefebre's background in Algeria, the Congo, and Uganda. I had assumed he had been out of Africa from 1965 to 1971. However, a sabbatical from turmoil would have been most uncharacteristic, so I placed additional inquiries, and I must admit, I found our dossier to be incomplete." He looked for a comment. Scotty said nothing. "I am now certain Lefebre was in Africa operating right under my nose off and on during the entire period. In Biafra, to be exact."

"Nigeria?"

Houghton laughed. "At the time, Biafrans would have bristled at any suggestion they were part of the Federal Republic."

Scotty's curiosity brimmed. "You say you were there?"

"Off and on. And involved enough to have gained a good understanding of the issues."

"I'm not much of an expert on world affairs," Scotty said, "but if I remember correctly, there wasn't much confusion about the issues."

Houghton's expression changed, his eyebrows rising. "Oh? Then perhaps you can enlighten me, Mr. Bruce."

"The government and major tribes were persecuting the Ibo tribesmen, so the Ibo who lived in Eastern Nigeria seceded from the republic, calling themselves the nation of Biafra. The federal government genocidally starved the Ibo into submission. Biafra lost the war. Millions died."

Houghton laughed. "Very good, Mr. Bruce. You are living proof propaganda works. Living proof history remembered by the masses rarely reflects the truth. But there is a truth. Whether you are aware of it or not."

"Are you telling me there was no genocide? No starvation?"

"As to genocide, absolutely not. Yes, the northern Hausa tribe, which lived under federal jurisdiction, hated and slaughtered the Ibo. In fact, the prime reason for Biafran secession was the return of the northern Hausa to a share of power in the government after a complicated series of coups and countercoups had forced them into isolation. But there was still no organized federal policy of genocide. Throughout the war, several million Ibo lived under federal jurisdiction. The truth is, genocide was a myth perpetrated by the Biafran hierarchy, notably by their leader, Col. Emeka Ojukwu, to scare the Biafran masses into unyielding and ferocious resistance."

"What about the starvation?"

"There was much. Many Ibo died. But both sides must be blamed. Yes, there was a blockade. Yes, there were federal Nigerians who wanted to starve Biafra into submission. But starvation was also a policy of the Biafran leadership, their only hope for outside recognition. Although Biafra fought heroically, it never really had a chance to win the war militarily. It needed the sympathy of the world to survive. Starving civilians fostered sympathy. So civilians were allowed to starve. Compromise and negotiation were vehemently rejected by Ojukwu. The world's conscience was stoked into action."

"Where does Lefebre fit into the picture?" Scotty asked.

"Ah," Houghton said. "The infamous Mr. Lefebre." He aligned his mercurial features thoughtfully. "Mercenaries were deeply involved, though at first neither the federal nor Biafran sides were enthusiastic about recruiting them. But expediency gained the upper hand. Though federal forces refused to employ ground-combat mercenaries, they did employ mercenary pilots while quite expectedly denying it. The Biafrans, however, had less to lose, and before long, mercenaries were fighting on the ground. Pierre Lefebre was one of them. However, Lefebre, who led a special guerrilla battalion, immediately clashed with Biafran field officers. He refused to obey their orders. He was also accused of murdering one of his own soldiers and on several occasions, according to eyewitness reports, personally raped and murdered half a dozen Ibo women. In mid-1968, Ojukwu ordered Lefebre the hell out of Biafra. Lefebre immediately disappeared, reappearing two years later in Uganda."

"It's all very interesting," Scotty said, "but I've heard worse about Lefebre."

Houghton smiled. "There was another man in Biafra. A man we are certain was in the oil-refining city of Port Harcourt at precisely the same time as Lefebre. A man named William Whittenfeld."

"Whittenfeld?" Scotty exclaimed, shocked, remembering Whittenfeld had claimed the North Sea to have been his first foreign experience. "What the hell was Whittenfeld doing there?"

"There's oil in Nigeria. Mr. Whittenfeld was employed by a small company named Colorado Standard Petroleum. While the civil war raged over the issue of sovereignty, there was also a war over drilling rights and oil revenues. Prior to the fall of Port Harcourt in May 1968, the Biafran government, needing foreign exchange, decided to lease oil land for exploration. Several companies bid. Colorado Standard won the concessions. However, federal forces overran Port Harcourt soon after. Colorado executives fled. Eventually, the oil leases were given to Royal Dutch Shell and BP."

"Did Whittenfeld meet Lefebre there?"

"Most definitely. Their first meeting took place at a reception held by Ojukwu."

"And after that?"

"I don't know. There are dead spots in the record, but we are working on them for you. I do know there was quite a bit of intrigue centered about the lease decisions, and there's evidence which suggests Mr. Whittenfeld was involved in considerable skullduggery."

"Which might have included Lefebre?"

"I put little stock in coincidence."

They re-entered the building, then walked out to the jeep.

"When will I hear from you?" Scotty asked.

"When I have something to tell you," Houghton replied retreating. "And by the way, I suggest you say nothing to Whittenfeld."

Scotty stared. He wasn't sure what all this information meant. Or where it would lead. However, he guessed it might lead to an understanding of Whittenfeld's need for the Frenchman. Christ, he knew he should let well enough alone. But he also knew he couldn't. He was incurable. He'd go slowly, gather additional information, see what developed.

Climbing into the jeep, he shook himself out of his trance and drove off.

*   *   *

Returning to Inverness, Scotty parked his car along the River Ness and walked toward the docks. The streets were deserted. Though official interest in the salvage operation remained high, the frenetic atmosphere had subsided.

A brisk wind was seeping inland. The shallow river bottom was visible. The Loch Ness monster, if it existed, had never navigated inland by means of the river; it would certainly have run aground long before reaching the loch's deep waters.

As he reached Douglas Row, he eased into a doorway to remain unobserved by three men who climbed into a car outside a corner building. He recognized one of the men, Girard. Judging by their movements, they wished to remain unseen.

The car disappeared down a side street.

He entered the corner building and examined the building's directory; the offices of the Transport and General Workers Union were listed.

He climbed to the second floor. The union's office door was open. He entered. The place had been ransacked.

He stepped into Sutherland's private suite; Sutherland's name was on the door. It, too, had been torn to shreds. A file cabinet had been opened and emptied.

Hearing footsteps, he turned.

"Did you find what you were looking for, Mr. Bruce?" Hugh Sutherland asked sarcastically.

Sutherland was standing with two burly men.

"Now before you get any ideas," Scotty said, realizing an alarm had been tripped. "I suggest you listen to me."

"That is precisely what I intend to do before I call the police." He looked inside the file cabinet, inspecting a severed pouch. "Where are the papers?" he asked.

"I don't know."

"Don't bullshit me."

"I'm not bullshitting you. I didn't break in here, and I didn't take anything. Here, search me! I was walking down the street, and I saw three men run out of the building, climb into a car, and race away."

"Three men? I see. Did you recognize them?"

Scotty hesitated. He'd promised himself he'd go slowly. And this was better left for Geminii internally. "No. But I goddamn well knew something was up. I entered the building and noticed the union listing in the directory. I came up here and found this."

"You're lying!"

"I swear to you!" Christ, once again trouble had found him. First, the beating incident. Now this. It was as if he couldn't avoid disaster.

Sutherland called the police, then turned on Scotty. "You dirty bastards think you own the world. Think you can step over anyone. Well, you're wrong. The one man you're certainly not going to step over is me. I'll see your gizzards rot before that happens." He clenched his fists, almost striking out. "Dirty rotten bastards!"

The police were in the offices a short time later.

Scotty stood on the command barge's bow next to Whittenfeld. The wind was churning between the loch's mountains like desert dervishes. Beyond the barge was the salvage flotilla. Three diving barges were nearby; several sets of divers were currently working on the bottom. Two huge hoisting rigs were anchored, and hoist lines had already been attached to the hulks. The largest ordnances, though, were supply tugs loaded with flotation material; their huge feed lines were visible descending into the water. According to schedule, the divers would soon be attaching the feed lines to the airtight chambers of the *Columbus* and sonar tug. Then pumping would begin.

"Fortunately," Scotty was saying as he stared across the silver-blue waters, "an old man who lived in a garret across from the union offices also saw the three men leave the alley. He corroborated my story. MacGregor bought it."

"How long did they have you there?"

"Two hours."

"You didn't tell them about Girard?"

"No, and the old man was too far away to ever be able to make a positive identification."

Whittenfeld looked off, his facial expressions registering little. "Good," he finally said. "I appreciate your discretion."

"Why did the men ransack the offices?"

"They were looking for information. Lefebre discovered a tie between Sutherland and the Jacobites. I asked him to uncover more."

"Why didn't we turn the information over to MacGregor?"

"Because it was sketchy. And because neither MacGregor nor the Special Branch could have followed it up properly."

Scotty braced himself; the barge was rolling heavily. "Why is that?"

"Use your head, Scotty. The police are limited in what they can do. They're governed by British common law. They just can't go breaking into private offices digging for information. Their resulting impotence is fairly well documented. They've had little success in opening up the radical movement. Hell, Scotty, we're in no position to wait for the police. Nor can we put the safety and success of the Loch Ness project in their hands. There is a guerrilla war underway. The *Columbus* might very well have been a victim. And damn, you have to fight guerrillas with guerrilla tactics."

"We've been breaking the law as a matter of policy," Scotty said angrily.

"We've had no choice," Whittenfeld countered.

"Was Lefebre's raid successful?"

"Yes. There were papers in a pouch which conclusively linked Sutherland to the New Jacobites. I have the material— letters, propaganda documents, what have you. We'll find a way to get the information to the police without incriminating ourselves, then, apart from keeping a sharp watch, we'll leave the rest to them."

Scotty paced slowly away. Whittenfeld watched him. Scotty returned.

"How are security decisions made?"

"Lefebre and I make them."

"I want to join the deliberations."

"I'm sorry, but that's impossible."

"Why?"

"Lefebre won't tolerate it."

"Order him to tolerate it."

Whittenfeld breathed deeply. "I force him to operate in front of a third person—especially you—and Lefebre will leave. I can't let that happen."

"And if I leave?"

"I won't let that happen, either. I will get on my hands and knees and beg before I would let you go."

Scotty looked out at the flotilla. Scores of men were busily moving about the decks of the tugs and barges.

"Why did you hire Lefebre?" he asked, finding it hard to envision Whittenfeld on his hands and knees begging him to stay. Hell, he did not see himself as invaluable to Whittenfeld's future; there were always other engineers.

"I think the answer is obvious. To allow me the freedom to operate without interference. Scotty, Lefebre stands between

Geminii—my dreams, everything I live for—and those who would destroy it all."

"You hired Lefebre from Schlumberger, right?"

"Yes."

"You'd never worked with him before?"

Whittenfeld narrowed his stare. "I'd never even met him before. But I assure you, I interviewed him thoroughly. I knew what I was getting—the positives and the negatives." He patted Scotty's shoulder. "I know you have a problem with Mr. Lefebre. You'll just have to learn to accommodate it."

Scotty bristled. Should he challenge Whittenfeld about the lie? Invoke the specter of Africa? It would serve no purpose now. He had something more important to challenge. "I'll accommodate Lefebre," he said, realizing he was about to issue the type of challenge he'd sworn to avoid. "But I won't tolerate the bullshit. I won't be involved in security excesses anymore!"

"I understand your feelings."

"I want to be part of security deliberations. I want to be able to veto dangerous gambits. I need not meet with Lefebre. You do that. Then you and I can caucus together alone."

"You've got it."

"Good!" He was shocked it had been that easy. Appeasement?

Whittenfeld smiled. "You're a good man, Scotty. An asset. You're a trusted confidant. I want to see you happy, and I tell you, even in the face of all our problems, I'm going to make you happy. Or I'll die trying."

Scotty looked out at the flotilla. All the ships and barges were in place. The men, too. The derelicts were fully prepared for liftout as well, filled with air sacks, their compartments closed, their structures free from inhibition, and according to to chief salvage engineer, precisely buoyant enough for the dangerous and time-consuming hoist maneuvers.

Tony Spinelli approached.

"Everything is ready," he advised.

"Good," Scotty replied.

"We just need your order," Spinelli said.

Whittenfeld's words—"I'll die trying"—rang in his head, just as they had been ringing in the last week during the final stages of the salvage prep.

"Bring the *Columbus* up!" he declared.

Chapter 16

The sky brooded like a black, heavy sledgehammer as Scotty crossed from the executive office building toward the makeshift plastic bubble that had been erected over the remains of the *Columbus* and sonar tug. Ignoring the light spray of snow that had already covered the ground, he checked through security. The last three weeks, since he'd seen Houghton, had been living hell. Even though this was the first snow, it had been relentlessly cold, and they'd had more than a winter's share of driving wind already.

The salvage operation had proceeded remarkably according to plan. He'd expected much worse. The *Columbus* and tug had settled on a narrow plateau over the wellhead, a precariously short distance away from the loch's deepest trench, which had presented the reality of slides. In addition, the center section of the drill ship had been impaled on the marine riser, and the riser's extraction had created a gauntlet of problems. There was no way to minimize the difficulties they had encountered in deploying the air bags and then raising the remains to the surface. And, of course, they had started operations fully aware they'd had an open well bore below them.

He entered the bubble.

The vision inside was surreal. Before him were three mounted sections of the *Columbus* and the sonar tug, framed in precisely the position they'd been found on the loch bottom, the tug's bow buried in the drill ship's superstructure. Though severely damaged, the derrick had been replaced over the moon pool. On the ground lay a five-hundred-foot length of marine riser. Portions of broken and melted drill pipe were also arranged nearby. Along the far side of the room were several body bags. The total body count had reached sixty-one. Fifty-one bodies were still missing, presumed lost forever.

Security inside the building was heavy. The inspection crew, however, was minimally staffed. There were several Geminii structural and mechanical engineers involved as well as two representatives from the Energy Petroleum Directorate and, of course, senior Geminii staff.

Whittenfeld and Spinelli were perched on one of the inspection platforms. Seeing them, he climbed the access ladder.

"Are they ready out there, Scotty?" Whittenfeld asked after Scotty had reached their level.

"Yes. We've cleared out most of the salvage vessels and have keyed in the lead dive support ship. They're about to send down one of the RCV remote eyes. We'll have a good map before the divers go down."

"I want the best men."

"You've got them."

Scotty realized they were slightly behind schedule. The divers should have completed the final recovery phase over a week ago. However, wind conditions had not been accommodating, and after they had hauled the remains of the drill ship and tug to shore, they'd had to place the on-loch operation on hold.

"How long until we're able to dispatch the recovery teams?" Whittenfeld asked.

"We need a day or so for planning, and then we can go, although I don't think we should move until after the funeral services—out of respect."

"We'll wait," Whittenfeld said, then turned to Spinelli. "Show Scotty the newspaper," he added.

Spinelli held up a newspaper he'd been carrying in his hand. Scotty scanned the front page. There was a lead article on the New Jacobite coalition, which included extensive coverage of Hugh Sutherland's involvement and a statement by the Northern Constabulary that Mr. Sutherland had been called in for questioning.

"I see the material found its way into the proper hands," Scotty said.

"The very proper," Whittenfeld observed.

Scotty glanced at Spinelli. Obviously, Tony Spinelli was aware of what had happened.

"Will it affect Sutherland's position with the union?" Scotty asked.

"I'd assume so," Whittenfeld speculated. "I contacted the National and suggested Sutherland is not the proper man for the Inverness post. I can't imagine them not agreeing, especially in the light of the threatening letters we received. However, I haven't gotten an answer yet, though I know the National is squirming. When I hear from them, you'll be the first to know." He paused, looking up at the hulk. "Right now, though, I'm more concerned with Sutherland's Jacobite connections, making sure Sutherland is defused."

Joined by Energy Department officials, they began to walk along the wooden catwalk, inspecting the hull. The three broken segments of the ship had been superficially joined together. The gas explosions and fire itself had roasted and twisted much of the deck metal, fusing numerous discrete parts into one. Unfortunately, as of yet, they had no firm leads to the cause of the blowout, though they had seen enough to intelligently formulate theories and ask leading questions. Assuming the kill operations had been completed, as the radio transmissions suggested they had been, a loss of mud circulation was suspected. The drill pipe had obviously been blown out of the well. But had it bent prior to its expulsion, thereby stopping the downward flow of mud? And if so, why hadn't the crew foreseen this and closed the preventer? The drill pipe was there, and its inspection had been scheduled. However, the control hoses and blowout preventer were still on the bottom, and until their recovery, a complete investigation and its resulting conclusion were impossible.

A call from inside the ship captured their attention. One of the inspectors had located another body, pinned by twisted metal. They waited as several acetylene workers cut a hole in the side of the hull and removed the virtually unrecognizable remains. There was one means to determine its identity, however. The corpse's clothes, and Scotty did not have to look long before he felt as if he would pass out.

It was Bob Reddington.

A horrible vision of Reddington's decomposed body hung before his eyes, and as Scotty walked behind the horse-drawn hearse down High Bridge Street. Listening to the clop of hoofs and the grind of wheels, he could not contain a swirling surge of nausea.

Reddington's coffin was last in the funeral cortege; sixty-one horse-drawn hearses preceded it, along with an empty hearse representing the men whose bodies had not been recovered. The entire route was lined with stern-faced Scotsmen. A light snow was falling. However, a weather window which would allow the final phase of the recovery, was rapidly approaching. Though it was just short of noon, the sky was dark and brooding, and the air was exhaustingly cold.

The end of the cortege crossed the River Ness Bridge and approached St. Andrew's Cathedral.

The crowd grew larger.

The pace slowed. Scotty dug deep for breath, nodding to Grabowski, Nunn, and Foster, who were standing at the edge of the church lawn. Scotty was crying heavily, and he couldn't remember the last time he'd cried for anything.

He left the hearse, started up to the cathedral entrance then stopped. Mary MacKenzie was standing on the church's top step. She was staring at him. She was crying, too.

He entered the cathedral.

Someone knocked on the front door.

"Come in," he called.

The door opened; he turned in the desk chair.

"Hello," Mary MacKenzie said as she appeared in the den doorway.

"Hello," he said, thoroughly taken by surprise.

"Can I come in?" she asked timidly. "I hope I'm not intruding. I know this has been a difficult day. But—"

"I'm glad you came," he said, walking around the desk and taking her by the hand. "Why don't you have a seat. Perhaps I can get you something. Some coffee. Or tea. My housekeeper is off today, so it will take me a few minutes."

"I'm not very thirsty," she said, sitting.

He sat across from her. "I don't suppose it will surprise you to know you've surprised me!"

"No. But it was not easy for me to come here. I've broken official procedure, something I don't think I've ever done before. There were a lot of conflicting thoughts and emotions. In fact, I feel most embarrassed right now."

"Why'd you come?"

"To apologize."

"For what?"

"Have you forgotten our last meeting?"

He shook his head. "Well, to tell you the truth, I tried. But

guess I didn't do a good job of it because I still have your
voice ringing in my ears."

"I was a little excited, overly so."

"To say the least."

"I'm sorry."

"I understand. You know, it's not the easiest thing for a
hardheaded American jerk to learn to think like a Scotsman."

"Or for a hardheaded Scotswoman to learn to listen."

They sat silently for several moments, staring at each other,
the drawn window shades admitting just enough light to generate appealing shadows.

"Why suddenly the change of heart?" he asked, breaking
the ice.

"I saw you at the church. I saw the tears."

Scotty said nothing.

"Remember what I told you about my father?" she asked.

"You told me a lot of things."

"I said he was a big man, with square features and a rock-
hard constitution. And he could be as stern as the Lord but
also as soft as a lamb. Strength and gentleness. Few people
possess both. My father did. I think you do, too."

"You find that appealing?"

"Yes. It gives added insight, too. I think you're an honest
man and have been honest with me."

"Just because you saw me cry?"

"That's part of it. I also read feelings in your face. Living
here gives one great knowledge of expression, Mr. Bruce."

"Scotty."

"Yes, Scotty."

"So does this make our relationship more personal once
again?"

"In part. You are still Geminii. I am still an inquisitor.
Once I leave here, I will not be able to speak to you until the
hearings are over. Any contact between you and me would
only create an inference of collusion. I cannot allow that to
happen."

"Can't we just sneak around a little?"

She smiled, shook her head, glanced around the room at
reams of unfolded charts and maps. "You look busy."

"These are our salvage plans. I can put most of them away,
except for the few involved with tomorrow's final haul-up."

"What about the weather?"

"We're in for some relief overnight. I promise you I won't

be blown overboard, though if we Geminii executives we
all winded off to the Land of Oz, I don't think we'd be to
missed around here."

"In general? You're right!"

He pulled up the sleeves of his ski sweater and placed h
feet on the coffee table, boots and all. He stared. She wa
wearing a plain blue dress and very little makeup. Yet sl
still looked very sensual. And her sense of propriety enhance
the impression even more. She was almost something unattai
able, something not to be touched.

"What if I told you I care about you?" he suddenly said.

"Excuse me?" she countered, taken by surprise.

"I'm attracted to you. I care about you."

She looked away. "Words of the moment," she stammere

"Absolutely not," he said.

The admission unsettled her. She shifted awkwardly on th
couch, then stood and meandered about the room, glancin
finally at a book lying open on the desk.

"Were you reading this?" she asked, needing time to thin

"Yes."

"A history of Scotland?"

"I decided I ought to find out something about Rober
Bruce since it's become the standing line around here that I'
his successor, maybe even his reincarnation."

She picked up several pamphlets that were lying on th
desk. "A history of Scottish nationalism. The platform of th
Scottish National Party." She turned toward him. "Are thes
just ornaments?"

"No."

She placed the material on the desk again and sat. "Do yo
think you'll be able to digest it all?"

"I'm going to try, but I make no promises."

"What made you suddenly so ambitious?"

"Our talk at the inn. But don't praise me too enthusiastica
ly. They've lain there for a while. I've barely bent the pages

"The intent is good."

He smiled. "I'd like to return to my words of the moment
he declared.

"If you must," she parried.

"You make it sound painful. Feelings between men ar
women are not always painful."

She did not respond.

He pressed. "I told you I care about you. You didn't r

ply. I'd like to know if my admission meant anything to you."
He hoped Mrs. Munro had been right.

She looked away, very disturbed. "This is Scotland. Not
America. This is not the wild and woolly West. Things are
done differently here. Things take time. Feelings just don't
pop out of nowhere."

"I asked you a question. I'd like an answer. Did it mean
anything to you?"

"Yes."

He smiled. "I see."

"You don't see me."

"Don't I?"

"I told you I've sworn away the privileges of the unburdened. I'm also not one for emotional attachments."

"You're not a teenager anymore. I'm sure there've been a
lot of emotional attachments in the past. I'm also sure one or
two of them went kind of bad, judging by the way you've
shut everything out. 'Cause that's the reason people close
themselves off emotionally. Political convictions or historical
burdens have nothing to do with it. You say you have an
obligation to feel no emotion. I don't buy it!"

"You're a very direct man."

"Honest is the word. You said it yourself. So if you're
seeking honesty in me, I expect it in you."

She took a deep breath. He touched her hand. She held
for a moment, then pulled her hand away. "I do feel," she
said, softly, almost hiding the words. "It puzzles me. Frightens
me, too. And I can't let it interfere with my responsibilities."
She stood abruptly. "I have to go."

He stood, too. "Are you sure?"

"Yes."

"When can we see each other again?"

"After the hearings. Maybe."

He walked her to the door. As she was about to leave, she
kissed his cheek. He wrapped his arms around her, pulling
her close, embracing her. She resisted, then relaxed and submitted. He held her tighter and kissed her neck. She breathed
heavily, squeezed once, then pulled back.

"I must go," she said.

He opened the door. "I'm glad you came," he declared.

She eased through and walked down the path, stopping
near the gate, turning. "So am I," she said.

Chapter 17

The machine-gun sputter of the inboard engine slowly die~~d~~
as the motor launch pulled alongside the diving support vessel
allowing William Whittenfeld and two security officers t~~o~~
board.

"They're in the command cabin," a boatswain said.

The deck was crammed with equipment. A huge cran~~e~~
stood ship center. Two other cranes were at the bow an~~d~~
stern, respectively. The command cabin stood in the back
ground; the huge Martcon Saturation Diving System, dec~~k~~
decompression chamber and diving bell included, was locate~~d~~
directly in front.

Whittenfeld followed the boatswain into the cabin, a rec~~-~~
tangular module packed with sophisticated instruments an~~d~~
television screens.

"So do we see the light at the end of the tunnel?" he asked
ambling to Scotty Bruce's side.

"Could be," Scotty replied, pointing to one of the tele~~-~~
vision monitors. "The RCV remote has done a good job."

"Let me take a look." Whittenfeld buttoned his coat. It wa~~s~~
cold in the cabin, perhaps even colder than outside. "Th~~e~~
blowout preventer first."

"We've got a clear view of her," Scotty said. "Take the ey~~e~~
in!"

The RCV console operator began to manipulate his han~~d~~
controls; the bright lights and television eye of the thruster~~-~~
propelled RCV module focused on the twisted pile of debri~~s~~
520 feet below the surface.

"There's a lot of junk still down there," the module eng~~i~~
neer said as he tilted the module's eye. "There! There's th~~e~~
blowout preventer."

"Closeup," Scotty ordered.

Upon command, the RCV module moved directly to the blowout preventer and its twisted guide frame. The blowout preventer was still firmly attached to the wellhead. However, the guide frame was mangled, and strangely, none of the hoses or guide wires were connected or visible nearby.

"What do you think, Scotty?" Whittenfeld asked, his expression as grim as the monitor view.

"Don't know," Scotty replied.

"Shouldn't the hoses and wires still be attached?"

"They should. But obviously they've been torn away."

"Are we ready?"

"Yes. Both teams of divers have been compressed to five hundred and twenty feet."

"Let me see the area again."

The RCV engineer thrust the undersea eye into action, moving it across the twisted mass of silt-covered metal.

"Goddamn hoses and guide wires," Whittenfeld mumbled plaintively, turning to Scotty. "If the divers find any one or all of them, have them brought to the surface first—before we bring up the blowout preventer. Then we can clear the remaining debris." He addressed the senior diving engineer. "Got it, Hox?"

The diving engineer, a grizzled veteran named Hoxley, nodded. "We find them, we get them."

Whittenfeld walked across the cabin. "I'm going to order a tender tug to moor up. As soon as any of the hoses or guide wires are recovered, I want them transferred to the tender. When the divers have prepared the target objects for liftout, notify me. In the interim, I'll be at my office or in reach of base radio. If anything unexpected happens, call me immediately."

"Do you want to speak to the divers?" Scotty asked.

"Yes."

Scotty handed Whittenfeld a headset equipped with voice descrambler. Because of the magnitude of the dive, the divers would not be breathing compressed air but an oxygen-helium mixture, which would prevent deep-water nitrogen narcosis and oxygen poisoning. Although essential for such deep dives, helium made the normal voice unintelligible without an intervening electrical aid that was contained within the telephone equipment.

Whittenfeld issued instructions, then left the cabin. Scotty followed. Passing the deck decompression chamber, Whittenfeld looked in at the divers, then turned.

"Go get it," Whittenfeld said with a smile.

"I'll call as soon as we have something," Scotty promised.

Whittenfeld looked around the loch, then returned to the launch, taking the two security men with him.

Max Furst and Rudy Blasingame had entered the deck chamber several hours before with another dive team, starting decompression to depth. Apart from time spent in the diving bell itself, it would be their week-long home during return to-surface rest stops and the eventual arduous four-day process of decompression.

Blasingame looked through the chamber porthole, holding the telephone receiver. Scotty Bruce was outside, wearing the deck headset.

"Saddle up," Scotty said.

Furst and Blasingame stripped off their clothes, put on wet suits, which they would wear underneath their hot-water garb for additional thermal protection, then wiggled through the narrow chamber entrance trunk into the attached diving bell.

They donned their hot-water suits. Outside, the hatches were closed and sealed, and the bell was unmated from the deck chamber. Inside, Furst and Blasingame belted themselves to their seats while the bell was attached to the deck crane.

"Cameras activated," Scotty called, a slight veil of static smearing his voice.

There was a television camera inside the bell and one attached to its outer shell. In addition, both diving helmets were equipped with television eyes. The entire undersea operation would be monitored and directed from the surface.

Furst and Blasingame felt the bell rise, swing through the air, then descend with a jerk into the water. Soon the bell moved smoothly downward and reached its target depth, the floor hatch popping open due to the equalization of external and internal pressure.

Furst fastened the open hatch to prevent it from flapping. Below the hatch, water pooled around the exit rim, held out by the internal pressure. Blasingame looked out one of the portholes. The bell's floodlights illuminated the area. Though everything was dense with silt, they could see twisted piles of debris almost within reach.

"We're picking up the work area," Scotty said, his voice descending through the telephone cables from the surface.

"Good," Furst said as he donned mixed-gas headgear and checked the hose connections, his voice audible at the surface through the diving suit's internal telephone system.

Equipment in place, Blasingame helped edge Furst into exit position, then handed him a preliminary run of tools. Smiling, Furst slipped down through the bulkhead into the water next to the ballast line, attached the bell guideline, and started off toward the metallic graveyard.

The support vessel was bobbing gently as Scotty watched ash-colored clouds cast shadows over the water. Urquhart Castle stood beyond the stern, rising like a majestic gravestone. The wind was surging across the loch's surface, bringing subtly lower temperatures. He rubbed his hands together, bending frostbitten fingers. His face, however, remained warmly protected. He had not shaved since the *Columbus* had gone down, and the beard covering his cheeks and chin had grown full and dark. He'd never worn a beard before, but this growth did not feel resented. It was a marker, his own peculiar epitaph for associates now dead.

He stared at the descending bell life line. Furst and Blasingame had been under for five hours already. During the tour, he'd been in the control room directing the assault. Just prior to his present break, Blasingame had returned to the bell, releasing Furst to duty. So far, they had cleared the blowout preventer and guide base from debris and had scoured the area looking for the missing control hoses and guide wires. They had failed to find them.

"Scotty," Hoxley suddenly yelled, body half out of the control cabin.

"Yeah?" Scotty said, jolted from reveries.

Hoxley was visibly excited. "We may have something."

Scotty jumped past Hoxley into the cabin, moving to the television console, simultaneously placing the communications headset in place.

"What do you have?" he asked, peering at the television screen, whose view was hopelessly clouded with silt.

"I got the lower part of a control hose," Furst replied. "The free end has been torn apart."

"A band or compaction tear?"

"No."

"Can you be more specific?"

"I don't want to sound like an idiot. You'll see soon enough."

"Sound like an idiot!"

"It looks like it's been chewed!"

Scotty quickly glanced at the others in the control room—he was the only one who'd heard the words—then cleared his throat. "Say again."

"I said it looks like it's been chewed!"

"TV reception's bad. Could you clean your lenses?"

"Can't. There's a lot of oil and grease residue down here sticking to the glass." He paused. "The hose is the damndest thing I ever saw!"

"Bring it up to the camera eye."

A thick wire passed close to the television, but the resolution was still poor.

"Can you see it?"

"Not very well."

"As I said, you'll see it soon enough."

"Is the other end about?"

"Haven't seen it. There are a couple of more places it can be buried within reach, but the edge of the plateau is not too far away, and I'm sure we've lost some of the material to the real deep pits."

"Is the hose free?"

"Yeah. You get me some sling hooks and shackles, and I'll rig to a hoist and oxy-arc off a usable segment right quick."

"How far are you from the bell?"

"I've got seventy-five feet of guideline with me."

"The compass heading?"

Furst spit out a figure. Scotty advised Hoxley to order the crane operator to swing the giant hoist into position and drop a lifting line down to the work site. Hoxley immediately left the cabin. Scotty stayed behind, entered the radio shed, contacted Whittenfeld ship to shore, and informed him they had found a suspicious control hose section.

"Suspicious?" Whittenfeld asked.

Scotty held his breath; he knew it was coming. "The diver says it looks like it's been chewed apart."

Silence!

Then: "Is the transfer ship there?"

"Yes." He could sense Whittenfeld was trembling.

"We're on our way out."

"Right."

"Scotty, I want you to clear the deck of the support vessel."

"I don't understand."

"You don't have to understand, Mr. Bruce. Just do it."

Whittenfeld had never called him Mr. Bruce before. "Of course," he said.

"How many men heard Furst's appraisal?"

"Just me." He'd never heard Whittenfeld's voice so strained.

"Was the hose visible on the television monitor?"

"Not really. Too much silt and grease down there."

"Good. Now clear the deck, Mr. Bruce! And keep your telephone channel to the divers closed!"

Static crackled; the transmission died. Scotty looked at the radio mike, then dropped it on the radio console.

A launch arrived twenty minutes later. Lefebre and Girard boarded the diving support vessel.

"Mr. Whittenfeld could not come out," Lefebre said while approaching Scotty cross-deck. He was chewing a huge wad of tobacco, a habit Houghton had suggested Lefebre had picked up from American mercenaries in the Congo. "He sent me in his stead. With his full proxy."

"What does that mean?"

"That means you will do as I say."

"And if I refuse?"

Lefebre walked toward the crane. "You won't." He pointed toward a boatswain. "Get that man off the deck."

Scotty demurred. "He's needed there. Someone has to guide the hose on to the tender tug."

"Girard will do it. Whittenfeld considers the hose a sensitive matter. He wants no one on board. He has ordered everyone to comply with those wishes. If not voluntarily, then with my assistance. Do I make myself clear, Bruce?"

Scotty ordered the boatswain off deck. Only the crane operator remained in the vicinity of the lift-up. Scotty grabbed the deck phone and asked Furst if he had rigged the hose. Furst replied affirmatively. Scotty ordered the crane operator to bring the material up.

The hose was out of the water a short time later.

"Get it on to the tender," Lefebre ordered.

The crane operator swung the rigged hose into position over the tender tug, which was also clear of deck hands.

Scotty stared at the swinging hulk of hose, but the hose was too far away for him to make any kind of appraisal.

Girard climbed down onto the tender tug, eased the hose into position on a rack, and disattached the lift line. Then he covered the hose with a tarpaulin.

Scotty jumped on to the tug; Lefebre stepped into his way.

"Off the tug," Lefebre ordered.

Scotty tried to pass him. "I want to look at that hose."

Lefebre again interceded. "No one looks at the hose. Those are Mr. Whittenfeld's orders."

Scotty stiffened. "I've had just about enough of you, Lefebre."

Lefebre smiled, his tobacco-stained teeth glaring. "I'm afraid that's too bad. Very surprising, too. I've been very nice to you, Bruce. Mr. Whittenfeld has ordered me to treat you gently. I have been doing so. If you find my good nature difficult to handle, I'm afraid you will not like to see my disagreeable side once more. No. You will not like to see that at all, and you will see it sooner than expected if you try to examine the control hose. It is to be covered and transmitted to shore at once. That is my responsibility, monsieur. I will see the responsibility carried out."

"You're a pathetic man, Lefebre."

"Foolish words are a fool's paradise. Now get off this tug."

Scotty walked to the tug's edge, stopping, turning. "Now is not the time or the place."

"For what?" Lefebre asked pointedly.

"To allow you to try and fulfill your deepest desires. To allow you to try and break my neck."

Lefebre sniffed at the cool air. "I told you, I court the day. Pray for it."

"It will come. And I may very well boot your ass back to Africa."

Lefebre's expression changed; he was startled. Had he said too much too soon, Scotty wondered.

The lift line moved over Scotty's head and back to the command vessel. Lefebre took two steps in Scotty's direction. "Get back to your duties, Bruce!" he said.

Scotty felt his entire body freeze. He did not like being ordered around that way. Especially by Lefebre. The restraints popped off. Christ, he'd known he could only rationalize himself into inaction for just so long. He charged at the Frenchman but stopped dead in his tracks. Lefebre had unbuttoned his holster guard and had started to remove his gun. Girard was similarly set, hand on pistol.

Scotty breathed deeply, realized he might very well get shot, then stepped off the tug.

The crucial exhibit in place, Lefebre ordered the pilot to take the tug to shore. Scotty remained on the diving vessel, supervising the change of diving teams and the return of the blowout preventer and associated guide frame to the surface. Then, after the tender tug had returned, this time without Lefebre, to take the additional material to base, he remained again to command the final phases of the operation.

All the while thinking of the control hose.

And Whittenfeld.

And Pierre Lefebre as well.

Scotty returned to base late that night. Whittenfeld was still in his office. Scotty barged inside. Whittenfeld was visibly disconcerted, nervous to excess.

"Why wasn't I allowed to see the hose?" Scotty asked angrily.

Whittenfeld's face drew blank. "What are you talking about?"

Scotty reviewed the episode on the barge.

"Lefebre exceeded his authority, Mr. Bruce. I told him to make sure no one on the crew saw the material. He was not supposed to inhibit you."

Was this bullshit? Scotty asked himself. Maybe, maybe not. Although Whittenfeld had kept parts of his past a secret for whatever reason, Whittenfeld had not yet lied to him about anything substantive in Inverness. "Lefebre has a way of exceeding authority," Scotty declared.

"Fortunately, no harm was done. And no guns were actually pointed."

"Can I see the hose?"

"It's gone. I sent it to our Aberdeen research complex this afternoon. It will be analyzed there."

"Furst still insists the hose looked chewed, that something alive chewed it!"

"The hose was severely damaged. Furst's conclusion is off the cuff, an inexpert opinion. Until the hose is analyzed, there's no way to tell what happened."

Scotty stared. Whittenfeld's hands were shaking badly. His skin was anemic, almost white.

"Did you tell Furst to keep his observations to himself due to the sensitivities?" Whittenfeld asked.

"Yes," Scotty replied.

"Is the work finished?"

"Almost. We have another dive or two to do."

Whittenfeld stood and held out his arms, almost begging. "Then let's both go home and get some sleep. It's been a long day."

Scotty stood, too. Thoughts were cascading through his head, a review of recent events. "All right," he said reluctantly.

Whittenfeld was obviously barely hanging on to the edge of control. He'd had the shock of his life.

There was no reason to pursue the subject any longer.

Chapter 18

The helicopter landed on the Geminii roof.

Scotty stepped out. It was warm, but he welcomed the slumberous air after six blistering days out on the Moray Firth, supervising the inception of a new seismic study.

He breathed deeply, looked around—the bubble and its contents were still there—then walked toward the roof staircase, setting time and place. The last two weeks, starting with the recovery of the control hose section, had tumbled by as if they'd been weighted with barbells. Yet, instead of being easily defined, they'd passed as a peculiar blur, punctuated by a maze of questions.

As soon as Whittenfeld had been notified that the hose section had arrived in Aberdeen and had been placed under lock and key, and when he learned that the final group of divers had been unable to locate any other critical material, he called a staff meeting to discuss the remaining phase of the investigation. Then he followed the hose section east, accompanied by Pierre Lefebre, who had packaged the control hose section himself to ensure its safety.

In retrospect, Whittenfeld's discomfiture, annoying insistence on airtight security, and decision to subject the hose to classified scrutiny away from Inverness had not really surprised Scotty. Again, Whittenfeld's "child" had come under attack, along with the *Columbus;* clearly, the nature of the control hose's damage had visibly unhinged the man. Scotty had no doubt that Whittenfeld had already been painfully trying to come to grips with the inevitable conclusion Scotty had reached from the first—that there was a strong possibility something alive had eaten through the control hose.

Certainly his phone conversations with Whittenfeld had only reinforced his suspicions.

While the final phase of the inspection was winding down and a preliminary report was being written, he'd had several such exchanges, but every time he'd asked about the control hose analyses, Whittenfeld had said only that they were continuing to study the specimen and had not even reached any preliminary conclusions as of yet.

Christ, the charade had been obvious. Whittenfeld's voice, its nervousness, its echo of paranoia, had been unmistakably evasive. So had Whittenfeld's behavior.

The week before, Whittenfeld had scheduled a brief return to Inverness. Scotty had expected to hear something definitive. However, prior to Whittenfeld's arrival, a telex had arrived, sent from Aberdeen, requesting Scotty to proceed out on to the North Sea to hook up with one of the company's North Sea seismic teams. The order had confused him. Although they'd completed the investigation, the last place he'd expected to be sent, or expected to be needed, was the North Sea. Nevertheless, he hadn't questioned Whittenfeld's order and had helicoptered out to the work site the following day.

Between that day and this, Whittenfeld had been in and out of Inverness twice, but though he'd spoken to Whittenfeld three times ship to shore, Whittenfeld had continued to be evasive, paranoid, a bundle of nerves.

Whittenfeld had sent him away for a purpose—he suspected that the man did not want to face him—intending to keep him away until the start of the commission hearings.

The question was why.

Christ, he knew the realities were terrifying. And the ramifications mind boggling. But the inordinate subterfuge had stupefied him. He wasn't about to start wild rumors without proof. And as far as he could tell, Furst and Blasingame had kept their mouths shut as well.

He entered the deserted building. It was Saturday. A lone guard, stationed at the end of the third-floor hall, appeared.

He walked into his office. Mail was stacked. So were phone messages. He examined both stacks and then phoned Tony Spinelli, who informed him he'd just completed a final meeting with the inspection team and that they had reviewed all the documentation intended for the commission tribunal. Scotty asked for copies. Spinelli said copies were already on his desk.

Scotty located the copies and returned to Travis House. Mrs. Munro met him at the door. Giving her the day off, he secluded himself in the den and read the fact sheets, reports, and test data. All checked out. His work was only interrupted by thoughts of Mary MacKenzie, whom he had not seen in quite a while. He did not call her.

Finishing the review just after sundown, he fixed himself something to eat, then decided to go into town. Hell, he'd been on a boat for almost a week. He was in sore need of a pub.

Scotty walked into the pub next door to the railway station, sat at the bar, and ordered a lager. The pub was crowded.

When the lager arrived, he sipped off the head and swiveled around, facing smiles, animated eyes.

Hugh Sutherland was staring at him. Sutherland was seated at a corner table, alone.

Surprised, he bowed; Sutherland ambiguously moved his head.

He walked to the table. "Mind if I sit?"

Sutherland shrugged. "No. But why would you want to?"

"I have no quarrel with you."

"You say that with great pain, Mr. Bruce."

"Not at all. I want to talk."

Sutherland pointed to a facing chair; Scotty slid on to his rump.

Neither moved. Neither spoke. Sutherland's mug sat untouched on the table. Scotty sipped from his.

"You said you want to talk," Sutherland finally said. "So talk."

"I'm thinking of something intelligent to say."

"Try a confession. Try admitting you were involved in the burglary, after all. I invited you to visit our offices. You took me up on the invitation—surreptitiously."

"Sorry. Can't admit that. 'Cause it's not true."

Sutherland smirked, staring ahead. He looked even more ghastly than Scotty had remembered—his cheeks sunken down to the bone, his forehead roadmapped with crossing veins, his lips chapped, stained with tobacco, covered with remnants of recently used rolling papers.

"I've been gone from Inverness awhile," Scotty declared.

"Good for you," Sutherland countered cheerlessly.

"Before I left, I read the newspapers. I read about you. This New Jacobite group."

"Do you believe everything you read?"

"I believe the truth."

Sutherland lit a cigarette. "For what earthly reason should I discuss this with you, Mr. Bruce?"

"There's none."

Sutherland lifted his mug and drank. He wore a gray cardigan. It had several holes, a button missing. "You read some truth. There is an organization called the New Jacobite Coalition. I am a member. I am a radical nationalist." He paused, swallowing heavily. "I am also a member of the Transport Workers. I am a senior rep for them."

"Still?"

"For the moment. Though that status may unfortunately change. I am attempting to see it doesn't. I may fail. You see, Mr. Bruce, unions are very conservative organizations; no matter that they are usually considered to be of the left. Apart from their own parochial concerns, they have few interests and very little guts."

"Then why do you want to remain a member?"

"It's my job. I believe in the union's work. I desire to serve it."

"As well as the New Jacobite movement?"

"Yes."

"The article said the New Jacobites have been implicated in several murders."

"The word 'implicated' implies an absence of proof. The New Jacobites have never been positively tied to any murders.

Nor certainly have I. And to answer your next question even before you ask it, the New Jacobites and I had nothing to do with the destruction of the *Columbus*. Nor with any of the incidents which took place on board."

"But you did compose threatening notes!"

"I know nothing about notes—any notes."

"If you're so inactive, what are you doing in Inverness?"

Sutherland chafed, his face reddening. "I was sent here as a union rep! I came here to do a job. As a free man, an honest man, I can go wherever the hell I please, whenever the hell I wish!"

"Well said!"

"Is that all?"

"No. I have a question."

"Then ask it and leave me alone."

"Do you believe in violence?"

"As a means to an end? The philosophical answer is yes."

Scotty shifted uncomfortably. "Violence does not earn respect. Nor does it lead to rational compromise." He thought back to his own rebellions; they'd always been relatively peaceful, based on facts, reason, dialogue. "Ever."

Sutherland started to laugh. "What in God's name are respect and reason?"

"Relationships are based on respect and reason. The world runs according to their dictates. And as a union rep, you've resorted to dialogue, the use of reason to compromise. Give and take. Mutual respect. Nonviolent sit-downs at worst."

"Mr. Bruce. You are talking about business. The Jacobites are involved in politics. In politics, respect is irrelevant. So is reason. The political world runs on fear. Strength and power beget fear. Violence begets fear. An oppressor will only negotiate when confronted with strength and power. Where they are not present, negotiation is a sham. No, in the face of such disdain, one must then resort to the threat of violence and possibly violence in fact until enough fear is instilled that the oppressor will cower and submit." He shook his head; his face was a mask of ridicule. "Go. Talk of respect and reason. Go talk like a fool. But you are not talking about this world. You are not talking about the subjugation of Scotland by England."

"Scotland united with England in 1707 to save herself from ruin. It was not subjugated!"

"Nonsense!" Sutherland nearly screamed, his face turning

a shade of crimson. "The two countries were united by status-seeking traitors—nobles in Edinburgh who wanted to take their phony pomp to the English court. Scotland was betrayed, not saved. Scotland could well have survived without England—alone, allied with France—in so many, many ways. And it can certainly survive without England now!"

"You sound like a bitter man."

"On the contrary, I'm a happy man, a man at peace with himself. I am content in the political world because I have earned the glory of resistance. I have tasted the buds of freedom!"

"What do you want of Geminii?"

"I want Geminii to disavow the English. To get the hell out of Scotland. To leave Scotland's oil for the Scots."

"Then there would be no jobs for your people."

"Wrong. We or our representatives, maybe even a company such as Geminii working by our rules, would provide all the jobs needed."

Scotty shook his head. "You don't have a rat's ass chance with your political demands because Geminii does not have the right to grant them."

"Maybe."

"And as a Jacobite, Geminii won't listen to you."

"Why is that?"

"Geminii doesn't respect you, and you do not have sufficient strength and power to make it submit."

Sutherland stood. "Mr. Bruce. It's time I should be going."

Scotty stared. "If Geminii won't listen to you because you don't have the strength and power, then you must, according to your own admission, resort to violence."

Sutherland put his empty mug on the table. "I said I believe in violence philosophically, but I reject it as a human being and a dreamer. I recognize the truth, but I am far too weak to exercise it."

"Then why be a Jacobite?"

"To try to explain the truth. No, Mr. Bruce. If you're looking for a violent act from me or my associates, you'll grow old fast. I only hope to explain to Geminii what it can expect and might already have received from radicals far less human and idealistic than I or my other Jacobite associates."

"You're contradicting yourself," Scotty challenged. "Resorting to the very thing—reason—you believe to be impotent."

Sutherland smiled sadly. "Good night, Mr. Bruce," he said, and left the pub abruptly.

Scotty jogged Sunday morning, played soccer with several Geminii engineers—he needed the exercise—slept most of Sunday afternoon—he needed the rest, too—and then, after dinner, fell asleep.

He arrived at his office the next day, midmorning.

A message was waiting; Whittenfeld wanted to speak to him.

He immediately went to Whittenfeld's office.

"Sit, Mr. Bruce," Whittenfeld said as he stood behind his desk.

He dropped into one of the lounges.

Whittenfeld looked as if he'd been through the wringer, far worse than he'd looked the day they'd spoken after the recovery of the hose. He hadn't shaved in a week. His eyes were red. His hands were shaking ever so slightly. Even his tie, which was always knotted perfectly, was slightly askew.

"Don't mind my appearance," Whittenfeld said disconcertedly. "I flew in late last night from Aberdeen with Mr. Lefebre, and I spent the rest of the night reviewing the investigation documentation."

"I hope you've found everything in order," Scotty said, also noting indecision and an awkward quality of fear in Whittenfeld's usually steady voice.

"They're in order. In fact, I think we're ready. And I've confirmed the readiness of the inspection investigators as well. I am going to notify the London office to notify the Department of Energy that we and the inspection investigators are prepared to present our findings to the commission."

"Are you sure you're all right?" Scotty asked.

"Just tired, Mr. Bruce," Whittenfeld replied, unsteadily lighting a cigar. "How was the seismic work?"

"It went well."

Whittenfeld walked to the window and looked out. Scotty examined Whittenfeld's face. He sensed severe strain. No physical. But mental. He was sure Whittenfeld had been through an emotional cyclone.

It did not surprise him.

"What about the blowout prevent control hose?" he finally asked.

"I finished the inspection."

"And?"

A bead of sweat ran down Whittenfeld's face. "I reached a conclusion."

"Do you want to let me in on it?"

Whittenfeld blew a ring of smoke into the air. "Of course." He walked toward Scotty. "There is nothing I keep from you. But I would like you to bear with me for a few days. The information I have is startling. The proof I have found is frightening. Only I know the particulars. I would like to keep them with me until I face the tribunal."

My God, Scotty thought. "Of course," he said.

"I have information that will focus the spotlight of the world on Scotland."

"I understand."

"Good, Mr. Bruce."

They stood in silence, facing each other. Then Whittenfeld returned to his desk.

"I will speak to you later," he said.

Scotty said nothing and left the room.

Chapter 19

That afternoon, Geminii Petroleum's London office notified the secretary of state for energy that the *Columbus* investigation had been completed.

The investigation commission convened immediately thereafter. As Fallworth had noted, the commission tribunal was composed of members of select governmental departments. Andrew Farquharson, its chairman, and Peter Droon had been drawn from the Scottish Office, Mary MacKenzie from the Highland Regional Council. There were also individuals from the Petroleum Engineering Division, the Home Office,

the Department of Trade, and the Health and Safety Execu
tive.

The inclusion of Droon and MacKenzie had drawn con
siderable attention from the start. The press considered thei
selection a canny political maneuver, a device to suggest im
partiality and a high regard for Scottish nationalism. Cabine
spokesmen, however, insisted they'd been chosen by lot fron
lists provided by their respective departments.

The public inquiry was gaveled into session in the executiv
chamber of the Highland Regional Council, Inverness. Th
preliminary sessions focused on a description of the *Columbu*
and the environmental impact of her destruction, while th
succeeding ones concentrated on the salvage operation and
description of the recovered drill ship and sonar tug. It wa
only after the committee obtained a complete preliminar
picture that it shifted the focus to the chain of events leadin
to the catastrophe, the causes, and a possible assignment o
blame.

Peter Droon, of the Scottish Office, scanned the packe
gallery, especially the press section, then, while fiddling wit
the end of his tie, looked back at the witness.

"Mr. Bruce," he said, "am I correct making the followin
assumptions based on the expert testimony elicited so far? Th
Columbus was found in three discrete sections, though par
of her had broken free. The bow of the sonar tug wa
imbedded in the drill ship's hull, and much of the drill ship
stern section, behind the impact point, had broken loose
Parts of the drill pipe were imbedded in the remains of th
derrick. The blowout control hoses and the guide wires wer
missing, presumably having been burned off the ship by th
fire and explosions?"

"That's correct," Scotty said, leaning back in his chair, ob
viously disquieted; he had finally been called to testify, th
next to last witness, after having listened to seven days c
brutal testimony.

"We'd like to pose several questions based on these facts,
Droon explained. "We'd like you to elaborate."

"If I can."

"That's all we can ask of you," Droon said, glancing brief
at Mary MacKenzie. "Several expert witnesses have su
gested the tug was caught in the gas blowout and sucked int
the heavier drill ship. Would you agree?"

"Yes."

"That obviously implies the tug was close enough to the drill ship and wellhead to have been caught in the gas funnel."

"Yes."

"But, Mr. Bruce, according to testimony and Geminii's carefully documented operational orders, the tug was to have remained at least half a mile away from the ship."

"That's correct."

"Well, then. Perhaps you can tell me what the hell the tug was doing alongside the *Columbus?*"

"We're not sure. We tried to check the tug's instruments. However, they had been totally destroyed, as had all of her records. We can only guess the tug was either steaming toward the drill ship to offer help or to warn the drill ship of impending danger."

"To warn the drill ship? Mr. Bruce, the tug had a radio."

"Unfortunately not. We recovered the tug's radio. The radio had multiple shortings, which we determined had occurred prior to the catastrophe. So if there was a warning to be given, it would have to have been given at close range."

"Couldn't visual signals have carried the distance?"

"No. You've heard the testimony concerning the weather conditions on the night of the blowout. The fog was so thick the tug had no choice but to make a near approach."

"Could the tug have been closing to offer aid? Might they have seen the blowout?"

"Of course they saw the blowout. But I doubt they were closing because of it."

"Why?"

"Because there was too little time between the blowout and the aeration to have allowed the tug to reach the danger zone. No, the tug was closing before the blowout—closing to warn of impending danger."

"How could the tug have known of such a danger?"

"It had highly sophisticated equipment on board designed to detect foreign objects in the loch."

"Then you're suggesting there was a foreign object present which the tug perceived could endanger the *Columbus* and therefore the tug was moving to warn the ship's crew of the foreign object's presence."

Scotty glanced back at Whittenfeld, who was seated in the rear, next to Lefebre, Foster, and a team of company executives, then turned toward Superintendent MacGregor and

Inspector MacKintosh, who had attended every session. "I don't know," he said. "We do know one of the control hoses, parts of which we were able to find, was severed a hundred feet below the water surface. We suspect the drill pipe was bent as well, pinching off the downward flow of mud, thereby causing the blowout."

"What could have pinched the drill pipe?"

"The disalignment of the riser."

"How might the riser have been disaligned?"

"Based on our prior experience—and the committee has reviewed the record—we suspect something might have pushed it out of whack."

"What severed the blowout control hose?"

"You'll have to ask Mr. Whittenfeld. He examined the hose."

Farquharson interceded, tapping his cane. "Mr. Bruce could you possibly reconstruct the sequence of events aboard the drill ship prior to her demise?"

"I would have to make many assumptions."

"We understand that. But we would still appreciate an attempt."

Scotty fiddled with his notes. "As you know, the *Columbus* had taken a kick and had instituted kill procedures. During these procedures, the blowout preventer would have been closed, sealing off the well. With the blowout preventer closed, there could not have been a blowout unless the preventer had structurally failed or the well wall itself had collapsed. Neither occurred. We examined the well. It is intact. I personally examined the blowout preventer, Exhibit D, and there is nothing structurally wrong with it. It did not fail. Therefore the preventer would have to have been open at the time of the blowout, and we have to conclude the kill procedures had been completed and the drill team had returned to normal operation, which would correspond to the radio messages received from the ship."

Farquharson arched his brow, puzzled. "Then what caused the blowout?"

"As I said, the drill pipe was pinched closed by the movement of the riser after drilling had been resumed. The pinching cut off the downward flow of mud, which had kept the gas from flowing to the surface. Then, suddenly, without down pressure, the well flowed."

"Why didn't they close the preventer again once they realized the riser was out of alignment?"

"First of all, everything happened very fast. And secondly, they might well have tried to close the preventer only to discover they were unable to. I told you one of the control hoses had been severed."

"But there was another, a backup."

"Yes. But we never recovered it. Since one hose had been severed, it's highly likely the other had been, too. Therefore, there would have been no way to activate the blowout preventer."

"Then what happened?"

"Based on the evidence, the drill pipe blew out of the well and up through the ship. Gas followed. There was an explosion and fire. Then the aeration."

"How did the gas get into the water beneath the ship?"

"It ate right through the lower riser joints."

"The crew was helpless?"

"Correct."

The Trade representative pointed. "Couldn't the crew have moved the ship away at the first hint of trouble?"

"No. The events happened very quickly, sir. Plus, there were restraints. The ship was held in place by half a dozen anchors. It was attached to the riser. They would have had to close the blowout preventer before moving, which I told you might have been impossible from the first. And last but not least, there was no tug to pull the ship. The *Columbus* is a ship, but it has no engines. Due to drilling-space demands, engines were omitted in the design stage. When you want to move the *Columbus,* a seagoing tug provides power, and there were no seagoing tugs in position at the time."

Mary MacKenzie spoke. "Mr. Bruce. After the *Columbus* and tug were recovered, there were subsequent dives made to recover additional material. Correct?"

"Yes."

"What were the results?"

"You have our written statement."

"I'd like to hear it from you."

"We were missing four entire guide wires and both blowout preventer control hoses. In addition, the blowout preventer, guide frames, wellhead, and TV monitors were still on the bottom. We recovered most."

"What didn't you recover?"

"The guide wires. One entire control hose. The upper section of the other."

"Why?"

"Most likely they had fallen off the plateau where the wellhead was located and had sunk into the loch's deepest abyss."

She glanced at the exhibit table. "We seem to have everything but the recovered control hose."

"Mr. Whittenfeld will present it."

"You say the control hose was severed?"

"Yes."

"Did you see the control hose upon its recovery?"

"Only from a distance."

"Well, do you think the severance might have been caused by structural failure?"

"I don't know," he said. "I didn't get close enough to examine the hose. Nor did I get a chance to inspect it on shore. As I said, Mr. Whittenfeld took control."

"Has anyone examined the control hose other than Mr. Whittenfeld?"

"You'll have to ask Mr. Whittenfeld."

MacKenzie glanced at Droon, who formulated the next question.

"From your testimony, Mr. Bruce," Droon said, "you suggest the entire matter comes down to the severed control hose, correct?"

"I would say so."

"Assuming your analysis is correct, Mr. Bruce, could anything have been done to save the ship after the hose had been severed?"

"In my opinion, if both hoses were cut? No."

"And prior?"

"That's problematical. We don't know—or at least I don't know—why the hose broke, so I can't begin to even guess at preventive measures. And even if I knew, the real question is whether the crew knew there was trouble."

"Where were you while all this was occurring?"

"In a helicopter racing to the scene."

"What did you see when you arrived?"

"The *Columbus* and the tug going down. The water aerated. Fire. The riser sticking out of the water. The *Columbus* slid down the riser like a fireman on a firehouse pole."

"Did you ever think such a thing could happen?"

"No."

"What were the odds?"

"Gigantically long."

"You would have bet against it?"

"With my life."

"Yet it happened."

"Yes."

"So you are saying it's virtually impossible to ensure complete safety on your rigs."

"Now wait a minute. The *Columbus* was a safe ship. The chance such a sequence of events would ever happen again is remote. Until we know what happened to the hose, Mr. Droon, and why the ship went down, I think we should avoid conclusions."

"Mr. Bruce is right," Farquharson said, waving Droon to silence. "Does anyone have additional questions?"

Several committee members posed more questions, but they were inconsequential. When Scotty's testimony ended, Farquharson announced they would call the final witness, William Whittenfeld, after recess.

Scotty stood alone in the hall, staring through the windows. He'd wanted to say more. Based on Furst's assessment, he suspected the control hose hadn't broken by itself, nor had it been cut. But Whittenfeld alone had examined the material and had the results in hand, and as Whittenfeld had so clearly implied, there was to be no discussion about the blowout preventer control hose until Whittenfeld himself faced the tribunal.

Returning to the hearing room, Scotty took a front seat near the exhibit tables. Whittenfeld walked immediately to the witness stand. Prior to the first question, an exhibit was wheeled into the room: the recovered portion of the blowout control hose.

Looking extremely nervous once more, haggard, too, Whittenfeld fielded a barrage of preliminary questions, then moved to the exhibit. Describing how the exhibit had been analyzed, he then dropped the bombshell.

"I submit that the control hose was severed," he screamed, near frenzy. "And I submit the severance was caused by an oxy-arc torch, a work of sabotage. Yes! The sonar tug was steaming toward the *Columbus* to warn her. The tug had picked up the trace of a submersible in the loch, a submersible which cut the control hose and presumably the other hose and guide lines and pushed the riser, bending the drillpipe, setting off the sequence of events leading to the destruction of the drill ship!"

Shocked, the committee attempted to clarify the specifics. Whittenfeld was ready. He let the committee examine the hose and then read a report written by a prominent structural engineering firm based in London. According to the report the inference of sabotage was overwhelming.

"This is a grave accusation," Farquharson said, returning to his seat. "A ship has gone down. Men have died. Because of sabotage? May God help us!"

"Who could have done this?" the trade rep questioned.

"I don't know," Whittenfeld replied.

The gallery commotion grew.

"Can we run our own analyses?" the Home Office rep asked.

"Of course," Whittenfeld declared. "You can subject the material to any test you want. But I assure you, the result will be the same, and the decision of this committee will become patently obvious. It will allow Geminii to bring in a new drill ship and resume operations. It will allow us to institute the strictest security measures." He raised his voice, almost to a fury. "And it will recommend the Crown undertake a thorough investigation aimed at routing out the savages who killed so many good men!"

Droon suddenly leaned forward. "After the hose was recovered," he asked suspiciously, "what was done with it?"

"It was placed under lock and key in Aberdeen."

"Who examined it prior to the arrival of the structural team?"

"I did."

"Did anyone else get a close look at the exhibit other than you prior to the appearance of this structural team?"

"My aides—Pierre Lefebre and Brian Girard." He paused, swallowing heavily. "And the diver who recovered the hose from the loch floor."

Droon turned to Farquharson. "I would like the diver to testify."

"Who was the diver?" Farquharson asked.

Again, Whittenfeld swallowed heavily. "Messr. Furst," he replied.

Farquharson pointed to the committee's counsel. "Would you please subpoena the diver?"

"That will be impossible," Whittenfeld suddenly said.

"Why's that?"

"Furst and his diving mate Blasingame died two days ago during a compressed air dive in the Moray Firth."

Stunned again, the committee adjourned. The gallery left the hearing room. However, Scotty remained behind, seated in the first row of the gallery, trembling, trying desperately to contain the fury that was racing through his body. He hadn't really seen the control hose specimen after it had been brought to the surface. But he had heard Furst's appraisal several times. Christ, Furst was a pro. He wasn't prone to exaggeration or whimsy. The hose lying on the exhibit table could not have been the hose Furst had recovered. The hose on the table had clearly been oxy-arced and indented with tool-face imprints. Furst surely knew the difference.

Could a phony exhibit have been substituted for the real specimen? Could Furst have been murdered?

He didn't know, and he had no proof. He could only suspect. Suspect that something alive, powerful, and vindictive had chewed the hose, leading to the destruction of the *Columbus*. Suspect that someone, notably William Whittenfeld, had conspired to hide the truth.

The committee reassembled for public inquiry the next morning at ten. The entire staff of Geminii was present. After the committee interviewed Lefebre and Girard, who verified the authenticity of the hose specimen, they began to review relevant testimony. They were stopped by an unexpected development.

Receiving a note from counsel, Farquharson stood. "We seem to have a witness," he said, "who claims he personally helped destroy the *Columbus*." He looked to the rear of the room. "Would the clerk please usher Father James MacPherson into the room?"

The clerk opened the rear door. Father MacPherson moved to the witness docket. Scotty, who had spent the night lying in bed unable to sleep, going over the revelations and their implications, stared, dumbfounded. So did Mary MacKenzie and most of the other committee members and spectators.

"What is this about, father?" Farquharson asked, perplexed.

MacPherson raised his hands. "The manifestation of the

false prophet has been destroyed," he cried. "Sent down to hell from whence it came."

"What do you mean?" Droon asked.

"Mean?" the priest screamed, his mane flowing. "What do you think I mean? The drill ship was a manifestation of the son of Satan. And I, a soldier in God's army, did battle to destroy it!"

There was laughter. Confusion. Whispering.

"Could you be more specific?" Farquharson asked, caught up in the levity.

"Heathens!" MacPherson cried. "You all shall incur the wrath of the Lord."

"How did you destroy the ship?" Droon asked.

"By invoking the power of the Almighty!" MacPherson replied. "The Word of God came to me, entering my heart and mind. It said the vessel must be destroyed, for it carries the seed of Satan. And you are to lead the flock, my son. You are to gather the flock and pray for the ship's destruction. And I, the Lord, shall infuse thy prayer with my power, and thy prayer shall smite the wicked."

"Were you near the loch, father?" Mary MacKenzie asked, distraught.

"No," MacPherson replied, standing straight, eyes blazing. "But the Word of the Almighty empowered my prayers. It was His will that sent the ship to the bottom. Thank the Lord for it. The world will be the better. Now only the beast itself need next be destroyed."

Droon was furious. "Father. With all due respect to your position and the power of the Almighty. The sinking of the *Columbus* was a worldly disaster, either an accident or the intentional work of man. You cannot seriously claim your prayers destroyed it. Such declarations are appropriate for a Sunday school session, not a governmental inquiry."

Blood red, MacPherson stood on the chair, pointing at the panel. "You are the followers of the beast and the false prophet. You are the legion of the damned. You shall be destroyed, as was the drill ship, cast down into eternal hell to burn in sulfurous fires. How dare you deny the power of the Almighty. How dare you question His ascendancy." He contorted his face. "You have chosen to follow the devil, and you shall suffer the consequences. I destroyed the ship by invoking the Word of God. I shall destroy any other ship brought into the loch, any other manifestations of the false prophet.

I shall destroy the beast's followers who work for Geminii. And I shall destroy you. I carry the sword, the power of the Lord, and I ride behind the Rider, Faithful and True."

MacPherson's parishioners began to bang their chairs, screaming. MacPherson cried his defiance. Farquharson rapped his gavel, asking the orderlies to remove the priest from the room. MacPherson resisted.

"How dare you defy the Word of the Lord!" MacPherson bellowed, racing up and down the aisles, arms raised, eyes flared. "How dare you defile the truth! God Almighty has sent me here to lead you to salvation. Follow me. Forsake Satan. Applaud the destruction of the drill ship. Stand with me. Stand with Christ."

"Remove him, please," Farquharson ordered.

The orderlies grabbed the priest. The priest's followers attacked, crying the name of the Lord. The hearing room was reduced to chaos. Chairs were overturned; observers were pummeled to the floor; exhibits were damaged. And MacPherson stood amid it all, screaming defiance, invoking God's power.

Scotty watched in disbelief as MacPherson and his followers were finally subdued by MacGregor, MacKintosh, and several court officers.

"My God," Farquharson said after order had been restored. "Father. You cannot tell me the Lord would condone this behavior."

"The Lord condones the struggle against the beast," MacPherson cried, struggling.

"Father MacPherson," Mary MacKenzie pleaded, moving to the priest's side. "Please. For me. For God Almighty. This must stop!"

"You do not understand, my child!"

"I do, father. We will talk. But by disrupting this hearing, resorting to violence, you only serve the cause of the beast."

Father MacPherson stopped resisting and looked around. The cacophony of sounds died. Motion ceased. Everyone waited.

MacPherson walked to the door, turning, pointing at the panel. "I destroyed the drill ship. If any other manifestation of the son of the beast enters the loch, I shall send it to the bottom, too. This is the command of the Lord. This I shall do as his servant."

MacPherson defiantly walked out. Silence enveloped the

room. Farquharson asked Mary MacKenzie if the priest was
dangerous. She assured the panel he was not. If anything, he
was merely a crazed, overzealous cleric, harmless. However,
seated in the back of the room, William Whittenfeld did not
seem to share the opinion. Discomforted, expression blank,
anger barely concealed, his eyes focused on nothing, his stare
frozen.

Chapter 20

The day after the commission had adjourned, Whittenfeld
called another meeting of the senior staff and announced he
would be spending the following two weeks—while they were
waiting for the tribunal report—at company headquarters in
New York, planning for the expected resumption of operations. He briefly reviewed responsibilities and duties to be
undertaken by the staff in the interim, and, satisfied his operating orders were understood, left Scotty Bruce in command
while investing Pierre Lefebre with veto power over most
nontechnical decisions.

After the meeting, Whittenfeld explained the rationale behind his orders to Scotty in private—there were enemies
everywhere, and it was essential that Lefebre be left with
significant latitude and control. Scotty objected, but when
Whittenfeld refused to budge, Scotty decided not to press
Whittenfeld into an explosive response. He also decided not
to confront the man, who was still visibly on edge, about the
control hose section. Christ, only a lunatic would think that
Whittenfeld would admit to subterfuge and murder, assuming
those acts had actually been committed.

Frustrated, he almost quit his job but stopped himself. Hell,
he'd quit the NFL only to leave others behind to wage the
battle. And he'd vowed after that experience never to quit a

difficult situation again, a decision that had propelled him into countless entanglements and had kept him involved long enough in each to have tasted success or pink-slip failure.

No, he would stick this out, especially with the specter of the *Phoenix* incident staring him right in the eye, reminding him that Max Furst might well have been wrong about the hose and that Furst's death might have been an accident, after all.

The *Phoenix* incident had been the final straw, the fatal crusade that had gotten him booted out of his last job and into private consultancy. The *Phoenix* was a drill ship. At the time of the incident, it was stationed off the coast of northern California in a highly controversial lease territory. Shortly after he took command, a senior company manager, who was involved in the *Phoenix* program, died in a suspicious car accident. A short time later, Scotty was approached by a group of environmentalists who claimed the executive had been murdered after discovering falsifications in the company's original environmental impact reports. The environmentalists claimed the company had hidden information that not only projected the possibility of a major environmental catastrophe but also the inevitability of a dangerous accident aboard the drill ship due to unstable underlying gaseous formations. Convinced of the plot's authenticity by intracompany memos obtained by the environmentalists, he led a rebellion. The drill ship was shut down, and the state of California began an investigation, which ended in disaster. The memos were discredited, discovered to have been forged. The death of the executive was conclusively shown to have been an accident. And he was shown to have once again followed his wild instincts, thereby causing the loss of millions of dollars.

That Geminii had hired him after the *Phoenix* incident had never ceased to amaze him. He could not let the current affair become another *Phoenix*. No, if he was going to make noise, it would have to be with a gun loaded with bullets, not blanks.

Whittenfeld left Inverness. He remained behind, determined to avoid a fruitless, meaningless confrontation with the Frenchman while preparing for subsequent operations at Black Isle and Highland B.

Three days after Whittenfeld's departure, however, Highland B turned up dry and was plugged and abandoned. He ordered a new hole spudded a short distance away from the

first, concluding they had missed the prime producing interval
due to a freak twist of geological chance. The Black Isle hole,
on the other hand, hit pay dirt several days later—some good
news for a change—and he immediately authorized a program
of delineation.

Apart from the actual business, though, he attempted to
find ammunition for the gun. Furst and Blasingame were the
point of departure. A week after Whittenfeld had left Inverness, he drove to the dive base at Lossiemouth where the
fatal accident had occurred. Department of Energy investigators had already arrived. Joining the interrogation team, he
spoke to the diving rig's senior staff and to its diver tenders,
pinpointing the cause of the disaster. Someone had placed a
welding machine near the divers' air compressors. Unfortunately, before anyone had noticed there was trouble below,
the two divers had absorbed a fatal amount of carbon mon-
oxide.

Along with the Energy staff, he then questioned the welders
and work crew. The effort was fruitless. In fact, based on
these interrogations, the absence of strangers on board the
barge, and any apparent motive, he was convinced there
might never be any actual proof that the deaths had been
effected intentionally. He was also convinced the Energy
interrogators would make a finding of accidental death.

On the other hand, there might very well have been a motive, though he was the only one who suspected its existence.
If a phony hose had been substituted for the real one, there
would have been good reason to eliminate the divers, one of
whom could positively identify a forgery.

The possible disappearance of the original blowout preventer control hose remained the key.

He couldn't ask Lefebre to provide particulars, and he
doubted whether any of Lefebre's employees would prove to
be loose tongued.

He realized he would have to follow the trail himself.

By questioning Aberdeen base guards and other peripheral
personnel, he discovered the original hose segment had been
placed in a guarded storage area in the company's Aberdeen
compound. He was also able to determine that Whittenfeld
and Lefebre had visited the spot on numerous occasions alone
or together. But he could find no one who had seen the
original control hose section removed, nor the new hose

rought to the site. And inquiries into the reputation and
ackground of the London-based company that had inspected
ie phony hose bundle had been unproductive; their reputa-
on was immaculate, their honesty unquestioned.

Two conclusions were unavoidable. First, if a hose switch
ad taken place, it had taken place in secret and had been
arried out in Aberdeen by Whittenfeld or Lefebre or men
orking under their supervision. Second, he had absolutely no
roof of anything.

The two-week interim period drew to a close without any
dditional discoveries or insights. Tony Spinelli called him
Ionday night and informed him that Whittenfeld had re-
irned to Inverness. He accepted the news stoically. Based on
ie evidence presented, he expected a favorable decision by
ie tribunal. He was sure he knew exactly how Whittenfeld
ould react.

He also suspected how he would proceed as well.

Scotty sipped from a cup of coffee, feet up on the desk, an
nlit cigar in his mouth. His office was stone-cold silent.

According to Jerry Foster, who had called earlier, the
olumbus inquiry report was to be delivered precisely at
oon. Until then, he had nothing to do but prepare for his
rst contact with Whittenfeld since Whittenfeld's departure
r New York.

The buzz of the intercom interrupted his thoughts. Jerry
oster was outside. He shouted an invite, and Foster entered.

"Whittenfeld here?" Scotty asked.

"Yes. He just arrived. As did a representative of the
ibunal."

"What's the word?"

"Don't know."

"What if they stop operations?"

"We'll appeal."

"To whom?"

"You're asking the wrong guy. Legal procedures aren't my
ecialty."

"Then what is?"

"Drilling holes."

"True. But I also hear you've become an amateur detec-
ve."

"Now who told you that?"

"Hey, Scotty. The investigation is over."

"I'm aware of that."

"Then the Q and A sessions should be over, too."

"Sometimes I wonder about you, Foster. Are you the com
pany protocol adviser? The guidance officer for the wo
force?"

"No. I'm your friend."

"Maybe."

"I also know what sets Whittenfeld off. Snooping and que
tions drive him up a wall."

"Is that so? Well, then. Maybe it's time someone started
do a little driving around here."

"What do you mean?"

"Just what I said." Scotty knew he should keep his mou
shut, but he needed to explode. "Whittenfeld isn't God. N
is he the president and chairman of the company. He's ju
the project manager. When he's wrong, he should be que
tioned. When he adamantly rejects correct advice, he shou
be fought. When he's out of control, acting against the com
pany's best interests, he should be stopped."

"Has he been doing any of those things?"

"Maybe."

"Barrett had similar ideas about fighting. He clashed wi
Whittenfeld over Lefebre. Look what happened to him."

"Barrett had a heart attack."

"And it looks like you're working your way to one you
self." He paused, staring. "Scotty, what are you looking fo
Why the questions?"

"That's my business."

The intercom buzzed, and Scotty flipped the interco
switch. The secretary notified him Whittenfeld's secretary ha
called, asking Scotty to proceed to Whittenfeld's office
once.

"I appreciate your advice," Scotty said, moving to the doc
"I'm sure it's been offered honestly. But, Foster, I can ta
care of myself."

Foster stared. "I hope so," he said.

William Whittenfeld walked ebulliently around the jamm
conference table, waving the investigation commission's
port, then turned the pages to Part II, FINDINGS AN
RECOMMENDATIONS, and read the final section aloud:

Foreword. In accordance with enabling legisla-
tion and the recommendation of the prime minister,
an Interdepartmental Committee of Inquiry was
established to investigate the loss of the drill ship
Columbus and the sonar tug *Excalibur*. The following are the findings and recommendations relevant
to facts presented in Part I, said facts established
during public inquiry. The initial investigations were
overseen by Geminii Petroleum International and the
Petroleum Inspectorate of the Department of En-
energy.

1. FINDINGS

1.1 The catastrophic events aboard the *Columbus*
occurred after a kick and the completion of a subsequent kill operation.

1.2 The immediate cause of the disaster was a gas
blowout, the gas aerating the water beneath the
drill ship, causing loss of stability and buoyancy, the
vessel eventually sinking.

1.3 The tug *Excalibur* was captured by the gas
blowout funnel and sunk as well.

1.4 The blowout was eventuated by the bending of
the *Columbus*'s drill pipe, the cessation of mud circulation, and the loss of overburden pressure.

1.5 The blowout preventer was rendered inoperative by the severance of the subsurface control
hoses.

1.6 The available control hose was severed by an
oxy-arc cutting device, manipulated by and subject
to human control.

1.7 A finding of sabotage is unanimously supported.

1.8 The committee accumulated no findings relevant to the assignment of felonious culpability.

2. RECOMMENDATIONS

2.1 Upon compliance with existing regulations, Geminii Petroleum International shall be allowed to introduce a new drill ship to Loch Ness.

2.2 Said drill ship shall be allowed to reattach to the existing wellhead and to proceed with drilling operations.

2.3 Geminii Petroleum shall be required to institute strict security procedures to protect her floating installations, procedural guidelines to be established by Geminii Petroleum under the guidance of the Ministry of Defence, United Kingdom.

2.4 The committee recommends the immediate inception of criminal investigations by local police authorities and any and all national police organizations who possess jurisdiction pursuant to relevant parliamentary statutes.

The men around the conference table clapped enthusia tically; Scotty's participation, however, was restrained.

Whittenfeld dropped the report on the table. "Scotty?" asked, singling out the district supervisor, "is anythi wrong?"

"No," Scotty protested as diplomatically as possible. think the results are excellent."

Whittenfeld clapped his hands. "Better than excellent. A there's more. Just prior to your entering the room, I spoke New York. The *Columbus*'s sister drill ship, the *Magella* is on its way. We're back in business."

Whittenfeld seemed legitimately convinced of it. His e pression exuded life. His eyes danced with excited expect tion. A seductive smile lay on his lips. His entire manner ha returned to normal—his look, voice, temperament. There been a rebirth. And "Mr. Bruce" was now "Scotty" on more.

"How soon will it arrive?" Scotty asked, aware of t transformation.

"Soon enough," Whittenfeld said. "You're to begin pre

arations immediately!" He glanced down the table. "Spinelli!"
Spinelli looked up. "You're out on the *Magellan*. We'll find
someone to take over your duties on shore. The *Magellan*
comes first, and I want my best men on it." He looked to
Lefebre, seated away from the table. "Mr. Lefebre. You are
immediately to contact the Ministry of Defence and establish and coordinate new security procedures. You are also to
liaison with the local police, and you are to attend every one
of our management meetings. Security is now top priority!"
Lefebre didn't respond, remaining silent. "And Foster. I want
press releases issued over my signature congratulating the
tribunal, thanking everyone involved, predicting future suc-
cesses, and noting our new security awareness. I want this
goddamn place back in gear."

"Is it safe to put out another ship?" Scotty asked.

"We'll make it safe!" Whittenfeld said. "You will help
make it safe. Everyone in this room and on this base will help
make it safe."

"Absolutely," Scotty said, struggling to agree.

John Fallworth called from London. Whittenfeld placed
Fallworth on the speaker box so everyone in the room could
hear. Fallworth offered his congratulations and challenged
the staff to a renewed effort—it was a good company pep talk.

Whittenfeld returned to business, then dismissed everyone
except Scotty.

"You don't seem enthusiastic or joyous, Scotty," Whittenfeld declared as he sat behind his desk. "I want you to welcome the future."

"I'm very conservative," Scotty replied. "I remember the
past too well, and I'm afraid of the danger up ahead."

"That is why I like you as much as I do. That is why I
trust you. Regard you so highly. You care. You're concerned.
You are a very valuable man. I doubt we could function without you. But you're being overly cautious, and there's no
need to be. I promise, saboteurs will not reach the *Magellan*.
We will be ready. I also promise you we will identify the men
who attacked the ship and killed its crew. We will exact revenge. I give you that commitment. In return, I want yours.
I want you to steam ahead. Refrain from looking back. I
want your emotion. I want you to help us reach the wealth
below the loch. I want you to help reach 'my child.'"

Scotty was sickened. Whittenfeld's approach, the way he
formed ideas, was now so obviously contrived, so self-serving.

He would have to do all he could to prevent himself from throwing up.

Whittenfeld apologized for his recent behavior; the terrible truth had demanded secrecy while frazzling his nerves; Scotty accepted the apology, knowing otherwise.

"Could I see the report?" he asked.

Whittenfeld handed over the manuscript. He read. Part I contained the gist of the public findings. Part II was as announced. Part III had gone unnoted. It was the minority report, written by Droon and MacKenzie. In general, it accepted the committee's findings but violently objected to its recommendations. Droon and MacKenzie critically opposed allowing Geminii's return to the loch. The new drill ship would be in danger. No matter the cause of a future disaster, the results would be the same. There were also reasons to doubt the evidence presented at the tribunal. They questioned the curious deaths of the two divers and Whittenfeld's handling of the most crucial piece of evidence: the blowout preventer control hose.

He gave the report back to Whittenfeld and announced he was ready to proceed full blast. Satisfied, Whittenfeld advised he was heading home.

"I want to see you here tomorrow morning," Whittenfeld concluded, "raring to go!"

Whittenfeld smiled. Scotty did not.

"Ay, Mr. Bruce," Detective Superintendent Angus Mac-Gregor trumpeted as he walked back and forth behind his desk like a moving metronome. "This is a sad day for Scotland. For the Scots. For Geminii. For all of us."

"Yes," Scotty said.

"Mr. Bruce, I asked you to come here because I'm going to need your cooperation, because my job and the job of the Special Branch is not going to be easy. We have no leads. No clues. Oh, yes, we do have some slithery radical groups in the region, as I've mentioned before, and we will be grilling them like a piece of haggis, but I'm sure you can well imagine that we're going to have our work cut out for us without more specific directions."

"What about the Jacobites?"

"They're about. Purring like garden cats. Right proper little angels."

"I take it you've spoken to Sutherland."

"Of course. We interrogated him before the tribunal proceedings, and I've also spoken to him since. No, I've got a good bead on Sutherland, and he is a right proper Scottish radical with all the standard prejudices and hatreds. But I can find no link between Sutherland, his New Jacobites, and the *Columbus* disaster. And as I'm sure you're no doubt aware, in this society, we cannot incarcerate people for their thoughts or speeches. Though, of course, we can watch them carefully."

"You'll be watching Sutherland?"

"We and the Special Branch will be watching everyone who deserves watching, including Sutherland and his Jacobite friends. This is where you come in. Once you begin operations again, I want you to watch, also. I want you to keep an eye open and let me know if something—anything—out of the way occurs. Even little things—"

"Such as?"

"Suspicious occurrences. Conversations. The like."

"I will do anything I can to help you."

MacGregor pounded his fist on the desk. "Now you are a man I can count on." He walked around the desk and sat in the seat next to Scotty. "Before I let you go, I want to ask you something about the tribunal proceedings, specifically your reaction to Mr. Whittenfeld's testimony."

"What do you mean?"

"I was watching you carefully while Mr. Whittenfeld was speaking. I watched your face when he announced his findings and conclusions. You did not look pleased."

Careful, he thought. The *Phoenix!*

"I was disturbed."

"I seemed to see something else. Anger. Disagreement. Disapproval. All of those things. Did I read you right?"

"No."

"You weren't angered? You didn't disagree? You didn't disapprove?"

Scotty stood. *"No* to all of those things. I was disturbed. That's it. That's all."

MacGregor stood, too. "Thank you, Mr. Bruce," he said abruptly. "I appreciate your time and consideration."

"Anytime," was Scotty's reply.

Scotty closed the front door of the Carn Dearg Inn. The reception parlor was deserted. He pounded the desk bell. Mary MacKenzie appeared.

"Hello," he said.

She smiled. "That's right quick of you."

"I had the accelerator pressed to the floor."

"You didn't have to call first. You could have just stopped in."

"It's not proper."

"I did it to you. You had one coming in return to me."

"I guess we can talk now, be seen together. Even though your minority opinion poked at every one of us at Geminii."

She breathed deeply. "I guess we can."

She led him into a lounge, a lovely little room with comfortable furnishings. He looked at his watch. It was eleven-thirty. She must have just closed the pub.

"Where's your niece?" he asked.

"Staying with friends," she replied.

"You mean we're alone?"

She glanced at the picture on the wall. "Not quite. My father is watching us."

He looked at the picture, too. MacKenzie's father was wearing a kilt, bonnet, kilt jacket, and sporran.

"Handsome man," he said.

"He was."

"I like his kilt. His sporran, too. I have a particular thing for sporrans. Mrs. Munro, my houselady, made one for me, though she was disappointed I didn't have a kilt to wear with it."

"Do you have one now?"

"No. I can't bring myself to get one. I guess I don't feel like the kilt type."

"You'd look good in one."

"I can't see it," he said, shrugging, touching her hand. "You know, I have an admission to make."

"What?"

"It wasn't easy to sit in front of you during the inquiry."

"Well, it was kind of uncomfortable for me, too."

"I don't mean the question and answer part. I mean the emotional part. I wanted to reach out and put my arms around you. I want to now."

She blushed. "I'm still torn between where I sit with you. There are conflicting feelings. Conflicting thoughts."

He kissed her gently. "I have none. You shouldn't, either."

She touched his lips with her hand. "We're just two people? Plain and simple?"

"Yes."

"But that's not true. That's not the way it is. There are things between the strong emotions."

"Then you admit it. There are strong emotions?"

"Yes."

He kissed her again. Once more she resisted, fought herself. Then she submitted. She put her arms around him, holding him tight. Touching her skin, he kissed her neck, her face, her lips, pulling tighter and tighter.

And suddenly the conflict was gone.

The morning sun held little warmth. The sky was clear. He stood in the open field, pummeled by a frigid wind. The skin on his face was cold; he'd shaved the beard off the night before. Scores of gravestones lay before him, the final resting place of the *Columbus*'s crew. Some of the gravestones were marked. Robert Warren Reddington's was specifically drawn.

ROBERT WARREN REDDINGTON . . . PETROLEUM ENGINEER . . . FATHER . . . HUSBAND . . .

HUMAN BEING.

A wreath of flowers sent by Reddington's children lay on the ground.

The memory of the *Phoenix* rattled through his mind once more. He could not allow another *Phoenix* incident to occur. One more screw-up, one more self-induced eruption over any scheme, let alone an imaginary one, and he'd be through. On the other hand, he could not let a real danger perpetuate itself right before his eyes.

Was he imagining all of this? The hose? The nature of Furst's death? Maybe. Maybe not. But he would have to find out, especially since the lives of the crew of the new drill ship might well hang in the balance.

If ever there was a reason to investigate a horror, this was it.

What had Whittenfeld said? He was a gunfighter who had put away his guns for good. Yes, that's how Whittenfeld had phrased it. Very clever.

But Whittenfeld had also told him to keep the guns ready. Invited him to take them out of mothballs if the need arose.

The need might very well have arisen.

All he needed was proof.

Part III

≈≈≈≈≈

THE
MAGELLAN

Chapter 21

The driller pushed the control levers. The *Magellan*'s engines roared. The rotary table began to turn.

Isolated on the drill ship's forward helipad, Peter "Scotty" Bruce listened to the sounds while shielding his eyes from reflected sunlight. The loch was covered with small craft, packed with spectators. There were a dozen crowded company vessels, and the road around Urquhart Bay was jammed with cars.

Scotty positioned himself on the helipad staircase. The engine noises suddenly ceased; the machinery had only been activated briefly for public display. Because of safety and legal requirements, actual operation would wait until all non-certified persons had been removed from the ship.

He could clearly hear Whittenfeld's voice. The project manager was situated on the drill floor, surrounded by dignitaries from the Scottish Office, the Highland Council, the Department of Energy, the Northern Constabulary, and the Ministry of Defence. There were also several shadowy figures who had accompanied the defense specialists and who were reputed to be members of MI5. Fortunately, though, the defense and secret service operatives were scheduled to depart as soon as the ceremonies had been completed.

The constabulary contingent, however, would remain, pursuing its investigation. Although squads of detectives had fanned throughout the region, the constabulary had uncovered no leads. He was convinced Geminii would be inundated with police operatives for the foreseeable future. He also suspected their investigation would be a total waste of time.

He searched for familiar faces. Bill Nunn and Mike Grabowski were both present, having assumed their normal duties. Tony Spinelli was there, too, having replaced Bob Reddington.

And, of course, Jerry Foster was aboard, scooting about like a roadrunner.

He marked the absentees. Undersecretary Farquharson, who had been scheduled to attend, had conveniently begged off, ostensibly bedded by the flu. Peter Droon and Mary Mac-Kenzie weren't there, either. He couldn't speak for Droon, but he knew MacKenzie had declined the company's invitation, determined not to impart the slightest suggestion of approval to the *Magellan*.

There was another familiar face, too: Malcolm Abercrombie, the reinstated local representative of the Transport and General Workers Union. However, it was not Abercrombie's presence but Hugh Sutherland's absence that augured trouble. Relieved of official duties because of his New Jacobite connections, Sutherland had refused to recede into oblivion. Rather, he'd been waiting in the wings, quietly counseling unemployed local oil workers.

Listening to the pop of champagne corks—the strict alcohol taboos had been suspended for the occasion—he noted he'd almost forgotten the most significant celebrant of them all, Pierre Lefebre, who was standing alongside the drill floor. The ship was brimming with security guards; the base itself had become an armed camp. And Lefebre had been given control of a vast assortment of intricate ordnance, supplied by the Ministry of Defence, the most notable being Dover class, tube-launched, heat-seeking torpedoes and fathom-rated depth charges, both under the supervision of defense personnel, permanently assigned to the drill ship.

The inclusion of the depth charges intrigued him. Only if a non-heat-producing target was sighted would they be preferable to the torpedoes. The Ministry of Defence had argued against their deployment. Whittenfeld had countered, demanding maximum potentialities. Whittenfeld had won the joust, won it without revealing the precise reasons for the requisition.

Other than Whittenfeld and Lefebre, he, alone, knew them.

He turned the binoculars on the tower of Urquhart Castle. He could see Father James MacPherson's angry face. Mac-Pherson, who had occupied the ruin along with his parishioners at the inception of shipboard ceremonies, had conducted a ritual mass, damning the false prophet, the beast, and their various manifestations, all under the scrutiny of constabulary police and Geminii security guards.

It was all very peculiar. Almost comical. A circus. Frightening.

He glanced around.

Three new sonar tugs were on line, under the command of Capt. Eamonn Harrigan, a retired Royal Navy antisubmarine specialist with unblemished credentials. Each tug was assigned to a sector and equipped with far more sophisticated equipment than Captain Olafsen's tug had been, including high-frequency, short-range Sectascan sonar, 3-D display stacked profile plot systems, and advanced acoustic imaging hologram units.

Sonic listening devices had also been imbedded beneath the *Magellan* on the loch floor. There were two surveillance helicopters permanently berthed just beyond the shore of Urquhart Bay in a newly built security installation, and loch shore security itself had been augmented with additional guards and special surveillance teams at each intersect point on the Caledonian Canal, preventing any transglen barge or work ship from carrying a submersible into the loch.

In fact, Scotty couldn't imagine anyone getting anything into the loch undetected anymore, except perhaps if delivery were made by a helicopter or airplane, and even that contingency had been blunted by the presence of the security choppers and their radar tie-ins.

Geminii was ready for almost anything.

He descended into the moon pool. There was no one about. He could hear the laughter and noise above. He could see the marine riser ahead. He watched the loch water lick against the riser's shell, then sat on the moon pool railing and stared. It had been three weeks since the *Columbus* tribunal report had been issued. He'd made no progress toward finding hard proof to support his suspicions, nor did he have any fresh insights concerning a new direction in which to proceed. Yet he did have a haunting fear, a fear that if there were to be a breakthrough, it would be provided by a new attack on the drill ship. The terror dream had kept him awake, sleepless through many long nights.

He expected it would continue to do so.

Shortly before six, Scotty returned to Travis House. A van was parked in front of the main gate; a man and woman stood alongside. The man was holding a small black suitcase.

Scotty walked toward the front gate.

"Mr. Bruce?" the man asked with a heavy New York accent.

"Yes," Scotty replied.

The man was thin, studious in appearance, balding. "Could we possibly have a word with you?" he asked.

"About what?"

"Your cooperation," the woman said.

The man smiled aggressively. "My name is Dr. Allen Rubinstein. This is my associate, Dr. Janice Fiammengo."

Scotty bowed. "You want my cooperation?"

"And your help."

"To do what?"

"To save the *Magellan!*"

Scotty had already started to ease toward the mansion's door; Dr. Rubinstein's statement stopped him in his tracks.

"What do you mean?" he asked.

Dr. Rubinstein removed his bifocals and placed them in his pocket. "Mr. Bruce, unless we can secure your cooperation, the *Magellan* will be destroyed just like the *Columbus*. It'll be sent to the bottom of the loch and all its crewmen will die."

"What makes you think—?"

"I don't think! I *know*."

Scotty stared at Dr. Rubinstein, then Dr. Fiammengo. "Haven't I seen you before, Dr. Rubinstein?"

"Perhaps," Dr. Rubinstein said. "If you had scanned the gallery at the *Columbus* hearings. I was there. At first, just a curious spectator. But then a very concerned one."

"And what inspired this miraculous transformation?"

Dr. Rubinstein could barely hide his excitement. "A long conversation with Max Furst."

Scotty's interest intensified. "When did this take place?"

"Several days before he died."

Scotty turned to the woman. "Were you at the hearings, too?"

Dr. Fiammengo parted her lips. Tall, dark-haired, dark complected, she was regally built with long arms and legs and had very sensual bohemian features, though her tortoise-shell eyeglasses gave her a studious appearance. "No," she said, bearing the remnants of a Georgia twang, "but I arrived soon after the hearings had adjourned."

"Dr. Fiammengo invariably accompanies me in my work," Dr. Rubinstein added.

"What work is that?" Scotty asked.

"I represent a privately funded scientific research organization." He handed Scotty a business card. "The Phenomena Research Institute."

Scotty turned from a gust of biting wind. "Did Furst say anything interesting?"

"Mr. Furst was a very intelligent and curious man," Dr. Rubinstein remarked. "He said many valuable things. But it's what he showed me that impressed me most."

"What was that?"

Dr. Rubinstein looked around, almost as if he feared they were under surveillance. "Could you possibly invite us inside? I think you'd like to hear what we have to say in private."

Scotty stared at the woman; she was shivering. His own hands were trembling slightly, too. What the hell had Max Furst shown them?

"Yes," he said, pointing toward the house. "Please."

The man and woman thanked him, then followed him through the mansion's front door.

Mrs. Munro placed a tray of coffee and cakes on the coffee table, then handed out cups. "I don't think I ever heard such a collection of accents in my life," she said. "You Americans have really butchered the language if you ask me."

Scotty poured coffee for his guests. "We're not asking you, Mrs. Munro."

"I'd bet you're not," she said indignantly, "because you're the worst of the lot, Mr. Bruce. It's only by the Lord's grace and kindness that I can even understand you. You and that California garble of yours. Let me tell you, you should only speak as well as this gentleman here!"

Dr. Rubinstein laughed; his feet were straddled over the black suitcase. "That's the first time I've ever heard a New York accent complimented over a Californian."

"Well, you're hearing it," Mrs. Munro declared. "Mr. Bruce hardly even speaks the Queen's English."

Scotty shook his head; he doubted whether Mrs. Munro would ever change. And, in a funny way, he was glad for it. As persistently aggravating as she could be, he'd grown quite used to her. In fact, if pressed, he would have had to admit he'd even come to like her. But there were times she was better being neither seen nor heard. Certainly this was one of them.

"Thank you, Mrs. Munro," he said. "Please close the door on your way out."

Mrs. Munro stood straight up, her chin held high.

"Thank you, Mrs. Munro," he repeated.

"You're welcome, Mr. Bruce," she replied, finally leaving the room and shutting the door.

Scotty waited, assuring himself Mrs. Munro was gone. Then he turned to Dr. Rubinstein. "Tell me about Max Furst."

"First, let me tell you about us."

"You're a phenomena researcher. Which means you're interested in the Loch Ness monster."

"There are other phenomena in the world."

"Not around here."

Dr. Rubinstein laughed between chews at his nails; he was a nervous little man, the type who could rarely sit still or relax. "We stand exposed," he said. "But there are many people interested in the Loch Ness monster, though there are few with sufficient credentials to appreciate it or to engage in any kind of properly designed scientific study."

"But you are."

"Dr. Fiammengo is an experienced scientist," Dr. Rubinstein declared. "She has undergraduate degrees in zoology from Columbia University and graduate degrees in paleontology and anthropology from Harvard. I did my undergraduate work in electrical engineering and postgraduate studies in physics and marine biology. I am also currently on the faculty of M.I.T. and have been in charge of NASA's hyperbaric experimental program for the last five years. And, of course, I lead the Phenomena Research Institute." He indicated the card in Scotty's hand. "The institute itself undertakes many diverse investigations. The Loch Ness monster being one. We're particularly equipped for a study of the monster. worked with the Academy of Applied Sciences. I also directed two of our own research expeditions."

Scotty unwrapped a cigar and lifted it to his mouth. "What were the results?"

"They were unrewarding, though we did work with some very experienced and talented people like Max Furst."

"What did Furst do for you?"

"He set cameras, probes, underwater sensors, the like."

"And he asked you to come to Inverness after the recovery operation?"

"No. We were prepared to make the trip, anyhow. This *Columbus* thing was very intriguing, very exciting. The possibilities and ramifications were enormous."

Scotty glanced at Dr. Fiammengo again. "You thought a monster bore some of the responsibility for the loss of the ship?"

Dr. Fiammengo smiled, baring perfect teeth and a pair of attractive dimples. "Yes. And now we're convinced of it."

"What did Max Furst tell you?"

Dr. Rubinstein stood. "He said the ship's blowout preventer control hose had been torn apart. Chewed, if you will. Chewed by something alive, something very strong. He also said the hose had been seized by Whittenfeld and no one had seen it since recovery. He suggested I monitor the hearings because the revelations could be very startling. Of course, they were. Max Furst was very possibly eliminated, and Whittenfeld unveiled a preventer hose which was certainly not the hose Max Furst had recovered. Isn't that right, Mr. Bruce?"

"I have no way of knowing."

"But you suspect that to be the case."

Scotty didn't reply.

Dr. Fiammengo smiled. "We *know* that to be the case."

"How?"

Dr. Rubinstein paced in front of his host. "Max Furst took pictures of the chewed hose with a small, revolutionary, handheld camera." He puffed his chest proudly. "A camera I designed."

Scotty felt a surge of excitement. "Do you have those pictures?"

Dr. Rubinstein smirked. "We didn't come here just to titilate you!" He opened the suitcase and removed several pictures, handing them over. "You should find these interesting."

Scotty carefully examined the prints. They seemed genuine, and the pictured hose had been masticated like a stalk of licorice. However, he cautioned himself that the prints could have been fraudulently prepared.

"Impressed, Mr. Bruce?" Dr. Fiammengo asked.

"Yes," Scotty replied.

"Good," Dr. Rubinstein announced, patting his thighs. "Now we're getting somewhere."

"What do you think could have done this?" Scotty asked.

"Something big and strong enough," Dr. Fiammengo answered, "to have moved the marine riser and the drill ship.

Dr. Rubinstein reached back into the suitcase and pulle out an object covered by a cloth. "Mr. Furst gave us anothe bit of material which he was able to secretly recover fro the loch floor and smuggle ashore." He removed the clot Beneath was a two-foot-long section of ship's hull, dented b a row of incisions. "This was part of the *Columbus*'s hull. was found by Furst, lying in the debris."

"What are the holes?"

Dr. Rubinstein brought his nails to his mouth, his eyes e: citedly dancing in his skull. "Teeth marks, Mr. Bruce!"

Stunned, Scotty just stared, then shook his head. "How ca you be sure?"

"We carefully analyzed them and matched the measur ments against paleontological controls. The results have le no question. In addition, we found particles of living tiss embedded in the sharp edges of the metal. We analyzed then too. They're mucous tissue. From gums."

Dr. Fiammengo interceded. "Of course, the mucous tiss is highly specialized. It belongs to a highly evolved, ancie animal, and as we expected, the tissue does not fall with any one categorizable group of species, though it seems re tilian in derivation."

Scotty digested the information. "What kind of reptile cou it be?" he asked.

"We're not sure," she said. "There are several possibilitie but it would take some time to cover them all."

"Which we can do later," Dr. Rubinstein declared, inte rupting. "Just be assured this thing is ancient. Unknown as this moment on the face of the earth. And quite big."

"How big?"

"One hundred feet. One hundred twenty-five. About there

Scotty remembered the tug tracings, the dimensions r corded. "It seems impossible."

"On the contrary. Blue whales reach enormous dimension Sometimes eighty feet in length. And then, of course, the are the giant squid."

"A Jules Verne fantasy."

"They exist, Mr. Bruce!"

"Of course. I've even seen some. Up to thirty or forty fe long."

Dr. Rubinstein corrected him. "The attack-class submari

Montauk was cruising the Mindinao Depths shortly before the Battle of the Coral Sea. The captain lost directional control and stability. He surfaced the sub. The crew found a giant squid wrapped about the sub's superstructure. The crew had to fight the thing hand to hand. Six men were lost. The squid's body itself measured almost seventy feet. But from the end of the largest tentacle to the nose, the squid stretched the entire length of the sub, over two hundred feet. Want more? A South African trawler, the *Transvaal*, went down in a typhoon in the Indian Ocean in 1951. Two lifeboats were floated. Shortly after the lifeboats had entered the water, a giant squid rose up from the depths and destroyed one of them. The survivors in the other boat witnessed the tragedy. The lifeboats were forty feet long. The survivors testified the squid's body had dwarfed the ill-fated lifeboat by at least three boat lengths."

"So much for size," Dr. Fiammengo said. "Because size is not in question. There are ample examples among currently accepted marine species to support spectacular dimensions. Only a *what* is in question."

Scotty thought for a moment. "You said Furst smuggled the chewed hull piece ashore?"

"Yes," Dr. Rubinstein said.

"Why?"

"Max Furst had an acute interest in the Loch Ness phenomena. He knew we did, too, and he wished to supply us with the material because he considered it so incriminating. He did it secretly because he was convinced others would not share his enthusiasm, particularly the management at Geminii. Subsequent events, of course, seem to have proven him correct.

"I have some problems with all this," Scotty said, sitting forward. "This thing has been talked about for years, spotted for years. It hasn't lived forever, has it?"

"Of course not," Dr. Fiammengo declared. "But we believe the continuous sightings suggest a simple conclusion. There is more than one, or at least there has been more than one, and there has certainly been a lineage."

"Then why isn't the bottom of the loch littered with bones?"

Dr. Rubinstein explained. "Many species do not die where they spawn. We believe the loch is the creature's spawning ground. The site where the young are born and nurtured, which would explain reported discrepancies in size. We also believe the animals live and die elsewhere, the Arctic Sea, to be exact."

"How the hell do they get from here to there?"

Dr. Rubinstein jabbed at the air. "They swim. And we believe they have a means to navigate from the loch to the sea, and vice versa."

"The loch has no tides. It isn't connected to the sea."

"We disagree. We believe there is a connecting cavern, much of it above sea level. We believe there's an entrance somewhere in the loch walls and that the cavern rises up beneath the surrounding mountains, heads toward the sea, then descends again."

"Do you have proof?"

"No."

"Then how can you be so sure?"

Dr. Rubinstein looked at his associate, who wetted her lips. "Simple," he said.

"Logic," she declared. "A cavern is the only conceivable way an animal could get in and out!"

Scotty broke into an amused grin. "Let's apply logic across the board, doctor. This creature has always been shy and harmless. Why did it attack the ship when it has never attacked anything in the past?"

Dr. Rubinstein smiled confidently. "It's become aggressive because Geminii Petroleum has introduced an object the creature, or no creature before it, has ever experienced: drill ship, equipped with a drill, which grinds irritatingly right into the floor of the loch."

"You think the drill vibration has attracted this thing?"

"Yes. And angered it. And these conclusions are supported by history. First, as I'm sure you're aware, the last major incidence of sightings occurred in 1933 when a road was blasted around the loch. Certainly, the dynamite explosions and vibrations might have awakened our quiet friend. And secondly, as a petroleum engineer, you're well aware that the drilling vibration attracts fish by the millions. I've even had chance to study the phenomena in the Gulf of Mexico, and we once found a drill ship's marine riser literally covered with fish, all brought to the spot by the hypnotic drill vibrations."

"Christ!" Scotty declared. "The damn ship was drilling

everal weeks. Yet this thing of yours appeared only two, maybe three, times. Where was it? Swimming in the sea?"

"Possibly," Dr. Fiammengo said. "But there might be another explanation."

"It may be the frequency!" Dr. Rubinstein declared.

"What frequency?"

"The frequency of the vibration. There might very well be just one vibration pitch that the creature responds to. You do drill with different sizes and types of bits. You do drill through different formations. There are different frequencies attached to each variable. The question is whether we can find a constant."

"That's why we want your help," Dr. Fiammengo pleaded. "You can help us find this constant by getting us copies of the *Columbus*'s drilling and bit records as well as cutting correlation logs and any cutting samples from the well you might have had on shore."

"That might be a very difficult thing for me to do."

"I see," Dr. Fiammengo said.

"But not impossible," Scotty added, realizing he had to follow this up. "Assuming I do this, what then?"

Dr. Rubinstein stood, his mood more forceful. "We'd want you to become an ally. I listened to you at the hearings. I saw your reactions. I asked discreet questions about you. I know all about you now. Your NFL experiences. Your engineering career. Your escapades. The *Phoenix* affair. We think you're the right man to help us."

"To do what exactly?" Scotty asked.

Dr. Rubinstein answered coyly. "We suspect Whittenfeld's trying to hide the existence of the creature because he fears the ensuing attention might affect his drilling operations. We're also aware he might have gone to considerable lengths to protect this knowledge. But with you behind us, supporting us, we might be able to convince Whittenfeld that the *Magellan* is in terrible danger. We might also be able to ultimately convince him to allow us to use the drilling sector to establish the creature's existence beyond dispute."

"How the hell will we be able to do that?"

"By threatening to take our information to the authorities!"

"If you're so concerned about the drill ship, why don't you go to the police right now? Why wait?"

"Simple. If the police believe us and shut down the drill

ship, we lose our means to attract and positively identify th
creature. We will never really know if we were right. If yo
go to the police with us, you will roughly wind up in the sam
predicament you faced after the *Phoenix* affair blew up i
your face. But more to the point, if the police don't believ
us, if they consider us charlatans, crazy Nessie freaks, the
we lose our trump card over Whittenfeld, and you might ver
well lose another ship."

Scotty stared, thinking; they'd done one hell of a job re
searching his background.

Dr. Fiammengo pressed. "Will you help us? Help us fin
this creature? Help us save the drill ship and its men?"

Scotty switched his attention from the woman to the mar
"I'll get you the logs and cuttings," he finally said.

Dr. Rubinstein was ebullient. "Now we're cooking." H
was quite a character, bitten nails, sloppy attire, and al
"Yes, let's positively establish the existence of the creatur
and then, if you want, we can walk into the constabular
headquarters en masse."

"Where can I reach you?" Scotty asked.

"The Claidheamh Mor."

"You'll hear from me tomorrow."

Dr. Rubinstein suggested he and Dr. Fiammengo return 1
the hotel. Scotty accompanied them out to the van.

"It's been a pleasure, Mr. Bruce," Dr. Fiammengo sai
shaking Scotty's hand.

Dr. Rubinstein joined. "Yes, absolutely. There are genuir
prospects for some very exciting scientific findings."

Scotty realized this might be a broad understatement, b
he said nothing more as the two researchers climbed into the
van and drove down the street.

Déjà vu!

It was almost as if the script had been written by the san
supernatural hand. The *Phoenix!* The suspicious death of th
project executive. The sudden appearance of the environmer
talists along with their damning evidence. His total but car
less involvement. Then disaster. And now Loch Ness! Th
recovery of the suspect hose after the loss of the drill shi
The suspicious death of the divers. The mysterious activiti
of Whittenfeld and Lefebre. And now the sudden appearan
of the concerned scientists along with their own form

damning evidence. Did disaster lay ahead once again? Maybe. But the new crusaders were not asking him to follow them blindly into opposition. They were asking him to help amass unassailable proof. That alone gave them credibility and set them apart from the zealots of *Phoenix*. But damn if he was going to wander blindly into the valley of death again. No, this time, as he had promised himself before, he was going to be very careful.

The following day, he telexed the New York office, asking New York to compile profiles on Dr. Rubinstein and Dr. Fiammengo. Before committing himself to action, he had to determine whether the two researchers were oddballs or frauds, whether their evidence was fraudulent, too.

A telex returned that night.

It painted a brief but satisfying picture.

It verified Dr. Rubinstein's self-appraisal and that of Dr. Fiammengo. Although it warned that some colleagues regarded Dr. Rubinstein as a bit of a dreamer, he was uniformly considered honest, a genius, an outstanding academician, an aggressive and innovative researcher.

And most importantly, he was highly regarded by NASA.

The telex also briefly addressed the Phenomena Research Institute.

The organization was legitimate. Most of its funding originated from private sources. However, it had also received major grants from several Eastern newspapers, including the *New York Times,* as well as grants from various philanthropic foundations, and it had directed expeditions under institutional auspices, too, notably one for *National Georgraphic.*

Satisfied, Scotty placed the telex in his pocket.

Chapter 22

―――――――――

"This building, this estate, is a shrine to many Scotsmen," Mary MacKenzie was saying as she stared past an open bottle of white wine. "Because the most famous battle in Scottish history took place on the Culloden Moor just beyond the grounds." She paused. "But I suppose you've read all about it in your history book."

Scotty embarrassedly cleared his throat as a young waitress placed some rolls on the table. "I haven't gotten quite that far," he said.

"How far have you gotten?"

"Oh, about a page or two beyond the page I was reading when you first saw the book."

"Then you're really moving along. Let me guess. A word a day?"

"The intent is good. You said it."

They both laughed. He kissed her hand, her warm, soft hand. He could read affection in her eyes, feel excitement in her touch, and he was sure she sensed the same in him. Since the first night they'd made love, their emotions had intensified crazily, their inhibitions and distrust consumed by their desire for each other. He'd helped her break down the barriers, and she'd finally permitted herself to go beyond Scotland and politics and love a man. Hell, he knew the conflicts had made it difficult for her, but at the same time he'd had to face his own special obstacle course. He'd had to unbridle his feelings, allow them to seek fulfillment while facing the terrible and intricate realities of Loch Ness. In fact, he was convinced the struggle had prevented him from giving totally, just as he was sure her internal conflicts had inhibited her. The words "I love you" had not been voiced by either, though when their eyes met, a sense of the words was there.

"Tell me about the battle," he said as he glanced around the room.

"Smile for me first," she demanded.

He did; she loved the look of happiness on his face, the warmth of his smile.

"I know you know Scotland and England merged in 1707," she began, "but I suppose you don't know the crowns were united a hundred years before, in 1603."

"Of course I know that!" he declared, grimacing. "Doesn't everyone?"

"When Queen Elizabeth I of England died in 1603," she said, laughing, "James VI of Scotland, a member of the House of Stuart, became James of England as well, inheriting the English throne. You see, his mother, Mary, Queen of Scots, was the great-granddaughter of England's Henry VII, and even though Elizabeth had Mary executed, the line of succession to James remained intact."

"You expect me to follow this?"

"I'll make it simple. There were two separate countries with the same king! Unfortunately, James and the succeeding House of Stuart kings preferred the court in London to the one in Edinburgh."

"Sounds like a prescription for trouble."

"It was. And things took a turn for the worse in 1688 when James VII was removed from the English throne and William and Mary were brought in from the Netherlands to rule. You see, there were many clansmen in the Highlands who remained loyal to the original Stuart monarchs even though the Stuarts had whisked themselves off to England. These clansmen opposed the usurpers. They were called Jacobites."

The connection was obvious!

"Let me hear more," he said, suddenly very interested.

"I have an audience," she remarked, surprised. "The Jacobites attempted several insurrections prior to the union of states, but all were unsuccessful. James VII died in 1701. His son, James Edward, became pretender, and after the union of states, the Jacobites rose again in 1715. Their rebellion failed. This time, the government in London took steps to ensure such rebellions did not reoccur. Highland estates were forfeited. Hundreds of Jacobites were expelled from the country. An attempt was made to disarm clans disloyal to London, and the use of the native Gaelic language was proscribed."

She looked at him; he was eager for more.

"Everything remained fairly stable until 1744, when Prince Charles, the son of James Edward, returned to Scotland. By this time, the union of the states was very unpopular, and the relations between England and Scotland were at a low. Charles was a far more vigorous leader than his father or grandfather, and he was able to rally the Jacobite clans once again. A huge insurrection erupted, and the decisive battle was fought right here at Culloden. The Jacobite army was destroyed. Wounded men were burned alive or chopped to pieces while lying on the battlefield. The government in London moved to eliminate the clans forever. More estates were forfeited. Clan leaders were executed. The possession of arms was banned, and so was the wearing of kilts and tartan colors." She paused; the conclusion was obviously painful. "And the Highland clans never rose again."

"Are you sure?"

"Of course I'm sure."

"Have you ever heard of the New Jacobites?"

"Yes. It's a radical offshoot of the SNP. One the SNP has disavowed."

"They're operating in Inverness."

"So I've read. But I can assure you, they are not a Jacobite reincarnation. Neither in principles nor fierceness." She arched her head. "Hey, we were going to have a romantic dinner, and we were not going to talk about Highland Council business, Scottish politics, oil, or Geminii Petroleum. You made me promise over my severe objections, and I'm going to hold you to the promise as well."

Leaning forward, he kissed her cheek, capitulating. The main course arrived. They began to eat.

"Would you be surprised if I told you I'm still uncomfortable with my feelings?" she asked a short time later.

"No. Not really."

"I'm still afraid I made a mistake letting myself get so close to you."

"No mistake. I'm hung up."

"What does that mean?"

"It means—well—it's an American way of saying— Damn, I'm not so good at voicing these things. I feel emotion better than I express it."

"When we're alone. Can you?"

"There's a lot better chance." He knew he would have to be the first to say, "I love you." After that, he suspected she would be able to bridge her own psychological dam, the same dam that made her resort to nationalist rhetoric and tales of Scottish history every time she felt herself being overcome with passion and the loss of control.

She touched his lips with the tips of her fingers, then kissed his hand. "Let's wait, then," she said.

Leaving the Culloden House, they drove by the Culloden battlefield graveyard.

She stared at the gravestones; clan names were etched into the rock faces.

"I know you can't feel what I feel when I look at these markers," she began somberly.

"No," he replied. "But I understand."

She squeezed his hand. "I look at the clan names, and I can visualize the men, their faces, the zeal they felt for Bonnie Prince Charles, the zeal they felt for Scotland. I told you they died terribly, but if they had known their sacrifice would one day become a symbol of a free Scotland, they would have felt their deaths worthwhile. I feel very strongly for these men. In fact, when I was young, my father would tell me their story, and I would wish that I had fought and died here. Is that peculiar?"

"Not for a child."

"Sometimes I still dream. Sometimes I think my duty is still martyrdom."

He flinched; the words that sprang from her mouth seemed anachronisms for a twentieth-century woman. Yet there was a lot about Scotland still trapped in the past. "I don't want to hear it. I wouldn't allow it. I'd take you back to the States before I would let that happen."

She stared at him, the moonlight lighting his handsome face. "I couldn't let you do that. I left once. I can never leave again. My father and mother lived and died here. They lie in the ground behind the inn, and I will, too, someday. My soul, the cells in my body, are made of Scottish soil. I can never leave without seeing Scotland free. That is a trust God has given me. A duty. I can never abandon it again. If I did, I would betray everything!"

Left once? Abandoned the trust? What was she talking about? He asked her what she meant. She did not reply.

*   *   *

They headed back toward Inverness.

Reaching the loch, they drove to Drumnadrochit and then, deciding to drop in on Father MacPherson, proceeded to the parish.

The parish parking lot was jammed with cars. The lawns were covered with books, broken pews, glass, all strewn indiscriminately.

Someone had wrecked the church and MacPherson's home next door.

They entered the chapel. The building had been completely ransacked. The huge crucifix, which had hung resplendently behind the altar, had been hurled to the floor; the body of Christ had been shattered. The place was filled with parishioners, sorting through the rubble, moaning, crying. MacPherson was there, too, holding a bible.

They approached.

"What happened, father?" she asked.

MacPherson turned, tears running, lips quivering. "Destroyed!" he screamed. "All of it. By the followers of the beast and the false prophet!"

"Who?" Scotty asked.

"The men from the oil company."

"Are you sure?"

"By God's word, I'm sure. May hell's fire singe me if I'm wrong, I'm sure."

"Did anyone witness this?"

"I do not know. And it does not matter."

"Then—"

The priest turned angrily. "They've watched us. They surveilled us. And, finally, they thought they could subvert the power of God by the use of the sword!"

"Have you called the police?" Mary asked.

"The police?" MacPherson cried. "What good are police? What power can they bring forth against the minions of Satan? No, I have not called the police, and I shall not. I have prayed to the Lord, and he has answered; another manifestation of the false prophet, another drill ship has been brought to the loch. This I shall destroy first. Then I shall march against the armies of the night."

"Father," Scotty said, "I think we should try to discover who did this before something is done that someone will regret."

MacPherson bristled. "You speak a dolt's language. The power of the Lord stands supreme. I need not fear, nor do I fear the folly of man."

MacPherson exited the church, called his parishioners together and mounted a stone, his face as wild as the night.

"Immediately afterward," he exclaimed, his expression a vision of lunacy, "while dismissing the crowds, Jesus insisted that his disciples get into a boat and precede him to the other side of the lake. When he had sent them away, he went up on the mountain by himself to pray, remaining there alone as evening drew on. Meanwhile, the boat—already several hundred yards out from shore—was being tossed about in waves raised by strong headwinds. At about three in the morning, Jesus came walking toward them on the lake. When the disciples saw him standing on the water, they were terrified. 'It is a ghost,' they said, and in their fear they began to cry out. Jesus hastened to reassure them. 'Get hold of yourselves. It is I. Do not be afraid.' Peter spoke up and said, 'Lord, if it is really you, tell me to come to you across the water.' And Jesus said, 'Come.' So Peter got out of the boat and began to walk on the water, too, moving to Jesus. But when he perceived how strong the wind was, becoming frightened, he began to sink and cried out, 'Lord, save me.' Jesus at once stretched out his hand and caught him. 'How little faith you have!' he exclaimed. 'Why do you falter?' Once they had climbed into the boat, the wind died down. Those who were in the boat showed Jesus reverence, declaring: 'Beyond doubt you are the son of God.'"

Scotty turned to Mary MacKenzie. "What the hell is this about?"

"I don't know," she said.

"The Lord has spoken," the priest screamed, waving his arms. "The battle is joined."

"I want to talk to him," Scotty said.

But before he had a chance, the priest was gone. Scotty looked around. He saw MacPherson halfway up a nearby hill.

MacPherson had gone to pray.

Scotty spent the night at the Carn Dearg Inn, then arrived at Geminii base early the next morning and chaired a staff meeting. Afterward, he returned to his office. Dr. Fiammengo called shortly after ten to advise him they had received the bit records as well as the cuttings. When she said the cuttings were excellent, he wasn't surprised. Bill Nunn was a superb geologist, and he'd consistently recovered the best downhole formation samples available from the return flow of mud.

He asked how long they would need to make a correlation study. Not long was her reply.

Scotty checked with Foster about the events in the Loch Meiklie parish. Foster advised he'd heard nothing about it, and doubted anyone at Geminii would have been involved in such a self-defeating enterprise, though certainly, if Scotty wished, he could take any suspicions he had to Whittenfeld.

Coincidentally, Whittenfeld summoned Scotty to his office a short time later. Entering, Scotty sat at the conference table across from Pierre Lefebre. Hugh Sutherland was also in the room.

"Mr. Sutherland crawled out of the woodwork this morning and asked to meet with us," Whittenfeld said as he walked from his desk. "He specifically requested that you be here, Scotty. Perhaps he senses your past sympathies for radical causes."

"I doubt it," Scotty said.

Sutherland lit a cigarette, self-rolled, holding it to his wrinkled lips with callused hands. "I would like to make Geminii a right-proper proposition." He glanced surreptitiously at Scotty. "Ay, I would like to see Geminii and the local population begin a collaboration."

Whittenfeld thoughtfully rubbed his jaw, hiding a smile. "What do you have in mind?"

"I want a statement made by Geminii accepting the fundamental primacy of the Scottish nation. A statement setting new company policy. A commitment by the company to employ Scottish workers on their own soil. A commitment by the company to use their good and powerful offices to plead the Scottish position—Scotland for the Scots—to the British Parliament, the Cabinet, the public. A commitment by the company to work for a more equitable distribution of Scottish oil revenue. A commitment by the company to enter into a partnership relationship with the population and terminate forever the anachronism of slave and master. And I want a commitment by you to run the tartan colors up the *Magellan*'s mast!"

"This sounds like a very one-sided collaboration," Whittenfeld declared.

"There are commitments on the other side, too," Sutherland quickly added.

"Why should Geminii do all this?" Whittenfeld asked, moments later.

Sutherland smiled for Scotty's benefit. "Reason dictates it. Mutual respect demands it. It is only just and proper. And last but not least, it is in Geminii's best interests. Pacify the population honorably, the people will work with you, and you will not find your drill ships attacked."

Whittenfeld's temper flared. "Our drill ships will not be attacked again! Do I make myself clear?"

Sutherland raised his hands. "You need not make anything clear to me. I did not attack the *Columbus,* and I don't know who did. But I do know why it was attacked. And I'm giving you the means by which you can prevent further turmoil forever."

"Guns," Lefebre said, interjecting himself into the conversation. "Guns and bullets."

"Guns and bullets silence voices," Sutherland said, "not ideas."

Whittenfeld glanced quickly at the Frenchman; no more violence, the gesture said. "Reason demands I do the opposite of what you suggest, Mr. Sutherland. My franchise issues from the Crown and Parliament. I look to the Department of Energy and the Scottish Office, and both receive their power from the state. The state is not Scotland. It is *England. England* controls Parliament and the Cabinet." He shook his head. "So you can't expect me to do the one thing that will certainly provoke English anger, can you?"

"I want you to do what is just, what reason demands."

"Justice and reason are not the real world, Sutherland. The real world is strength and power!"

Sutherland looked at Scotty. "Is that so?"

"Besides," Whittenfeld said, "these things you ask are outside the province of our business. Our job is to find oil, not to lead a political movement."

"Think!" Sutherland challenged. "Reason!"

"If I reason, I throw you out. Because I goddamn well know a known Scottish radical does not come to my office to beg and cajole. I know goddamn well there's something else in his mind."

"You make me out to be deceitful."

"I make you out to be what you are. And I want to know what the hell you really want?"

"I was told reason and mutual respect run the world."

Whittenfeld appraised the Scotsman with precision, then returned to his desk, sat on the edge, and stared. "I see," he said.

Scotty held open the front door of the building. Sutherland was just beyond.

Sutherland smiled. "You challenged me, Mr. Bruce. You challenged me to recognize what isn't, and I don't like to be challenged. So I think I have shown you the truth, though I'm quite sure you knew it already. It's amazing how often even the most experienced of men will dredge up a glimpse of utopia from within."

"So now what? Violence?"

"From me? No. I told you I am too human. Too much the dreamer."

"Then from someone else?"

"Perhaps."

Scotty returned to the office and sat behind his desk. Rubbing his face, he looked out at the loch. Christ, between the fraud of the investigation, the danger to the ship, and the cast of angry characters in Inverness, he could hardly even begin to calculate the different possibilities for disaster.

But then again, he was convinced he didn't have to.

Events would surely take care of themselves.

Chapter 23

~~~~~~~~

t was as dark a night as he could remember. A heavy cover
of clouds had rolled in early in the evening, blocking out a
bare crescent of a moon. Apart from the sonar tug's lights
and the *Magellan*'s own torches, the loch and surrounding
mountainside looked like an endless black funnel.

Entering the geologist's office, Scotty watched Bill Nunn
catalogue some cuttings, then wandered outside toward the
drill floor and exchanged some drill-bit penetration data with
Tony Spinelli and Mike Grabowski. It was just after midnight.
According to a new procedure, he would be spending at least
two nights a week aboard the drill ship, carefully monitoring
operations. This was tour number one.

Leaving Spinelli and Grabowski, he walked to the bow
past a heavily armed security guard. The night was cold and
windy. The loch current was strong, and whitecaps rose high,
their movements a rhythmic assault against the hull.

A strange sensation of light caught his attention. It was
situated along the north loch shore beyond Urquhart Castle,
about three miles toward the west and partway up the
mountainside. He unsuccessfully tried to determine the source.
Then he turned away as the light flickered and darted in the
direction of the wind.

The station wagon moved slowly down the unlit street,
passing merchant vesels moored to empty docks. Hugh
Sutherland was seated in the rear. There was another man in
front alongside the driver.

The wagon reached the end of the street and pulled into a
parking zone behind a boarded warehouse. The zone was
jammed with cars, all empty, all dark.

225

Sutherland climbed out of the wagon, accompanied by tl
man; they walked toward the warehouse entrance.

"What time is it?" Sutherland asked.

"Twelve-ten," the man replied.

Sutherland knocked on the warehouse door. The do
swung open, held by a bald, emaciated worker. Sutherlar
entered alone and then, as the door closed behind him, walke
down a corridor and stepped into one of the warehouse
main storage areas.

The area was packed with men seated on folding chair
They were lower class, poorly dressed. Though some we.
whispering, most were quiet.

Sutherland walked along the front row, shaking hands, th
mounted a makeshift stage.

"You don't seem as angry as you should be," he sai
staring, "but you will become angry. You must first learn
think in angry terms. For too long have we walked like laml
under the heavy feet of oppressors. For too long have v
allowed our blood to be sucked by the English vampires." I
pointed to the banner. "All of you *are* Jacobites. It is throug
us that Scotland shall be reborn." His voice began to rise, h
mannerisms becoming more exaggerated, more forcefu
"Where are your jobs? How do you support yourselves, yo
families? The jobs have gone to foreigners, and you cann
support anyone!" He listened as voices responded, cries, agre
ment; men began to stand, to feel, emote. "Where is your o
It is in England. Where is your future?" He pointed out. "Y
have no future. None. Unless you act!"

Pierre Lefebre buttoned his jacket over the bulge of
shoulder holster. A Gitanes cigarette dangled from his lip
Girard stood just inside the security office door along with tv
other security men.

Lefebre opened the door and ushered the men outsic
They climbed inside a waiting car, which roared off.

"When did the meeting start?" Lefebre asked.

"Ten minutes ago," Girard replied.

Lefebre pinched the end of the cigarette between his colc
less lips, then spat a sliver of tobacco on the floor. "Who
the tail on Sutherland?"

"MacNamara," Girard said.

Lefebre smiled. "Good," he declared. "One of their ow

t is poetic." He hummed a few bars of the "Marseillaise."
Any idea what they're up to?"

"No," Girard said. "But they've rounded up every unemployed oil and mechanical worker in the region."

"Interesting."

"Maybe they just want to hear themselves talk?"

"No," Lefebre said, slowly savoring his words. "Sutherland not a talker. He is a man of action. He issued an ultimatum; e meant it." He looked at Girard. "You are too ignorant to nderstand, Mr. Girard. But I respect this Sutherland. Even hough he is proud of a stupid, weak people, he has my admiation."

Lefebre glanced at the passing streets as he removed a nall knife from his jacket and began to clean his nails, the itanes still dangling from his lips.

Several minutes later, the car stopped; Lefebre stepped out. irard joined him.

"Where's the warehouse?" Lefebre asked.

Girard pointed to a protruding side of a building. "There. e can wait by the fence."

Lefebre ground the Gitanes into the cement. His face vitching, he followed Girard across an esplanade, then eased nseen into the shadows.

A shaft of light interrupted the darkness for an instant; two en squeezed out of a nearby doorway. Girard pointed, then alled. The men approached.

"Who's the man with MacNamara?" Lefebre asked.

"A contact," Girard replied.

Lefebre listened to the night sounds. "What's your name?" e asked as MacNamara and the contact stepped alongside.

"Reynolds," the man replied; he was the emaciated worker ho had opened the door for Sutherland as well as the man irard and Lennox had nearly beaten to death on a lonely ll several months before.

Lefebre turned to Girard. "Reynolds?"

"Yes. We've slowly educated Mr. Reynolds. He's a very luable ally now."

Lefebre smiled; Girard's initiative had pleasantly surprised m. "What's going on in there, Mr. Reynolds?"

"Sutherland's inciting the crowd."

"To do what?"

"To turn against Geminii. He wants to use Geminii to

create a rallying flag for the nationalist movement. That's wh
the Jacobites are here. That is why Sutherland was sent."

"When is this to happen?"

"Tonight!"

"By what means?"

"They're going to seize the drill ship, claim her for Scot
land."

Lefebre could not help laughing. "These mice?"

"They're going to use the boats in the Urquhart Ba
marina and board the ship."

Recalling his laughter into a sadistic smile, Lefebre grabbe
Reynolds by the hair and pulled back his head. "You will b
there, too, Mr. Reynolds," he said. "You will be with us. Yo
will watch us teach a lesson to these foolish Scotsmen onc
and for all."

Releasing his hold, Lefebre pressed a wad of chewin
tobacco into his mouth, then walked back toward the car.

Hugh Sutherland's face was a maelstrom of movement, th
furrows and crags carrying streams of perspiration. His once
powerful voice had grown hoarse, though it still could b
heard above the frenzied cries. Before him, two hundred angr
men were screaming, waving fists, having lost the ability t
reason and think. And that was precisely what he had wante
Emotion had replaced all else.

"Violence is the only true language, the only universa
tongue." Sutherland was screaming as he raised a lead bar i
his right hand. "It earns respect. It earns victory. It forces th
adversary to listen. Talk cannot gain attention. Talk is n
power. Scotland has been talking too long. You've bee
cowed like sheep. Brainwashed to believe you can reason you
way out of two centuries of servitude." He angrily smashe
the bar against the lectern. "You cannot reclaim what
yours by begging. You must take what is yours with forc
You must cry your defiance!"

He raised the lead bar in the air; a deafening roar erupte
He could almost smell the hatred, the anger.

He smiled.

Puzzled, Scotty leaned against the bow rail. The mounta
light he'd been watching for the last half hour had move
down to the water. However, it wasn't the only disturbi

stimulus. Cars had begun to arrive at the Urquhart Bay security installation, and the ship's communications officer had been unable to raise the installation radio as of yet.

He scanned the darkness; he could see the sonar tugs. He listened; someone called his name. He turned; Tony Spinelli moved toward him, carrying a pair of binoculars.

"The infrareds," Spinelli said, placing the binocular strap around Scotty's neck.

"They get to shore yet?"

"No."

"What about home base?"

"Base doesn't know a damn thing. They're trying to raise the installation, too."

Scotty trained the binoculars on the loch shore; the infrared lenses peeled away the darkness. The light was emitted by small fires. There was movement, too, although the resolution was not quite strong enough to give him definition.

"Torches," he announced.

"Are you sure?" Spinelli asked.

Scotty held out the binoculars. Spinelli looked through, then agreed. Scotty turned the lenses toward the shore installation.

"Trouble," he declared.

"What?"

"About sixty or seventy men with clubs!"

"Why the hell don't they answer our calls?"

"Maybe they don't want to."

Spinelli looked down at the drill floor. The crew was drilling ahead, though they had noticed the shoreside commotion as well.

"Get Grabowski," Scotty said. "Take the launch in. I want to know what the hell's going on."

Spinelli retreated. Scotty climbed on to the forward helipad. Finding a good observation point, he trained the binoculars on the shore installation, then moved them toward the northwest. The torches had come closer together; several seemed to have moved on to the water.

He was even more confused now.

Dressed in flowing white robes, Father MacPherson stood on the jagged shoreline like a Biblical prophet, his hands raised toward the sky, his white mane unfurled from his scalp by a fierce shoreward wind. He was a dance of flames, reflecting the light of a hundred burning torches, held by fanatic, white-gowned followers.

They had all moved toward the shore down the mountain, overcoming a Geminii shore guard. There they had waited while MacPherson had prayed.

Before them, bobbing on the water, was a huge wooden raft that they had assembled.

"Jesus walked on the water," MacPherson began suddenly. "So shall we. So I have been commanded by the Lord God. And woe be to him who is clutched by the beast. And woe be to the world, for the manifestation of the false prophet stands before us."

The men and women prayed. The wind howled. Leaves blew.

"There!" MacPherson cried, pointing into the darkness. "See. The heavens have opened. There is the white horse. There is the Rider Faithful and True. Justice is His standard. Look! See! The cloak! It is dipped in blood. His name is the Word of God. Behind Him is the army of heaven. The soldiers are riding white horses. They are dressed in white. There is a sharp sword. Look! There is a name on the cloak. King of Kings and Lord of Lords."

"Hallelujah!" the man beside MacPherson cried.

The crowd echoed the call. They moved in around Mac-Pherson. MacPherson was crying, wailing.

"God's glory shines. The image of the Christ has appeared. We have been blessed. We have been called into His service. We are the armies of the Almighty. We are His sword. We ride behind the Rider Faithful and True. We shall slay the manifestation of the false prophet, and then we shall follow the Christ into war against the beast itself."

The clamor grew. Screams echoed. Benedictions arose.

MacPherson climbed down from the rock and walked through the crowd to the raft. A tiller man was already on board. There were also a half dozen oarsmen.

MacPherson stepped on to the wooden planks. The torch bearers followed. The planks groaned. The raft settled. Water trickled over the side. MacPherson took his position along the forward edge. An oarsman threw the raft's tether line ashore; the tiller man pushed them off. The raft floated on to the loch; the current grabbed it. The torchbearers began to pray. Torches flickered.

MacPherson turned to the host. "I command you to battle,"
he cried. "In the name of God and Christ."

The helicopter maneuvered over the main road to Urquhart
Bay. Below it, a stream of cars raced westward.

"They're below me!" Whittenfeld said.

Whittenfeld had been awakened less than a half hour before; he had ordered Lefebre to deal with Sutherland without
the assistance of the police.

"Have you notified the *Magellan?*" he asked, speaking into
the helicopter's comm-phone.

"No," Lefebre replied above the static. "I was waiting for
you."

"Call the ship. They are to continue operations. Assure
them we will handle the problem. Then order the sonar tugs
to station themselves between the shore installations and the
drill ship. Give Captain Harrigan strict orders. No one is to
reach the *Magellan.*"

Whittenfeld clicked off the microphone and turned to the
pilot.

"Take us down," he said.

The pilot dropped the chopper to the fore of the lead car
and switched on the floods. The car was encased in light.

The occupants of the car looked up. Sutherland was seated
in the front. The rear of the car was filled.

Captain Eamonn Harrigan, an impressive man with an
Irish-red beard, a peasant's earthy complexion, and a decath-
lete's body, stood in the guard tug's bridge watching readouts
and displays on a dizzying array of scopes and meters.

Seated before him were six technicians monitoring the heat
and noise detect scopes and the elaborate, multidimensional
sonar systems. Two other technicians sat at a data panel tied
to the underwater sensors.

The first officer called. "Mr. Lefebre is on the wire."

Harrigan quickly moved across the bridge and put on a
headset. "Yes?"

Lefebre relayed Whittenfeld's message.

Harrigan asked if he should issue weapons.

"Yes," Lefebre replied.

Harrigan signaled the crew. "Swing us around!" he ordered.

* * *

Scotty and Bill Nunn moved quickly along the main-deck catwalk, avoiding several security men who had positioned themselves next to the starboard rail, facing the shore, then climbed on to the drill floor and notified the driller to prepare to close the blowout preventer. If the situation worsened, they would shut down the rotary and the bore.

The roar of ship's screws neared. The three sonar tugs were rounding the drill ship, heading for a position between the ship and the shore.

"Here they come," Bill Nunn suddenly said, pointing.

What had been a distant glow suddenly became discrete headlights, cars snaking inbound to Urquhart Bay. A heli copter, which had been hovering over the installation, landed. Scotty looked through the binoculars. Lefebre's security guards were strung along the road between the installation and the marina. In order for anyone to reach the boats, they would have to fight through a gauntlet of club-bearing men.

He left Bill Nunn and headed toward the radio room. A light caught his eye. Christ, he'd forgotten the torches, and now, incredibly, the torches were burning on the loch. He raised the binoculars again, and then, gasping, climbed up on to the forward helipad to get a better view.

A raft was heading toward the ship; on the raft, a hundred men and women, holding torches, were dressed in white. Among them stood Father James MacPherson, his arm raised high, his head bobbing wildly about, along with the violent sway of the raft.

The sonar tugs had taken their new positions. They could not be moved. The radio was worthless. There was nothing he could do about the priest. He remembered: MacPherson's threat to destroy the new drill ship.

He held his breath, incredulous.

The goddamn lunatic was going to try and burn the *Magellan.*

Hugh Sutherland opened the car door and stepped out. A line of autos stretched behind him. He held up his hand. Other doors opened. Men appeared holding pipes and bats, then moved forward, gathering around the lead car. Suther land pointed toward the drill ship.

"There is your trophy," he cried. "We take that ship, we bring the oil company to its knees. We take her, we seize the media. We take her, we seize history." He looked around there was no one in sight. "Hold your clubs ready. They will fight!"

They reached the marina perimeter moments later.

The marina fence was lined with security guards. Lefebre stood in front. Whittenfeld sat in the rear of a guarded sedan, parked off to the side. Spinelli and Grabowski were standing helplessly nearby.

"I would suggest you return to your cars," Lefebre announced, once more dangling a Gitanes between his lips, his hands wrapped around a club. "Although I would personally like to crack your skull, Sutherland, we must put Geminii first. Go home. Take these fools with you and let them return to their families."

No one moved; Sutherland stepped forward.

"Get away from the fence!" he cried.

"Go home," Lefebre ordered. "We do not want to see anyone hurt."

Sutherland inched forward again and raised his club.

"We're going to take the ship," he warned. "Step aside or we go over you."

Lefebre tightened his grip on his club. A smile creased his lips. The wind tossed his hair. His face twitched angrily.

Sutherland looked behind him at the workers. He had driven them into a frenzy, and now their anger was waiting to explode.

He pointed out toward the drill ship. "Take that sacrilege!" he cried. "For Scotland!"

A wild whoop erupted. Clubs raised high, the men stormed toward the gates, Highland clansmen reborn, screaming for blood.

Lefebre and the security police moved forward. Suddenly, bodies melded. Clubs flashed. Blood trickled, flowed. Men dropped to the ground. Wails rose. Hell broke out.

Whittenfeld locked the door of the sedan. But he couldn't lock out the sounds. Moments after the battle started, he heard it, the scream of police sirens.

Captain Harrigan stood watching on the deck of the lead sonar tug. He was wearing a holstered automatic pistol. Two crewmen, holding rifles, were next to him. Set on either side of the lead tug were the other two guard vessels.

He'd taken a position to intercept. However, he doubted they would be forced to act.

Although he could see the violence, no one had reached the boats and barges, and there was still a reserve force of security men positioned behind the lines on the docks.

Most important, a large detachment of constabulary police had already left their vans and were proceeding toward the melee.

The first officer moved to his side. "What do we do now?" he asked.

"We hold," Harrigan replied.

Scotty peered down from the helipad. A lifeboat moved away from the side of the drill ship, heading toward Mac-Pherson and his raft, its crew prepared to stop the priest from reaching his objective.

He watched the launch pitch headlong into the breakers. There were six men on board.

He placed the binoculars back to his eyes.

The chant of voices melted into the wind as the raft moved ahead. The tiller man frantically held to the rudder; the oarsmen stroked. Father James MacPherson stood upright, his right arm pointed straight toward the drill ship, the confusing stimulus of converging lights on shore nothing more than a momentary distraction.

"The Lord did anoint His Son to carry the battle to Satan," he was crying. "And the Son did obey, mounting His Father's holy chariot. The chariot did convey Him to the horse. On the horse, He led forth His army. And we are part of His army, for in us, we have the power of the Almighty! We shall destroy the drill ship, for it is foretold in the book of the living."

The raft turned heavily into a side wash of whitecaps. Water rushed over the sides. The raft spun about.

"Give us a sign of your power, Lord," MacPherson called. "Show us your sword so my people might not fear for your ascendancy."

MacPherson beckoned to the black, unanswering sky. Then suddenly, the raft jerked wildly around, moving back against the current, rocking partway into the water. Terrified, the torchbearers moved to the center.

"Do not fear," MacPherson cried. "God has given us His sign."

The raft shifted again. The water around it began to churn and wave into eddies. The raft turned wildly, as if it had been caught in a maelstrom. The water rose even more and parted as if something had surfaced.

A huge black object moved amid the waves.

"It is the beast!" MacPherson suddenly thundered.

Terrified, the torchbearers wailed. The object moved under the raft, pitching it upward. Three men fell into the water. One grabbed to the raft's edge as the raft rocked askew. The other two disappeared beneath a surge of foam.

"The Lord has brought us face to face with the beast!" MacPherson called. "Praise be His name. He has honored us. He has chosen us to destroy the beast." He pulled an old dagger from a sheath and waved it in the air. "I challenge you, Satan. Summon you forth."

The water stopped churning. The raft ceased to pitch. The current caught them once more. They waited.

Then the jolt hit!

Torches fell. Robes caught fire. The putrid smell of burning flesh spread. People dropped into the water. The churning began again, sucking the living under.

"Strength!" MacPherson cried, violently pummeled about. "Believe in Him and we shall prevail . . ."

MacPherson fell on to the wet planks. He looked around. The torchbearers were helpless. A terrible sound split the air. The raft began to rise. Something was lifting it. Up it went, tilting, crashing down; bodies fell into the loch. A black object rose, poised to attack, and then crashed down, smashing the raft into pieces. Survivors held on to the free planks, but the black object came crashing down again and again, vengefully crushing everything below.

The current pulled the debris down. The survivors screamed, flailed at the water, and then sunk, enveloped by the horrible, wet darkness.

Trembling, Scotty lowered the binoculars. He did not hear the sirens. Nor did he see the arrival of the police vans. He was too stunned. MacPherson and all the others were gone, sucked down into the loch. But it wasn't just their deaths. He'd seen it all through the infrareds; he had seen the thing. It had come up under the raft and had lifted it from the water. It had thrown its enormous tail into the air and had smashed it down.

Yes, he'd seen it, highlighted in the torchlight. This huge, black glistening beast, this horror.

He'd seen it.

And he was the only one.

Chapter 24

Scotty eased the jeep into his parking space in the Geminii base parking complex, killed the engine, and followed Dr. Rubinstein and Dr. Fiammengo out of the vehicle.

The ground was wet; it had rained early that morning. Although Dr. Rubinstein was wearing a large pair of galoshes, both bottoms of his baggy corduroy pants dragged on the ground, and the sun, which had finally broken through the overcast, reflected brilliantly off the bald spot on the top of his head.

"This will be a momentous day, Mr. Bruce," he said. He began to move in an awkward, storklike canter toward the main building.

"Maybe," Scotty remarked, his powerful athletic stride in vivid contrast to Dr. Rubinstein's comic gait.

They entered the building, checked through reception, and proceeded down the hall toward the elevators.

Detective Superintendent MacGregor intercepted them.

"Mr. Bruce," he said. "Just the man I want to see."

MacGregor smiled; he was particularly well dressed this day, almost as if he were about to go on the political stump.

Scotty introduced the police officer to Dr. Rubinstein and Dr. Fiammengo, referring to them merely as associates. MacGregor guided Scotty off to the side.

"Have you been in seclusion, Mr. Bruce?" MacGregor asked.

"No," Scotty replied. "Why would you think that?"

"I've been trying to find you for the last two days. Even Mr. Whittenfeld has apparently been ignorant of your whereabouts."

"I've been busy."

MacGregor lifted his heavy brow. "You'd think you would have wanted to be about here at a time like this." He waved his arms. "This has been an exciting week, don't you think?"

"I wouldn't use those exact words."

"No? That's curious. One hundred or more religious fanatics die in the loch. A massive brawl erupts in Urquhart Bay between Geminii security and the resident unemployed. You don't think that's exciting?"

"No," Scotty said, releasing a whoosh of breath. "I think it's tragic."

"That, too! Most definitely so, Mr. Bruce."

"Look, Superintendent—"

"Yes. Yes. I know. You've been busy."

"If you have any questions—?"

"A few."

"I'm all ears." He did not want to be curt or edgy, but he was in no mood for this. More human beings had died, and after two days of preparation, he was about to strike at the indirect cause.

"I've come to understand you took no part in the civil unrest," MacGregor declared.

"Correct," Scotty affirmed.

MacGregor skeptically clapped his massive hands together. "Geminii should have informed the authorities of the approach of the radical aggrieved and should have let the authorities handle the matter. There is also the question of excessive force. But, of course, no one was critically injured, and I suppose—"

"I wasn't involved in any of the decisions, either."

MacGregor gestured curiously. "Yes. Yes. I know. But it's neither here nor there. I don't want to question you about the melee. I want you to tell me about Father MacPherson and his deceased associates."

"They drowned."

"Precisely."

"What else?"

"I spoke to several crew members who told me you were watching the priest with infrared binoculars."

"That's right."

"What did you see?"

"I saw MacPherson and his parishioners on a very unstable raft. I saw the raft caught up in the current."

"And you dispatched a launch."

"Yes. But it reached the raft too late, after the raft had capsized. The men aboard the launch found no survivors. The water was ice cold. The current was ferocious."

MacGregor leaned against the wall. "The men and women on the raft had voiced clear threats against Geminii and the drill ship—at the tribunal hearings in particular."

"So what?"

"You knew that!"

"Of course, I did."

"Tell me about the parish. Tell me what happened."

"I don't know what you're talking about."

"The parish church in Loch Meiklie was ransacked, and you happened by to see the remains."

"How do you know that?"

"I spoke to Councilwoman MacKenzie this morning. She had a surprise for me. She told me about the church. She said she'd been there with you."

"Then you know everything there is to know."

"You heard the priest threaten to attack the ship again."

"All right. You've got me."

"Your attitude, Mr. Bruce. It is surprisingly antagonistic."

"As is your own."

"You were well aware of Father MacPherson's threats. You were well aware of the approach of his raft. I submit the launch you dispatched sunk the raft under your orders to protect the drill ship."

Scotty started to laugh. "You've got to be kidding."

"No."

"Did someone in the crew tell you this?"

"No. But I wouldn't think they would even if they knew."

"Superintendent, I've grown to respect you. I think you're intelligent. Dedicated. Serious. Please don't destroy my impressions. Now is that all?"

"Where is Sutherland?"

"How the hell would I know?"

"I'm taking a stab."

"Sorry. No blood."

"Think hard."

"Still zero."

MacGregor smiled accommodatingly. "If you find out by hance, you, of course, will let me know. I would most like ɔ talk to him."

"I promise," Scotty said, knowing full well that MacGregor vas baiting him across the board. But damn if he was about ɔ bite and open up to the authorities yet. He was well aware e alone had seen the creature destroy the raft. There had been ɔ corroborating witnesses, and no physical evidence had been ·ft behind. The fears of *Phoenix* had been forgotten—this ne the danger was real—but not all the lessons. Apart from is own isolated testimony, he had no more usable proof than ɔ'd had before. Their personal observations, their suspicions, ɪd the photographs of the hose were insufficient and certain-open to rebuttal, and Scotty was still very cognizant of Dr. ubinstein's warning: they could not blow their trump before ɔtaining irrefutable evidence! Besides, he hoped that after ɔtaining solid proof and backing Whittenfeld against the all, he'd be able to persuade Whittenfeld to shut down the ɔject without a public spectacle. Whittenfeld and Lefebre ɔuld have to deal with the fraudulent hose and the death of e divers, but those were secondary considerations compared the welfare of the drill ship and her crew, and no matter 1at proof they might be able to obtain concerning the eature, he doubted such proof would be of any use in ming up the circumstantial nature of the Furst murder ɪsiderations. No, the options and his choices were fairly ·ar. "Now is that all, superintendent?" he concluded after almost interminable period of thought, remembering Mac-·egor was watching.

MacGregor stared, then suddenly walked toward the front trance, disdaining to look back. "This time, Mr. Bruce," he d. "That's all."

William Whittenfeld pivoted away from the picture window 1 walked along the conference table behind Lefebre.

'You have a wonderful imagination, Dr. Rubinstein. Ex-ordinary. In fact, you would make a sensational novelist. t I must deal with the real world. I run an oil company, : a publishing firm. Therefore, I can't waste company time fiction."

Dr. Rubinstein chafed. "This isn't fiction. This is scientific t!"

'No," Whittenfeld declared curtly. "This is supposition and

drivel. And I cannot allow either to endanger the Loch Ne
project."

"I'm warning you!" Dr. Rubinstein said. "If you do
listen to me, you are going to lose another ship." He laid o
a series of charts. "The proof is incontrovertible. Each tin
the ship was attacked, the crew was using a Lyon TX
carbide insert drill bit and the drill was working in very ha
chert silica."

"What does that mean?"

"It means the vibration produced by that combination h
been acting as a magnet for the creature."

Whittenfeld examined several of Dr. Rubinstein's char
"Where did you get this information?"

"I gave it to them," Scotty said.

"The bit and mud records are confidential company pro
erty."

"I felt it was in the company's best interests to allow D
Rubinstein the opportunity to examine them."

"You exceeded your authority!"

"There were no standing orders."

"But there were standing assumptions, and I assumed
member of senior management would not act contrary
policy."

"I told you I acted in the best interests of the company. D
Rubinstein's discovery might very well save the company
neck."

"We do not have time to chase monsters. You'd do bett
to keep your attention on submersibles and dangerous peop
like Sutherland!"

Scotty breathed deeply, ready for a confrontation. "The
was no submersible in the loch, and a submersible did not c
the *Columbus*'s blowout control hoses!"

"You say that with a great deal of conviction. Convicti
which goes directly against the evidence. You were present
the hearings. You saw the hose."

"I saw *a* hose."

"What do you mean?"

"The hose shown to the investigation committee was
the hose Max Furst found on the bottom of the loch!"

Whittenfeld suddenly walked to his desk. "This had bet
be good," he said. "Because I don't like what I'm hearing.
the inferences."

Dr. Rubinstein nervously bit his nails. Dr. Fiammengo tarted to speak. Scotty stopped her.

"The hose shown to the tribunal was not the hose re-ieved," Scotty declared. "Somewhere between its recovery nd presentation, a torched hose was substituted for one that as chewed."

"And you're accusing me of the fraud?" Whittenfeld asked.

"I'm accusing someone," Scotty replied sarcastically.

Lefebre shot to his feet, furious. "I took the hose after its covery. I handed the hose to Monsieur Whittenfeld. The ose shown to the tribunal was the hose I had in my posses-on."

"Bullshit!"

Lefebre moved toward Scotty. Whittenfeld stopped him.

Scotty could barely hide his contempt for Lefebre as he ened Dr. Rubinstein's suitcase and removed the pictures d metal fragment, handing them to Whittenfeld.

"Those are pictures of the real hose taken by Max Furst. he fragment of the *Columbus* hull, dented with teeth marks, as recovered by Furst, also."

Whittenfeld examined the exhibits, then handed them to efebre.

"Forgeries," Lefebre declared, throwing them back on the ole.

"They're not forgeries," Scotty snapped. "So let's bury the ap!" He pointed at the hull fragment. "The *Columbus* was acked by a living thing!"

"Nonsense!" Whittenfeld declared.

"And Father MacPherson was killed by the same creature, reature I saw. Yes, I saw it, goddamnit. I saw a giant thing, giant black thing come up under the raft and splinter it o pieces."

Dr. Fiammengo collected the fragment and pictures. Dr. binstein nervously tapped the table. Whittenfeld was visibly concerted.

A long silence followed.

"I assume you've kept this wild assertion to yourself, Mr. ace?" Whittenfeld finally asked, once more resorting to mality.

"So far."

"I see. And you, Dr. Rubinstein? Dr. Fiammengo?"

"We've only spoken to Mr. Bruce," Dr. Fiammengo said.

Whittenfeld smiled. "All right. Assume for one minute
believe this. What then?"

"You must move to protect your ship," Dr. Rubinstein sai

"We can stop using the Lyon bit."

Dr. Rubinstein vehemently shook his head. "I'm afraid yo
must do more than that because we must assume there cou
be other bit-formation combinations that might incite th
creature."

"You say creature. What kind of creature?"

"A sea-adapted animal will do for now. Perhaps one hu
dred and twenty-five feet in length."

Whittenfeld snickered. "So what do you suggest?" he aske

"Several things," Dr. Rubinstein replied. "First. I agre
You must not use the Lyon bit. Secondly, we must attem
to absolutely locate and identify the creature."

"How do we do that?"

"We introduce a specialized submersible to the vicinity
the drill ship and use the precise vibrations which anger th
creature to draw it near."

"Won't that endanger the ship?"

"We won't use the ship. We'll duplicate the vibrations in
lab, record them, and introduce the sounds to the loch wate
Then, once we attract the creature, we will carefully phot
graph it so we can determine its size and our best course
action."

"Sounds fascinating," Whittenfeld said, barely able to ma
his derision.

Dr. Rubinstein continued. "We can do all this with t
utmost discretion. This way, we won't attract attention, a
your drilling operation will be able to proceed unhindered

Whittenfeld asked Dr. Rubinstein and Dr. Fiammengo
wait in the executive lounge; he wanted to speak to Mr. Bru
alone.

"How dare you bring these charlatans in here!" Whitte
feld screamed after Dr. Rubinstein and Dr. Fiammengo h
left the room. "How dare you give them confidential co
pany documents. Christ! For all the hell you know, they
with another oil company, and they wanted our cuttings
they could make strategic assessments concerning the Mor
Firth bids!"

Scotty detailed Dr. Rubinstein's background. Then I
Fiammengo's. He produced the New York telex. Whittenf
threw it on the table.

"Get rid of both of them," Whittenfeld ordered. "And find a way to destroy the pictures and hull fragment!"

"No!"

"What do you mean *No!*"

"You heard me."

"Either you do it or I fire you!"

"I don't give a damn what you do. The creature exists. I saw it. And I won't let another man die because of it."

"It's the wrong time and wrong place to go back to your old ways, Mr. Bruce! This isn't a cause. This isn't something to shake the world about."

"You don't believe that yourself."

Whittenfeld's anger flared. "I took you out of the garbage."

"I know."

"When no one else would have you. And I can send you right back. You disrupt another company, create a public furor over nothing again, and you're finished. You'll have to become a high school football coach!"

"Maybe."

"You imagined you saw this thing."

"I didn't imagine jack shit!"

"Goddamn you!"

Scotty angrily pointed; he was going to enjoy this. "Now you listen to me, you bastards. The bullshit is finished." He turned directly to Whittenfeld. "If you do not do what Dr. Rubinstein suggests, I'm going to go to Fallworth. I'm going to tell him everything. Then, if that doesn't work, I'm going to go to MacGregor. Then MacKenzie. Then Farquharson. Then the secretary of state for energy and the secretary of state for Scotland. Up to the prime minister if I have to. I'll go to every one of them and tell them what I know." He paused. "Think about it. Those are your choices. You either do what Dr. Rubinstein suggests or I blow the lid."

"You don't mean that!" Whittenfeld challenged.

"You bet your ass I do!" Scotty said, using Dr. Rubinstein's trump, the threat to approach the authorities, "and I want an answer by the morning."

Scotty informed Dr. Rubinstein and Dr. Fiammengo that Whittenfeld would give them an answer by noon the following day. Then he drove Dr. Rubinstein back to the hotel and took Dr. Fiammengo with him into town for lunch. Finding a seat in a window booth at one of Inverness's "otherwise" Scottish coffee houses, Dr. Fiammengo placed a looseleaf folder on the table.

"See if you can recognize one of these," she suggested.

He flipped pages, staring at artists' renditions of prehistoric animals.

"Some nasty-looking critters," he observed.

She watched. A waitress delivered some coffee and two cheese-filled potato skins, a Scottish speciality.

"There's been a lot of conjecture about just what this creature might be," she said matter-of-factly. "Some have suggested it's an invertebrate, some form of giant annelid worm. Others, a mammalian species, highly evolved. Amphibians and fish have received some support, and so have reptiles."

"What do you think it is?" he asked, staring at her. As attractive as Dr. Fiammengo was, there was something coldly scientific about the way she spoke and gestured; she did not have Mary MacKenzie's warmth and smile or even her visible depth of emotional commitment.

"I lean toward the reptilian theory. Eyewitness reports would support some form of aquatic dinosaur, in particular the *Plesiasaur*, which grew to enormous size and roamed the seas millions of years ago. And we have the reptile-like mucous sample. But, of course, there are strong arguments against!"

"Like what?"

"It is presumed dinosaurs were cold-blooded like modern reptiles and therefore would prefer warm water over cold, certainly water warmer than the loch. And *Plesiasaurs*, like other reptiles, breathed air. Now we're going to have a hard time accepting a creature which only breathes air because such a creature would be a very visible landmark."

"It could have evolved to breathe in water. Like an amphibian. Couldn't it?"

"Maybe. But amphibians can't breathe in both environments simultaneously. When an amphibian is young, it breathes in water through gills, but when it comes on to land it loses the gills and solely utilizes lungs."

"Maybe this one has learned a different trick."

"Maybe."

He continued to span the pages. Suddenly, he stopped. She

leaned over. His facial expression changed rapidly; he was disturbed.

"This is it—almost."

She turned the book around. On the page was a giant black dinosaur with a long neck, a huge bulbous body, and four immense flippers.

"You've chosen a *Plesiasaur*," she said excitedly.

"I did?"

"Yes. But you said almost—"

"Yes. I saw the body. The rear flippers, too. But I also saw two huge arms, tipped by enormous claws."

"Where?"

He pointed to the picture. "Where the front flippers are shown here."

She looked up, puzzled. "It's possible," she said, reflecting. "Anything's possible. But this creature certainly would have to be a very evolved organism. Your description suggests it. The mucous samples we studied do, too. If it can breathe underwater, it is one hell of an incredible thing."

"Are we dreaming all this, lady?" he asked.

"No," she answered.

"Sometimes I wonder. And when I wonder, I confront logic again."

"Specifically?"

"If this creature's a dinosaur, how and why did it survive its brethren?"

"I don't know, and we may never know."

He digested the disclaimer, grabbed the book, studied the picture and the proportions. "Incredible," he said in conclusion. "Just incredible."

Chapter 25

Whittenfeld called the following morning and informed Scotty he could not make a decision without additional documentation on the background of Dr. Rubinstein and Dr. Fiammengo.

Scotty protested. Whittenfeld demurred. They were not about to embark on a Sunday school picnic. Dr. Rubinstein's proposed gambit was beyond the ken of a novice. Before he would give the project a "go," he wanted to be damn sure Dr. Rubinstein and Dr. Fiammengo were the genuine articles.

And he wanted the additional information quickly.

Scotty agreed, strangely pleased by Whittenfeld's intransigence. He, too, was concerned. He now had no doubt about Dr. Rubinstein's and Dr. Fiammengo's honesty, but he wanted to be doubly sure about their abilities, too.

He informed Dr. Rubinstein there would be a slight delay, then placed additional inquiries with New York. Three members of the New York security office were placed on the matter full time, told to complete dossiers on both principals within two days.

Business completed, he drove the jeep to the Highland Regional Council offices and picked up Mary MacKenzie. They shared a lager at a pub in town. The day before, they had spoken at length about Father MacPherson's death. She still seemed as upset about it now as she'd been then. He mentioned his conversation with Superintendent MacGregor, then informed her he'd let the cat out of the bag about their relationship. She said she didn't care. She also said she wanted to visit the parish.

They motored to Loch Meiklie, arriving after the sun had set.

The church was dark and intimidating. The silence was

246

eafening, almost supernatural. It was as if MacPherson's
eath had placed a shroud over the building, burying it.

The impression disturbed him; he cursed it away.

Her footsteps rang clearly as she approached the altar. He
watched her kneel and pray. The sound of crickets suddenly
ntruded. Life was reborn. She stood erect, her expression
ontradictory, remorseful, yet strong. Then she raised her
ands and recalled MacPherson's vision—the beast, the false
rophet, the rider on the white horse—recalled it as if she
ad been meant to take up the standard.

"Why did you say all that?" he asked after they had re-
urned to the jeep.

"I felt it appropriate."

"Out of respect?"

"Yes. But there's another reason. I think Father MacPher-
on was right."

"About the Loch Ness monster?"

"No. About good and evil."

He said nothing. Based on what he knew, he also felt that
MacPherson, in a very real way, had been right.

He drove the jeep back on to the road.

They ate dinner together at the inn. They did not mention
MacPherson again. In fact, as soon as they had left the parish,
Mary MacKenzie's entire mood had changed. She was now
miling, upbeat. It was as if the visit to Loch Meiklie had
urged emotions.

After dinner, she conscripted him for service in the pub
nd then, after closing, retired with him to the inn's drawing
oom along with a bottle of wine.

The room was attractive, its decor subdued, mixing tones
f brown and beige. The furniture was old, the atmosphere
timate.

"Can I ask a question?" he asked after they had settled in.

"Of course."

He poured two glasses of wine.

"Remember the day of the *Columbus* funeral service? Re-
ember our conversation, how I'd guessed you'd had a bad
motional experience and that's why you'd closed yourself
f."

"Yes."

"I never asked for specifics."

"I know."

"I'm asking now."

"Why?"

"Because I care about you. Because I'm not as uninterested
as I made myself out to be. Because I'm human."

"There was no experience," she said, touching his hand
running her nails softly along the inside of his fingers very
sensually. "At least not with a man."

"Then with what?"

"A city—London—a country, England."

"I don't understand."

"Sometimes, when I think back on it, I don't, either."

"You were in London at the time?"

"Yes. I was a student at the London School of Economics
I felt the experience would be good for me, that a taste o
England would expand my horizons. And my father was ther
quite a bit—a member of parliament."

"What happened?"

"Culture shock! Mr. Bruce, whether you know it or not, w
Highlanders are very provincial people. London was a revela
tion. I was just twenty-two years old and had grown up wit
very narrow ideas. I was raised in a provincial nationalis
home with a very rigid outlook. London and the ideas
found there were very different."

"You began to understand the English."

She seemed embarrassed. "Yes, but London seduced me
The night life seduced me. The good times seduced me. T
this day, I don't know how it happened."

"It happens to young women all the time."

"But it shouldn't have happened to me. I was too com
mitted. Too dedicated."

"Did your father find out?"

"Yes. He was hurt and angry. He was convinced I ha
desecrated the spirit of our nation, desecrated our dead. W
argued incessantly. I was temporarily insane. But I woke u
with a jolt. I came out of a restaurant one night with som
friends. A young couple was waiting for a taxi. They wer
wearing tartan colors. They were attacked by an Englis
street gang because of the colors. I tried to stop the brutality
Others did, too. It was terrible, a nightmare. The young bo
died in my arms."

"And you blamed the English?"

"No. Of course not. Just like I wouldn't blame the Scots
some Scottish ruffians killed an English tourist. But I wa

lted nevertheless, reminded of what I am, what Scotland is, hat I had subconsciously chosen to forget."

"And you reacquired your burden?"

"Yes."

He laughed to himself. "Then it wasn't a man, a boy friend." his then was the betrayal of trust she'd spoken of at Culoden.

She grinned teasingly. "Oh, I've had boy friends. You know hat. It just wasn't *a* boy friend until you. You've caused me o let some of the burden slide again. That frightens me."

His face registered recognition. "You were seduced by a ountry. I was consumed by ideals."

"Your causes. The pursuit of the truth."

"And a headlong rush to disaster."

He sat quietly, thinking, then took her step by step through he *Phoenix* incident. He was convinced he had to provide er with the last piece in the complex puzzle that was his life. ooner or later, she would learn the truth about Loch Ness, arn that he had kept critical information from her. The *hoenix* incident might help her to understand and accept his ctions, and so might the eventual revelation about the death f Max Furst. He was convinced she'd instantly attempt to ort-circuit the loch project if she knew the truth. He was so convinced she might then be in terrible danger. If Whitnfeld and Lefebre had disposed of Max Furst, they would ertainly be capable of eliminating her—or him, for that atter. No, if and when the time came for action outside the ompany, he would approach a broad spectrum of governing uthorities. No matter that Mary MacKenzie might hate his uts afterward; she was going to be the last one to know. She as not going to become a footnote on one of Lefebre's asualty lists!

She embraced him as soon as he had finished the recitation. We all make mistakes," she said.

"Not all of us," he replied. "Some of us are just destined."

The New York-compiled dossiers arrived the following day. hey were painstakingly complete.

Scotty delivered them to Whittenfeld, who reluctantly uthorized the project and then informed Dr. Rubinstein and r. Fiammengo. The researchers were elated. They instructed eminii procurement to obtain the chert-silica blocks and set

out to assemble the drill apparatus in a basement lab provide
by the company. When the blocks arrived three days late
the apparatus had already been completed.

It took thirty-six hours to prepare for the actual recording
Dr. Rubinstein estimated the entire process would last tw
days.

The recording sessions began.

Scotty entered the lab during an early recess and invite
Dr. Fiammengo to the executive lounge for coffee.

"Tell me more about Dr. Rubinstein," he said. "Tell m
how you met."

"I was doing graduate work at Harvard. He was on th
faculty. He was giving a lecture series on unexplained phe
nomena. I caught his second session on UFOs."

"Does he believe in them?"

"Yes."

"UFOs and the Loch Ness monster. What about the Abom
inable Snowman?"

"He's skeptical there. But on most things Dr. Rubinstei
has a very open mind. He accepts possibilities until they ar
conclusively disproven. He is a very thorough man."

"A nervous man as well."

"Call him energetic. He has more than enough energy fo
ten men. And he's an achiever. That's what attracted me t
him. Immediately. And that's what attracted us to you. You
activist past. You are a doer, too."

They finished their coffee and left the lounge. Dr. Fian
mengo returned to the lab.

Later that day, both researchers joined Scotty in his offic

"I would like to procure this vehicle for the enterprise,
Dr. Rubinstein began after placing a submersible spec o
Scotty's desk. "The submersible is the MV-7. I've carefull
studied the alternatives and our requirements, and I'm co
vinced it's the best vehicle I can obtain for the price and th
job."

Dr. Rubinstein handed Scotty a booklet. Scotty scanned i

"Impressive," Scotty said.

"I have used the vehicle before," Dr. Rubinstein declare
"It is reliable and very advanced."

"The crew?"

"The best. The pilot is a Liverpudlian named Malcol

Conner. The engineer and copilot is a Dutchman named Johannes Aard. I know them both. They are crack."

"Who owns the sub?"

"London Surveying and Marine."

"I assume it's available."

"Yes."

"Have you spoken to them?"

"Yes."

"When can it be here?"

"They promised they can fly it in within twenty-four hours of commission."

"Get it!"

Two days later, Dr. Rubinstein completed the recording procedures. The submersible arrived at the airport, and Scotty ordered it helicoptered into the loch. Then he and Dr. Rubinstein welcomed the submersible team to Geminii base.

Johannes Aard and Malcolm Conner were the most conspicious members of the group. They were outgoing, garrulous, confident, radiating the aura of men who knew what they were about, adventurers, daredevils.

Scotty liked them immediately.

He also liked Conner's ribald sense of humor as well as the information he read off their resumes.

"So what is this all about?" Aard asked, burying his words in a jarring Dutch accent.

"You'll find it interesting," Dr. Rubinstein predicted.

"The company doesn't know why the submersible was chartered."

"That was intentional."

"They told us," Malcolm Conner added, "that if we don't like the assignment, we can turn it down."

"That was the deal," Scotty explained.

"Then let us hear," Aard said, draping his body over a chair and stroking his beard.

"This conversation is confidential," Dr. Rubinstein advised them.

"Of course," Conner assured.

Dr. Rubinstein explained the nature of the assignment. Aard and Conner were astonished.

Dr. Rubinstein asked if they would accept.

Aard and Conner just stared.

* * *

Submersible planning commenced. Apart from the two operators, the submersible team was kept in the dark about the ultimate objectives.

A command barge was floated and placed on line. Several planning sessions were conducted. Captain Harrigan was included, though he was given only a minimum of information.

One week after Whittenfeld had given his authorization, they were ready. Scotty notified Whittenfeld, whom he had barely seen in the intervening days, of the status.

Whittenfeld gave final clearance.

Scotty informed all the participants.

They would begin operations the following morning.

Scotty paced down the street. Travis House stood in the background. Rarely had he ever felt so unhinged.

The moon was out, and the sky was clear. Weather service had predicted a perfect day for the first dive.

He looked at his watch. It was time to go to bed, but he was too keyed up.

He returned to Travis House, said good night to Mrs. Munro, then retired to his room and called the Carn Dearg Inn.

Mary MacKenzie answered; she was in the Carn Dearg pub, working.

"I love you," he finally said, tearing down the last remaining emotional block between them.

A long pause intervened.

Then she said, "I love you, too. Very much."

Chapter 26

~~~~~~~~~~~

The day was perfect, the loch's surface uncharacteristically quiet.

The command barge and the twelve-ton, thirty-foot-long, deep-water probe were the only vessels in the active drilling sector apart from the drill ship and lead sonar tug. For purposes of secrecy, the two support sonar tugs had been docked.

They were nearly ready. Soon the submersible would start its engines and descend to one hundred and fifty feet. Then the *Magellan*'s crew would stop the rotary system, the submersible would begin to broadcast the lab recordings, and if anything alive appeared, it would be photographed by the submersible's ejectable cameras as well as by surface-supported camera equipment previously lowered into the loch.

The plan seemed perfect.

"They're ready in the probe," Dr. Fiammengo called as she entered the cabin.

"Good," Dr. Rubinstein observed. He was perched in a chair behind the console, his bald spot concealed by a woolen ski hat. "Turn on the surface camera."

One of the technicians hit a switch. A television monitor flashed. The interior of the submersible's command module appeared on the unit, photographed by an interior television that transmitted pictures through a tether while the submersible was moored. Conner and Aard were both visible, prone, facing the sub's controls, which operated the vessel, its video, floodlight, and sonar systems, as well as its telechiric arms.

The submersible's surface officer ran a checklist with the crew. The systems okayed, Dr. Rubinstein assumed command.

Scotty walked out of the cabin.

The submersible was moored. He peered through one of its portholes, able to see Aard and Conner. He retreated to

midship, and moments later, the boatswain untethered the
probe. Easing out of the barge's way, the probe executed a
series of maneuvers, then descended, leaving its radio communication buoy bobbing on the surface.

The test would last two hours.

Capt. Eamonn Harrigan wound a rubber band around the
fingers of his right hand as he oversaw the operation of the
lead sonar tug. Ahead, he could see the command barge and
the *Magellan*.

He scanned the water. As expected, he saw nothing; the
submersible had disappeared more than ten minutes before.
He was uneasy. He had attended three planning sessions
during the week, but they had only been peripherally informa-
tive. He still had no idea what the barge team was actually
doing or why Geminii command had placed strict security
over the entire operation. He had been told just to record; he
had not been told what to expect. It made their work all the
more difficult, all the more nervewracking.

God Almighty, he thought he'd been employed to protect
the drill ship from saboteurs and submersibles, not religious
and political fanatics and imponderables!

He walked onto the bridge, entered the observation area,
and examined a side-scan printout. The *Magellan*'s riser was
visible. So were the television cameras suspended from the
flotation pontoons and the submersible.

He checked his watch.

They had an hour and forty minutes to go!

Scotty looked out the window at the *Magellan*—she was a
beautiful sight on a beautiful day—then scanned his instruments, finally focusing, for want of anything else to do, on
his hands.

They were strong hands, covered with calluses and bruises.
Years on the football field had gnarled them into abstract
sculptures. Strangely, though, his fingers were trembling.
Even though he'd always considered himself impervious to
pressure, the incredible tension in the cabin had apparently
gotten to him, too.

A technician called out the operation time. They were an
hour into the exercise; absolutely nothing had happened yet.

A short time later, though, the sonar tug's crew informed
them that they had picked up a suspicious trace. The barge

am sprang into action; the tension level rose precipitously.
n minutes into the alert, however, the sonar tug radioed
mmand that the trace had been incited by a school of fish.
Dr. Rubinstein called off the emergency.

Scotty telephoned the submersible team.

"Sorry about the false alarm," he said.

"So are we," Conner countered. "We're getting lonely.
ll, it seems this creature of yours isn't very friendly."

"It's shy. It has to be coaxed. It likes music. So keep play-
;."

"It's one hell of a tune."

Scotty took a breath, stood, poured himself a cup of coffee,
en returned to his seat.

"That's it," he announced some forty minutes later.

"Damn!" Dr. Rubinstein declared.

Scotty put on his headset. "Conner. Aard," he called. "Bring
e probe up."

Dr. Fiammengo swiveled toward him. "Can't we hold? Just
ew more minutes."

Scotty shook his head. "Whittenfeld gave us two hours. We
errupt operations any longer and there's going to be a
sh." He glanced at Dr. Rubinstein. "There's always to-
orrow."

Submersible operations continued the following two days.
e results were the same, nothing. The sonar tug recorded
traces of significance. The barge crew itself showed little
its labor.

Scotty arranged a breakfast meeting with Whittenfeld.

"So where is this huge monster, Scotty?" Whittenfeld be-
a.

Scotty noticed the "Mr. Bruce" had been dropped for the
ment. "I don't know."

Whittenfeld buttered a sweet roll. Behind him, a bright
re of sunlight invaded through the suite's picture window.
erhaps even monsters take vacations. This one seems ened. It has worked very hard on the imaginations of my
cutives."

"I saw it."

"Of course."

"You know damn well I didn't imagine it."

"Of course."

Scotty sat back in his chair, staring.

Whittenfeld leaned forward after loosening his carefu
knotted tie. "Why don't we cut through the pretense. Speak
confidence? Just between ourselves?"

"I'm game."

"All right," Whittenfeld said. "I substituted the phony co
trol hose. I took the hose Furst and Blasingame had recover
and destroyed it. Then I had Lefebre create a counterfei
He punctuated the admission with a pause. "I hope that cle
the air?"

"Why'd you do it?"

"I told you the world is illogical, its population nea
devoured by its own stupidity."

"I remember."

"And that fortunately there are enlightened men determin
to see the battle through against onerous odds."

"So you said."

"The commission was an illogical exercise. Its memb
were stupid. They would illogically and stupidly have cut th
own nation's life line. They might well have stopped lo
operations if I had allowed them to draw the illogical co
clusion I knew they would draw."

"What conclusion?"

"They would have ruled a living thing had attacked
Columbus."

"A living thing did attack it."

"Scotty. This is the twentieth century. Dinosaurs and
monsters do not exist. However, if the commission had se
the real hose, they could not possibly have arrived at
truth."

"And you know the truth?"

"Yes. And I'll say it again. The Columbus was sabotag
and the sabotage vehicle was designed to simulate the appe
ance and work of a monster."

"You don't think the commission could have seen that?"

"No. These are superstitious people. Their history is fi
with tales of dragons, goblins, creatures. Subconsciously a
maybe even intellectually, they can well accept the existe
of a monster. Scotty, I really did nothing wrong. In fac
helped the tribunal arrive at the truth. I eliminated a h
which would only have confused them and substituted
which more accurately reflected actual events."

What a crock of shit, he thought. "What about Furst?"

"His death was an accident. There was no reason to prev

rst from testifying. The hose was right there. Living proof.
Furst had raised objections, the conditions of his inspection
ıld have been brought into question as well as his motives.
you are aware, Mr. Furst was a Nessie aficionado."

"So I'm told."

"Lefebre and Girard were also there to corroborate my
timony."

"How fortunate."

"And, as an added precaution, we paid Mr. Blasingame a
tain sum of money to impugn Furst's testimony."

"How clever."

"Unfortunately, the accident intervened."

"Unfortunately."

"Scotty. My friend. You gave Dr. Rubinstein the drilling
a. You said you were acting in the company's best interests.
ıen I gave the tribunal a torched hose, I was acting in the
ıpany's best interests, too."

"But I acted for the men. For their safety."

"Didn't I?" He smiled. "Look what I've accomplished. The
gellan is guarded like a saint. What does it matter if we
preparing for a monster or a submersible? Protection is
tection. We have it."

"We have what you wanted. Continued operations. If the
ımission had found evidence supporting the existence of a
ature, they would have closed us down. And that's precise-
ʌhat you could not allow."

"Because I had the good of the company in mind."

"No. The *good* of the company is safety. The *good* is a
tdown of operations."

"Our opinions differ here."

"They differ across the board because the sabotage theory
sn't hold."

"Oh?"

"For the hundredth time, I saw it!"

"You saw something. Perhaps the same thing that severed
control hoses. This thing made to look like a monster.
ı saw the thing under less than ideal conditions. It was
ı black. You were far away. There was a great deal of
fusion, trouble on shore. And there are no survivors to
ıoborate your observations. In short, there is still no
ıf."

ıcotty was aware of it. He was also aware Whittenfeld was

trying to manipulate him, appease him, keep him quiet by mitting the incontestable truth, the control hose substituti and then coloring the truth with praiseworthy objectives destroy any inference that there had been self-serving heinous reasons behind the deed. But did Whittenfeld tr think he would buy this bullshit about disguised submersibl Did Whittenfeld think anyone would?

"We'll find the proof," Scotty declared as he watche desperate man grasp at random defenses helter skelter.

"How? By continuing to sit like nesting chickens on loch? By broadcasting foolish noises, a symphony for fi Please. Have some regard for my intelligence. And my d cult situation. I can only conceal a drill shutdown for so lo Sooner or later, some cost-conscious, ambitious desk wor in London is going to notice the lag. When I'm asked ab it, what am I going to say? We're out looking for a monste

"No, you can say we're conducting additional security te It will hold."

Whittenfeld looked out the window, shading his eyes. " sorry you have so little trust and faith in me."

Scotty refused to comment. "We want to continue tests," he said.

"Your symphony?"

"In part. But the recorded sounds won't do the trick al We want to locate an actual chert-silica formation and the Lyon TX-1 bit to create a tremendous vibration on loch's rock bottom to draw the animal. Once the ani approaches, we'll shut down the *Magellan*'s rotary and sw to the less powerful matching recorded broadcast."

"You want to drill? Endanger the ship?"

Scotty smirked. "How in the hell can we endanger the if there is no creature to attack it? This sinister submers of yours won't know the game plan. So if we're wrong, monster will appear, and you'll have your proof. But if w right, something will appear. We'll close down the rotary fore anything reaches the *Magellan*. We'll photograph identify the creature, and then we will have *our* proof."

Whittenfeld unsuccessfully tried to hide signs of an "And if I say 'no'?"

"You won't. For fear I may march into the constabula "I'll give you one dive. One shot."

Scotty damn well knew that Whittenfeld's only safe

was their inability to find the creature. Whittenfeld would patiently wait, popping mad theories. It was only after definite proof existed that Whittenfeld might be forced to act, and only then did Scotty suspect he might be in danger. "That's all we need," he said.

Chapter 27

"Take a team through those reeds and rushes," Detective Superintendent MacGregor ordered as he closed the top button of his raincoat and drew his hat closer to his eyes. "And check that bog area just behind."

Chief Inspector MacKintosh led several investigators off the dilapidated jetty, located just inside the entrance to Inverness harbor.

MacGregor turned; a fine spray of mist tickled his face. At the end of the jetty, three detectives entered a utility shed. Beyond the shed, several patrol cars sat on a dirt access road. Heavy clouds massed overhead. There were no spectators. It was still early morning. A man's body lay on the end of the jetty; it had been fished out of the water less than an hour before. The man had drowned. Apart from the anonymous message received by the police that morning indicating the dead man had been forcibly held under water, the police had nothing concrete.

MacGregor looked at his feet. His socks were uncomfortably wet, and his shoes were covered with dark clay. Walking landward, he glanced through a note pad and then moved under the eave of the shed.

A police car appeared moments later. It stopped alongside the jetty. A plainclothes officer stepped out, leading Scotty Bruce, who had also eased out of the car, to the shed.

"Mr. Bruce," MacGregor said, extending his hand.

Scotty ignored the gesture. "Why the hell was I dragged out of my house at six o'clock in the morning?"

MacGregor smiled; his teeth looked severely white against the backdrop of unshaved cheeks. "You weren't dragged. You were invited to come."

"Why?"

MacGregor pointed to the covered body. "There's been a drowning. And, as of now, the presumption is murder."

"What does this have to do with me?" Scotty asked.

"Would you please follow?" MacGregor said, delaying an answer.

Scotty slid behind MacGregor to the side of the corpse. MacGregor pulled back the corpse's shroud. The victim was Hugh Sutherland.

MacGregor smiled obliquely. "The fanatical Mr. Sutherland, who, I'm sure, has not been held in the highest esteem by Geminii management."

"Nor by the Transport and General Workers Union. Nor by the SNP. Nor by any number of radical national splinter groups. Nor most probably by his own opponents within the New Jacobite coalition. He failed, didn't he?"

MacGregor lit a cigarette, saying nothing.

Scotty stepped around the body. "Why am I here?" he asked.

"You're our prime suspect."

"What?"

"Why do you look so surprised?"

Scotty flicked some water off the edge of his Stetson. "I think the answer is obvious," he said angrily.

MacGregor smirked. "Where were you at three this morning?"

"Where the hell do you think I was?"

"Here?"

"No! I was in bed!"

MacGregor ground out the cigarette after just two puffs. "You seem to have made a habit of pursuing Mr. Sutherland. First the break-in at the union offices. Now this."

"I told you! I was in bed."

"Do you have a witness?"

"No."

MacGregor covered the body. "Well, we have one. An anonymous one, but one nevertheless."

"What do you mean?"

"A phone caller told us he'd witnessed the murder. Unforunately, the caller wanted to remain anonymous, didn't want o become involved. Nevertheless, he told us he saw two men emove an apparently unconscious man from a tan jeep, drop im in the bay, and hold him under the water. You have a an jeep, Bruce. And as a member of Geminii, you certainly ad no love lost for Sutherland."

"Look, you," Scotty said evenly. "There are probably a undred tan jeeps in Inverness."

"By registration? Only three. We already checked. And he other two owners are well known in the community and ighly respected, I might add."

"I didn't do this!" Was the presence of a tan jeep a coincience? he asked himself. Or had he been set up, presumably y Whittenfeld and Lefebre? Christ, a setup made absolutely o sense. Whittenfeld and Lefebre might have wanted to get id of Sutherland, but implicating him served no purpose hatsoever. It could not possibly seal his mouth about the ontrol hose fraud and the presence of a creature, and it had ertainly served to draw unwanted police attention to Geminii nce again.

"Mr. Bruce. Believe me. I am not conducting a vendetta. I ave nothing personally against you, nor am I intent on aaking you an example. But I have a very difficult job which getting more and more difficult with each passing day. here is still the *Columbus* investigation, our number-one riority, and so far it has been unsuccessful. There is a connuing query into the circumstances surrounding Father Macherson's death. And now, there is Mr. Sutherland. Geminii es at the heart of each of these matters, and unfortunately, ou have not been in an unassailable position. So bear with e."

MacKintosh returned from the shore side, acknowledging cotty. "There are no tire tracks anywhere," he said, gesturing MacGregor. "The jeep must have remained on the road. utherland must have been carried or dragged, though it esn't look like he was unconscious at the time. There are a t of scuff marks and movement. No, the caller was misken. We'd bet a good lager that Sutherland was alive when e was placed in the water."

"Anything else?"

"We've taken casts of the footprints."

"Any bits of clothing? Paper? Whatnot?"

"Nothing."

MacGregor thanked MacKintosh, who then retreated.

"Mean business, murder," MacGregor declared. "I've seer a few in my time, but I never get used to it. No one ca Don't you think?"

"Superintendent, what do you want from me?"

MacGregor led Scotty back to the patrol car, then allowe him to get back inside with two of the officers.

"I want you to answer a question."

"All right."

"Where were you last night at three in the morning?"

Exasperated, Scotty replied, "For the last time, in bed."

MacGregor stared hard. "Thank you, Mr. Bruce. You ma go."

MacGregor signaled the driver; the patrol car pulled awa

Scotty liked the prospect of noise. It would help him forg the incredible pressures. Goddamn day had just crawled. Ma Gregor had set the snail's pace. Nothing had altered it. N even a planning session for the next dive.

He crossed the parking lot toward the pub door of tl Carn Dearg Inn. The windows were ablaze with light. Thei was movement, too.

He entered. The pub was jammed, as it always was at nin evening time. He grabbed the only available bar stool. Ma MacKenzie was standing over a booth. She did not see hir

He called to her, but she did not hear him. He noted tl paradox—she was one of the region's most powerful politic figures, but she was also an innkeeper, bartender, barmaid.

Only in Scotland, he thought.

She suddenly approached the bar. "I didn't think you'd I here so early," she said, pleasantly surprised.

"Couldn't wait to see you."

She poured him a lager. "How was the day?"

"Interesting."

She moved from the bar carrying a tray and glasses. Sl was dressed in a tartan skirt and white ruffled blouse. I liked the look. Very innocent. Very feminine.

"You seem very preoccupied," she said, returning to b position behind the counter.

He pressed his cheek to hers. "I want your body."

"Shh. There are people."

"They can't hear. And besides, they don't care."

"You're such an American."

Several patrons ordered. She catered to them. He noticed a box with a ribbon behind the bar.

"What's that?" he asked, pointing.

"A present for you," she said nonchalantly, as if she gave him a present every day.

He broke a smile. "For me? Why?"

"Because I love you," she whispered.

"Let me open it."

She handed him the box. He removed the wrapping, lifted the top ever so gently, and peeked inside. A magnificent plaid kilt, kilt jacket, bonnet, belt, and shirt lay in tissue.

"I don't believe it," he said incredulously.

"Now you'll be able to wear the sporran," she advised.

"I'll be laughed out of the country if I'm seen in this."

"Nonsense."

He motioned her close once more. "What about underpants?" he asked, whispering.

She was shocked. "Underpants?" she whispered back. "You can't wear such things. It's not done."

"I'll freeze my balls off!"

She glanced nervously at the patrons. "You'll find the strength. My father wore his kilt all the time, even in blizzards."

Once again, he looked inside the box, then moved his mouth up to her ear. "Must I really put this on?" he asked.

"Well, if you want my body," she replied *sotto voce*, "you're going to have to pay the price." She pointed to the box.

"Damn!" He burrowed into thought. "All right," he finally said.

Her expression was her reply.

Happy.

She sat on the edge of her bed. Her hands were clasped together in her lap. Her eyes were wide open. She was wearing an especially childlike smile.

"What's taking so long?" she called.

His voice tumbled out of the bathroom. "This is not easy, goddamnit."

"You're just making excuses."

"The hell I am."

Something dropped. Something rustled. She listened, trying

to stifle inadvertent laughter that would only discourage him. But she could tell he was flopping all over the place. She only wished she could see the confusion and watch him twist himself into a knot.

His face appeared moments later, peeking around the bathroom door, and then, head slouched, he stepped out, dressed in the kilt and accompanying outfit.

"Well, damnit, how do I look?" he asked, blushing, feeling momentarily guilty about wallowing in levity in the midst of death and terror.

She walked around him, palms to cheeks, pressing her effusive smile into an oval. "I think you look wonderful."

"I do?"

"Yes." She adjusted his jacket. "For some reason, I wasn't sure I'd get you to put the kilt on."

"Well, I did, and now you see me exposed. So laugh at me."

"You don't laugh at those you love."

He turned toward the wall mirror and broke into hysterics. "The hell! I'm ridiculous!"

She looked into the mirror, too, studying the powerful long legs that descended beneath the kilt bottom and the look of pain in his face.

"I love you very much," she said as she began to laugh as well.

The rush stripped him bare. He'd never felt like this with a woman before. Nor had he ever experienced such intensity, the conquest of the unconquerable.

He pressed himself between her legs. Her arms were wrapped around him, biting into his body like scissors. No more did he feel the fear, the reluctance, the inhibition. She was totally committed. As was he.

They reached orgasm. Their bodies fused; perspiration flowed together. Their breathing quieted.

Then silence.

He continued to look blankly into space, as if she wasn't even there.

"Something is wrong," she said as she moved her head on to his chest. "You've been off somewhere for the last ten minutes."

He said nothing.

"Is something wrong?" she asked.

"Yes."

"Is it me?"

"No, of course not." He could feel her heart suddenly begin to pound. "Superintendent MacGregor will probably ask you some questions."

"About what?"

"About do you know where I was last night at three o'clock in the morning."

"Why will he ask that?"

"Because Hugh Sutherland was murdered. At three. And I'm the prime suspect."

She jerked upward. "That's impossible."

"You heard me."

"Some suspect. You were here. In bed with me. You didn't leave to go home until three-thirty."

He grabbed her wrist. "That's the last thing I want you to tell him. Because that's the last thing someone in your position need announce. Can you picture it? The number-one opponent of the loch project having an affair and sharing a bed with the number-two man at Geminii. I love you. I don't want you injured. And in this medieval place, populated by all these medieval minds, that's exactly what will happen."

"My career is one thing. This is another."

He kissed her again and again. "I know. But I want you to promise you won't say anything. I didn't do it. The police will realize it without your help."

She turned on the bed light. "Mr. Bruce. This is me you're talking to. Don't you ever forget it. Nobody tells me what to do. Ever. If I can't come forward for a man I love, then I'm not worth the very salt in the sea. So if I decide to come forward, no one, and that includes you, is going to stop me. Understand?"

He rubbed his eyes, kissed her. "I love you," he said, then closed the light once more.

He left the inn at three-thirty, arriving home at four, managing three hours' sleep.

Noting he had another dive-planning session at ten, he showered, dressed quickly, then hustled down into the kitchen. Mrs. Munro, who had already prepared breakfast, was glancing out the window, her view impeded by a thick frost.

"The spring just doesn't seem to want to come, Mr. Bruce,"

she declared as she shuffled dishes from right to left, then back. "Ay, it's right cold this morning."

He buttered some toast, nibbled at his eggs. "It looks cold."

Mrs. Munro was exasperated. "Now isn't that what I just said? Lord help me, you'll never learn to listen. And I'm not a mite surprised. Coming in at all hours of the night isn't good for the senses. Numbs them."

Shaking his head, he continued to eat, glancing quickly over the lead articles on the front page of the *International Herald Tribune*. Behind him, Mrs. Munro put on her coat, intent on starting and warming up the jeep, as she did each day.

"I'll give the gas a good pumping today, Mr. Bruce," she said as she glided through the door. "The jeep'll be warmer than a goblin's fire."

"I appreciate it, Mrs. Munro."

She walked out the front door. He left the dining room for the den. Reaching the front of the hall, he heard the first turn of the engine.

Then a terrible explosion.

The door blew open. The windows shattered. Plaster fell.

Shocked, he ran out the front door. The smoke was incredibly thick. Debris lay all around. The jeep was burning with the rage of a sun. Mrs. Munro's charred remains were in the front seat.

Sickened, senses ravaged, he stumbled back against the wall of Travis House. Mrs. Munro was dead. That was the only impulse that registered.

It took him several minutes to come to grips with the fact that she had not been the target.

Chapter 28

Detective Chief Inspector MacKintosh and a detachment of homicide police arrived shortly after the explosion. MacKintosh conveyed an apology to Scotty from MacGregor—the superintendent had unavoidably been detained on another matter but would be there as soon as he could—then proceeded to question him extensively while a squad of police searched the house and car. Scotty had nothing to say because he knew nothing.

The medical examiners arrived.

Then Whittenfeld.

"I was just told!" Whittenfeld explained as he marched into Travis House.

"I appreciate your coming," Scotty said, noticing that Whittenfeld was wearing a light-colored tie for the first time he could remember. "And your concern."

"Concern alone is worthless," Whittenfeld countered. "We're going to do something about this!"

They entered the den. MacKintosh was speaking on the phone. They waited while MacKintosh finished the call. Then Whittenfeld swooped in on him, demanding the apprehension of the men who had planted the bomb.

"We will do the best we can," MacKintosh declared.

"So far, your best has been very inadequate," Whittenfeld scolded as he pressed down his lapels, adjusted his tie, twisted his watch band, mannerisms designed to distract.

"I'm sorry you feel that way."

"Where is MacGregor?"

"At the constabulary, involved in an important matter."

"Nothing is more important than this!"

"I have kept him informed, and he will be here as soon as he is able to come."

"Are there any clues?"

"As of this moment, no. However, the bomb squad has recovered most of the bomb fragments and a good portion of the capping mechanism, and we will be subjecting it to intense scrutiny."

"People!"

"Excuse me?"

Whittenfeld pointed out at the jeep. "If you had placed people under the intense scrutiny you will claim for the fragments, then this wouldn't have happened."

The phone rang. MacGregor was on the line, informing MacKintosh that he was on his way. MacKintosh relayed the message.

"I suggest you wait for the superintendent," MacKintosh mumbled.

"I certainly will," Whittenfeld declared.

MacKintosh left the den.

"Why was your house lady in the car?" Whittenfeld asked, turning to Scotty.

"She was warming it for me," Scotty replied.

"Did she do it every day?"

"Yes. She enjoyed it. Just like she enjoyed doing everything else around here."

"Then perhaps the bomb was meant for her."

Scotty whooshed a breathless laugh. "You're reaching. 'Cause the goddamn bomb was meant for me. Meant to blow my brains and gizzards all over Scotland!"

Whittenfeld seemed genuinely puzzled. "But why would anyone want to do that?" he asked.

Scotty lit a cigar. "That's exactly what I'd like to know," he replied, staring suspiciously at his superior.

Detective Superintendent MacGregor arrived a half hour later.

"We seem to be spending a great deal of time together, Mr. Bruce," MacGregor said as he opened his raincoat and sat on one of the lounges.

"I would rather it were otherwise," Scotty observed.

"I'm sure you do," MacGregor agreed, turning to Whittenfeld. "You know, until Geminii arrived in Inverness, this was a quiet place. Murder was uncommon. In fact, unnatural death of any kind was doled out sparingly." He shook his head. "Unfortunately, times have changed for the worse."

"What do you mean by that!" Whittenfeld challenged.

"Just a thought posed by a long-term resident who cannot help but be disturbed by the painful turn of events. And I can predict your reaction, Mr. Whittenfeld. You will challenge me once again. If the police were doing their job, you will say, this would not have happened."

"Precisely."

"It is always the police. The poor police." He laughed, gestured to Scotty. "I might have been better off following Rob Roy's lead, Mr. Bruce."

Scotty didn't reply. Whittenfeld impatiently shuffled across the floor. MacGregor removed a telegram from his pocket.

"I was detained on an important matter. A matter related to the bombing." He waved the telegram. "This telegram was received at constabularly headquarters a short time after you had called, Mr. Bruce, informing us of the death of Mrs. Munro. The transmitter claims responsibility for the bombing and indicates the bomb was planted to avenge the death of Hugh Sutherland."

"Why the hell me?" Scotty challenged. "I had nothing to do with Sutherland's death!"

MacGregor seemed embarrassed; he handed the telegram to Scotty. "The transmitter was aware we suspect you of the crime—how, I don't know. But one way or the other, the transmitter claimed to defer to the department's expertise. Since we suspected you, they were satisfied with your guilt."

"Great," Whittenfeld commented bitingly.

Scotty handed the telegram to Whittenfeld. Whittenfeld read it.

"The sender identifies himself as a Jacobite," MacGregor began again. "We have spent the last several hours trying to verify the missive's authenticity. That is why I was not able to appear here earlier."

"What have you concluded?" Scotty asked.

MacGregor stood. There was a Rand-McNally road map of Scotland pinned to the wall. He placed his finger on Glasgow.

"The telegram was sent from a precinct on the north side of Glasgow. We located the particular office and questioned the clerk. The clerk remembers the man who sent the telegram, a working man, muscular, stern-faced, lowest of class. Unfortunately, Glasgow is filled with such men."

"Why didn't the clerk notify the police when he saw the telegram?" Whittenfeld asked.

"Precisely my first query," MacGregor replied. "But you will notice the cryptic language. My associates in Glasgow informed me the clerk was of meager intellect—a veritable twit—so you can imagine his difficulty with words posed in such a manner."

"What else did you uncover, detective?" Whittenfeld asked, interrupting the detective's train of thought.

"We spoke to our informants," MacGregor declared. "They confirmed that Sutherland's death invoked a great deal of anger among known Jacobite sympathizers and operatives. But we were unable to uncover any evidence of planned reprisal. Nevertheless, the reprisal came very quickly—within the day—which only supports a suspicion of legitimacy to the Jacobite message. The Jacobites are particularly capable of mounting a strike on short notice due to the widespread nature of their organization and its top-heavy inclusion of zealots."

"So far, you've told us nothing," Whittenfeld declared.

"I'm sorry you feel that way," MacGregor said.

"What do you intend to do now?"

"Follow the leads. Examine the bomb fragments. Discover the identity of the man or men who did this."

"What about my executives? How will you protect them?"

MacGregor lit a cigarette and breathed deeply, inhaling the harsh tobacco fumes. "Apart from Mr. Bruce, I can only protect them through diligence and a thorough investigation. I trust your Mr. Lefebre can provide for internal cover. However, we will supply Mr. Bruce with an escort."

"Forget it," Scotty said. "I don't want an escort. I would prefer to protect myself. So far, because of your efforts, I am now both a murder suspect and an assassination target."

MacGregor raised his brow disconcertedly. "As you wish," he said, preparing to leave.

"There is one more thing," Whittenfeld declared.

"What?"

"I would like our people to assist you in the investigation."

"Absolutely not!"

"Lefebre and his team in particular."

MacGregor fumed. "This is the province of the Criminal Investigation Division. I will tolerate no interference from private parties."

"We can be of great help," Whittenfeld advised. "We have ways—"

"I'm sure you do. But you will dream about them." He pivoted to Whittenfeld. "I will not tolerate a repetition of the worker-melee incident. Nor will anyone else in an official capacity around here. You will keep your security men within the confines of Geminii base. They are not to sortie out into the general area. Nor are they to engage in any pursuits properly within the jurisdiction of the police." His expression was hard, definitive. "I trust I make myself clear. But if I don't and your security people do roam where they should not be, I will have them arrested, and I will ask the procurator to prosecute. Understand?"

Whittenfeld did not reply. MacGregor left Travis House.

Angry, Whittenfeld departed a short time later. Scotty called Jerry Foster and asked him to expedite the shipment of Mrs. Munro's remains back to her home. Foster advised he had already contacted Mrs. Munro's immediate family and had arranged to send the body out on the eight P.M. train.

Scotty then contacted Mary MacKenzie at the Carn Dearg and told her what had happened. She was shaken; she wanted to come right over. He stopped her, preferring she meet him at the railroad station that evening.

Shortly before eight, he drove a company car through the darkness and a damp, penetrating mist to the terminal, situated in the center of the city. Jerry Foster had already left after seeing to the particulars. Mary MacKenzie was still there.

She embraced him, squeezing tight, refusing to let go, tears running down her face.

"I'm scared for you," she mumbled. "And ashamed for Scotland."

They stood in the mist together, then walked to the northbound train. An empty hearse was sitting next to a freight car. They looked into the car. Mrs. Munro's coffin was inside, propped securely.

"The poor woman," Mary MacKenzie said. "I can still hear her voice. You know, she was very un-Scottish in many ways. Her sternness better fit a big Irishwoman. Yes, she had an Irish way about her."

The train belched a cloud of smoke; it began to move.

"She was some piece of work," Scotty said as a requiem. "I'll miss her."

Scotty and Mary MacKenzie spent the night together again at the Carn Dearg Inn. He stayed until the morning, leaving the inn at seven A.M. and arriving at Geminii base shortly after nine.

A message from Bill Nunn was waiting. He had hit pay dirt, a hard chert-silica formation, and was on his way to shore. Scotty summoned Dr. Rubinstein and Dr. Fiammengo.

The two researchers arrived at the complex just after Nunn; Scotty immediately forbade discussion of the assassination attempt.

"The chert-silica samples are identical," Nunn declared as he led Scotty, Dr. Rubinstein, and Dr. Fiammengo into the base geology office.

Nunn broke open a package he had in his hand along with several he'd removed from the cutting shelves. He placed four samples on a microscope stand.

"The two on the left," he explained, "were taken from the return flow of mud at the time of the first attack. The two on the right came out an hour ago. I took the initiative. The rotary is down."

Scotty looked through the microscope and manipulated the slide. "That's it!" he declared.

Dr. Rubinstein and Dr. Fiammengo looked next. They agreed. Nunn read his composition breakdown; it matched the controls.

"Does this mean we're on?" Dr. Rubinstein asked, knowing the answer already but wishing to hear it out loud.

"Yes," Scotty said. "As soon as we get the Lyon bit in place, we're on."

Chapter 29

～～～～

The submersible swung into position. Johannes Aard noted the fathometer reading and set the ballast tank controls to depth.

Dr. Rubinstein's voice echoed through the communications equipment, corroborating a position fix.

Malcolm Conner, who lay next to Aard, looked out the forward porthole; as usual, visibility was minimal.

The air-purification unit hummed softly. Static rippled through the comm-phones. Sound blips ticked off the control meters.

Conner reset the position of the exterior tape cameras. Aard put on a sonic receiver headset. He listened to the purr of the *Magellan*'s mud pumps, then checked his sound-oriented DME. They were three hundred feet due south of the *Magellan*'s riser, lying two hundred feet below the surface. All propulsion systems were still active. If anything was sighted approaching, they would shift position to intercept, manipulating ballast and thrusters.

Aard felt the buoyancy, the sensation of weightlessness. One never quite got used to it. He could also feel their center of gravity shift counter to the intermittent upthrusts of the engines, which held the submersible in position against the current.

He and Conner had both felt uneasy that morning. It wasn't the operation's requirements. Rather, it was the whole concept. Though they had enthusiastically accepted the assignment, they'd begun to have second thoughts. Neither could pinpoint anything in particular that had set them off. Nothing extraordinary had happened yet; rather, their imaginations had started to run rampant. Damn, it was creepy—the anticipation of a confrontation with the unknown.

Aard moved close to the observation window. He coul
see suspended particles of peat dancing in the water. Christ
what a hell hole. That something huge might live in it wa
almost unimaginable.

Almost!

Scotty mated disjointed stimuli, the movement of the barge
the sight of the floating pontoon rafts, the sense of tension in
the command room, snips and pieces of conversation. Alone
they meant little; together, everything.

He placed his hands on Dr. Fiammengo's shoulders. Sh
looked up, touched his arm. She was dedicated, as hard
working as Dr. Rubinstein, who was running back and fortl
across the room, supervising the start-up. It occurred to hin
he'd never gained an insight into the mechanism that drov
the researcher. All he knew was that a man of boundles
scientific skill had decided to devote a large portion of hi
time to monsters.

Dr. Rubinstein approached, holding out a clipboard. Scott
grabbed it, and taking off his headset, picked up a differen
set of communication gear. It was time to contact the sona
tug and the *Magellan*.

They were ready!

Captain Eamonn Harrigan felt a surge of excitement. Sev
eral seconds before, he'd received Scotty Bruce's operationa
command.

He looked out the window toward the *Magellan*. Off he
port, the submersible was lying waiting, its position indicate
by the radio buoy. He glanced at one of the side-scan prin
outs. There she was, the sub, her needle-shaped nose pointe
toward the deep loch trench.

He massaged the curled ends of his beard. There wer
beads of sweat on his palms. He hadn't been told anythin
specific, but Mr. Bruce had made it clear they were lookin
for something other than a submersible.

He looked up—ominous black clouds, borne by fierc
winds aloft, traversed the Scottish sky—then walked throug
the bridge cabin, his communications headset linked to i
console by a long cord. He scanned several scopes and mor
itors, sat, removed a rubber band from his pocket, wrapped
around his fingers, and began to wait.

*   *   *

A communications officer relayed Scotty Bruce's operational order. Tony Spinelli, who'd been given only the bare essentials of information, walked toward the drilling platform.

"Start the rotary," he ordered.

Moments later, a roar of machinery exploded, and the rotary table began to turn, twisting the Lyon TX-1 bit at the bottom of the bore.

It had begun.

Johannes Aard listened carefully to the sounds punching through the headset. He could still pick up the muffled roar of the *Magellan*'s mud pumps, but the preeminent sounds were now issuing from the rotary engines and the drill itself.

He glanced at Conner. Conner seemed transfixed, his face pressed up against the viewing porthole.. Aard looked out, too. Nothing.

"Anything worth hearing?" Aard asked, taking off the headset.

Conner cracked a smile. "No. Not really."

"You're smiling about something."

"I'm trying to keep my mind on the job," he said. "On this thing out there, assuming it exists. And I get funny thoughts. Kind of ridiculous."

"Like what?"

"I have a vision of a beautiful mermaid swimming up to the front porthole and embracing the manipulators."

"You're nuts."

"It's no more unimaginable than the chance of a giant wanker appearing. And I'd much rather have the mermaid. This wanker may not be very cordial. It wasn't to the *Columbus.*"

"We're mobile. The *Columbus* wasn't."

"How mobile?"

"Mobile enough."

"No bets! We're going to stick ourselves right in the wanker's way if it appears—if it exists—and the wanker may not like it. You think about that. I'll think about mermaids. At least till we're put to the test, I'll keep me cubes warm."

Aard laughed.

"Captain!" the chief sonar officer screamed.

Harrigan appeared. "What?"

"Take a look at these printouts and sectascans."

Harrigan studied several traces. "What's its position?"

The engineer pointed first to one set, then another. "Here it's right in the center of the trench at about eight hundred feet. Here it's at six fifty. Here it's at the same depth, but it' moving northwest."

"Toward the *Magellan?*"

"Can't tell yet."

Harrigan checked with the other engineers. Nothing had shown up on their heat or noise scopes, and as expected nothing had registered on the subsurface sensors, either.

Harrigan called the command barge.

"How big is it?" was Scotty's first question.

Harrigan caucused with the sonar engineers. More trace had been taken. The velocity of the target object had in creased. It had also moved up to six hundred feet, and it direction was now more determinable. It was heading righ for the *Magellan*.

"An estimate? A hundred feet or more."

Harrigan checked the printouts again, then, biting his li nervously, walked to the bridge cabin door. He looked at th loch. It seemed so serene, so peaceful.

It was hard to believe they were confronting the unknow beneath its waters.

The tension was palpable. Technicians worked in a frenzy The cabin was nearly silent.

Aard and Conner had been informed the target object wa rapidly moving in their direction.

The television eyes had not yet picked up anything. Neithe had the barge's own simple sonar unit.

Scotty felt a lump rise up his throat, cutting off the air, feeling of suffocation.

He looked at Dr. Rubinstein and Dr. Fiammengo. Both were white, drained of color.

The lead sonar tug relayed additional data.

The target object had moved closer.

Tony Spinelli nervously peered out at the command barge One. Two. That was it. Two blips from the barge's beacon

"Shut down the rotary," he ordered.

*   *   *

Johannes Aard and Malcolm Conner quickly worked their controls while watching their sonar unit and the view through the porthole.

Moments before, they'd started to broadcast the vibrations, coincident to a shutdown of the *Magellan*'s rotary.

"Anything yet?" Scotty asked, his voice their only contact with the surface.

"We have it on sonar," Aard replied.

"It will be coming up below you just a bit," Scotty advised. "About two hundred feet off your bow and a hundred feet beneath."

"Affirmative," Conner said haltingly, "but we have no visual contact yet."

"Hold it!" Scotty said, pausing. "Sonar advises target object has now moved under you and is stationary. Do you confirm?"

Aard and Conner checked their instruments.

"We're not picking it up anymore," Conner said. "It must be inside a dead cone for sonic."

"Hold for instructions," Scotty advised.

Captain Harrigan raised the command barge on the command phone.

"Mr. Bruce?"

"This is Bruce."

"We've got a strange trace here. Can you verify?"

"What have you got?"

"The target object is pointed up like an arrow, right into the center of the submersible. We have it just floating there if it were taking aim."

Scotty's voice cracked back. "Affirmative for us."

"We'll continue to monitor," Harrigan said.

Aard and Conner had just received a relay from the command barge when the jolt hit, turning the submersible over on its side.

Sparks erupted from the instruments. The sonar unit and several of the submersible's directional controls shorted out. A small fire ignited. Conner instantly extinguished it while Aard informed the surface that they'd been hit.

"Is your sonar unit working?" Scotty frantically asked.

"No. And some of our stabilizers are out. Though we have our engines and directional and surfacing controls."

The submersible, which had been listing severely, sudden[ly] righted itself. Aard reported the curious recovery.

"Can you see out the portholes?" Scotty asked.

"No," Conner replied. "It's just black out there. Our floo[d] must be out."

Scotty shot back. "Sonar informs us that the target obje[ct] is directly in front of you."

"What do you mean?"

"Get the hell out of there!"

Aard turned off the vibration broadcast, then hit th[e] thruster controls. The thrusters surged, but the submersib[le] didn't move. He unloaded ballast. Still no movement. He trie[d] several pitching maneuvers. Nothing. He reported their i[n]ability to navigate.

"Are your controls inoperative?" Dr. Rubinstein aske[d], having cut into the circuit.

"No," Conner replied, checking electrical connection[s]. "Everything is working. But we can't move!"

Surface checked sonar again. Aard and Conner regauge[d] their instruments. They listened. The silence was eerie. The[y] exchanged transmissions. Then the submersible began to roc[k].

They were thrown against the bulkhead. More spar[ks] flashed. Bleeding heavily from a gash on his forehead, Conn[er] passed out. Terrified, Aard called to the surface.

"What is it?" Scotty cried.

Aard tried to answer. His headset popped off. More shor[ts] and small fires flashed. Frantic, he tried to regain control [of] the craft.

Suddenly, a hideous sound ripped through the cabin, t[he] skirl of metal buckling. The hull started to collapse. Wat[er] poured in.

Aard looked up.

There were teeth! Hideously sharp! Extending into the cab[in] through the shell!

Aard grabbed the headset while jettisoning the sub's car[m]eras.

"It's bitten through!" he screamed. "We're in its mouth[!]"

Scotty Bruce, Dr. Rubinstein, and Dr. Fiammengo board[ed] the sonar tug and followed an officer into the bridge cabin.

Captain Harrigan and the chief sonar engineer were hu[d]dled over a slew of sonar records.

Harrigan pointed. "Look at those!"

They carefully examined the printouts.

The truth was obvious. The creature had the submersible's nose in its jaws and was dragging the sub down into the deepest loch trench.

They watched the printouts, scans, and holograms. Depth readings continued to advance. The submersible went down, dragged by the unknown. Then, suddenly, it disappeared.

"Where'd it go?" the sonar engineer asked.

"God knows," Dr. Rubinstein struggled to say.

Scotty slammed the cabin door. "We're going to shut down the *Magellan* and keep her shut," he screamed.

Dr. Rubinstein charged back. "Think, man. Think about the opportunity!"

"I am thinking!" Scotty screamed, shaking. "I'm thinking about the two men who just died. Thinking about the crew of the *Columbus*. I don't want any more corpses."

"Let's wait until we see the pictures," Dr. Fiammengo pleaded.

"I don't need any pictures. Forget it! The *Magellan* is down."

Dr. Rubinstein grabbed Scotty by the arm, turning him face to face. "You can't do this! You can't shut down!"

Scotty looked deep into the man's eyes. He did not like the view, but he should have expected it. "Why not? You have what you wanted. We've found the creature. Identified it. Taken its picture. Obtained enough information to orchestrate the salvation of the *Magellan* and her men. And if I remember correctly, you were going to walk with me into constabulary headquarters. Walk with me en masse!"

Dr. Rubinstein did not reply.

Dr. Fiammengo stepped forward, glancing out the cabin window at the launch, which had just returned with the submersible's tape cameras.

"Now is not the time to argue this out," she suggested. "There's too much emotion at play. Let's wait. Then talk. Let's allow the emotion to die. Then we can reason. Use logic."

Scotty stared. "Logic?" he asked, his voice dripping with anger.

Chapter 30

The examination table came to life with a spray of fluorescent light. Dr. Rubinstein hovered close, waving a pointer. The table was divided into two sections, one containing selected sonar records, the other an extensive series of glossies.

Dr. Rubinstein traced the sonar material chronologically, tying the records to actual communications, which were reflected in the transcripts he held in his hand.

Then he turned to the glossies.

"It wasn't until we'd returned to the command barge that we realized the crew had been able to jettison their interior and exterior tape cameras," he was saying, his usually agitated voice pulsating with excitement. In fact, since the loss of the submersible the day before, he hadn't slept or eaten, having spent most of his time poring over notes, command barge records, sonar data, and the recovered prints. "Fortunately, Aard and Conner had their wits about them in the face of almost certain death. Or else we wouldn't have had these fantastic exhibits. Fortunately, too, I chose the MV-7 submersible laboratory, among whose prominent systems were the detachable tape units with flotation jackets." He paused, obviously proud of himself, then forlornly shook his head. "I was well aware there might be considerable danger, and I wanted to make sure there'd be a recoverable record even if something went wrong below."

He glanced at Scotty, who was standing at the end of the table next to Tony Spinelli and Jerry Foster. Scotty glared back, a prophecy of imminent explosion written across his features.

"The pictures on the right were obviously taken by the exterior tape cameras and the ones on the left by the interior system. Let's look at the exterior views first."

Whittenfeld focused his attention on the exhibits. "Go head," he said, opening his collar button and loosening his ie.

"Look at this," Dr. Rubinstein said, pointing, "This frame hows part of the creature's body. Notice the scales; they are ery reptilian. You can also see part of a flipper. We think he flipper may be vestigial, but of course we can't be sure." Ie swung the pointer with precision. "This is interesting. The ppendage is an upper arm, and if you look behind it, you an see part of a flipper, too. We think it's the same flipper ve saw in the previous picture. In fact, the proximity of the wo appendages has led us to the vestigial theory."

"And this?" Whittenfeld asked, tapping a glossy.

"That is a claw," Dr. Rubinstein declared. "A huge one.)ne of several that sit at the end of each armlike appendage." Ie shifted his eyes, looking into space, almost into another limension. "What a fantastic creature!"

Dr. Fiammengo slid along the table; she also had a pointer. Notice these shots," she suggested. "They capture the head. The speck in the corner of this frame is part of the eye. And these blurred white lines were made by teeth moving apidly by the lenses."

"How big are the teeth?"

"Six or eight inches."

"And the size of the open mouth?"

"Let's say big enough to surround the nose of the submers- ble, whose diameter was six feet."

Whittenfeld examined several other prints, interior views. Fascinating," he said.

"We've even been able to determine exactly what Aard and Conner were doing at each interval," Dr. Rubinstein advised. Ie moved closer to the table, explaining each frame, finally inpointing the concluding print. "Notice the hull impacting," ie said. "You can see the first hint of water entering. And here. The white points. Believe it or not, they're teeth. Coming through the hull. Just think of the power in that bite. t's a wonder it didn't bite the *Columbus*'s marine riser in wo."

"It didn't have to!" Scotty said caustically, his downbeat oice intruding into the euphoria.

Whittenfeld shut off the fluorescent examination light, lanced at Lefebre, then turned to Scotty Bruce.

"So," he said. "This thing of yours exists."

"Yes," Scotty replied coldly.

"What do you suggest we do?"

"I don't suggest anything. What I have to say is a demand
We're going to stop operations before the *Magellan* is de
stroyed. Before more innocent men lose their lives."

Dr. Rubinstein squirmed; he seemed near panic.

"I'm sorry," Whittenfeld said. "I told you nothing stop
operations. Ever. And your demands mean nothing to me
This thing has killed. We will kill it."

"You can't," Dr. Rubinstein implored, interrupting, moving
back and forth along the table, eyes pleading.

Whittenfeld ignored him. "We will kill it," he repeated.

"We have no right," Dr. Rubinstein argued.

"The thing is a killer!"

"Yes," Scotty suddenly said, realizing so far he was speak
ing to deaf ears. Didn't Whittenfeld fear the information he
possessed? Did Whittenfeld's fixations make him immune to
reality? "It's a killer. It killed my best friend. But we invade
its home. We've invaded its spawning grounds. The thing
doesn't have a logical mind. It can't think. It can only defend
itself. So we're going to shut down the ship."

Dr. Rubinstein burst between them, frantic, jerking hi
head from side to side. "Listen to me! You must listen." He
thrust his hands outward through the air, a vision of constant
motion. "We can't shut down the drill ship, and we can't kill
the creature. We must try to catch the creature and show i
to the world." His eyes blazed. "Think of it. The past reborn
Legend come to life. We can't let this opportunity go to waste
We can't avoid our responsibility." He looked to one man
then the other, desperate. "Think of what we could learn
This thing survived the destruction of every other member of
its species. Why? How? We get the answers; we solve the
riddle of the past and might very well unlock the key to the
future. Think what this could mean to Geminii! Think of the
international furor if you killed it. No, it must be caught. I've
waited an eternity for this. This opportunity comes once in a
lifetime to so few men. You must let me catch it."

Scotty watched Dr. Rubinstein beg and plead. Obsession
Whittenfeld was obsessed with the loch. With what lay beneath
it. Dr. Rubinstein was obsessed, too. With what lived in its
waters. The creature was obsessed with defending its home
Mary MacKenzie was obsessed with the politics of nationhood
MacPherson had been consumed with the drill ship and the

beast. And Sutherland had been obsessed with violence. It was almost incomprehensible, all this intensity fueled by the loch. Almost every person involved except, paradoxically, the men who had died had been sucked into Loch Ness's gut and had been spit out, cancerized with dizzying passion.

He could only ask himself where it would lead if he didn't stop it in its tracks.

"We may not have to kill it," Whittenfeld suddenly said. He turned to Tony Spinelli. "Does anyone on board the drill ship know what happened?"

"No," Spinelli said. "They were all told the submersible had surfaced further west, near Fort Augustus, and had been removed at that point."

"Harrigan?"

"Harrigan and his crew passed stringent security checks which were conducted by the Ministry of Defence and ourselves. They are totally trustworthy. No, they have not revealed what happened, and they won't."

Whittenfeld stepped back from the table. "No one in this room will say anything, either, including you, Mr. Bruce, and I'm sure we can count on the cooperation of the submersible's base company if we can couch the submersible's destruction and the men's death in terms of a national emergency. I'll handle the priorities. There's the insurance problem, but that can be sidestepped momentarily." He turned to Foster. "Can you close off any possible leaks?"

Foster filled his puffy cheeks with air. "If I can't, no one can."

"I don't mean just the submersible thing. But we'll need a cover."

"If we come up with a convincing cover, I can make it stick."

"What are you talking about?" Scotty asked, incredulous.

"We're talking about Geminii Petroleum. The company good. The Loch Ness project. You want us to stop operations. That is impossible. I want to kill the thing. That might be counterproductive. But Dr. Rubinstein may have something." He turned to the researcher. "Suppose I say all right. Suppose I let you try and catch this thing. Tell me how. Tell me how you would do it without interrupting well progress and without endangering the drill ship."

Dr. Rubinstein jumped awkwardly away from the table and returned with a briefcase, which he opened.

"I always knew I would find *Nessiterus Rhombopteryx*," he said, removing a handful of documents. "I knew when I did that I might have an opportunity to try to catch it. I knew I would have to be prepared. The institute commissioned a team of naval architects, structural engineers, and NASA docking and computer specialists to work out and program a method of entrapment." He spread two huge blueprints across the table, covering the glossies. "This is the fruit of their labor. An undersea snare, a metal venus fly trap floated to depth by ballast tanks and actuated through surface controls."

Whittenfeld snapped on the overhead fluorescent lights again and studied the blueprints.

"How do you close the trap's spokes around the thing?" he asked several minutes later.

Dr. Rubinstein pointed to the bottom of each U-shaped spoke. "The spokes are hinged at the base center of the U, and each hinge contains a watertight motor. The moment the creature is lured inside, we actuate the motors, closing the spokes. It takes less than sixty seconds, and if we can keep the creature inside during closure, we have him."

"How do we know when the creature is in the trap?" Whittenfeld asked.

"The trap is lined with sonar and television units which feed information into a command barge computer whose programs were designed by NASA engineers. The computer works like satellite docking hardware. It assembles data and prints out digital readings and pictorial schematics which represent the actual position of any target relative to the trap."

"What are the spokes made of?"

"High-grade structural steel coated with a very strong titanium shield."

"This thing has bitten through metal before."

"I don't think it'll bite through this combination before we can bring the trap to the surface."

Whittenfeld motioned Lefebre to the table. "What do you think?" he asked.

Lefebre stared at the blueprints, chewing viciously into a chunk of tobacco. "Anything is possible. But you'll have to ask an engineer if it will work or not."

"I'm not asking you for an engineering opinion. I want to know whether you can work out the logistics and security."

"Of course I can."

Whittenfeld walked behind Dr. Rubinstein. "How do you lure the creature into the trap?"

"The same way we lured it to the submersible. We use the *Magellan*'s rotary to bring it close; then we cut off the rotary and cut in the recorded vibrations, which we will feed into the trap through surface connections from a command barge."

Whittenfeld smiled at Dr. Fiammengo. "Do you think this will work?" he asked.

"I was part of the team that designed it," Dr. Fiammengo replied.

Whittenfeld smiled, bowed, then turned back toward Dr. Rubinstein. "All right, suppose we catch it. Then what do we do with it?"

The energy generated by Dr. Rubinstein's enthusiasm was infectious. "We study it. Then return it to the sea. Which is its native home. You and Geminii receive the glory of its capture. And I humbly present the story to the scientific world."

Whittenfeld, very reflective, began to pace. "You say you return the thing to the sea?"

"Yes."

"But you've told me when you walked in here that you're convinced this thing has a route into the loch."

"Absolutely convinced."

"How long can we keep it in the trap out of the water?"

"I don't know. We can't let it die! And it might, even if we keep the cage water suspended. It might have trouble breathing in air for extended periods. We might be forced to return the creature very quickly."

"Then it will swim its ass right back in here and go after the *Magellan!*"

"Not if we find the access tunnel and block it until you've completed your drilling operations."

"How do we do that?" Lefebre asked.

"I'm not sure," Dr. Rubinstein said, "but we must address the issue immediately. Look at the sonar records. The creature dragged the submersible down into the loch's trench, and then both disappeared. It might have pulled the submersible under a ledge. But it might very well have dragged it into the mouth of its cavern."

Whittenfeld shook his head. "We can't send divers down there. It's too deep."

"I'm aware of that. We'll just have to figure out a way to search for the route on the land mass."

Whittenfeld shifted his attention back to the blueprint. "Do you have an estimate on construction time, doctor?"

"Three weeks once the materials are on site."

"The materials are no trouble."

"There's London," Spinelli said.

"I'll take care of London," Whittenfeld snapped.

Whittenfeld bore in on the design specifics while Dr. Rubinstein explained. Everyone waited. Then Whittenfeld looked straight at Dr. Rubinstein.

"We do it!" he said. "We start tomorrow."

"No, we don't." Scotty suddenly declared, returning from the oblivion to which he'd been relegated. He'd tried to deal with Whittenfeld internally, tried to prevent disaster without having to approach senior company management or outside authorities. But Whittenfeld seemed bound and determined to prevent him from stopping disaster painlessly. Whittenfeld was asking for a showdown, and the goddamn maniac was going to get it! He was going to move quickly on the one issue that mattered, the presence of the creature in the loch. The hose fraud and the death of the divers were no longer of imminent importance. They were old business. The drill ship and the safety of its men were now.

"The only way you can proceed," he declared, staring right at Whittenfeld, "is to endanger the drill ship and its crew. And I'm not going to let it happen. If you don't shut down voluntarily, I'm going to shut you down. Understand?"

No one replied.

He'd lost Dr. Rubinstein and Dr. Fiammengo, and he was angry about it. He did not like being used, and damn, they had used him but good.

The conversation he had with both doctors after Whittenfeld and the others had left the room could not have bagged the truth more clearly. He'd given them credibility. He'd eased their feet in the door, helped them maneuver past Whittenfeld. And now that Whittenfeld had come around to embrace their ultimate objective, Whittenfeld had become the sole object of their attention and allegiance, the classic switch-off having occurred.

He was furious that he'd waltzed blindly along without suspecting their true motivations, furious he'd failed to realize that the last thing they'd been concerned about, even from the very first, was the fraud of the tribunal, the deaths of the divers, and the safety of the human beings aboard the drill ship.

He let them know precisely what he thought of them; they did not like it, nor his promise that he would one day kick both their asses to the other side of the moon.

He then left the base, driving from Dores to Inverness, juggling his options. He could continue to press Whittenfeld for a shutdown of operations, but he knew the effort would be fruitless. He could go immediately to the authorities, but he preferred to go to John Fallworth, who he hoped would react quickly and decisively. However, he had no illusions. The switch-off by both researchers had chased illusions away. If he did not get the reaction he wanted from Fallworth, the next calls would be to Superintendent MacGregor and Mr. Farquharson.

Reaching Travis House at nine P.M. he placed a call to London. Fallworth was out to dinner. He left a message.

An hour later, Fallworth had still not called back.

He heard a noise.

He walked into the foyer from the den. Lefebre was standing there.

"How the hell did you get in here?" he asked, feeling his body turn rigid.

"I walked through the back door," Lefebre replied.

"What do you want?" He had to get the Frenchman out of there!

"You once said the project is more important than you and I. You said you wanted to talk. I came to talk."

"Don't give me that shit, Lefebre!"

Lefebre smiled. "I appreciate your impatience. I am an impatient man, too. I will get to the point."

"You do that!" Scotty ordered.

Lefebre moved slowly around him; Scotty pivoted, keeping himself face to face with his antagonist.

"We're concerned," Lefebre began, "that you might do something stupid. Cause a furor in London. Even go to the authorities. We hoped you would not go back to your old ways, but your threats this evening convinced us otherwise and left us no option but to give you an incentive to remain quiet." He dropped several pictures on the lounge—pictures of Scotty and Mary MacKenzie—obviously photographed surreptitiously. "We're aware of your relationship with the councilwoman. We're aware of its intensity. She is our incentive."

"What the fuck are you talking about?" Scotty challenged the flush in his cheeks unseen in the darkness.

"There are two men in Inverness equipped with deadl weapons. Their weapons are loaded. Their identities are un known to all but a few. Their ammunition has Madame Mac Kenzie's name written on it. If you say anything to anyone i London or anyone in authority, they will blow out her brains No matter where she goes or who tries to protect her, she wil be eliminated."

Scotty exploded at Lefebre, grabbed Lefebre by the throa and bashed the Frenchman's body against the wall. "I'll ki you," he cried as he continued to bore in.

Suddenly, he stopped. He'd felt it almost instantly. H looked down. A high-caliber automatic was jammed into hi groin.

"I only wish I could kill you!" Lefebre struggled to say Blood dripped from a cut on his scalp, and he fought to catc his breath. "You touched me, and I should kill you, bu you're going to stay very alive for now." He pulled away. "It' the woman who'll be dead if you open your mouth or do any thing I don't like."

Lefebre disappeared. The phone rang. Scotty did not an swer it.

Scotty's new jeep moved rapidly along the dark road to ward the city's residential neighborhood. Scotty had just lef the Claidheamh Mor Hotel where Dr. Rubinstein had re viewed the trap graphics and logistics, convincing him tha there was a legitimate chance the trap might work well enoug to perform its mission without any additional loss of life.

He'd been shaking since Lefebre had left Travis House and his brains had been shifting around the options so fas that he sensed it was about to come apart at the seams. Onc again, he'd been given painful choices, but now the choice carried even more intense personal stakes. If he opened hi mouth, Mary MacKenzie would be killed. Lefebre was no one to bluff, nor was murder beyond his ken. True, Whitten feld and Lefebre would then face a murder rap far more diffi cult to avoid than one that might issue from the cleverl conceived deaths of the divers, but he suspected that Whitten feld was absolutely convinced he would not endanger Mary MacKenzie's life. On the other hand, if he stayed silent, th

ves of the men on board the *Magellan* and the support tugs
ight well be endangered. Before speaking to Dr. Rubinstein,
ho'd been puzzled by his appearance and almost sudden
hange of heart, he'd thought his decision would have to lay
a favor of the men. But now that he realized the trap scheme
ight succeed, he had a new option. He could work with the
esearchers and the Geminii team to insure the trap's success
nd thereby shield both Mary MacKenzie and the crew on the
rill ship. And then, afterward . . .

He stopped the jeep in front of Whittenfeld's home. Two
ars, filled with the security officers, were visible nearby. He
imbed out and knocked on the mansion's front door. Whit-
enfeld appeared moments later and escorted him into the
ansion's living room. Both men sat. Whittenfeld was ex-
emely nervous.

"Lefebre visited me!" Scotty began.

"I know," Whittenfeld said faintly.

"Why are you doing this?"

"The vile bitch. The loch. My child."

"Did you consider the consequences if I don't go along?"

"You must go along. You don't want to see the girl hurt.
certainly don't. You must help us succeed. We need you."

"And if I help?"

"I will be forever grateful."

Did he actually hear those bizarre words? "And after the
atch?"

"The creature will be gone. The ship and men will be safe.
ou will be satisfied. The girl will be free of danger."

"Then I could go to the authorities?"

"I would deny everything. Your word against mine. You
ve no proof of a threat to the girl. No proof concerning
ything else that will stand. And you no longer have Dr.
ubinstein and Dr. Fiammengo."

Scotty wrenched Whittenfeld off the couch and pulled him
ose, so close that he could smell Whittenfeld's stale breath.
You're sick!" he screamed. "A fucking sick, miserable, de-
aved sonovabitch!"

Whittenfeld didn't reply; he just pushed Scotty's hand off
d walked out of the room.

Scotty breathed deeply, trying to control himself. There
uld be an aftermath. They would have to reckon with him.
But for now he would have to join the hunt.

Chapter 31

Detective Superintendent MacGregor walked down the pa[th]
to the east shore of Urquhart Bay. Ahead stood a huge plas[tic]
bubble, the same one that had overlain the remains of t[he]
Columbus and sonar tug. The bubble was heavily guarde[d.]
Pierre Lefebre appeared, to lead MacGregor to the bubb[le]
entrance.

MacGregor entered alone.

"Mr. Bruce!" MacGregor called, staggered by the sight i[n]
side.

Rising high beneath the bubble roof and extending o[ver a]
hundred and fifty feet along its length was the strange[st]
amalgamation of metal he'd ever seen. It looked like the inn[er]
frame of a giant boat. However, it did not look like a tr[ap]
because the end spokes had not been attached and would n[ot]
be attached until the trap was ready for submersion.

"Be right there," Scotty called, looking down from high [on]
a scaffold where he was perched with Tony Spinelli, I[ra]
Rubinstein, and two Geminii structural engineers.

MacGregor meandered around the work site, popping [a]
nut or two into his mouth. Scotty descended a scaffold ladd[er.]
MacGregor moved to meet him.

"Science fiction has come to Inverness, Mr. Bruce," Ma[c]
Gregor said. "No wonder there have been so many whisp[ers]
and questions."

"We haven't made the project's design a secret," Sco[tty]
said.

"No, but this place has been designated off limits for mo[nths.]
Isn't that correct?"

"Yes. Out of necessity. We're building a protective dev[ice]
to be installed around the drill ship's marine riser. It wo[uld]

290

e unwise to allow those who wish us ill to get a good look
t it."

"Well stated," MacGregor declared. He opened the center
f his raincoat, revealing a very conservative business suit
eneath. "Mr. Bruce. Is there a place we can talk? In private?"

Scotty pointed to an enclosure. "We'll be alone in there."

They entered a work room.

"Take a seat, Mr. Bruce," MacGregor suggested, sitting
imself. "There are several open matters we must address.
he attack on the drill ship. The death of Father MacPherson.
he murder of Hugh Sutherland. And, unfortunately, the
ssassination of your house woman."

"I was the intended victim!"

MacGregor just stared. "We are no closer to uncovering the
lentity of the party or parties who attached the drill ship. As
told Mr. Whittenfeld yesterday and repeated to Mr. Le-
bre just moments ago, that has not been for want of effort.
/e've worked closely with the Special Branch and the Gram-
ian Police in Aberdeen, particularly the Grampian units
ssigned to offshore matters. And I'm afraid Scotland Yard,
orking on the national level, hasn't fared much better, even
ith the assistance of MI5." He shot a quick smile. "What
others all of us is the departure from pattern."

"What do you mean?"

"In the past, the radical groups have been very vocal after
ttacks, claiming responsibility, blaring the trumpet. But
ey've been right quiet about the *Columbus* thing. Not a
ord. Not a claim. Ay, it's very strange indeed."

"What ghoul would want to lay claim to the destruction of
e *Columbus?*"

"Don't play the fool, Mr. Bruce. You're intelligent enough
 realize that it would have made no sense for a radical group
 have destroyed the ship without claiming responsibility
d the resulting political capital."

"Perhaps there are new motives. And I wouldn't overlook
e possibility of industrial espionage."

"We haven't."

MacGregor took out a notebook, opened to the first page,
d laid the book down. There were a series of notations. He
ecked one.

"The death of Father MacPherson. You are exonerated.
e *Magellan*'s crew vehemently supports your position. We
so spoke to members of the Waterway Authority, and they

assured us the current on the night in question could we
have overturned the raft."

Current? Scotty thought to himself, realizing a quick refer
ence to the real reason might bring all the activity under th
bubble to a jolting halt.

MacGregor applied another check to the book. "The mur
der of Hugh Sutherland."

"I didn't do it. And you know it."

MacGregor smiled. "You are exonerated there as well."

Scotty was taken by surprise.

"I received a call from Mary MacKenzie this morning,
MacGregor said, continuing. "She was distraught. She sai
she'd made a difficult decision, one which ran counter to you
wishes. She admitted being with you at the time of the murde
I asked if there'd been other witnesses. She said there hadn
because the two of you had been in bed together."

Scotty's face flushed. "She's lying. To protect me."

"You needn't protest. Councilwoman MacKenzie has neve
told a lie in her life. And I promise you, her reputation won
be impugned either as a woman or as a public official." Mac
Gregor added another check to his book. "The murder c
Mrs. Munro," he said. "We're now fairly well convinced th
Jacobites were behind the attack, and the new evidence sup
ports it."

"What evidence?"

"We traced the purchase of the bomb's fuse mechanism t
Strathclyde, which is the clandestine home base of the Ne
Jacobite movement."

"Then I'm no longer under suspicion."

"Not on these matters; though, of course, you were neve
under suspicion vis-à-vis the drill ship and your house woman

Scotty asked if there was anything else. MacGregor sai
no. They left the enclosure and walked back toward the e
trance.

"Thank you for your time once again," were the Superi
tendent's final abrupt words.

Scotty returned to Travis House a short time later an
found a limousine parked in the driveway. The driver hande
him a note. After reading it, Scotty climbed into the limo
rear seat.

The limousine drove across the Black Isle Bridge and d
posited Scotty in front of a small pub in Cromarty, whic

aced the Highland Fabricator's Nigg construction complex
about a mile and a half away across the Cromarty Firth.

John Leslie Houghton was seated at a small outdoor table
sipping tea, his face turned into the sun; he wore an exquisite-
ly tailored white suit and hat.

"You continue to surprise me," Scotty said, joining him at
the table. That was an understatement. He'd virtually forgotten Houghton's existence, let alone his request for Hough-
on's further assistance.

Houghton smiled, placing a cigarette in his holder. "Diligence is uncommon to you?" he asked.

"Not usually."

"Then you shouldn't be surprised by mine. I made a commitment to you. My undertakings are always completed. Besides, I've taken a liking to you, Mr. Bruce, and have devel-
ped a degree of sympathy for your situation."

A waitress appeared; Scotty ordered a lager, which was
promptly delivered.

"Why are we here?"

"Cromarty is a good place for discretion. Besides, I had
some business at Nigg." Houghton glanced off. "Incredible,
isn't it?"

The huge construction complex, characterized by enormous
gantries from which thousand-foot-high platforms could be
assembled, looked like something from the future. Though no
assembly work was underway at the moment, the sight of a
latform sliding down the launch ramp into the firth was
easily imaginable.

"I suppose you wanted to see me for a reason," Scotty said.

"Yes," Houghton declared. "I've set the last pieces of the
uzzle into place. I thought you'd be interested."

"Of course, I am," Scotty said, though he no longer knew
hy; echoes of the past seemed academic right now.

"If you remember, Mr. Bruce," Houghton began, "the
Biafran civil war broke out in June 1967, and Port Harcourt
was overrun in May 1968. A year's period. However, the war
idn't reach Biafran soil until November '67. Although there
was an unease in Biafra about the effects of the blockade
during the first six months, there was a simultaneous mood of
onfidence. In Enugu, the capital, and in Port Harcourt, the
l city, there was a bustle of activity. Armies were being as-
mbled. A sense of nationhood was about. And, of course,
Lieutenant Colonel Ojukwu's presence was everywhere, his

voice ringing out over every radio. Ojukwu was a talker. H
speeches could go on for hours. He could incite the crowd
Ojukwu was Biafra!"

"And Whittenfeld was there."

"As I told you, the Biafrans were leasing new drilling terr
tories. Whittenfeld, who was the senior Colorado represent
tive, became involved, emotionally so. He felt Biafra was b
break, the key to his future. Succeed in Biafra and he coul
name his price. The lease parcels became living things to hir
According to other oil executives, he became obsessed wit
them."

Scotty squirmed. It sounded familiar.

"Whittenfeld commuted between Port Harcourt, the c
fields, and Enugu. He got to know Ojukwu. Other Biafra
officials, too. He also met Lefebre. They got along famousl
Whittenfeld was fascinated by Lefebre's past and present. L
febre was intrigued by oil, most probably because he had
thing for money."

"Who did Whittenfeld answer to?"

"Colorado had a regional office in London as well as
home office in Denver, the U.S.A. However, Whittenfeld w
in complete charge in Biafra, assisted by a man name
Charles Bagley, who unfortunately met an untimely death."

"How?" Scotty asked, interrupting.

"The head of the concession administration was a ma
named Christopher Mbanjoku. Mbanjoku was a fierce Biafra
nationalist. However, he also had sticky fingers. Whittenfe
attempted to reach Mbanjoku through intermediaries. Th
connection was made. A bribe was offered. Charles Bagle
warned Whittenfeld the bribe attempt could prove to be cou
terproductive if the Biafran regime learned of it and aske
Whittenfeld to withdraw the offer. Whittenfeld refused. Ba
ley threatened to notify London. Bagley was found dead tw
days later."

"How'd he die?"

"He had a severe heart attack."

"He died of natural causes?"

"No," Houghton said, lighting a new cigarette and smilin
through a veil of smoke. "Lefebre murdered Bagley, fulfillin
a contract."

"You said Bagley died of a heart attack."

"There is a drug known to Yoruba tribesmen in weste
Nigeria called manijuju. It is a coronary artery vasoconstri

tor. It cuts off blood flow to the heart muscles. Lefebre fed the drug to Bagley. Bagley died four hours later."

Scotty stared, stunned. All he could think about was Jim Barrett, the incredible parallels. "Could a doctor detect the drug in a heart attack victim?" he asked.

"A medical examiner could in an autopsy, though it would not be easy."

Scotty finished his mug of lager. Houghton could tell Scotty was disturbed, but he continued.

"There is more," he said. "The bribe was paid. The bids were entered. However, before the bids were opened, a government official named Anthony Arisika, who had been charged by Ojukwu to stamp out corruption, received a call from a man named Martin Pettibone, the managing director of a competing oil company, Oxford Gas and Oil. Pettibone told Arisika about the bribes. Arisika confronted Mbanjoku. Mbanjoku denied the charges and asked to meet with Pettibone. A meeting was arranged. Arisika and Pettibone entered a room at the Presidential Hotel where they were to wait for Mbanjoku. Mbanjoku never arrived. Someone else did. Arisika and Pettibone were murdered. The murder was never solved."

"What happened to the bids?" Scotty asked, feeling a chill of terror.

"The bids were opened secretly. Colorado was awarded the concessions. Unfortunately, the federal army intervened."

"I assume Lefebre killed Arisika and Pettibone," Scotty said.

"Yes. Mbanjoku told Whittenfeld about the meeting. He asked Whittenfeld to do something or else both of them would be finished. Whittenfeld located Lefebre, paid him a large sum of money, and gave him the assignment. Lefebre, ever efficient, carried it out."

Scotty now realized why Whittenfeld had kept his presence in Africa a secret.

"Both men are murderers," Houghton said as he crushed out his cigarette. "But you are dealing with two very different animals. Lefebre is a killer. Pure and simple. He was trained to kill without emotion. He is a machine of death. His foible is that he has learned to enjoy killing. Lefebre is a simple man to understand. However, Whittenfeld is far more complicated. He is not a true killer. I doubt he would ever kill a person himself. In fact, his orders to Lefebre were always 'Do something.' The words *kill* or *eliminate* were never used. Whittenfeld is very pathologic, very disturbed. His insecurities have always manifested themselves in a quest for success, and though he is a respected manager, he has never achieved the personal success he's craved. And every project, at least by what I know of Biafra, has become an obsession. In Biafra, he talked about fathering the concessions. Of discovering the best parcels. They were his 'children.' He was their father. Their defender, Mr. Bruce. A man will protect his offspring with his life—not only defend them but do so without fear of injury. Such a man, or such a father, will abandon rationality, do anything to preserve what he loves. This I suspect is Whittenfeld, and if that is so, Whittenfeld is a very dangerous man, more dangerous than Lefebre."

"Why?"

"Because he is unpredictable, capable of anything, rational behavior or irrational."

Scotty stared. "Loch Ness is a mirror image of Biafra."

"How so?"

Scotty described the death of Jim Barrett. The death of the two divers. The murder of Hugh Sutherland. The murder of Mrs. Munro. Whittenfeld's repetitive references to his "child."

"It fits the profile," Houghton said.

"Could you verify my suspicions, perhaps get me proof?" Scotty asked, determined to keep Houghton involved, convinced there was a role for Houghton to play in the ultimate denouement of the drama, especially since he suspected that Whittenfeld might move to silence him permanently once the trap caper had been completed.

Houghton remained silent for a long time, eying Nigg askance. "I had thought my work for you was done."

"Had thought?"

Houghton's expression was oblique. "As I said, Mr. Bruce, I like you, and I appreciate your predicament. You will hear from me."

Scotty thanked the man. Moments later, Scotty was back in the limousine, heading toward home.

Chapter 32

The air was still. The sky was clear, a joy. Scotty felt relaxed at the stick of the helicopter. Mary MacKenzie was comfortable, too.

The view from three thousand feet was magnificent. She indicated landmarks, prominent geographical points.

He flew the chopper over the Black Isle, headed back to Cannich, and then turned to Loch Ness, flying out of the mountains over Urquhart Bay.

Below them, Geminii workers had already started to disassemble the bubble. The trap itself was visible in the Urquhart Bay marina. Mary MacKenzie knew all about it; she'd been part of the council committee that had reluctantly approved Geminii's proposal to build it.

She continued to describe the surrounding countryside, avoiding any mention of the trap. He tried to listen, but his thoughts were focused on the dizzying sequence of past events and those that were about to occur.

Since the start of the trap project, Scotty had spent most of his waking hours inside the bubble. He'd seen Mary MacKenzie only twice. Work had monopolized his time, he had explained. However, the work excuse had been merely that, an excuse, and he knew she knew it. He suspected she thought a problem had arisen between them; he damn well hoped it wasn't more than that. He had intentionally distanced himself from her physically while at the same time trying to keep their relationship alive by phone, sure the less time they spent together, the less she'd be endangered. If she knew the truth, there would be no way he would be able to convince her to remain quiet or leave Inverness. Rather, she would undoubtedly stick her neck right in the guillotine.

He lowered the chopper. The trap was truly amazing. But

what fascinated him nearly as much was what Whittenfeld
had told Fallworth, the cover. He'd spoken to Fallworth
several times since the night he'd refused to answer the phone,
and even when prompted, Fallworth had avoided any detailed
discussion concerning the trap. It was as if between him and
Fallworth, the subject was taboo.

They crossed the loch, flying over the foothills of the
Monadhliath Mountains, then returned to Geminii base,
boarded the jeep, and drove back toward Travis House.

"You're not happy," she declared as they passed the mid-
point of the journey home.

"Why would you say that?" he asked, trying to brush away
her concern.

"I've shared your bed," she said. "I know when you're
troubled, and you're troubled now."

He ached to tell her the truth. "There's nothing really. Just
intracompany problems. Pressures. We have to get the new
web into position, and I've been working night and day."

"I'm not stupid. There's more. Are you still angry I spoke
to MacGregor? Is there something more seriously wrong with
us?"

"Don't be ridiculous."

"I'm not. But we've seen very little of each other the last
three weeks. We talk on the phone. We say romantic things.
I know you're busy, but it's as if you've tried to avoid me."

"Now you're being paranoid."

"Does your unhappiness have anything to do with the submersible?"

Where did this come from? "What submersible?"

"There's an unsubstantiated rumor that a two-man sub went
down in the loch."

"Unsubstantiated and untrue. If such a thing had happened,
Energy inspectors would have been all over the place, and
there would have been no reason for us to hide such a thing."

"No apparent reason!"

"Remember what I was? Remember how I found plots under every rock? Remember I said you reminded me of me?
Well, it's happening again!"

"Sometimes you were right!"

"Rarely."

"What about the web?" She had asked Scotty to take her up
in the helicopter so she could get a good look at the device.

She was suspicious. She'd been suspicious in council. The view from the air had not allayed her concerns.

"What about it?"

"What's it really for?"

Goddamn woman, he thought! At times, he wished she wasn't so intelligent, so quick. "You heard everything there was to hear in council. You know everything there is to know."

They reached Travis House. Her car was parked outside. It was three-thirty.

"I wish you could stay, come in, relax," he said, though that was the last thing he could allow her to do. In fact, he'd been careful to keep her out of the house since it was full of documents and materials relevant to the trap operation. "But I have that important meeting at four, and I have to prepare."

"I know."

"I want you to know something."

"What?"

"I love you very much. Don't ever doubt it."

"I love you, too." Her voice was strained.

He smiled. "In a week or so, the work load will lessen." In actuality, the snatch would have been completed. "Then we're going to sit down, talk about us."

"I hope so," were her final words.

She sat in her car staring through the windshield. Travis House was visible, two blocks away. She was deep in thought, trying to piece together a myriad of impulses. It had been a strange three weeks. Before, their relationship had been almost idyllic. She'd never allowed herself to open up so. Then, suddenly, everything wonderful had screeched to a halt. Either Scotty had started to fall out of love, or something extraneous had occurred to interfere in his private life. She'd cried herself to sleep several times, but now, after spending the day with him, she'd begun to sense that sadness had been the wrong state of mind. Instead, curiosity and maybe even anger should have been the ruler of her actions. There was nothing she could point to in particular; rather, there had been an accumulation of puzzling developments: his behavior, the rumor about the lost submersible, the sudden rush to build the curious-looking web, and today, a very transparent effort to keep her out of Travis House. Was there something in the house he wished to hide? And what about the van occupied by a man and a very attractive woman that had driven up just after she'd departed? She'd seen the same van in front of his house several times over the last two months while passing by, but he'd never quite answered her request for a simple explanation. Was the van and its occupants part of the problem? Was she being overly paranoid, as he'd suggested, a mirror image of his former self? Was she jealous of the attractive woman? She didn't know, but her intuition had already raised a warning flag.

She looked at the note pad on her seat. She had scrawled down the license number of the van. At the very least, she was determined to find out something about its occupants. She would do it tomorrow.

Scotty looked out the fourth-floor window of Travis House. He could see Inverness Harbor below. Beyond, the Black Isle Bridge.

Sunday afternoon, navigation was light.

He chewed through the end of a new cigar, his attention recalled by Dr. Rubinstein, who had gruffly cleared his throat.

"Here's a representational graphic," Dr. Rubinstein said, pointing to an Inverness Firth Navigational chart on the wall.

Scotty moved closer. They were in the Travis House attic, which Scotty had set up as an alternative headquarters to their offices at Geminii base, where they could work, free from Geminii oversight.

"You'll notice the flags," Dr. Fiammengo said. "They represent each of the dives already made."

They had established five dive teams to explore the Inverness Firth for the cavern entrance. Dr. Rubinstein had drawn up the suggested dive points. It had been over a week since the first dive.

"Has anything looked promising?" Scotty asked.

"Not really," Dr. Rubinstein replied. "One team of divers picked up some current anomalies." He pointed to the chart. "But they proved to be red herrings."

Scotty turned to Dr. Fiammengo. "Did you get the quake seismic material?"

She held up a looseleaf notebook. "All that was available. All the Richter readings. We spent yesterday going over them. It doesn't seem promising. All the known faults have had significant seismic activity. If there's an offshooting unknown

"Sorry, but that's the way it has to be right now. You'll get full rundown before any attempts. For the time being, though, just go about your jobs and keep your mouths shut."

Whittenfeld and Lefebre, who had left the helipad, appeared below them.

"We're ready," Whittenfeld called.

Scotty climbed off the drill floor and joined Whittenfeld and Lefebre in a launch.

The launch pilot maneuvered the craft away from the drill ship and slid it parallel to the trap, which had nearly been set into position.

"Are those the cameras?" Whittenfeld asked, pointing toward bulges on the spokes.

"Yes," Scotty replied. "There are sixteen, two set on every other spoke. However, we changed camera models. The plans assumed standard water conditions, and we damn well know that's not the case here. We've substituted Hydro TC-125-ITs, which have very high resolution at very low light levels. All but two of the cameras are Hydros. The other two are Bebikoff color underwaters."

"And the sonar systems?" Whittenfeld asked; he'd made it plain that the responsibility for construction lay with Mr. Bruce and had therefore involved himself in the prep only sparingly.

"Just as the plans specify. There's passive and echo ranging inside and out. We'll know the moment something approaches and then enters the jaws."

The launch drew closer. Set at water level were the ballasts. There were four main ballast tanks for submersion and surfacing and several sets of smaller tanks for trimming and depth control. Four spools, two each at either end of the trap base, were all part of an ingenious anchoring system. The trap's four anchors would be cemented into the loch walls, much like the anchors of the *Magellan*. As the trap descended and ascended, the anchor lines would be spun in and out in order to keep the trap in a fixed position, held taut.

In addition, the four tugs would maintain connections, assuring additional horizontal stability.

Whittenfeld pointed toward the rear center of the trap. "The speakers?"

"Yes," Scotty said. "We've increased the amplitude range, too." He pointed to the top of the spokes. "There are the

clamps. Once we're sure the trap has closed around the cre
ture, we'll activate the mechanism, which will bind the oppo
ing spokes."

"What if the creature doesn't move into the trap?" Lefeb:
asked.

"It will," Scotty answered.

He stared at the two men, now fully aware of their bac
grounds, the bond between them. He also had a good idea
what made them tick and how the beat was anything b
predictable and sane. Lefebre, the trained murderer, Whitte:
feld, the obsessed manipulator of lives. They made him si
and angry.

The launch pulled up to the barge. They boarded and e
tered the command cabin. Captain Harrigan, Dr. Rubinstei
and Dr. Fiammengo were inside.

There were no other technicians on board.

"We were just discussing the tie-in of the barge to tl
trap," Dr. Rubinstein said.

"Then we arrived at the right time," Whittenfeld declare
turning to Harrigan. "Did you review the operational orde
with the other tug captains?"

"This morning," Harrigan said.

"How long until you're operational?" Whittenfeld asked.

"Two more days," Dr. Fiammengo advised, injecting he
self into the conversation.

"The tie-in?" Lefebre inquired.

"It will also take two days," Dr. Rubinstein said. "We pl
to begin first thing in the morning. The end spokes will l
attached first. The electrical crews will make the power cc
nections; then we'll follow with the television and son
teams and, finally, anchor and inspection divers. No, ever
thing has been covered in detail. Everything is timed an
scheduled. It should go like clockwork."

"You sure this will work, doctor?" Whittenfeld asked.

"It will work!!" Dr. Rubinstein replied, brimming with co
fidence.

Dr. Rubinstein began to explain the systems, particula
the computer and its associated display units. Dr. Fiammen
joined. Whittenfeld listened carefully. Lefebre seemed d
tracted.

Scotty just watched.

*   *   *

The telephone rang. Several times. Jolted from sleep, Scotty placed the receiver to his ear.

Sounds were garbled.

He turned on the table lamp. The windows were black. He consulted his alarm clock. Three A.M.

"Okay, Foster," he said, rubbing his eyes, clearing off cobwebs. "Say again."

Foster's voice barked out of the phone. "They had a breakdown at Carrbridge."

Scotty sorted impressions. Carrbridge. The new exploratory well. Twenty-two miles east of Loch Ness.

"What kind of breakdown?" he asked.

"Loss of circulation!"

The words invoked terror. The closed circulation of drilling mud had been interrupted. Some of the mud was disappearing from the well below ground, and the down pressure was obviously being reduced.

"Did they blow out?" he asked.

"No, but they shut down. Whittenfeld's on his way to base. You're needed, too. There's a chopper on call."

He climbed from under the covers. His clothes were next to the bed, thrown over a chair. He began to put them on.

"Why'd they lose the circulation?"

"Don't know. You'll have to ask them."

Scotty dropped the phone, finished dressing, left the house, drove quickly to the Geminii base, and proceeded directly to the roof.

A helicopter was already primed.

"Take her up," Whittenfeld cried after Scotty had climbed inside and the door had been shut.

"What do you have?" Scotty asked, huffing, exhausted. His shirt was askew; he'd buttoned it incorrectly in the rush.

"Just what you have."

The helicopter flew eastward into the black sky. They watched points of light recede into darkness. Several minutes after liftoff, floodlights appeared below. They'd reached the well site.

The pilot landed the chopper. They climbed off. The Carrbridge company manager was there to meet them. The well was a beehive of confusion.

"What the hell's going on here?" Whittenfeld asked, visibly perturbed.

"We lost mud circ," the manager answered.

"How bad?" Scotty asked.

"Total."

"Why?"

"We're not sure," the manager said; he was very agitated. "We were at eight hundred feet. There was no sign of abnormal pressure, and we were in an extremely consolidated formation."

"There's been no loss of drilling mud before?" Scotty asked. "Even small quantities?"

"No. It's all been very hard stuff. We didn't even find unconsolidated formations in the shallow part of the bore. And no fractures."

They walked to the well; there was some minor damage to the drilling assemblage. Most of the crew was clear of the derrick.

"What about injuries?" Scotty asked.

"Cuts and bruises," the manager replied.

Scotty looked around. "Let me see the mud and bit records."

The manager fetched the records. Scotty examined them in the bright glare of the floodlights and asked several more questions. The manager fired out answers.

"What do you think?" Whittenfeld asked after Scotty had reviewed all the parameters.

"I think we punctured into an underground cavern!" Scotty replied.

Whittenfeld looked to the company manager, who nodded indecisively.

"Look at the pump rates," Scotty said. "The other parameters. The loss of all the mud. The lack of gas or other fluids. No kick. Hell, we punctured a big space filled with air."

"What now?" the manager asked.

Scotty called for the well-site geologist. The geologist confirmed they had crossed no abnormal pressure zones. Nothing that would cause any problems.

"Pull the drill pipe!" Scotty ordered. "We may have our cavern!"

"But we're in Carrbridge. Nowhere near the Inverness Firth."

"I know!"

The rig crew began preparations to pull the drill pipe and shut in the well.

Scotty collared the manager. "Do we have the ability to

eam out a new hole so that I can get down in there? Say to
orty-six or forty-eight inches in diameter?" They couldn't
use the old hole; casing had already been inserted and cemented.

"We do, but—"

"Don't but me. Just get the material here for a big workout. Then contact base and have them ship in some television
equipment with extension electricals for a long drop. Say two
thousand feet. Make sure base sends the right kind of TV unit
and have it blimped for moisture protection. And it's going to
need a powerful strobe. Then contact whoever you have to
contact and get a descent jacket and harness here."

"Lefebre will go down with you," Whittenfeld said.

"No, he won't," Scotty countered. "He's going to keep his
limy ass up here."

"I understand your feelings," Whittenfeld said. "But I suggest your feelings be placed secondary to your safety. If you
encounter this beast of yours, you will be most grateful for
Lefebre's well-equipped presence."

Scotty called for the geologist again; the geologist appeared
moments later.

"Where are the seismics for this area?" he asked.

"I have the Carrbridge sections."

"What about the stretch between here and Loch Ness and
here and the Moray Firth?"

"I have them, too."

Whittenfeld's expression had shifted; he was astonished.
The Moray Firth?" he asked.

"It's just a thought," Scotty answered, turning back to the
geologist. "Let's get the sections out!"

The geologist retreated to the company office.

Scotty looked to Whittenfeld. He'd been afraid Whittenfeld
would allow Dr. Rubinstein to proceed without locating the
outlet. But he was sure his fears were now moot. His gut
feeling told him they were standing right over the object of
their search.

"You know, Scotty," Whittenfeld said, "it's a pleasure to
watch you work. You exude confidence. You make decisions
quickly. Issue orders with authority. Yet there is no conde-
scension in your attitude. You communicate to your under-
lings very well. They respect you. They act quickly when you
orchestrate. The demonstration I just saw was a classic example of an experienced and confident executive in action. I

should have recorded it for posterity. No, I'm morally grati-
fied I hired the right man for the job. You are definitely an
asset." A smirk crossed his lips as he surveyed the well-site
activity, blazed by the bright night lights. "However, I do
notice a change in attitude. Only a short time ago, you were
reluctant to participate in the venture. You were an adversary.
Now suddenly, there's this explosion of enthusiasm and dedi-
cation."

"You've given me no choice, you sick bastard," Scotty said.

"I know," Whittenfeld rejoined, smirking. "But I sense
some self-interest at work now, too. Something about this cavern, if it is a cavern, excites you." He started to walk to the
chopper, stopping before boarding. "Or perhaps Dr. Rubinstein and Dr. Fiammengo have infected you," he added. "Perhaps you've sensed the thrill of the hunt. Perhaps something
deep in your psyche has been energized. The human instinct
for conquest of the unknown. Base desires of the hunter." He
laughed. "Think about it, Scotty—think about it."

Chapter 34

Dr. Allen Rubinstein was a vision of excitement, his face, his
voice, totally unable to constrain the emotions that had been
surging through his body since he'd received the call from
Scotty Bruce.

He'd stepped off a helicopter just a short time before popping questions, aggressively seeking answers. He shared
Scotty's gut feeling, too. This was it!

Dr. Fiammengo had also been unable to restrain herself.
She had hugged Scotty, kissed him, overlooking the tension
between them.

Not even his admonition that they had yet to determine

hat the drill pipe had actually penetrated had been able to
mpen their enthusiasm.

And certainly the seismic evidence had only fed the grow-
g sense of euphoria.

"Assuming a portion of the cavern lies below us," Scotty
id as he paced back and forth in the company shed in front
a series of seismic maps, "it's certainly understandable that
e missed it on the wiggle traces." He pointed to a graphic; a
iy wiggle had been circled in red. "The ground is very con-
lidated. The soil is tightly packed. The propagation wave
oved down unusually fast. The air interface was very small."

"How wide is the section below us?" Dr. Rubinstein asked,
rvously biting his fingernails.

"It's hard to tell," Scotty replied as he pointed to several
her circled wiggle traces. "The air interfaces we have located
ve been circled in red. We think each circle indicates a
rtion of the cavern. One section suggests a stretch of the
vern goes down to almost four thousand feet. Others sug-
st it rises up well above sea level."

"The roller coaster," Dr. Fiammengo observed.

Scotty looked out the shed window. Whittenfeld, Lefebre and
ny Spinelli were at the well site. The drill pipe had been
lled, and a new bore had been drilled. There had been no
idents. A television crew was presently lowering a camera.
monitor had been set up in the tent.

"Why didn't we pick this up before?" Dr. Rubinstein asked;
was dressed in overalls, a flight jacket, and heavy combat
ots. When he'd insisted on joining the expedition, Whitten-
d had agreed.

"We were looking in the wrong place," Scotty said.

Dr. Fiammengo protested. "The cavern runs eastward out
the loch and not northeastward, as we expected. But it still
s to double back into the Inverness Firth."

'It doesn't turn into the Inverness Firth," Scotty said, point-
. "It turns into the Moray."

Dr. Fiammengo was awe struck. "The length of it. It's im-
sible."

'I traced the route myself."

Dr. Rubinstein clenched a fist. "I knew it was there. I knew
ll along."

The company manager informed them the television camera
penetrated the cavern.

They moved to the drill floor.

"What do you think of Mr. Bruce's conclusions?" Whitte
feld asked.

"They're exact!" Dr. Rubinstein replied, eyeing the te
vision cable that ran into a transit box, mounted on the n
bore hole.

They walked into the monitor tent. Whittenfeld ordered
technician to hit an activator switch. A camera monitor
sponded.

"That's it!" Dr. Rubinstein screamed, pushing up close
the screen; he could make out walls, a floor, the cavern ceili
itself. "When can we go down?"

Whittenfeld looked to Scotty. "Well?"

"Now," Scotty said.

They left the tent. A crew member brought the desc
jacket and harness to the bore hole. The roustabouts move
hoist into position and pulled the camera from the bore. I
febre removed a case from the chopper.

Scotty watched as Lefebre placed the case on the drill flo
opened the top, and removed the contents: three high-po
ered rifles and a closed ammunition pack.

The claustrophobia was intense.

Scotty had only a few inches on either side of his shoulde
and he was continuously dislodging sharp fragments from
bore wall as he descended.

The harness fit tightly; it was painfully digging into
sides. Looking above, he could see a circle of sky. He co
not see down.

He maintained contact with the surface, describing sen
tions, receiving depth readings. His helmet had a commu
cations system and a lightweight communications line.

He would have preferred an unencumbered descent, but
helmet had been necessary. Even though there had been
trace of gas in the mud flow and no intermediate loss of
culation, there was always the chance of a bore wall fract
releasing methane from a hidden reservoir.

"Six hundred feet," Tony Spinelli called.

Scotty shifted his legs. They were down weighted by
hanging rifle. The feeling was uncomfortable.

The descent slowed.

"Seven hundred feet!"

He reached the puncture point, turned on his helmet tor
and jerked his body down into the cavern.

Eighty feet below was the floor.

"Let me down," he said. "I'm inside."

They lowered him to the basement.

Securing the rifle and removing his stomach pack, which
ontained a small camera and first-aid gear, he took off the
escent jacket and harness.

The jacket and harness quickly disappeared up the bore.

He sat on a boulder and looked around. He was perched in
long tunnel. He could hear water dripping. There were no
her sounds. It was very cold; fortunately, all three of them
ere wearing thermal suits beneath their outer garments.

Spinelli notified him that Dr. Rubinstein had started his
escent.

Scotty waited.

Pebbles fell from above. He could hear sounds in the bore.
r. Rubinstein appeared, dangled high near the ceiling, then
uched the ground moments later.

Scotty helped the researcher undo his jacket and harness
d then sent both pieces of equipment back up to the sur-
ce.

Dr. Rubinstein vigorously attacked the cavern walls, taking
mples, running a nonstop commentary with Dr. Fiammengo
ove.

Lefebre appeared through the opening and dropped to the
vern floor.

Scotty noted the irony; he was now locked in the cavern
ith the last man on earth he would have chosen as a com-
nion, a mass murderer as well as the man who held an ax
er his and Mary MacKenzie's heads.

"What's the cavern's composition?" Whittenfeld asked, his
ice crackling through the communications lines.

"It's metamorphic and representative of the surface," Scotty
plied, examining the piece of rock. "Highly metamorphosed
artz-feldspar-granulate with some evidence of igneous intru-
n. However, I'm sure as the cavern heads toward the sea,
begins to pick up some old red sandstone."

"Your intitial conclusions?" Whittenfeld asked.

"There's no evidence of cavern formation," Scotty replied.
f I had to guess, I'd say we're inside a miracle. A cavern
uctured out of an inactive fault. Maybe one that intersects
e Glen Markie fault. But a closed fault nevertheless."

Whittenfeld acknowledged the message. Scotty informed

him they were disattaching their communications lines an
would be heading toward the northeast.

"Let me check the rifles," Lefebre said.

Scotty and Dr. Rubinstein handed the Frenchman the rifle
receiving them back moments later.

"You don't think rifles will stop this thing if it appears,
you?" Dr. Rubinstein asked.

"No," Lefebre replied. "But I have ten grenades and se
eral packets of nitroglycerin that will!"

Scotty pointed. "We'll start out that way."

They began to walk.

The cavern ran level for several hundred feet, then slope
downward. The surface was surprisingly free from debris, an
it wasn't as slick as they had anticipated.

Their torch beams danced ahead of them, crossing indi
criminately. The sound of their footsteps echoed, as did D
Rubinstein's voice, as he made audible notes to himself. Bo
were accompanied by Lefebre's high melodic whistle of reco
nizable operatic melodies.

At first, Lefebre and the music seemed incongruous co
panions, but Scotty realized that no matter how inhum
Lefebre had become, he had still come from civilized hum
stock.

They stopped several times to take rock samples, paus
near a steep dropoff, listened to the trickle of moving wat
then carefully moved forward, hugging the cavern wall.

They reached an underground lake.

Dr. Rubinstein sampled the water. It was fresh.

Scotty checked his watch. They had been walking for
hour. They surveyed the underground lake. They could n
pass!

"You can probably reach the next cavern by swimmi
down under this," Dr. Rubinstein theorized.

Scotty suggested they rest there, then return to the bore h
and inspect the tunnel's other branch. They all sat. Dr. R
binstein tried to speculate on the source of the cavern's oxyg
supply. Lefebre finally stopped whistling.

"We've appreciated the accompaniment," Dr. Rubinste
said.

Lefebre removed a piece of ivory from his pocket and b
gan to whittle the edges with a knife. "Music calms the sava
beast," he observed cryptically, with the barest of smiles.

"You're an expert on opera?"

"Just an aficionado. There's much to learn in musical theory. There's a great challenge."

Dr. Rubinstein glanced at the lake; the water was almost black. "Then you're more than an aficionado."

"Call me a student, too. A serious student. I studied opera. I learned orchestration. I'm still intensely interested."

"Literature and music," Scotty said sardonically. "You've achieved a great deal."

Lefebre swiveled face to face with Scotty; the mutual revulsion was intense. It was obvious both were waiting for the moment when they could shed all pretenses. "It's not what a man achieves in life. It's what he overcomes."

"What have you overcome?"

"A rotting, rat-infested orphanage. Poverty. Pellagra. Cholera. A bullet wound in my skull. Ignorance! Does that satisfy you, Bruce?"

"You're a martyr, Lefebre!" Scotty said facetiously.

"No. I'm a man. And I've ascended. What have you overcome in your pampered existence?"

"Hatred. Bigotry. Anger. Greed. Everything despicable. Everything you represent!"

The ripple of water in the lake became the only sound. Dr. Rubinstein sensed that only the flimsiest of gossamer strands was holding the two men apart. He could see them seething to attack. Whatever it was that held them in check held with tremendous strength. He realized, though, the restraints would not last long.

Scotty stood, suggesting they start back.

With Scotty leading, they reached the opening in the cavern ceiling forty minutes later, reattached their communication lines, reported their progress, then disattached the lines and started in the opposite direction toward Loch Ness. The topography was identical to the conditions they had already encountered. The route rose initially, then began to descend again. They had walked no more than a quarter mile when the tunnel narrowed considerably.

"This is where we block it," Lefebre declared.

Scotty did not reply. Neither did Dr. Rubinstein. Instead, they moved past the constriction.

There was another underground lake directly ahead, also impassable.

"It appears we penetrated the cavern at the top of one of

its roller-coaster rises," Dr. Rubinstein said. "On either side, the tunnel slopes down to lower-level pools."

They examined the water margin; Lefebre, gripping his rifle tightly, split off.

A short time later, Lefebre's voice rang out. "Here!"

Scotty and Dr. Rubinstein came running.

Lefebre pointed to the shoreline. Part of an enormous print, a flipperlike foot, was embedded in the soft water boundary.

"My God!" Scotty said, stepping into the hole.

It was six feet across.

They searched for more prints. They found none. Scotty photographed the one exhibit. They returned to the well bore.

Scotty notified Whittenfeld they had found an enormous footprint. He could hear a jabber of excitement. He then asked them to drop the jacket and harness. Both appeared soon after.

Dr. Rubinstein was the first to be hoisted out.

Scotty followed many minutes later, after Pierre Lefebre.

Scotty returned to the cavern the following day with two company demolition experts and led them to the cavern constriction. The experts rigged charges to bring down a portion of the ceiling, enough to close the tunnel.

When the job was finished, Scotty set a television camera and strobe in a safe vantage point, then accompanied the demolition experts back to the surface.

Reaching the work tent, they joined Whittenfeld, Lefebre, Dr. Rubinstein, and Dr. Fiammengo. The demolition experts detonated their charges.

The television clouded with smoke and dust, but gradually cleared. They had the picture they wanted. The ceiling had fallen precisely as planned. Although the tunnel was not completely closed, enough had been sealed off to prevent any large animal from ever penetrating.

They were ready.

"We sink the trap!" were Whittenfeld's final words.

Chapter 35

≈≈≈≈≈≈

The air carried the pleasant scent of heather and mountain
pine. The breeze that whisked through the shopping district
was warm, energizing. Inverness was energetically alive beneath the northern sun. Or at least that was Mary MacKenzie's
impression as she hurried about, tending to chores and a carefully constructed schedule of meetings.

At three o'clock, she stopped by the executive offices of the
Highland Regional Council. A message was waiting from
Chief Inspector MacKintosh, who had obtained the information she'd asked for. She phoned constabulary headquarters,
and a desk sergeant suggested she come by.

Ten minutes later, she was in the constabulary's waiting
room. MacKintosh soon appeared.

"This is the rundown," MacKintosh declared, waving a
sheet of paper in the air. "The car was leased by a Dr. Allen
Rubinstein, an American citizen, residence Boston, affiliation,
the Massachusetts Institute of Technology. We checked his
passport declarations. He's here as a representative of the Phenomena Research Bureau, whatever that is. We also did a
back check on his previous entries into Great Britain. He's
been here several times, each time as a member of the Academy of Applied Sciences."

She felt her blood run cold. She was familiar with the
academy, the council having been asked to approve academy
activities in the past. Dr. Rubinstein was a Nessie researcher.
He was here dealing with Scotty Bruce on a regular basis.
There was the lost submersible, the web, the inconsistencies.
It all indicated just one thing, and she was suddenly convinced
the proof lay in Travis House.

She drove to Old Edinburgh Road.

Scotty's new jeep was parked in the Travis House driveway. She honked, but no one emerged from the house.

Walking through the gate, she knocked on the front door. Nothing. She called Scotty's name, knocked again.

No reply.

Even though the jeep was there, he obviously wasn't home.

She parked her car out of sight. Taking a screwdriver from the car's glove compartment, she returned to the house, walked around the side to the den, and looked through the window. The inside lights were out. The view was dark, uncommunicative. She pried open the window with the screwdriver, climbed inside, looked around, and sat at the desk, glancing through a technical book on oil-well fracture gradients. She then noticed several pictures and drawings piled on the side of the blotter.

She looked at the top photo—two terrified men in a mechanical vehicle, water pouring over them. Picking it up, she noticed the photo beneath, showing the head of an animal. She lifted the stack, examining the other photographs. More shots of the thing—a dinosaur? She looked at the drawings. The first few were design reductions of the metal web. The next sequences were artist's renditions of a dinosaurlike thing resembling the animal in the photos. And then the final set of renditions depicted the animal entering the web, getting deeper inside, the web closing around it, trapping it.

She put down the drawings. She felt sick. She was suddenly conscious of the rapid beat of her pulse. Her hands turned clammy cold.

She searched the desk drawers. There was nothing there. She looked around the room. A book was sitting on the arm of the lounge. She looked at the title: *Textbook of Paleontology*. She examined the book shelves. One shelf was completely filled with volumes on the Loch Ness monster.

She found the tribunal report.

Angry, she walked from room to room searching. She climbed the staircase, inspecting the bedrooms—again nothing —and then went up to the attic. The attic door was open. She entered.

She was awe struck. There were maps on the walls. Plans. Notes. Pictures. A blowup of a strange footprint. She rifled through reams of material. She found more renditions, then finally a notebook outlining procedures, the step-by-step plan to catch a creature that had sunk the *Columbus*.

She questioned her state of consciousness. Was this all real? Is this a dream?

Suddenly, she felt the pain, a terrible pain of hatred that fed into her soul.

He'd deceived her, lied to her, used her.

She left the attic, returned to the den, grabbed the phone. Dialing a number, she waited, then spoke.

"I'd like to speak to Mr. Droon," she said.

A Geminii company car stopped in front of Travis House. Otty stepped out. Since the jeep had not been working right that morning, a driver had been placed at his service.

He entered the house as the car disappeared, popped into the kitchen, and returned to the den with a beer. Sitting at the desk, he inspected the pile of pictures and renditions. Strange, he was sure he'd left them in a different order. Had someone been in there?

He heard a sound and looked up. Mary MacKenzie was standing in the den doorway. Her face was granite hard, furious.

"Good evening, Mr. Bruce," she snapped.

He said nothing, too shocked to speak.

She entered the room.

He glanced at the stack of photos; she'd seen them all.

"You've been in the house?" he asked almost inaudibly; she would never understand now.

"Yes," she replied coldly.

"How'd you get in?"

She pointed to the window. "There."

"It was locked."

"I pried it open."

"Why?"

"To find out the truth, and I found it here and in the attic."

She stood immobile, staring. Their eyes locked. He tried to organize his thoughts.

"You're a pig," she suddenly growled. "An animal. Just like everyone else at Geminii."

He rushed to her. "Now wait. I want you to listen to me!"

"Listen to you? Never again!"

"I love you. I'd never hurt you."

"You've hurt me more than you could ever imagine. And for your love, it is vile. I don't ever want to hear of it again.

And I won't. I am stone once more. May God strike at
soul. I have failed my country, my people, myself. I let
burden languish while I listened to your line of rot."

"You don't understand!" he challenged.

"I understand everything!" she cried, her petrified exp
sion suddenly breaking. She stormed to the desk and grab
the pictures and sketches. "I understand these! I know wha
going on in the loch. I know how the tribunal was deceiv

"I had nothing to do with it."

"You're lying!"

He moved to her; she threw the pictures in his face.

"I know why the *Columbus* went down. I know the lie
know what killed MacPherson. I know why the lies w
told!"

"You must believe me. I'm doing what I'm doing for
men on the *Magellan*. For Scotland. I'm trying to prev
more carnage."

Her face turned blood red. "You defile this land, its peo
You and your kind represent everything that has made
suffer. You did what you did to keep Geminii in operati
Just as I knew you would!"

"It's not me, damnit!"

"If it's not you, then it's all the worse. If you've been
ried along, you're a mouse, a vermin swallowed by the
porate being. But believe me, Mr. Bruce, you are no lor
of importance. The only things that matter are Scotland
Loch Ness. If this beast exists, it is a danger to the drill s
If this beast exists, it is part of Scotland and its history.
Mr. Bruce, it is ours. You hear me! Ours! You have ta
everything else that is Scotland. You and your kind h
sucked our lifeblood. Used us. Tried to destroy us. Ne
again! This thing in the loch is part of us. It has always be
And damn if I'm going to let you destroy it, too."

"I'm going to save the beast," he exclaimed, trying to m
her understand. "We're going to catch it and return it to
sea."

She whirled on him viciously. "Do you think I believe a
thing you say? The sound of your voice makes me sick. /
I'll tell you what else, Mr. Bruce. I never thought I'd
feel hatred like I do now. God forgive me for it."

She moved to leave; he slid in front of her.

"You're not leaving here!"

"The hell I'm not."

"You're going to listen to me. You try to stop this thing and you're dead. There's an execution order hanging over your head. That's why I agreed to help them. You must believe me. You mustn't interfere. Let me catch this thing and—"

"Shut up," she screamed. "I don't want to hear it."

She began to cry, jerking in breaths, no longer able to keep in the hurt.

"I love you," he said, crying, too. "I love you."

She smacked him, crying even more fiercely, fighting off his attempts to hold her, stop her, smacking and hitting again and again.

He didn't resist; he merely tried to restrain her until she exhausted herself.

She broke for the door; he grabbed her by the arm, pulled her back to the desk, pinned her down.

"You're staying here," he screamed, "if I have to lock you up!"

She cried out, kicked. He held her tighter. She reached back, grabbed the inkwell, and hurled the ink toward his face. The ink splashed into his eyes. He howled in agony and released his hold. Falling to his knees, he tried to grab her leg but missed. She raced out the door.

He stumbled to the first-floor bathroom, splashed water into his eyes and then, still in agony, rushed out the door. She was gone. He jumped into the jeep. It wouldn't start.

Rushing back into the house, Scotty called Foster and asked him to arrange for a car—fast.

Scotty doubted whether Mary MacKenzie would talk to him over the phone, and it was essential he get her to listen. Damn! He had no idea what she was going to do, though she would certainly try to stop them. Superintendent MacGregor? The Highland Council? Farquharson? She had a whole host of choices.

When the car arrived, he drove it to the Carn Dearg Inn. Mary MacKenzie's niece was tending bar. She said she did not know where her aunt was. He searched the place. MacKenzie wasn't there.

He returned to Inverness and tried the council building. The building was dark.

Next, he tried the constabulary. No one had seen Mac-

Kenzie there, and an inquiry at the headquarters of the Scottish National Party also proved fruitless.

He drove to Travis House, unsure of what to do. He couldn't tell anyone about what had happened. If Whittenfeld knew, she'd be dead. And if he knew her as well as he thought, she'd do the exact things calculated to send Whittenfeld into shock!

He checked the den desk and the attic carefully. She'd taken some pictures and artist's renditions. Damn!

He descended the staircase to the first floor again and sat down behind the desk to think.

The phone rang.

William Whittenfeld was on the line.

Chapter 36

"You don't know how happy I am that you were able to come over," Whittenfeld said as he sat behind his living-room desk, holding a glass of Scotch.

Scotty sat on the couch. The room was dimly lit. Whittenfeld was smoking a thin, effeminate cigar. He wore a silk shirt and, very uncharacteristically, jeans. And he drank from the glass as if he was struggling against an incurably dry mouth.

Scotty said nothing.

Whittenfeld frowned. "Scotty, I don't want you to regard me as some distant voice of evil. I'm not. We're a team. You're my right-hand man, a man I've relied on for many things. Sure, we've had disagreements, and there are still many problems. But the problems have been external. They've been foisted on us. Believe me, once this animal is removed, we will be able to pursue our goals without interruption. We will unlock the secrets of the vile bitch, and it will all be ours. And remember, it will be yours, too. When this is all over, I will you to take an even bigger role here. I want the loch to become an emotional thing to you. I want you to love it."

Scotty couldn't believe he'd heard this! Had Whittenfeld lost touch with his own mind? Was the man so disjointed he could believe there could ever be a positive aftermath? "Right now, I fear it. Hate it. And I didn't come here to listen to your bullshit. I came to put your fucking neck in a noose or make a deal!"

"There. See. Anger!" Whittenfeld declared, ignoring Scotty's declaration. "Thank God. The loch has become an emotional thing already. Love and hate travel together. They produce similar catharses. That you hate only tells me that you will soon love. Yes, you will love because you're the type of man who generates feelings, a man worthy of my faith. You're not like the rest of the cattle that work for the company. They obey orders. They do not think. They can never achieve greatness. Scotty, you can. You are a man who can be immortal. And I want you with me. Believe me, I have an ache in my heart because of our differences. Because we did not see eye to eye on the tribunal matter. Because of your unwarranted suspicions about the divers. Because of our different views. Because I had to threaten the girl."

Scotty sorted impressions. Whittenfeld was one of the most schizophrenic human beings he'd ever met. And the more he sat and listened, the more he was convinced that Whittenfeld's actions and reactions, his thoughts and ideas, were spun out at random through severely crossed wires, spun out so haphazardly that Whittenfeld was capable of the most bizarre and illogical of actions at any time. God knows what was in store for them!

"What does Fallworth think of the beast and the trap?" Scotty asked.

"He approves."

"What did you tell him about the hose, the tribunal?"

"Nothing. Saboteurs destroyed the *Columbus* as far as Fallworth is concerned. The beast is another matter. They exist together. Both are real to Fallworth. There's no need to confuse matters by introducing meaningless complications. No, you don't worry about Fallworth. You worry about the trap. That it works. That this creature does not endanger the drill ship. That we rid the loch of the creature once and for all."

Scotty leaned forward; a shaft of light crossed his face. "We rid the loch of the creature and then the entire world will know."

"Yes," Whittenfeld said. "But then it will be done. There'll be nothing anyone can do. Our detractors will be confronted by the finished reality, and we will be able to go about our business no matter how loud they howl. Yes, let our detractors try to introduce negatives in the face of an admiring world. We will be heroes. The world loves heroes. It loves to bestow garlands. You've been a hero. You understand. You know that with garlands bestowed on Geminii, no voice in this foolish country will be able to command the stage." He walked to the picture of his son. "My son would have understood. He would have liked you, been like you." He examined a cartograph of Scotland. "It's funny how my past is always with me. Though my son no longer exists, he haunts me. I sometimes sit behind my desk alone at night and talk to him, explain to him what we are trying to do here. In many ways a lot of what I do, I do for him, his memory, to show him what I can and have accomplished. You understand, don't you?"

Scotty stared. Talk to his son? "Yes," he said.

Whittenfeld's expression slackened; his eyes reflected anger. "And my ex-wife is with me as well. I never told you much about her, the vile bitch, did I?"

Interesting, Scotty thought. "You never said much."

"She's better off not mentioned most of the time. She deserves to be part of oblivion. You would not have liked her. Not the way she was when we fell apart. Oh, sure, when we met, she was young, vibrant, in love with love. Though she'd come from an upper-class family, part of society, there were many things about her that were simple and warm. It's what she became, though. A vile bitch. A temperamental, greedy, selfish, vile bitch. A vile bitch who left me when I was at my lowest, when things weren't going too well. We were living in Houston. I wasn't moving up the corporate ladder fast enough. You know how it is with the big multinationals. I didn't have the right connections. I wasn't wired. So it was taking time. But my wife never understood time. She only understood status. She looked at others, and she despised me because I could not give her the status she felt she deserved." Little beads of sweat formed on his brow. "She took my son and left me. In 1963. That was a long time ago. But I remember it like it was yesterday. She said I'd never become anything! She said I was a failure. A loser. She said I was a waste who would never accomplish anything in life, and she convinced my son of it, too, took him from me." He laughed a sick laugh. "But I proved her wrong. I became something. Now, I've nearly reached greatness. And I will reach immortality. I will show the vile bitch, shove it up her ass, if it's the last thing I ever do." He paused, breathing deeply. "Loch Ness is my ramrod. Nothing will take it from me. Because it is my ramrod and my child."

"Why are you telling me this?"

"Because you and I had problems. Because I want a future for us in Loch Ness. Because I want you to understand the link between love and hatred."

They sat in silence, watching each other. The clock struck the hour. Whittenfeld's breathing became audible.

"I told you I didn't come here to listen to your pathetic rantings and ravings," Scotty suddenly declared, realizing it was essential he give Whittenfeld a pointed and violent warning in view of the information Mary MacKenzie possessed and the possible moves she might make. "I came to extract a commitment."

"What?"

Scotty walked up to Whittenfeld. "I will complete the trap project. But I want you to call off the hounds. I want you to ensure nothing happens to Mary MacKenzie—no matter what."

Whittenfeld seemed to consider Scotty's request. "Of course, I promise. With your commitment, I promise you mine."

Scotty grabbed Whittenfeld's right arm and bent it behind his back. Whittenfeld cried out in pain. "I've learned about your promises, so this time I'll add the incentives," Scotty said. "If anything happens to Mary MacKenzie, I will strangle both you and Lefebre with my bare hands!"

Scotty returned to Travis House.

John Leslie Houghton's limousine was parked outside. Houghton was in the back seat.

Scotty climbed from the loaner. Houghton's chauffeur opened the rear of the limo. Houghton stepped out.

"Good evening, Mr. Bruce," Houghton said.

"Surprised again," Scotty remarked.

"I have the information you requested. Let's go inside. I have something to show you."

They entered Travis House.

"Take me to the den," Houghton ordered.

Scotty led Houghton into the room.

Houghton unscrewed the telephone receiver and removed a small disc.

"A bug?" Scotty asked, shocked. "Are there any others?"

"Your upstairs phones are similarly equipped," Houghton advised. "Your office is bugged, too. The bugs were placed after the tribunal hearings. Lefebre also gave you an elephant. There is a transmitter in the trunk!"

"You know what's going on here, don't you?"

"Yes. Everything."

"What do you think about all this?" Could Houghton help him find Mary MacKenzie? He would ask.

Houghton lit a cigarette, held at the end of his holder. "I find some of it amusing. I find some of it disturbing. However, the only business I have here is you. The rest of Geminii's adventures are superfluous."

They both sat.

Houghton began. "You must understand that Whittenfeld only reacts when his 'child' is endangered, and he will protect his 'child' with his life. Lefebre, on the other hand, carries out orders without question but also reacts on a personal level to a challenge. You lashed out at him, grabbed him, physically attacked him; he lashed back at you. Mercenaries learn to respond quickly to attack. Their reactions become instant, automatic, vicious!"

"Was Barrett murdered?" Scotty asked.

"Yes," Houghton replied emotionlessly.

"Because he endangered Whittenfeld's 'child'?"

"Whittenfeld had nothing to do with it. Whittenfeld respected Barrett. Yes, Barrett and Whittenfeld argued about the excessive security. About Lefebre's presence. About Lefebre's operating procedures. But Whittenfeld wasn't overly concerned."

"Then why was Barrett killed?"

"He clashed with Lefebre. They argued. Then they fought one night outside of Gellions Lounge Bar on High Bridge Street. Lefebre was badly cut. The sight of blood sealed Barrett's fate. Lefebre fed Barrett manijuju."

"Whittenfeld didn't know?"

"He knew about the fight. He knew about Barrett's heart attack. I would venture to say he suspected Lefebre's comlicity. But he never asked nor accused. The Barrett problem was over. Simple as that. On with work."

"Furst?" Scotty asked.

"He posed a threat. Whittenfeld was very aware of it. He told Lefebre to take care of it, bribe the diver, secure the diver's silence. The diver refused the bribe. Lefebre sent the diver and the diver's associate to their maker."

"Then Whittenfeld ordered the murders."

"Not really. Whittenfeld told Lefebre to take care of the matter. Offer the bribe. Murder was Lefebre's initiative."

"But Whittenfeld knows what happened."

"I suppose. But to Whittenfeld's mind, the problem has just gone away. The two divers died in an accident. How it happened does not concern him. He has most probably closed it out, just as he's closed out many things in his life."

"Like the death of his son, the car accident, the pain."

Houghton's brow shot up. "Whittenfeld's son did not die in a car accident. He died of a blow to the head. Whittenfeld and the boy argued often about his mother. One night, Whittenfeld smacked the boy. The boy fell, hit his head, died."

Incredulous, Scotty breathed deeply, feeling closed in. He rose, opened a window, then returned to his seat.

"A priest named Father MacPherson might have been next in Lefebre's agenda had MacPherson not succeeded in getting himself killed first," Houghton said, returning to the subject at hand. "Whittenfeld heard MacPherson's threats during the tribunal proceedings. He told Lefebre to watch the old man, keep him under control, make things difficult. Lefebre ordered his guards to wreck the priest's church. The next step would have been a beating. Then death. Father MacPherson denied Lefebre the exhilaration."

"But Hugh Sutherland didn't."

"No, Mr. Sutherland didn't. And here I'm afraid Mr. Whittenfeld cannot hide his head in the sand. It's far too obvious. Sutherland tried to take Whittenfeld's drill ship, his means to reach his 'child.' Sutherland terrified Whittenfeld. Whittenfeld told Lefebre to do something about the Jacobite. Lefebre accepted the assignment with enthusiasm, then located Sutherland and had him taken to the harbor."

"And the call to the police implicating a tan jeep?"

"A message from one of Lefebre's associates."

"What about Mrs. Munro? Lefebre again?"

"Yes, though the bomb had been intended for you."

Scotty was not surprised.

"You clashed with Lefebre. Clashed violently. You challenged him aboard the recovery barge when the hose section was brought up. You mentioned Africa!"

"I also endangered Whittenfeld's 'child.' Endangered it like no other man could." Scotty stopped, thinking. He had mentioned Africa! But only Girard, besides Lefebre, knew it. Girard was the source! Girard was Houghton's pipeline to information. "I challenged Whittenfeld. Threatened to destroy his dreams."

"You did. But Whittenfeld had nothing to do with the bombing. You are much like Barrett. Whittenfeld respects you. Appreciates you. Though he obviously didn't at the start —didn't want you here at all."

"Wait a minute. Whittenfeld told me he flew to the States to fight for me, to get me this job."

"The truth, Mr. Bruce, is the opposite. Your Mr. Redding ton recommended you to Whittenfeld, London, and New York simultaneously. London and New York responded positively at once. Geminii is an honest company which generally does business honorably. The company was not afraid of your activ ities and past. In fact, it felt your reputation for honesty and fighting corruption would help immeasurably in the difficult atmosphere here in Scotland. Whittenfeld flew to the States to stop you. Your past frightened him. But support for you was too strong, and Whittenfeld couldn't say he didn't want you because of your honesty. He had to submit."

"But you say he grew to respect me?"

"Yes. He felt he could handle you, too, even after you re belled! However, he asked Lefebre to watch you from the first. Eavesdrop."

"Then why did Lefebre place the bomb?"

"I told you Lefebre never forgets. Never forgives. Besides the Sutherland murder set the bombing up perfectly. And a bombing made more sense than the use of manijuju. The bombing was designed to kill two birds at once. You and the Jacobite threat. Put the Jacobites on the run."

"What about Geminii's political opponents? Why didn't Whittenfeld strike out at them? They certainly posed a danger."

"Whittenfeld's psychoses do not dominate him completely. One does not murder political opponents on whim. No, Whit

enfeld had to eliminate a political figure in Biafra because he
ad no choice. I suspect he would only do so here if he felt
is back was against the wall."

"What about me?"

"You were probably saved by circumstances. After the de-
ision was made to build the clandestine trap, they realized
hat the last thing they needed was the death of another dis-
rict superintendent."

Scotty suddenly exploded. "We've got to stop them," he
aid; this was why he needed Houghton. To help him stop
hem.

"We?" Houghton asked.

"I need your help. I need your backing. After we catch the
east, you must help me deal with Whittenfeld."

Houghton stood; his voice was resentful. "Mr. Bruce, you
re free to fight all the battles you wish. But without me!"

"You know where the skeletons are buried, Houghton.
Vhere the evidence lies. You have the information. All I
ould have would be unsubstantiated allegations."

"I sympathize."

"You sympathize? That's all?"

"You expect something else?"

"Yes, I expect you to have a sense of justice, a respect for
w. You're a citizen of Great Britain. I expect you to have a
ritish citizen's sense of duty!"

Houghton broke up laughing. "Mr. Bruce, you are a very
inny man." He shook his head. "Justice? The law? Those are
oncepts for courts, judges, barristers, parliamentarians, phi-
osophers. I have no time for such games. As for my duty as
citizen, I can asure you, I have given my country far more
1an most and continue to give!"

"Lefebre has now committed crimes in Great Britain.
oesn't that bother you?"

"No. I have no business with Lefebre."

"If nothing concerns you, why did you agree to help me?"

Houghton smiled patronizingly. "I work for remuneration.
Vhen I'm paid by someone I respect and the job appeals to
1e, I do it."

"Just like Lefebre!"

"Not quite."

"But you weren't paid here."

"Wasn't I?" Houghton asked with a look of surprise. "You

must stand corrected, Mr. Bruce. I was paid. By Wessinghage. Though, of course, I wasn't paid in currency."

"Then how?"

Houghton walked toward the door. "Wessinghage asked me to do him a favor. One day, I will extract the payment, a favor in return, which, I assure you, often has far more value than mere coins or pieces of paper."

Houghton opened the door; Scotty sprung after him and grabbed his arm.

"You can't leave like this. You've got to help me! I have to find Mary MacKenzie. You must help me find her."

Houghton disdainfully removed Scotty's hand. "Don't touch, Mr. Bruce," he said. "Ever."

Scotty stepped back; a shiver had run up his spine.

Houghton smiled briefly, stepped out the door, and climbed into the limousine.

The limo roared off.

Chapter 37

The night air greeted Scotty coldly as he emerged from Travis House, climbed into the loaner, and gunned it down the Dores Road.

He yawned; he'd hardly slept. It was 4:30 A.M.

He'd spent most of the night placing phone calls, trying to locate Mary MacKenzie; he'd also sat up thinking, putting the final puzzle pieces into place. Christ, it was a horror. But it was all there—Whittenfeld's state of mind, the reasons for Whittenfeld's obsessions. He'd doubted it all at first, doubted a man could be driven so far off path by motives of revenge, but the doubt had been short-lived because he knew better. He'd known many men who, after being jilted, their ego

rushed, had harbored unending dreams of requital. Whitten-
eld was no different, just more pathologic.

He shivered. He was traveling in a mine field of insanity
nd murder, and the one person he cared about more than
nyone in the world—Mary MacKenzie—was traveling with
im.

He'd left messages all over the place, and he would con-
inue the search after they had sunk the trap.

He had to find her.

The A-9 road from Inverness to Edinburgh, framed be-
ween the intimidating Grampian Mountains, was narrow,
ortuous, unlit.

The drive had been difficult; more difficulties lay ahead.
Mary's arms felt like lead weights, her eyelids like stone. She
ad a throbbing headache; her insides ached from the pain
f betrayal and the shattered remains of her love.

She'd left Inverness at 1:30 A.M. Between the time she'd
aced out of Scotty Bruce's home and her departure, she'd
vaited at a friend's aparment for a response from Droon.

Droon had called at midnight. He'd told her he'd met with
is barrister and they'd decided to move against the findings of
ie *Columbus* tribunal, petition the Court of Sessions to re-
pen the hearings, and shut down the Geminii operation. All
e needed was her presence, along with the photographic and
arrative evidence she'd said she'd removed from Scotty
ruce's home.

Fly to Edinburgh, he'd ordered.

But flight had been impossible. The airport at Inverness, in
act, all the airports along the coast, had been shut down by
thick fog that had moved in from the sea.

She'd had to drive.

Scotty climbed aboard the helicopter. Jerry Foster was already inside.

"You coming for the show?" Scotty asked.

Foster placed the stem of his pipe in his mouth. "Yes, but
m not looking to be entertained. There's work to do. I have
ie cover story to handle. We'll have to release something
bout the inception of further security measures. You know,
dbits. Nothing anyone could bite into, chew around, find a
one."

The chopper rose. The noise was infernal. Scotty looked

out the window. He could see the demolition ordnance buil-
ing. There were several security cars parked outside and tw
vans from the constabulary.

"What the hell is going on there?" he asked.

Foster looked out the window, too. "They found some e
plosives missing early last night."

"Explosives!" Scotty repeated, shocked.

Foster swallowed awkwardly. "One thousand pounds «
ninety percent gelatin dynamite."

"What else?"

"Number-eight blasting caps. Ten thousand feet of prim
cord. A blasting machine. A timing mechanism."

"Does Whittenfeld know?" he asked.

"Of course," Foster said. "Hell, he nearly blew through tl
roof of his house when he was told."

"Why wasn't I called?"

"You were. Several times. Your line was busy."

"Do they know how long the stuff's been missing?"

"A few days."

"No clues?"

"Not yet. But the police are looking. Don't worry. Whi
tenfeld had the *Magellan* searched. The underwater hu
too. Nothing was found. And security was put on alert."

The helicopter started to move down the loch. Scott
crossed to the other side of the cabin and looked through tl
window. A massive white fog, highlighted by the moon, co
ered the harbor and part of the land mass. He'd known abo
the fog since the night before. He'd called the airport
check on flights, trying to locate Mary MacKenzie. They
informed him all planes had been grounded. But he'd had r
idea how huge the air mass had been.

He moved up next to the pilot.

"Anything on the fog bank?" he asked.

"The usual," the pilot replied. "It'll hold off the coast unle
there's a wind shift."

Scotty returned to his seat, concerned that the fog ba
could move in over the operation. He'd seen similar blanke
race in over the loch like gunshots.

He looked out the window again. First at the bank, then
the *Magellan*, which had come into view.

Damn!

*   *   *

The sound and sudden movement startled her into action. She gripped the wheel tightly, hit the brakes. The front right tire had blown out!

The car twisted wildly along the edge of the road, then settled to a stop in the blackness, turned sideways.

She couldn't believe it. Of all times and of all places. She looked around. She was surrounded by mountains, though there was a rift valley that extended eastward several miles. In the valley, about half a mile away, was a farmhouse. No lights were on.

Climbing from the car, she glanced at the tire. Blown to shreds. She looked in the rear. She had a spare but no jack. Unless another car happened along or someone lived in the farmhouse, she was stuck.

She had no time to waste.

She headed for the farmhouse.

Scotty leaned against the guard rail of the the drill ship. The trap was floating several hundred yards away, held in place by the four support tugs. Beyond were the command barge and the three sonar tugs. Interspersed, the television flotation rafts bobbed like buoys.

He could also see the top of the fog bank rising over the Inverness horizon, highlighted by moonlight.

The ship's rotary was quiet. The Lyon TX-1 bit was back on the bottom. They had located another chert-silica formation. Everything was ready.

"I can tell you've been thinking," Whittenfeld, who had flown out before Scotty, said as Scotty moved back away from the railing.

They had already discussed the theft of gelatin dynamite and the implications.

"I've been thinking about a lot of things," Scotty said.

"I hope about a future for you and Loch Ness. About greatness. Immortality."

Scotty didn't reply.

They entered the bridge deck's supervisor's quarters.

The place looked like the command room on the command barge—television monitors, trap controls, sonar screens, and a plethora of other instruments. This was now the alternative operations room. Whittenfeld, Lefebre, and Dr. Fiammengo would be here. He and Dr. Rubinstein would be aboard the command barge. Both Dr. Fiammengo and Lefebre were in the room.

This was the first time he'd seen Lefebre since Houghton had given him the last bits of information. He wanted to lash out, break the Frenchman's neck. But he knew he couldn't, not yet.

"So what do you think?" Dr. Fiammengo asked.

"The engineers have done a good job," he replied.

She pointed to the communications equipment. "If anything goes wrong with the barge, we're ready here."

Scotty and Whittenfeld left the cabin.

Pierre Lefebre watched the launch, which held Whittenfeld and Bruce, pull away from the drill ship.

He could still see Bruce's face.

He despised the face. He hated mice. Cowards. Life's flotsam.

He moved to the other side of the ship and looked toward shore through a pair of binoculars. There it was! The sailboat shed. Inside it were the caps, the blasting machine, the timer, the primacord and gelatin. After the trap had been lowered and before the inception of operations—the two events would be separated by a shutdown of all sonar and tracking systems for calibration—his divers would ring the trap with the primacord and the gelatin dynamite and would tie the timing device into the clamp closure electrical system.

Then, ten minutes after the animal had been snared, it would be blown into infinity.

He lit a Gitanes.

And smiled.

Mary MacKenzie knocked on the farmhouse door.

No one answered.

She looked inside the barn. There were no cars. The house didn't look abandoned, but obviously no one was home. She searched for a way to get in. The windows were barred; entrance was impossible.

She started to walk back to the road. She would have to wait for another motorist to drive by. There were no alternatives.

She crossed a grazing field, a sunken meadow below the level of the main road, then climbed back up toward the crippled car.

She stopped, surprised.

Another car was sitting right in front of hers.

She approached. No one was inside. There was also no one on the road. She turned toward the farmhouse. The missing driver had not gone in that direction. Intuitively, she sensed trouble. God, she was miles from nowhere on a sparsely traveled strip of highway, and suddenly a car had appeared, and the driver was nowhere in sight.

She felt a shiver of fear run up her spine. The shadows were suddenly very threatening. So were the sounds of the night.

She retreated to her auto and climbed inside, locking the doors.

A hand exploded up from behind her. A palm jammed shut her mouth. Nails dug into her cheeks. Heavy breathing gasped. She fought. She could not dislodge the hand.

Then she heard a man's voice; the voice was Girard's.

"There's a gun pointed at the back of your skull," Girard said. "One more move and I pull the trigger."

Scotty watched Dr. Rubinstein orchestrate. He listened to the cross of transmissions between the command barge, the sonar tugs, the trap tugs, and the duplicate control room on the *Magellan* while he tried to read Whittenfeld's very ambiguous expression, which was now colored by the light of the rapidly rising sun.

Dr. Rubinstein approached.

"It's as if God knows what we're about!" he declared, pointing through the command cabin window at the white wall of air hanging above the horizon. "It's as if God has sent His messenger carpet. An angelic fog."

"Or a satanic one," Scotty countered.

"Could the fog be a problem?" Whittenfeld asked.

"It should stay out there according to the weather reports," Scotty replied.

"What if it doesn't?"

"It shouldn't significantly affect us," he declared, looking to Dr. Rubinstein for support.

"Correct," Dr. Rubinstein said. "We do not need visibility to see. We have sonar. Television. Everything will happen beneath the surface, and all our controls are at hand. No, unless we get a storm in here that would affect our operating efficiency, we'll be all right."

A structural engineer informed them that all systems wer
operational.

Dr. Rubinstein's voice rang through the command cabi
Captain Harrigan and Dr. Fiammengo reported in from the
positions. The command barge's technicians hit a myriad c
switches. The electrical heart of the trap fluctuated to life.

Dr. Rubinstein opened the trap's main ballast tanks.

Scotty stared through the window. He could see the fou
anchor tugs moving, slow reverse. Suddenly, the water aroun
the trap began to churn. The ballast tanks were filling. A
orders flew around the command room, the churning in
creased; then, slowly, the trap began to sink, the tugs ease
back into anchor positions, and the trap's anchor spools dre'
in the slack of the anchor lines.

Several minutes after the trap's descent had started, it wa
gone.

Chapter 38

The time—eight P.M.

The fog bank remained off the coast.

The trap had been set at depth; the passive stage of t
operation, a thorough recheck of the inactive instruments ar
connections, had begun.

Scotty and Foster had already started the return to bas
Whittenfeld had moved to the Urquhart Bay installation.

Dog tired, Scotty reached Dores at 8:30, but he had thin;
to do other than sleep.

Pursuant to plan, Girard was to be in charge of Gemir
base security during the trap operation. But he was unable
locate Girard; according to key security people and those
charge of entry documentation, Girard had apparently n
been seen since the day before.

Could Girard be with Houghton? Did Girard know anything about the gelatin dynamite?

It seemed impossible that someone without formal access —Whittenfeld, Lefebre, himself, a nominee—could have removed the dynamite from the heavily guarded area.

His immediate suspicion was Whittenfeld and Lefebre. But why? To throw additional weight against the project's enemies? To keep the police off guard and away from the trap operation? Damn, he didn't know. But he was sure as hell Girard would. Besides, he needed Girard. Since Houghton had refused to come forward, he would have to forcibly make sure Girard, assuming Girard had been Houghton's source, made himself available.

He drove to Travis House and sequestered himself in the den. He phoned the Carn Dearg Inn. No one answered. Was it closed? He tried the standard places. No luck. He'd tried several key spots in Edinburgh, notably the Scottish Office, during the day. If Mary MacKenzie had gone to Edinburgh, she was keeping a low profile.

He'd never felt so helpless. He didn't know where the hell to look or what to do next, and he was fighting a terrible premonition that Mary MacKenzie would suddenly appear at the head of an assault team, beckoning for a bullet in the brain.

He rubbed his temples. His head hurt. He was tired. But he couldn't fall asleep. There were too many things to do!

The south side path along Loch Duntelchaig above Dores was narrow, overgrown. The area through which it ran was uninhabited and virtually unused.

Girard guided his sedan past the widest beam of the loch and stopped beneath an outcropping of rock.

A half hour later, a station wagon appeared with one man inside. Pierre Lefebre.

Lefebre stopped the wagon and slid out. Girard climbed out of the sedan and joined him. The path was covered with stones and gravel.

"Monsieur Girard," Lefebre declared, "you found the worst road in Scotland. Hell's road!"

"Very inaccessible. Nobody ever comes here. She'll never be found."

"Did you hear from Lennox?"

"Yes, it's done."

Lefebre looked above him. The mountains rose high int
the overbearing black sky.

"Where is she?" he asked.

Girard opened the trunk of the sedan. Mary MacKenziz
was inside, bound and gagged.

"A leader of the nation," Lefebre announced, laughing.

He placed a wad of tobacco in his mouth, then pulled Mar
MacKenzie out of the trunk. She fell to the gravel, face down
He dragged her some twenty feet by the hair, then turned he
over. Her face was scraped and bleeding. He removed her ga,
and jerked her to her feet.

"Are you afraid, Councilwoman MacKenzie?" he asked.

"No," she said.

"I'm going to kill you."

"I know."

"How do you know that?" Lefebre asked, his lips quiver
ing, a thin film of perspiration covering his face.

"I can see it in your face."

"Do you know why you're going to die, madame?"

"No. And it doesn't matter."

"It matters to me! You see, we bugged Monsieur Bruce'
phone. We heard you call Monsieur Droon. We did not lik
what you said or what you both intended to do. No, you wi
die. Then I will deal with Mr. Bruce, the fool with a con
science."

Her expression blazed with defiance. "You're pathetic." Sh
thought of Scotty; he'd tried to protect her from this. She fo
gave him under her breath.

"I frighten you, don't I?" Lefebre asked.

"It would take more than a slimy, foul-smelling anim;
like you to frighten me," she replied. "You, others like yo
have descended on Scotland for years. But Scotland sti
breathes. Stronger than ever."

"You're not Scotland, madame. You're flesh and blood."

"And you're the droppings of a cow."

He grabbed her by the hair. "Shut up!"

"Never."

"Frightened! Tell me you're frightened."

"They died at Culloden for their country. I'll die her
They were proud to die, and I am proud to die! Their deatl
inspired a nation. My death will somehow stop you, lead 1
your destruction!"

"What a brave and noble speech!" He smacked her.

She spat in his face.

Enraged, he punched her.

Blood poured from her nose and mouth.

He trembled, gasped. He preferred to see fear. He preferred to hear his victims beg. It excited him. They had always feared and begged. In Algeria. The Congo. Biafra. Uganda. "You're afraid!" he screamed, beside himself.

She spat on him.

He stood erect, eyes wild, face flooded with sweat, a knife in his hand, feeling the thrill, strong, pulsating, blinding.

William Whittenfeld sat in the corner of the Urquhart Bay installation operation's room, the lights on the desk turned down low. The office window was open; the blinds were up. He could see the *Magellan's* lights, feel a mild breeze whipping eastward across the loch, holding out the fog bank.

He felt his cheeks. He needed a shave. He smoothed the lapels on his black suit. He liked the suit. It had been made in London by one of the city's best tailors. Very expensive. It made him feel good, look good, distinguished. Everything English made his sensations soar.

He twisted his watch around and noted the time. Where in the hell was Lefebre? They did not have all night. If the explosives were to be set properly, the demolition team would have to begin their work at once. He would not tolerate any mistakes.

He hated fuckups. But here, especially. The trap was going to be mined, and the thing in the loch was going to be executed. Yes, he preferred the word "executed." The thing had killed. Sitting as judge, he had examined the evidence and had sentenced the thing to death. He laughed to himself, thinking about Dr. Rubinstein's sense of mission. All crap. Nonsense. The only duties that mattered were his duty to find oil and his duty to himself and his child. The thing had threatened his dreams. Threatened his child. The thing would die.

Of course, he'd told Scotty Bruce that if they caught the thing, removed it from the loch, and offered its existence to science, Geminii would receive the world's gratitude. But when the hell had mankind's gratitude ever really meant anything? When the hell had it ever run engines and cars or formed the base ingredients in plastics? The world's gratitude? Its accolades? Those were for megalomaniacs. The creature

would die, and if the world wanted to squawk, it would have
to do so after the fact.

To hell with the creature. He'd heard the world squawk in
Biafra. And what had the outrage caused? More deaths! Life
had taught him to disregard mankind's guilt and conscience
when it came to making important decisions. And behind this
decision was the most critical fact of all. If they caught the
creature and it lived, Geminii would no doubt be closed
down. The British government would certainly order the
creature returned to the loch and would place the loch off
limits. He could not allow that to happen.

A car pulled up to the building. Moments later, Lefebre
entered the office.

"Where is Mr. Girard?" Whittenfeld asked.

"Back at the complex."

"How is MacKenzie?"

"She is indisposed."

Whittenfeld sat at the desk. "Did you deal with the Droon
problem?"

"Yes. We convinced both Monsieur Droon and Madame
MacKenzize that their silence would be in the best interest of
Scotland."

"The trap?"

"The chariot is in the water. The divers are ready."

Whittenfeld stood again, turning off the light. "It's getting
late," he said as he walked toward the door.

"Yes" was Lefebre's reply.

The station wagon stopped inside a grove of trees along the
shore of the loch.

Lefebre and Whittenfeld climbed out.

Three security men were guarding a small submersible
chariot that contained the primacord, explosives, and automatic timing detonation device. There were two divers
equipped with scuba gear and compressed air cannisters.

The top of the trap was lying at one hundred feet below
the surface. The explosives and primacord would be set on the
trap at 140 feet. The timing device would be cut into the
electrical cable from the command barge, which operated the
trap clamp mechanism. Planned operation was one hour at
depth. On the way up, the diver crew would stop the submersible chariot for decompression. The dive time would be just
under two hours.

It was one o'clock. They would be finished by three if everything went well. The command barge was scheduled to reactivate its sonar and television systems at four-thirty. They had little time to lose. They could not allow Dr. Rubinstein, Dr. Fiammengo, or Scotty Bruce to discover the existence of the explosives. Of course, Captain Harrigan and his sonar tugs would normally have picked up the presence of the submersible chariot, but Lefebre had already seen to Harrigan's cooperation and discretion, the shutdown of the tugs' sonar systems during rigging and Harrigan's eventual total silence.

Lefebre spoke to the divers. Everything was in order. The two divers mounted the saddles on the chariot. Lefebre and Whittenfeld returned to the car. The divers started the submersible's engine. The submersible moved out into the loch, then descended and disappeared.

The station wagon departed.

A rooster crowed. A car roamed by, its engine screaming. Scotty opened his eyes. Morning light invaded the den window. He looked at his watch: 7:30 A.M.

Goddamn! He'd fallen asleep at the desk and had slept through the night.

He raced into the bathroom, threw some water on his face, then returned to the desk and once more tried to locate Mary MacKenzie. After several calls, he became convinced she was not in Inverness.

He called Edinburgh, the Scottish Office, and asked for Peter Droon. Droon's secretary answered the phone. He asked to speak to Droon. The secretary said that that was impossible. Droon was dead; he'd been killed in a hit and run accident in front of his home the day before. Shocked, Scotty asked the secretary if Mary MacKenzie was in Edinburgh. The secretary said that as far as she knew, MacKenzie was not.

He hung up, shaken. Droon dead.

It suddenly occurred to him that if Mary MacKenzie had phoned Droon from Travis House, using the bugged phones, she would have signed Droon's death warrant. And certainly her own.

However, there was little he could do now.

The safety of the drill ship and the men had primary importance. Even if he raced all over Scotland looking for Mary, there was no assurance he'd find her, alive or dead.

He had to be out on the loch by nine to test the trap.

The snatch was scheduled for one o'clock.

He stood and looked out the den window. The fog was still
there, lying off the coast.

Chapter 39

It was as if Scotty were looking at the world through a dream.
The command barge cabin, the instruments, the faces, the anticipation—all of it seemed to be veiled in a haze of suspended
time.

They had been there before. But then the submersible
operation had been no more than a dry run. This was the
highpoint of ambition.

The comand barge moved gently in the swells. All systems
were functioning. The morning test had been perfect. It was
five o'clock. They were four hours behind schedule. A post-
test short in an electrical connection had caused the delay.

Dr. Rubinstein, who had always been a waterfall of upbeat
emotions, suddenly seemed introverted, almost paranoic.
Though the doctor was still tearing at his nails and twitching
relentlessly around the room, there was something stoic about
his movements. Perhaps after all the anticipation, the reality
had cauterized his explosive energies.

Scotty had not escaped the tension, either, but his emotions
were divided. This was not finality for him. It was only an
intermediate stage. Once the preliminary drama had played
itself out, the beast caught and removed from the loch, then
the real end-run maneuverings would start.

Though he was unsure of exactly what he would do beyond
possibly securing Mary MacKenzie's safety, there was no way
he was going to allow Whittenfeld and Lefebre to march like
heroes into the sunset.

Where was Mary? Why hadn't he heard from her? Or about her? The obvious answer was too terrible to consider; he had to focus on one thing at a time. First, the ship and the crew, then Mary.

He joined Foster in the rear of the room.

"This will be quite a story when it can be told," Foster said, his stomach protruding over the waistband of his red polyester pants.

"Do you have it written yet?" Scotty asked, pulling an unlit cigar from his pocket.

"The beginning and middle," Foster said. "I'm waiting for the end."

"Where does it start?"

"It starts with Kreibel, Reddington, and myself."

"It starts with death. Let's hope the ending is better."

"You don't sound optimistic."

"I'm not optimistic. Or pessimistic. I'm realistic."

"Do you know something I don't?"

"No. I just appreciate the difficulties better. See me after the whole thing is over. Don't write the ending until you do."

Foster smiled circumspectly. "I remember when you first arrived here. You were excited. You had great expectations. What happened?"

"I told you. Reality."

Foster cleared his throat, confused. "Someday you'll explain all the double talk to me."

Dr. Rubinstein walked over. "We're going to turn on the monitors," he said.

The techs activated the flotation-raft cameras and the trap cameras. The monitors checked in simultaneously.

"As soon as we get a corroboration from the *Magellan*," Dr. Rubinstein said, "we can begin."

Capt. Eamonn Harrigan stood on the bridge of the lead sonar tug examining several side-scan printouts. There were a series of bizarre traces of the underwater trap.

He tried to control his discomfiture. He had a foreboding feeling, much of it attributable to the contradiction and secrecy. Just the day before, he'd been contacted by Pierre Lefebre, informed about the gelatin dynamite, warned to keep the information to himself.

The level of intrigue was frightening. Bruce, Rubinstein, Fiammengo, the three individuals who had organized the

operation, were being kept in the dark about its most critica
stage. God knows what other Machiavellian maneuvering
were underway.

He could only wonder if Captain Olafsen had encountere
similar difficulties. Did deception contribute to Olafsen'
death?

Did his sonar tugs and their crews face the same grue
some end? He could only go about his job and hope that tha
end was not inevitable.

Dr. Fiammengo felt relieved as she looked around th
Magellan's command room. Technicians were in place, a
were Bill Nunn and Mike Grabowski. But it was Pierre Le
febre's absence—he'd left just moments before—that allowe
her to breathe easily again.

There was something about Lefebre that unnerved her; per
haps the constant facial twitches, the Antarctic-cold eyes, o
the penetrating glare those eyes produced. She'd never see
anyone like him before and certainly had never felt so dis
sected by a man's attention. Lefebre reminded her of a rabi
animal. She sensed that beneath his silence was a reservoir o
hatred and malice, most of which was directed at Scott
Bruce.

She looked up at the monitors. Finally, it was about t
happen. They had drawn up plans for the trap three year
before. Though they had taken painstaking care to design th
mechanism properly, the entire design team had doubted th
effort would ever come to fruition.

It had been a pipe dream. It was now reaching fulfillment
There was an incredible feeling of destiny about it.

She picked up her comm-phone.

She could report to the command barge that they wer
ready.

William Whittenfeld walked along the main deck. The mu
pumps were running. The drill crew was on the drill floor
Tony Spinelli was with them. The deck was ringed with secu
rity guards equipped with high-powered rifles and grenades
The ship was also outfitted with extra lifeboats. The depth
charge ejection racks were armed, primed for use to repel th
creature in the event the trap failed.

He was ready for the public reaction. But more importan
he had already charted the moves toward the resumption o

ormal operations. After the creature's destruction, covert
nstructions would be given, and Dr. Fiammengo and Dr.
Rubinstein would be escorted off the vessels, returned to
hore, and prohibited from entering the Geminii complex.
Anything they had to say or do would have to be done elsewhere. Press silence would be maintained until Jerry Foster
ad issued a brief but clear-cut official version of the exercise.
Then he would channel his efforts toward official outrage,
nd, hopefully, they would be able to resume drilling within
matter of hours.

Drilling. The loch. His child. The petroleum reservoir
idden beneath the surface. That was all that mattered. All
nat had ever mattered. The rest was a nightmare.

Lefebre called his name. He turned.

"Look," Lefebre said, handing Whittenfeld a pair of binoc-
lars.

Whittenfeld trained the glasses on Lochend; the fog had
oved slightly inland.

"The wind has shifted," he said.

"Not the fog," Lefebre countered. "The launch."

Whittenfeld tilted the glasses downward. There was a police
unch headed directly toward them, throttled at full speed.

"Goddamnit," Whittenfeld said.

Dr. Rubinstein suddenly felt as if someone had encased him
ice. It was his recurring fear translated to fact, the constant
reat of interruption, something going wrong. As he watched
e police launch approach the command barge, he could see
l his years of work passing before him like an escaping
oud of gas.

"We've got to get them out of here!" he said.

"I know," Scotty replied. "I'll find out what they want." He
ointed to the trap monitors. "Turn those off."

Dr. Rubinstein ordered the technicians to deactivate the
ameras.

"Could they know about the operation?" he asked.

"Anything's possible," Scotty said, shrugging.

They walked out of the cabin as the launch pulled up. The
ommand barge crew tied mooring lines. Superintendent Mac-
Gregor and Chief Inspector MacKintosh climbed on to the
arge.

"You seem to have a big operation going," MacGregor
id, without his usual smile.

"The web," Scotty declared.

MacGregor glanced at the shore installation. A police heli copter was hovering over one of the helipads. "I hope you'r not essential to its fulfillment, Mr. Bruce," he added.

"I'm not," Scotty said.

"We'd like you to come with us."

"Is this an invitation, too?"

"No, it's a demand!"

Scotty turned to Dr. Rubinstein. "You'll have to begi without me."

"I'd prefer we didn't have to. But we must start."

Scotty moved toward the launch. "What's this about, Mac Gregor?"

MacGregor sighed. "I'd like to wait until we reach ou destination to give you an explanation, and I'd appreciate if you would accommodate me."

Scotty dropped on to the launch. He knew the explanatio already, knew it suddenly with a tremor of fear and horror But he had to get the police out of there. He could not pres now.

The police officers followed him on to the vessel. The moor ing lines were cast off. The launch pulled away.

The police helicopter moved south past the loch. Scott was seated directly across from MacGregor. Since he'd joine the officers, no one had said a word.

The chopper crossed the shore's rising mountains. He coul see a small, high-altitude loch ahead. The chopper slowed ove an isolated meadow. He looked down. A group of constable were moving near a gravel path. Most of the activity, how ever, was hidden under a cluster of trees. There were no car Everyone had obviously been transported to the site by th helicopter.

The chopper landed; the pilot opened the chopper door.

"Would you please step down, Mr. Bruce?" MacGrego suggested.

Scotty left the helicopter. MacGregor and MacKintos followed. MacGregor pointed up the road to the cluster trees. They walked ahead.

A body lay on the gravel, covered by a sheet. Nearby wa a mound of dirt next to an excavated grave. MacGrego glared at the covered corpse, then back at Scotty, sayin nothing.

Suddenly, Scotty couldn't breathe.

A constable removed the shroud.

Mary MacKenzie lay naked, her throat slashed, her body covered with blood and dirt, her death mask crying defiance.

Scotty held in the scream that suddenly tried to escape from his throat. The suffocating feeling became so intense he felt as if he were going to die. Tears poured down his cheeks.

MacGregor ordered the body covered once more.

"We were lucky to find her," MacGregor explained. "The grave was expertly concealed. Unfortunately for the murderer or murderers, a young shepherd boy happened by on the footpath high above during the final stages of interment and saw a solitary man dropping the body into the excavation."

Scotty said nothing, trying to stop himself from grabbing Mary's body and embracing it one last time. Had she died hating him?

"Who did it?" MacGregor asked.

Scotty looked at the superintendent. He knew the answer. But he was going to say nothing to the police right now. He could not allow the police to race back on to the loch and possibly dangerously interfere with the trap operation. But, more importantly, he was going to be the instrument of revenge for Mary MacKenzie's death—not the police.

"You don't suspect me of this, do you?" he finally asked.

"Officially, I must suspect everyone," MacGregor replied. "So must the procurator's office. But unofficially, no. Of course not."

"Then I can go?"

"Unfortunately not. We want to talk to you. So do the procurator's people. You may be able to help us. We will fly back to Inverness and talk for a while. Then, of course, you may go. And Mr. Bruce. I want you to know I understand the hurt you feel."

"I have to go back to the loch. It's a dangerous operation. Let me finish and I'll then come in for all the questions you want to ask."

"But you said you weren't needed."

"I am."

"I'm sorry. It will have to wait."

Scotty looked at the officers. No one seemed to be wearing guns.

"If you please," MacGregor said. "We will return to the helicopter."

Joined by Inspector MacKintosh, they walked back to the makeshift landing pad. MacKintosh held out his arm to assist Scotty into the chopper. Scotty pushed the inspector back against MacGregor, causing both men to fall. Several constables ran toward them. Scotty jumped into the chopper, closed and locked its door.

The pilot rose from his seat. Scotty punched him, knocking him unconscious, then strapped himself into the pilot's seat. MacGregor moved in front of the helicopter, screaming. Several officers tried unsuccessfully to open the chopper's door. Scotty checked the controls—the pilot had already started the engines—and took the chopper into the air. He looked down. The police had no cars. No radios. It would take them a good hour to reach civilization. That would give him just enough time.

He brought the chopper down a good distance away, eased out the unconscious pilot, then lifted the chopper into the air again, headed toward Loch Ness, raised Geminii base on the chopper's mike, and asked the director of helicopter operations to inquire if Girard had returned to base. Moments later, the director informed him that Girard had indeed shown up and could be found in Lefebre's office.

He turned the helicopter toward Dores.

Girard had disappeared just after Mary MacKenzie had left Travis House and had reappeared subsequent to the discovery of her body.

He clenched his teeth as tears ran down his cheeks. He felt his entire body tremble with hatred and loss.

He would speak to Girard.

Chapter 40

Girard stood as Scotty Bruce entered Lefebre's office, un-announced.

"Mr. Bruce," Girard said, surprised. "I thought you were out on the loch."

"I was," Scotty declared emotionlessly as he placed a small tape recorder on Lefebre's desk.

"Can I help you with anything?" Girard asked, staring at the machine.

"The police took me off the loch," Scotty said, turning on the recorder. "They flew me up to Loch Duntelchaig. They showed me a dead body. Councilwoman Mary MacKenzie. Murdered."

Girard seemed shocked. "That's terrible!"

"Where've you been the last two days, Girard?"

"Working."

"On what?"

"Well-site security."

Scotty meandered around the side of the desk. "Tell me about Houghton."

"Who's Houghton?"

Scotty walked behind Girard. Girard continued to look ahead.

"John Leslie Houghton?"

"I don't know the man."

Quickly, Scotty jolted Girard toward the window, rammed Girard's head through the glass, then forced his throat down on the shattered spikes.

Girard screamed. Scotty pressed. Blood flowed.

"One move and I slit your throat!" Scotty warned.

"Please," Girard begged, choking.

"I'm going to ask you questions," Scotty growled. "And

you're going to answer. You're going to tell me the trut]
shook Girard hard; Girard cried out. Scotty wanted t
cording, especially if anything happened to him; he wa
record for the police. "Understand?"

"Yes."

"Do you know Houghton?"

"Yes."

"How?"

"I'd never met the man before. I was contacted by an
mediary. Someone I had worked for in London. A p
sional hit man. He told me to speak to Houghton or
went to Houghton's farm. Houghton assured me ou
would remain confidential. I answered his questions."

"Who killed Barrett?"

Girard hesitated. Scotty pressed Girard's neck again
glass.

"Lefebre!"

"The divers?"

"Lefebre!"

"Sutherland?"

"Lefebre!"

"Mrs. Munro?"

"Lefebre!"

"MacKenzie?"

"Lefebre!"

"And your involvement?"

"I didn't do anything."

Scotty pressed harder. "You're lying!"

Girard choked; his body was a sponge of sweat. "I
cepted MacKenzie on her way to Edinburgh." His voice
"But I had no idea Lefebre was going to kill her."

"Barrett? The divers? Sutherland? Munro? You h;
idea?"

"Please . . ."

"Who took the gelatin dynamite?"

"Whittenfeld."

"Why?"

"They've rigged the trap. The trap is timed. Ten m
after they catch the thing, the trap will blow!"

Scotty felt a wave of dizziness. *It's ours,* Mary Mac]
had said! *Whatever is in the loch belongs to Scotlan*
Geminii is not going to harm it! He shook with fury.

feld had destroyed everything in his path. Now the beast
s next.

"Phony evidence has been planted," Girard declared. "The
truction of the trap will be blamed on the Jacobites."

"You fucking filthy scum bastards!" Scotty screamed, near-
a frenzy.

He pulled Girard off the glass and smashed Girard's head
o the wall. Girard recoiled, groggy, trying to resist. Scotty
led him down Lefebre's work table, through a row of
ry carvings. Pieces of ivory shattered to the floor. Girard
unconscious.

Scotty propped Girard up in Lefebre's desk chair, shut off
recorder, then contacted security and ordered them to
ne immediately to Lefebre's office and place Girard under
est.

Closed transmissions between the sonar tugs, the command
ge, and the *Magellan* began with Captain Harrigan's first
rm.

"We've spotted it!" he advised. "In the trench!"

Soon all three sonar tugs had picked up the target. The
mmunication channels were suddenly filled with a hiss of
ces, including the voices of Dr. Rubinstein and Dr. Fiam-
ngo, who began rapidly exchanging information.

As of the last transmission, which had suggested that the
st was angrily twisting in the trench, everyone in the
gellan command room had taken a position in front of
project controls.

t had begun!

The helicopter rose into the air over the Geminii complex.
ments before, Scotty had locked the tape recorder in his
ce.

He did not like the view he faced. The sky was dark. The
d had already shifted around toward the west and the fog
k had started to move rapidly over the loch. It was as if
an, the beast, controlled the elements.

He swooped toward the Urquhart Bay installation, trying
overtake the weather. The fog swallowed the *Magellan*,
n the barges and tugs. He pivoted to one of the landing
s. Then, suddenly, the pad disappeared, too, buried.

He looked over the surrounding terrain. Everything flat was

encased. The higher ground was unusable. It was gett
darker. He had to get down.

Eyes fixed on instruments, he started a descent. The ch
per entered the fog, pushed off trajectory by the light wi
Silent mushrooms of white billowed before him. It got dar
He watched his radar altimeter, his pitch and roll gauges.
held tight to his vertical controls. He was almost do
The tail caught something. The chopper lurched violently.
frantically tried to right it, but couldn't. The chopper ca
down tilted on one of its runners; the support collaps
sparks exploded in the cabin. Desperate, he lunged thro
the exit door as a fire broke out. He ran from the pad.

The chopper exploded.

"It's rising out of the trench!" Captain Harrigan cried,
voice echoing out of the receiver. "It's starting to move
ward the *Magellan*."

Dr. Rubinstein acknowledged the communication
checked his sonar screens and monitors. There! They had
too.

The object seemed to be moving, then stopping, turn
around, almost as if it were delaying, allowing its anger
build.

He informed the *Magellan*'s operations room that the
get had started to veer toward the drill ship.

"We've got it!" Dr. Fiammengo called out.

Bill Nunn and Mike Grabowski studied the high-freque
sonar screen.

"That's it!" Grabowski said. "Christ!"

Dr. Fiammengo called Captain Harrigan. Harrigan
mated the target object to be two hundred feet beneath
surface.

Dr. Fiammengo listened. The tension in the room was
most audible, and there were none who had been spared
strain, except perhaps Pierre Lefebre, who, since the star
the operation, had sat arms folded, looking straight ah
oblivious, almost as if he'd known the final outcome from
first.

Scotty rushed down the installation's main path. Bel
him raged an inferno of Dante, the firelight spread like a
by the breeze.

He reached the operations building, obtained a rifle and a
mpass, then ran down to the marina. A guard was stationed
ar the launches.

"Are they fueled?" Scotty asked, gasping.

"Yes, Mr. Bruce," the guard said. "All of them."

Scotty jumped into the smallest launch and started its en-
ne. The security guard untied the moor line. Scotty laid the
mpass on the console, planning to navigate by use of the
mpass and the sounds of the *Magellan*'s pumps and rotary.
He would certainly be able to hear both. Although the
ht fog had rolled in with a vengeance, it had not been
companied by high surface winds or foul weather. In fact,
surface of the loch was relatively smooth, and there were
v sounds. It was as if he was about to move into a vacuum.

The target object was less than two hundred yards off the
agellan's marine riser, closing fast.

Dr. Rubinstein ordered the *Magellan* to shut down her
ary. Seconds later, an affirmation returned; the rotary was
d.

He ran past an array of visuals, examining digital readouts
electronic pictorials. The creature had suddenly stopped
angered rush toward the drill ship and was lying still, no
bt confused. He waited several minutes, then punched on
broadcast system.

He held his breath—one minute, two—and then the target
ect, twisting angrily again, changed directions and started
ving toward the trap.

He swabbed his forehead with a handkerchief and vora-
usly bit his nails.

t would not be long.

The launch funneled through the thick fog like a sharp-
d knife. Scotty could barely see five feet in front of him
following the *Magellan*'s generated sounds for guidance
suddenly proved difficult. Only seconds before, he'd heard
rotary die. Although he could still hear the drill ship's mud
ups, he could not tell where the sounds were coming from.
nfused by the crossing echoes and the lack of vision, the
nds seemed to swarm directionlessly around him.

He cut the launch engine and listened. Apart from the
oes, the loch was almost supernaturally quiet. Yet he was
re that the beast was being lured into the trap.

Glancing at the compass, he headed southeast and dr
alongside flotation raft number 30.

He tried to remember the chart. The 30 raft, he recall
was just past the position of the command barge, and to t
south. Or was it?

He might already have passed by the *Magellan*.

Holding the compass, he turned the launch 90 degrees
the right.

Dr. Rubinstein watched the trap's outer television and so
monitors; the intent of the target was unmistakable.

The target was underneath the trap and was trying desp
ately to puncture the steel web to get to the interior broadc
cone.

"We'll just have to wait," Dr. Rubinstein said, answeri
Whittenfeld, who had nervously called from the *Magellan*.

"What if it doesn't come over the sides?"

"It will!"

Dr. Rubinstein looked out the command barge window
he listened to the incredible noises and vibrations picked
by the trap's sonic receivers. Everything was black, thou
the drifting fog was very discernible in the light of the barg
floods.

It seemed so peaceful and serene outside.

Jerry Foster moved up. "What's it doing?" he asked.

"Trying to tear all our work to ribbons," Dr. Rubinst
replied.

Dr. Fiammengo shot to her feet as whole columns of c
sole lights went dark.

"What the hell?" she exclaimed as she carefully chec
the instruments, joined by one of Geminii's electrical e
neers.

Whittenfeld and Lefebre rushed over.

"What's wrong?" Whittenfeld asked.

"I think the creature ripped one of our lines!"

"What do you mean?"

Dr. Fiammengo pointed to the flow chart over her positi
"Two hookups run from the *Magellan* to the trap. One car
the electrical cables, the other our television and sonar lin
She looked up at the monitors; everything seemed fine. "
lost electrical."

"What does that mean?" Lefebre asked.
"It means we can't operate the trap from here!"

Aware of the control failure on the *Magellan*, Dr. Rubin-
in quickly moved in front of the trap's interior camera
onitors and the computer pictorial display screen as they
gan to record the entrance of the creature into the trap's
ws.
The creature hung up near the top, and then, responding
the continued transmissions, attacked the broadcast cone,
ich was suspended between the number II spokes. Noise
ackled back.
"Close the spokes," Dr. Rubinstein ordered.
A technician hit a switch; the spokes started to close.
It took just seconds to ensnare the target.
Waving his arms wildly, screaming his ecstasy, listening to
es of emotion from the *Magellan*, Dr. Rubinstein checked
ery parameter to ensure they had the target encased, then
the activation switch, which joined the spoke clamps.
A flashing red light indicated the clamps had locked.
They prepared to ballast up.
A short time later, the technician cried, "It doesn't like
ng trapped!"
The creature was viciously ramming itself against the trap
ll, trying to breach the bars. The trap itself was moving
lently in the water. Dr. Rubinstein contacted the anchor
gs. The tugs reported they were under tremendous stress.
e command barge's instruments indicated the bottom an-
ors were also being strained. He watched closely. The crea-
e had gone completely berserk. They could hear the sounds
combat over their sonic receivers as well as what they per-
ved was the animal's cry, a terrible, high-pitched roar that
arly shattered eardrums.
The creature was fighting for its life.

Scotty slowed the launch. He could see the command
ge's floodlights up ahead.
He quickly pulled alongside, jumped aboard, and raced
o the cabin.
"Scotty!" Jerry Foster exclaimed.
Dr. Rubinstein turned as Scotty moved to his side.
"We have it!" Dr. Rubinstein screamed.

Scotty was sweating heavily. "What do you mean?" asked.

Dr. Rubinstein pointed to several pictorials. "It's in t trap. Fighting ferociously. We've had to ballast up quick than we wanted because it's ripping the trap from its mo ings!"

"How long have the clamps been shut?"

"Seven minutes."

"Let it go!"

"Are you mad?"

Scotty threw Dr. Rubinstein against a console. "The tr is mined. You've got three minutes until it blows."

A pall surged over Dr. Rubinstein's face. Scotty moved the controls. Dr. Rubinstein grabbed his hands.

"You're lying!" he exclaimed.

Scotty pushed him off. "Lefebre mined the trap for Wh tenfeld. Whittenfeld wants the beast dead. The hunt over. T return to normal operations. He does not want the world descend on the loch. Do you understand?"

Dr. Rubinstein just stared. Scotty started to manipul levers. Realization reached Dr. Rubinstein. He scream angrily.

Then he moved next to Scotty and began to help.

Whittenfeld grabbed Dr. Fiammengo by the shoulders a pointed to the myriad of monitors and pictorials.

"What the hell is going on?" he screamed.

Dr. Fiammengo looked on in disbelief. "They opened trap. The beast is out!"

Chapter 41

〰〰〰〰

The concussion was enormous; the trap had blown.

The command barge rocked out of the water and then settled back on to the top of violent swells.

Debris fell on top of the cabin.

Scotty peered through the window at the fog, the blackness, then moved next to Dr. Rubinstein. The trap graphic had been erased. The television monitors had blanked out, as had the trap sonar screens. Apart from a few scattered traces and images of debris, there were few representationals left of the capture.

As soon as the beast had been released, it had descended to the loch bottom, angrily moving toward the trench.

The *Magellan* called in. Dr. Rubinstein answered.

"Who opened the trap?" Whittenfeld screamed across the air wave.

"Mr. Bruce and I," Dr. Rubinstein replied.

"Goddamn you!"

"The trap was mined!"

"Goddamn you!"

"You lied to us!"

"What I did is none of your business!" Whittenfeld thundered. "Rubinstein! Get the hell . . ."

Dr. Rubinstein clicked off the radio.

Whittenfeld and Lefebre rushed on to the *Magellan*'s main deck.

"Can the defense people do it?" Whittenfeld asked.

"Yes," Lefebre replied, chewing his tobacco fiercely.

"We'll have to track the target."

"We can use the drill ship's sonar and the lead sonar tug."

"And Dr. Rubinstein?"

Lefebre smiled; tobacco juice dribbled over his lower li
"I will talk to him later. Then I will talk to Mr. Bruce."

Whittenfeld shook his head. "Are you sure the dep
charges won't endanger us?"

"The distances have been carefully calibrated. We will n
even feel a concussion."

They rushed up to the drill floor. Tony Spinelli met them.

"What exploded?" Spinelli asked, visibly disconcerted.

"The trap!" Whittenfeld replied. "The creature is loose!"

"What do we do now?"

"Start the rotary!"

"Are you mad?"

"Start it!"

"We're in a gas zone!"

Lefebre slammed Spinelli's head against one of the de
rick's ribs. "You get this drilling crew on the stick or I w
break your neck!" He threw Spinelli on the floor, then looke
at the crew. "Start the rotary!"

Spinelli pulled himself up; the driller primed the rota
table.

Lefebre summoned the depth-charge technicians up to
Whittenfeld returned to the command room, contacted Ca
tain Harrigan, and ordered him to bring his tug parallel
the Magellan, one hundred yards off her port, prepared
relay sonar data.

"What do I look for?" Harrigan asked.

"The target!" Whittenfeld bellowed.

Captain Harrigan did not reply.

The launch moved slowly through the darkness. Scotty he
tight to the wheel. On the console was the compass, the rif
and a radio beam tracking monitor, which Dr. Rubinstein h
requisitioned from command barge ordnance. There were i
termittent blips on the monitor screen; he was moving towa
the source of the Magellan's radio transmissions.

Scotty was puzzled. He could hear the echo of the Mag
lan's rotary, the last sound he'd expected to hear!

The beast had returned to the trench, licking its woun
God knew how it would react to a new provocation.

Sonsabitches!

*　　*　　*

"Bring her around!" Captain Harrigan ordered.

The first officer turned the tug's wheel, swinging the vessel parallel to the drill ship.

They had navigated to the spot by using the *Magellan*'s marine riser as a point of reference. They had also picked up the creature, rising explosively out of the trench once more.

"It's closing in!" one of the sonar engineers cried.

Harrigan looked at the scopes; the target was circling beneath them.

He ordered the tug hard astern. The tug swung around. The target moved off their scopes.

The tug jerked violently. The side-scan display went blank. The target had ripped off their sonar fish.

"Get the hell out of here!" Harrigan screamed.

A tremendous tremor hit. Men and equipment skidded all over the tug. Harrigan grabbed the controls and opened the throttle. The tug jerked forward. Another tremor hit, knocking Harrigan to the floor. Crewmen rushed on to the deck with life gear. Harrigan rose and grabbed the communications mike.

"It's attacking us!" he screamed.

The floor erupted beneath him. Planks flew into the air. A technician was impaled.

Harrigan crawled toward the wheel. Another eruption stopped him. The window shattered. Glass slivers rained down. The tug's radar unit crashed to the floor, shattering Harrigan's ankle. All the lights blew out; the cabin fell dark.

Harrigan cried out, consumed with pain, then cried out again as the beast ruptured invisibly up into the cabin, tearing a gaping hole in the vessel's floor.

Water surged upward. Harrigan held to the bulkhead. Freezing water flooded over his head. He tried to swim. The bulkhead collapsed. The roof of the bridge fell in.

There was water everywhere.

And then blackness.

He'd heard it all. The sounds of impact. The wail of dying men. The gut-wrenching gurgle of a sinking ship.

He'd also felt the water surge violently around him.

Could it have been one of the anchor tugs?

He cut the engine, listened. Were there any survivors? He heard nothing. No cries. No calls. He screamed. No reply.

Hell! He still couldn't see a damn thing.

He looked at the radio beam monitor. He was closing on the drill ship.

He reached for the engine primer. He heard a sound, a thunderous slush of breaking water. Waves suddenly beat against the launch's hull. An unearthly shriek split the darkness.

The beast had risen!

A shadowlike object slid through the fog, then descended. He'd seen only a blur, but he'd seen enough. The beast! Father MacPherson's beast!

He started the engine again.

He saw lights!

Directly ahead.

The *Magellan!*

Whittenfeld slammed the clipboard against the console.

"Bring those goddamn tugs in!" he ordered once more.

"I'm sorry!" a voice crackled back. "We will come in to aid the drill ship. We will not come in to patrol the sector!"

"Are you disobeying my orders?"

"I have a crew to worry about. The lead tug is down. Harrigan is dead. I'm now in charge, and there are superseding orders from the Ministry of Defence."

Whittenfeld started to scream. The sonar tug captain refused to comply. Whittenfeld smashed the microphone to silence.

"We'll use the drill ship's sonar alone!" he said, addressing the *Magellan* team.

Dr. Fiammengo protested. "Our sonar doesn't have sufficient range. It's not sensitive. There are dead sectors. We won't pick up the target until it's on top of us!"

Whittenfeld pulled Dr. Fiammengo from her seat. "You're no longer involved," he warned. "You just stand there and keep your mouth shut." He listened to the roar of the rotary, then asked the sonar engineer if the target was still being tracked. The engineer replied that they had lost it. "Well, find it! Grabowski! Take Fiammengo's seat and cut off all outside communications!"

Whittenfeld handed Bill Nunn his headset.

"I'm going topside," Whittenfeld explained. "You're to relay vectors!"

*   *   *

Dr. Rubinstein tapped his hand nervously on the cold metal of his console. There was stillness on all sides. No one was moving in the cabin. The icy stroke of terror had invaded. They had seen the lead sonar tug go down. They had also seen the creature follow the stricken vessel to the bottom, then disappear. The creature was angered beyond focus. The drill ship was no longer the sole object of its emotions. Every alien object was now an object of hatred.

They were all aware of their vulnerability.

A consumptive, frightened cough summoned attention.

"Contact," a technician yelled.

Dr. Rubinstein moved to the technician's scope.

"Where are you beaming?" he asked, confused.

"On the other side of the ship!" the technician replied. "The target's near the loch walls along the shore of Urquhart Bay."

"It has met opposition from the south," Dr. Rubinstein marveled. "It will now approach the drill ship from the north."

Dr. Rubinstein radioed the drill ship. There was no response.

He looked through the window.

There was nothing he could do.

"Goddamn fools!" he cursed.

They looked out into the milk-thick fog, leaning against the guard rail, their bodies aching from anticipation and bone-destroying dampness. Whittenfeld, Lefebre, and the two defense specialists were wearing headsets and flak jackets. Mounted on the guard rail were two sets of depth-charge ejection racks, ready for use. Next to them were the rack controls and additional rounds.

"Anything yet?" Whittenfeld asked.

"Nothing," Bill Nunn communicated from below.

Lefebre took off his headset. He listened. He could hear the pumps and rotary. Several minutes before, though, he thought he had picked up the sound of a launch, but no launch had appeared, and he had not heard the sounds again.

He started to reset his headgear.

The rotary stopped.

"What the hell?" Whittenfeld snapped.

They looked toward midship; they could barely see the derrick.

"Stay on the comm-channel," Lefebre ordered.

The defense specialists nodded.

Whittenfeld and Lefebre rushed midship and climbed to th
drill platform. The crew was in place. So was Tony Spinelli

"Start the goddamn rotary again!" Whittenfeld cried, besid
himself with rage.

No one moved. No one responded.

"Do you hear me!" Whittenfeld cracked. "Spinelli, wh
gave the order to stop the rotary?" His temper grew. "Star
it! Now!"

Lefebre rushed the driller; the driller stood aside.

"Lefebre!"

Someone had called Lefebre's name. Lefebre and Whitten
feld searched for the source. The call came again. The
looked up.

A man was standing high on the derrick platform, his bod
punching out at them through the fog.

Scotty Bruce!

Scotty trained his rifle on the drill floor, switching aim bac
and forth between Whittenfeld and Lefebre. "The rotary i
dead. The beast will be left alone." He stared at Whittenfeld
letting seconds pass. "You killed Mary MacKenzie!"

Whittenfeld was aghast. "Kill? I didn't kill anyone. She'
dead? Believe me, I had nothing . . ."

"Lefebre?"

Lefebre stared upward, unarmed. The nozzle of the high
powered rifle was pointed right at his head.

"I don't know what you're talking about," he said.

Scotty tightened his grip on the rifle. "The Magellan i
down permanently. And . . ."

A shockwave hit. The ship rolled. Everyone was thrown t
the ground. The derrick twisted on its frame. Metal buckle
Part of the drill floor gave way. Railings collapsed. Scotty fe
off the derrick. Two roustabouts were crushed. A huge met
girder caught Whittenfeld on the head. Men jumped off th
drill floor.

Lefebre ran down a staircase into the moon pool.

Scotty followed.

Dr. Allen Rubinstein, his face damp with sweat, stared a
the array of sonar screens. Several minutes before, he ha
ordered all systems trained on the Magellan's marine rise

And he and his staff had seen the creature rising out of the depths like a missile and ramming the hull of the *Magellan* near midship.

Now the horror grew. Shortly after impact, the beast had descended to the floor of the loch and had attacked the wellhead, trying to chew off the blowout preventer.

God help them!

The rifle extended in front of him, Scotty walked carefully along the narrow third-deck corridor, searching. The ship's interstices were illuminated by yellow ceiling lights; the atmosphere was surreal.

He had not found Lefebre in the moon pool or in any of the workrooms or crew quarters. Lefebre might have returned to the main deck, but his senses told him otherwise. He could feel Lefebre's foul presence. They were alone together below deck.

"Lefebre!" he called. "Listen to me! I'm here! Come! Get me! Get me, you fucking murderer!"

He moved between cement pods, listening. The mud pumps continued to run, camouflaging sounds.

He heard something. He turned, pointing the rifle.

Nothing.

Dr. Rubinstein watched the drama unfold.

He had seen the creature chewing at the wellhead—unsuccessfully.

Now he was a witness to the latest attempt at destruction.

The creature was ascending the marine riser toward the drill ship's moon pool.

Scotty jumped off the staircase through the shifting shadows on to the moon-pool catwalk. In front of him was the marine riser. Below the catwalk was water. There was a small hole in the ceiling where part of the floor had given way. Debris littered the area. The roar of the mud pumps was deafening.

He inspected each of the exits—nothing. He breathed deeply as his body trembled, his guts twisted by the tension. Had Lefebre fled?

A sound—movement.

Scotty turned, looked sideways, then up.

Lefebre was suddenly on him from above, twisting a guide wire around his neck, digging it into his flesh.

"You meet your God!" Lefebre cried. "Your God, monsieur!"

Scotty dropped the rifle, choking. Lefebre forced Scotty face down on the catwalk.

"I will make you suffer slowly," the Frenchman hissed through gritted teeth. "And I will enjoy it, almost as much as I enjoyed the death of the councilwoman!"

Scotty cried out, struggling.

"God has decreed your death, Bruce!" Lefebre's hands were bleeding from the tight grasp on the line. Scotty's throat bled, too. Their blood mixed. "You have never overcome. God has decided you are not worthy of life. God has asked me to execute His wishes!"

Scotty's hand crawled between the wire and his skin. Lefebre tightened his grip. Scotty gasped for air, then twisted.

They dropped off the catwalk into the water.

Dr. Allen Rubinstein and his team watched the holographic images splatter across the screens.

The beast was halfway up the riser.

Whittenfeld opened his eyes and looked across the drilling platform. Groggy, insensate, he rose to his knees, touched his face. He was covered with a ghoulish mixture of grease and blood; he could hardly see.

He heard the mud pumps. He heard screaming, men moving below on the deck. There was no one on the drill floor with him.

He tried to clear his thoughts. Blood flowed over his face. He crawled toward the drillers' controls, shivering. The rotary table wasn't turning. But that was impossible! Nothing ever stopped operations. Ever. No, the vile bitch—Loch Ness—never stopped him. He had to reach his child before the vile bitch destroyed everything.

He tightened himself into a ball, trembled, cried. Tears mixed with the blood. He felt fear and pain.

He rose shakily to his feet. The ship seemed to be listing slightly. Where had everyone gone? The crew of the *Columbus* hadn't deserted their posts! Why had these men?

He studied the panel. No, the rotary table had to turn. Progress! They had to drill ahead.

He hit the rotary engine switch!

* * *

Scotty could feel his strength ebbing. He could feel the wire noose tightening. All that remained between life and death were the bleeding fingers between his neck and the line.

Struggling in the water, they were now along the side of the moon pool. Lefebre was on his back.

Scotty smelled the odor of tobacco, the odor of death.

He heard the rotary, felt the incredible vibrations.

Summoning strength, he cried out and pushed backward into the marine riser.

Lefebre's head smashed into the riser's shell. The noose fell away. Scotty turned. Lefebre grabbed him by the throat. Scotty thrust out and clasped Lefebre's neck, too. They went under the inky water.

He could hardly see the Frenchman's face, but he could feel the Frenchman's hands on his neck, feel his own hands on the Frenchman's flesh.

They turned in a water ballet of death, strength against strength, will against will.

They drew themselves to each other—eye to eye, hatred to hatred, face to bulging face—the bursting lack of air in their lungs visible in their sallow expressions.

They rose to the surface. Scotty searched for something to give him strength, visions of Mary MacKenzie, Mrs. Munro, the others.

"God!" he screamed as he stared into the Frenchman's eyes and power surged through his hands, tightening his grip.

Lefebre's arms went limp, his hands floated off Scotty's throat.

Scotty grabbed Lefebre by the hair and, while treading water, brought the Frenchman's face close.

Lefebre was dead.

Crazed, he smashed the Frenchman's head into the riser again and again, until the water was red with blood and all those lives had been avenged.

He released his grasp.

Lefebre's body sank.

Scotty left the moon pool.

"Scotty!"

Scotty looked up at the drill floor. Whittenfeld was standing near the driller's station, bleeding badly, calling down to him.

"Scotty. Here. Come here. I need help. The vile bitch is trying to stop us. My child is in danger!"

Scotty looked up at the pathetic, delirious man who was covered with blood, crazed out of his mind.

There were several small fires. He had to still the rotary, close the blowout preventer, and stop the ship's mud pumps and electrical. And he had to do it fast!

He climbed on to the drill floor and pushed Whittenfeld away from the controls.

"No!" Whittenfeld cried as if his soul had been ruptured.

Whittenfeld grabbed Scotty by the arms. Scotty pummeled Whittenfeld to the ground, then quickly turned to the controls. He manipulated the drill pipe into the proper position, then activated the blowout preventer's slicing rams, which would simultaneously close the well bore and cut the drill pipe. He watched the lights, praying that the control hoses were intact. The lights flashed; the bore closed; the drill pipe separated below the ship. Quickly, he shut off the mud pumps, then the ship's electrical.

The *Magellan* was dead.

The drill ship shuddered. Something had hit it again. The impact had been directly below him. He heard a roar, then felt movement.

The beast was in the moon pool!

He began to drag Whittenfeld to the steps. Whittenfeld resisted, screaming, totally incoherent. He fought off Whittenfeld's hands, nails, teeth.

He moved on to the steps. Whittenfeld kicked him in the face. He fell backward on to the main deck.

"The pumps!" Whittenfeld screamed. "The rotary. We must drill ahead."

Scotty moved to the steps, prepared to climb up again.

Suddenly, the drill floor erupted. The entire inner section of the ship burst into the air, pushed up by the beast who rose unseen beneath them. Whittenfeld was carried up into the derrick. Scotty watched in horror as the deck crane swung around, its huge arm leveling parallel to the deck, careening into the derrick, crushing Whittenfeld into a mass of disintegrating flesh.

Water rushed up through the ruptures, and a vengeful beast cried out.

Scotty ran toward the bow as the beast smashed into the

ip repeatedly from below. All the lifeboats had been cast
f. As far as he knew, he was the only one left on board.
He dove into the water.

Dr. Rubinstein watched screens as the creature returned to
e bottom of the loch and attacked the blowout preventer
ace more. Moments later, the blowout preventer tipped off
e wellhead, and the creature disappeared.
Aeration again?
Dr. Rubinstein looked out at the loch. It seemed as peace-
l as ever.
"Look!" an engineer cried.
The sight stopped their pulses. Their scopes were filled with
aces as the hulk of the *Magellan* began a descent to the
ttom of Loch Ness, joining her sister ship, the *Columbus!*

Chapter 42

e car pitched through the fog along A-9, heading toward
rrbridge.
Scotty sat behind the wheel. One of the demolition men,
o had sealed the underground cavern, nervously peered
ough the window next to him.
Less than an hour before, Scotty had splashed into the cold
ter of the loch, swimming for his life. A lifeboat had
ked him up, taking him to the command barge. Dr. Fiam-
ngo, Bill Nunn, and Mike Grabowski had already reached
barge. Dr. Rubinstein had told him about the aeration.
'd had no time to grieve. Seizing one of the launches, he'd
hed to the Dores base, arriving just after the police. Realiz-
he couldn't enter the base, he'd located the demolition
n at his home.

Scotty stared at the winding road, transfixed. He'd be
vindicated. Damn, he wished he hadn't. He wished, in fa
there'd been no beast. That Dr. Rubinstein had been a frau
That there had been a submersible. That Whittenfeld had n
lied to the tribunal. He wished he had gotten himself
trouble, lost his job. He wished he had been kicked back
the States to disappear into oblivion.

If so, many of the dead would not have perished.

Mary MacKenzie would still be alive! Perhaps at his si

The car broke through the fog and arrived at Carrbrid
fifteen minutes later.

"Get the descent jackets," he ordered as he pushed t
company manager in the direction of the company shed. "A
give the demo man everything he needs!"

"What are you going to do?" the manager asked.

"Free an innocent!" Scotty replied cryptically.

The well site exploded with activity. Equipment was broug
to the access hole. The hoist was swung into position. Dy
mite and other blasting equipment were lowered into t
cavern.

The two men followed, reaching the cavern floor in ne
darkness, their helmet torches the only light. Walking slow
their backs bent over from the weight of explosives and equ
ment, they moved to the tunnel blockade.

The explosives expert rigged his charges and then dr
back a line to a blasting mechanism about two hundred f
away.

"Go back up top," Scotty ordered.

"But I have to detonate!" the demo man said.

"I'll do it! If anything goes wrong, I want only c
casualty."

The demolition man retreated. Several minutes later,
man was on his way up the bore.

Scotty waited, stared at the wall of rock that blocked
tunnel, then hit the plunger!

A tremendous explosion rocked the cavern. A cyclone
dust blew through the air. He trained the helmet beam. 1
wall was down, the passage open.

The vibration of the explosions continued to reverber
He felt a tremor. Rock chips fell off the tunnel wall.

Then the ceiling caved.

*   *   *

He coughed, gasped for breath.

His mouth was filled with dust. His right leg was pinned under a pile of rocks, broken. His helmet was just out of reach. Its torch was still shining under a mound of stone.

He tried to clear his head.

It was pitch dark; he could see nothing.

A horrible odor pinched his nostrils—the scent of mildewed flesh and rotted plankton.

He heard a movement in front of him, a heavy shuffle. Something was in the cavern, something alive. And it was staring at him!

He stiffened, terrified, realizing the impossible.

The beast!

He wanted to call out. He didn't dare; he couldn't.

He could hear the puff of ancient lungs, gigantic intakes of air that rustled a wind through the cavern.

He sensed the beast moving closer, watching, waiting.

Frantic, sure he would not survive, he reached for the helmet. He had to see the beast even if this was to be his last sight. He clawed at the rocks, desperately extending himself, then grabbed the helmet and turned the torch upward.

His mouth fell open; his entire body trembled.

The torch beam caught an eye, then part of a mouth. The head have must have been forty feet off the floor. The eye was fixed on him.

The beast roared. The entire cavern shook.

He could smell the beast's breath.

He pointed the beam again. The beast was bleeding heavily from the head and neck.

It moved down closer.

The torch flickered out.

He waited for death.

Minutes passed. The beast stood immobile. And then another hideous skirl ripped Scotty's ears.

The pain from his leg was so intense that he was sure he would pass out, making the beast's revenge unfelt. Suddenly, he heard a thunderous pounding. The beast was moving.

The sensation was unmistakable. The beast was moving past him toward the sea. It was going home.

He heard the rumble recede into the darkness, the sound captured periodically by a hideous call. The beast was badly wounded. It was in pain.

It wanted the sea.

He felt nauseous. His head spun.

Several minutes later, he heard a voice.

"Mr. Bruce!" a man called out.

He lost consciousness.

According to Jerry Foster, the chaos at Raigmore Hospital was a microcosm of the tumult occurring in Inverness. In fact, Foster assured him, the commotion far exceeded the commotion that had attended the loss of the *Columbus*.

Another ship and tug had gone down, and twelve more men, including Tony Spinelli, whose body had not been found, had probably died, but there was no question about the cause of the disaster this time or the identity of the perpetrator.

The word was definitive. The ships had been attacked by the legend!

Geminii's role in the caper had already been blazed across the headlines of every newspaper in Great Britain, if not the world. So had his own. In fact, based on information already supplied to the press, he and the two researchers had become the focus of the onslaught.

Damn, he just wanted to get out of the hospital and find some peace and quiet. He'd been there two days already, getting the bone in his leg set and various other bruises assuaged, and he'd virtually been a pincushion for Superintendent MacGregor, who, along with members of the procurator fiscal's office, had been in and out of the room like over-anxious interns.

Christ, he was sure this was just the start. According to Foster again, Farquharson had arrived along with the secretary of state for Scotland and the secretary for energy. And once more, an entire contingent of Geminii executives, including John Fallworth, had hustled to the spot.

The door opened.

Dr. Rubinstein and Dr. Fiammengo entered. He had not seen them since the evening before, and that meeting, according to his own wishes, had been short and unceremonious.

"They just told us you're to be released," Dr. Fiammengo said.

"So I've been informed," Scotty agreed.

"How do you feel?"

Scotty didn't reply.

"Scotty," Dr. Rubinstein declared, "we know what you think about us, about everything. But it's over. Finished."

"Is it?" Scotty asked bitingly.

"Yes," Dr. Fiammengo said. "What's done has been done!"

"Yes," Scotty declared. "The scientific expedition has ended. The research project has been drawn to a close. On to the next! But you've left a memorable legacy, my friends—death and destruction. You're as responsible for the hell as anyone. Write about it in a journal."

The two researchers looked at each other. There was nothing more to be said. They left the room.

A constabulary lorry picked Scotty up shortly after one and carted him across the highway to police headquarters. Superintendent MacGregor, he was told, was on his way up from the city.

However, John Fallworth and senior execs from New York were already there.

Their meeting was brief. Fallworth short-circuited any interrogation by announcing he knew everything, including the truth about Furst and Blasingame and the substitution of the false hose.

Scotty was puzzled. No one had heard the tape of Girard's confession because the police had been unable to find it. Someone had broken into his office, ransacking it, stealing the tape, and no one had been able to find Girard, who, obviously with the complicity of Lefebre's security officers, had fled the base soon after his arrest.

How the hell could Fallworth have gotten the information?

"I take responsibility for this entire thing," John Fallworth said. "I let Whittenfeld deceive me, convince me he had found evidence of a creature while pursuing a real submersible. I let him convince me to allow him to try and catch the creature. Though I had no idea of the true facts, I must solely accept the blame. And, Scotty, I let Whittenfeld convince me you were to be isolated. He showed me pictures, documentation, proving your involvement with the councilwoman and the Jacobites. He convinced me to ice you."

Scotty said nothing.

The Geminii staff left the building.

Inspector Superintendent MacGregor arrived shortly thereafter.

It was obvious from the first that MacGregor's tone had

changed since their last meeting in the hospital. MacGregor
seemed accommodating, even contrite, suddenly so desirous
of avoiding any discussion of lies and even Scotty's felonious
escape from custody.

"You're free to go, Mr. Bruce," MacGregor concluded
after some banter.

The police had not found the tape. Nor Girard. Yet they
now apparently believed him about everything. Why?

He didn't ask.

"Come around for some tea if you have a chance," he said,
just to say something.

And MacGregor smiled.

The next day, Scotty returned to Travis House. The following week, he would return to the States. Staying in Scotland
would be too hard, too painful.

Shortly before nine P.M., a car drew into the Travis House
driveway.

Scotty looked through the den window. John Leslie Houghton's limousine was idling behind the jeep.

He limped outside, assisted by crutches. Houghton rolled
down his rear window.

"My office called. They said you wanted to see me."

"Yes," Scotty said, leaning. "I want to thank you." Realis-
tically, he had not needed Houghton, but Houghton had made
everything easier.

"For what?"

"For going to the police. The government. Geminii."

"How do you know I did such a thing?"

Scotty smiled. "It could only have been you."

Houghton placed a cigarette into his holder. "I could deny
it."

"You could."

Houghton smiled. "I told you I had grown to like you," he
finally said.

"You also told me you only work for remuneration. Did
anyone pay you to come forward?"

"Directly? No."

"What about indirectly?"

Houghton lit his cigarette and drew deeply. "Not yet. But
one never knows."

"I don't understand."

Houghton slid closer to the window. "Suppose one day

come to you—wherever you are, I'm sure in a high position n the oil industry—and I ask you to do me a favor, even a little one. What would you say?"

Scotty stared. "I don't know. Depends what you ask. Depends the purpose. Depends what good would come of it."

Houghton nodded. "Well, then, there you have it. If you cannot accept my altruism, you can certainly accept that!"

Scotty stared.

"Good-by, Mr. Bruce."

The limousine backed out of the driveway and disappeared.

He gazed at the lights of Inverness below, shook his head, then hobbled back into the house.

Epilogue

A golden descending sun splashed spears of colored light across his face. The wind blew his hair. The warm evening air seemed to kiss his skin.

He stood transfixed, staring down at the gravestones. Behind him was the Carn Dearg Inn. Its windows were dark.

"My father and mother are buried here," she had said. "I will be buried here, too!"

Her stone was simple, dignified. It befit her.

The dirt hadn't settled yet.

"I love you," he said.

He looked out at the loch. She had loved it. She would always be near it, its glistening blue waters, the green surrounding mountains.

He looked back at the stone, tears rolling down his face.

He had thought after seeing her body near Loch Duntelchaig that he would never cry again.

He'd been wrong.